J. J. Connington and The Murder Room

››› This title is part of The Murder Room, our series dedicated to making available out-of-print or hard-to-find titles by classic crime writers.

Crime fiction has always held up a mirror to society. The Victorians were fascinated by sensational murder and the emerging science of detection; now we are obsessed with the forensic detail of violent death. And no other genre has so captivated and enthralled readers.

Vast troves of classic crime writing have for a long time been unavailable to all but the most dedicated frequenters of second-hand bookshops. The advent of digital publishing means that we are now able to bring you the backlists of a huge range of titles by classic and contemporary crime writers, some of which have been out of print for decades.

From the genteel amateur private eyes of the Golden Age and the femmes fatales of pulp fiction, to the morally ambiguous hard-boiled detectives of mid twentieth-century America and their descendants who walk our twenty-first century streets, The Murder Room has it all. ›››

The Murder Room

Where Criminal Minds Meet

themurderroom.com

J. J. Connington (1880–1947)

Alfred Walter Stewart, who wrote under the pen name J. J. Connington, was born in Glasgow, the youngest of three sons of Reverend Dr Stewart. He graduated from Glasgow University and pursued an academic career as a chemistry professor, working for the Admiralty during the First World War. Known for his ingenious and carefully worked-out puzzles and in-depth character development, he was admired by a host of his better-known contemporaries, including Dorothy L. Sayers and John Dickson Carr, who both paid tribute to his influence on their work. He married Jessie Lily Courts in 1916 and they had one daughter.

By J. J. Connington

Sir Clinton Driffield Mysteries

Murder in the Maze (1927)

Tragedy at Ravensthorpe (1927)

The Case with Nine Solutions (1928)

Mystery at Lynden Sands (1928)

Nemesis at Raynham Parva (1929) (a.k.a. *Grim Vengenace*)

The Boathouse Riddle (1931)

The Sweepstake Murders (1931)

The Castleford Conundrum (1932)

The Ha-Ha Case (1934) (a.k.a. *The Brandon Case*)

In Whose Dim Shadow (1935) (a.k.a. *The Tau Cross Mystery*)

A Minor Operation (1937)

Murder Will Speak (1938)

Truth Comes Limping (1938)

The Twenty-One Clues (1941)

No Past is Dead (1942)

Jack-in-the-Box (1944)

Common Sense Is All You Need (1947)

Supt Ross Mysteries

The Eye in the Museum (1929)

The Two Tickets Puzzle (1930)

Novels

Death at Swaythling Court (1926)

The Dangerfield Talisman (1926)

Tom Tiddler's Island (1933) (a.k.a. *Gold Brick Island*)

The Counsellor (1939)

The Four Defences (1940)

The Counsellor

J. J. Connington

An Orion book

Copyright © The Professor A. W. Stewart Deceased Trust 1939, 2014

The right of J. J. Connington to be identified as the author of this work has been asserted in accordance with the Copyright, Designs and Patents Act 1988.

This edition published by
The Orion Publishing Group Ltd
Orion House
5 Upper St Martin's Lane
London WC2H 9EA

An Hachette UK company
A CIP catalogue record for this book is available from the British Library

ISBN 978 1 4719 0637 4

All characters and events in this publication are fictitious and any resemblance to real people, living or dead, is purely coincidental.

No part of this publication may be reproduced, stored in a retrieval system or transmitted in any form or by any means without the prior permission in writing of the publisher, nor be otherwise circulated in any form of binding or cover other than that in which it is published without a similar condition, including this condition, being imposed on the subsequent purchaser.

www.orionbooks.co.uk

CONTENTS

Introduction by Curtis Evans

During the Golden Age of the detective novel, in the 1920s and 1930s, J. J. Connington stood with fellow crime writers R. Austin Freeman, Cecil John Charles Street and Freeman Wills Crofts as the foremost practitioner in British mystery fiction of the science of pure detection. I use the word 'science' advisedly, for the man behind J. J. Connington, Alfred Walter Stewart, was an esteemed Scottish-born scientist. A 'small, unassuming, moustached polymath', Stewart was 'a strikingly effective lecturer with an excellent sense of humour, fertile imagination and fantastically retentive memory', qualities that also served him well in his fiction. He held the Chair of Chemistry at Queens University, Belfast for twenty-five years, from 1919 until his retirement in 1944.

During roughly this period, the busy Professor Stewart found time to author a remarkable apocalyptic science fiction tale, *Nordenholt's Million* (1923), a mainstream novel, *Almighty Gold* (1924), a collection of essays, *Alias J. J. Connington* (1947), and, between 1926 and 1947, twenty-four mysteries (all but one tales of detection), many of them sterling examples of the Golden Age puzzle-oriented detective novel at its considerable best. 'For those who ask first of all in a detective story for exact and mathematical accuracy in the construction of the plot', avowed a contemporary *London Daily Mail* reviewer, 'there is no author to equal the distinguished scientist who writes under the name of J. J. Connington.'[1]

Alfred Stewart's background as a man of science is reflected in his fiction, not only in the impressive puzzle plot mechanics he devised for his mysteries but in his choices of themes and depictions of characters. Along with Stanley Nordenholt of *Nordenholt's Million*, a novel about a plutocrat's pitiless efforts to preserve a ruthlessly remolded remnant of human life after a global environmental calamity, Stewart's most notable character is Chief Constable Sir Clinton Driffield, the detective in seventeen of the twenty-four Connington crime novels. Driffield is one of crime fiction's most highhanded investigators, occasionally taking on the functions of judge and jury as well as chief of police.

Absent from Stewart's fiction is the hail-fellow-well-met quality found in John Street's works or the religious ethos suffusing those of Freeman Wills Crofts, not to mention the effervescent novel-of-manners style of the British Golden Age Crime Queens Dorothy L. Sayers, Margery Allingham and Ngaio Marsh. Instead we see an often disdainful cynicism about the human animal and a marked admiration for detached supermen with superior intellects. For this reason, reading a Connington novel can be a challenging experience for modern readers inculcated in gentler social beliefs. Yet Alfred Stewart produced a classic apocalyptic science fiction tale in *Nordenholt's Million* (justly dubbed 'exciting and terrifying reading' by the *Spectator*) as well as superb detective novels boasting well-wrought puzzles, bracing characterization and an occasional leavening of dry humour. Not long after Stewart's death in 1947, the Connington novels fell entirely out of print. The recent embrace of Stewart's fiction by Orion's Murder Room imprint is a welcome event indeed, correcting as it does over sixty years of underserved neglect of an accomplished genre writer.

Born in Glasgow on 5 September 1880, Alfred Stewart had significant exposure to religion in his earlier life. His father was William Stewart, longtime Professor of Divinity and Biblical Criticism at Glasgow University, and he married Lily Coats, a daughter of the Reverend Jervis Coats and member of one of

Scotland's preeminent Baptist families. Religious sensibility is entirely absent from the Connington corpus, however. A confirmed secularist, Stewart once referred to one of his wife's brothers, the Reverend William Holms Coats (1881–1954), principal of the Scottish Baptist College, as his 'mental and spiritual antithesis', bemusedly adding: 'It's quite an education to see what one would look like if one were turned into one's mirror-image.'

Stewart's J. J. Connington pseudonym was derived from a nineteenth-century Oxford Professor of Latin and translator of Horace, indicating that Stewart's literary interests lay not in pietistic writing but rather in the pre-Christian classics ('I prefer the *Odyssey* to *Paradise Lost*,' the author once avowed). Possessing an inquisitive and expansive mind, Stewart was in fact an uncommonly well-read individual, freely ranging over a variety of literary genres. His deep immersion in French literature and supernatural horror fiction, for example, is documented in his lively correspondence with the noted horologist Rupert Thomas Gould.[2]

It thus is not surprising that in the 1920s the intellectually restless Stewart, having achieved a distinguished middle age as a highly regarded man of science, decided to apply his creative energy to a new endeavour, the writing of fiction. After several years he settled, like other gifted men and women of his generation, on the wildly popular mystery genre. Stewart was modest about his accomplishments in this particular field of light fiction, telling Rupert Gould later in life that 'I write these things [what Stewart called tec yarns] because they amuse me in parts when I am putting them together and because they are the only writings of mine that the public will look at. Also, in a minor degree, because I like to think some people get pleasure out of them.' No doubt Stewart's single most impressive literary accomplishment is *Nordenholt's Million*, yet in their time the two dozen J. J. Connington mysteries did indeed give readers in Great Britain, the United States and other countries much diversionary reading pleasure. Today these works constitute an estimable addition to British crime fiction.

After his 'prentice pastiche mystery, *Death at Swaythling Court* (1926), a rural English country-house tale set in the highly traditional village of Fernhurst Parva, Stewart published another, superior country-house affair, *The Dangerfield Talisman* (1926), a novel about the baffling theft of a precious family heirloom, an ancient, jewel-encrusted armlet. This clever, murderless tale, which likely is the one that the author told Rupert Gould he wrote in under six weeks, was praised in *The Bookman* as 'continuously exciting and interesting' and in the *New York Times Book Review* as 'ingeniously fitted together and, what is more, written with a deal of real literary charm'. Despite its virtues, however, *The Dangerfield Talisman* is not fully characteristic of mature Connington detective fiction. The author needed a memorable series sleuth, more representative of his own forceful personality.

It was the next year, 1927, that saw J. J. Connington make his break to the front of the murdermongerer's pack with a third country-house mystery, *Murder in the Maze*, wherein debuted as the author's great series detective the assertive and acerbic Sir Clinton Driffield, along with Sir Clinton's neighbour and 'Watson', the more genial (if much less astute) Squire Wendover. In this much-praised novel, Stewart's detective duo confronts some truly diabolical doings, including slayings by means of curare-tipped darts in the double-centered hedge maze at a country estate, Whistlefield. No less a fan of the genre than T. S. Eliot praised *Murder in the Maze* for its construction ('we are provided early in the story with all the clues which guide the detective') and its liveliness ('The very idea of murder in a box-hedge labyrinth does the author great credit, and he makes full use of its possibilities'). The delighted Eliot concluded that

Murder in the Maze was 'a really first-rate detective story'. For his part, the critic H. C. Harwood declared in *The Outlook* that with the publication of *Murder in the Maze* Connington demanded and deserved 'comparison with the masters'. 'Buy, borrow, or – anyhow – get hold of it', he amusingly advised. Two decades later, in his 1946 critical essay 'The Grandest Game in the World', the great locked-room detective novelist John Dickson Carr echoed Eliot's assessment of the novel's virtuoso setting, writing: 'These 1920s [. . .] thronged with sheer brains. What would be one of the best possible settings for violent death? J. J. Connington found the answer, with *Murder in the Maze*.' Certainly in retrospect *Murder in the Maze* stands as one of the finest English country-house mysteries of the 1920s, cleverly yet fairly clued, imaginatively detailed and often grimly suspenseful. As the great American true-crime writer Edmund Lester Pearson noted in his review of *Murder in the Maze* in *The Outlook*, this Connington novel had everything that one could desire in a detective story: 'A shrubbery maze, a hot day, and somebody potting at you with an air gun loaded with darts covered with a deadly South-American arrow-poison – *there* is a situation to wheedle two dollars out of anybody's pocket.'[3]

Staying with what had worked so well for him to date, Stewart the same year produced yet another country-house mystery, *Tragedy at Ravensthorpe*, an ingenious tale of murders and thefts at the ancestral home of the Chacewaters, old family friends of Sir Clinton Driffield. There is much clever matter in *Ravensthorpe*. Especially fascinating is the author's inspired integration of faerie folklore into his plot. Stewart, who had a lifelong – though skeptical – interest in paranormal phenomena, probably was inspired in this instance by the recent hubbub over the Cottingly Faeries photographs that in the early 1920s had famously duped, among other individuals, Arthur Conan Doyle.[4] As with *Murder in the Maze*, critics raved about this new Connington mystery. In the *Spectator*, for example, a reviewer hailed *Tragedy at Ravensthorpe* in the strongest terms, declaring of the novel: 'This is more than a good detective tale. Alike in plot, characterization, and literary style, it is a work of art.'

In 1928 there appeared two additional Sir Clinton Driffield detective novels, *Mystery at Lynden Sands* and *The Case with Nine Solutions*. Once again there was great praise for the latest Conningtons. H. C. Harwood, the critic who had so much admired *Murder in the Maze*, opined of *Mystery at Lynden Sands* that it 'may just fail of being the detective story of the century', while in the United States author and book reviewer Frederic F. Van de Water expressed nearly as high an opinion of *The Case with Nine Solutions*. 'This book is a thoroughbred of a distinguished lineage that runs back to "The Gold Bug" of [Edgar Allan] Poe,' he avowed. 'It represents the highest type of detective fiction.' In both of these Connington novels, Stewart moved away from his customary country-house milieu, setting *Lynden Sands* at a fashionable beach resort and *Nine Solutions* at a scientific research institute. *Nine Solutions* is of particular interest today, I think, for its relatively frank sexual subject matter and its modern urban setting among science professionals, which rather resembles the locales found in P. D. James' classic detective novels *A Mind to Murder* (1963) and *Shroud for a Nightingale* (1971).

By the end of the 1920s, J. J. Connington's critical reputation had achieved enviable heights indeed. At this time Stewart became one of the charter members of the Detection Club, an assemblage of the finest writers of British detective fiction that included, among other distinguished individuals, Agatha Christie, Dorothy L. Sayers and G. K. Chesterton. Certainly Victor Gollancz, the British publisher of the J. J. Connington mysteries, did not stint praise for the author, informing readers that 'J. J. Connington is now established as, in the opinion of many, the greatest living master of the story of pure detection. He is one of those who, discarding all the superfluities, has made of deductive fiction a genuine minor art, with its own laws and its own conventions.'

Such warm praise for J. J. Connington makes it all the more surprising that at this juncture the esteemed author tinkered with his successful formula by dispensing with his original series detective. In the fifth Clinton Driffield detective novel, *Nemesis at Raynham Parva* (1929), Alfred Walter Stewart, rather like Arthur Conan Doyle before him, seemed with a dramatic dénouement to have devised his popular series detective's permanent exit from the fictional stage (read it and see for yourself). The next two Connington detective novels, *The Eye in the Museum* (1929) and *The Two Tickets Puzzle* (1930), have a different series detective, Superintendent Ross, a rather dull dog of a policeman. While both these mysteries are competently done – the railway material in *The Two Tickets Puzzle* is particularly effective and should have appeal today – the presence of Sir Clinton Driffield (no superfluity he!) is missed.

Probably Stewart detected that the public minded the absence of the brilliant and biting Sir Clinton, for the Chief Constable – accompanied, naturally, by his friend Squire Wendover – triumphantly returned in 1931 in *The Boathouse Riddle*, another well-constructed criminous country-house affair. Later in the year came *The Sweepstake Murders*, which boasts the perennially popular tontine multiple-murder plot, in this case a rapid succession of puzzling suspicious deaths afflicting the members of a sweepstake syndicate that has just won nearly £250,000.[5] Adding piquancy to this plot is the fact that Wendover is one of the imperiled syndicate members. Altogether the novel is, as the late Jacques Barzun and his colleague Wendell Hertig Taylor put it in *A Catalogue of Crime* (1971, 1989), their magisterial survey of detective fiction, 'one of Connington's best conceptions'.

Stewart's productivity as a fiction writer slowed in the 1930s, so that, barring the year 1938, at most only one new Connington appeared annually. However, in 1932 Stewart produced one of the best Connington mysteries, *The Castleford Conundrum*. A classic country-house detective novel, Castleford introduces to readers Stewart's most delightfully unpleasant set of greedy relations and one of his most deserving murderees, Winifred Castleford. Stewart also fashions a wonderfully rich puzzle plot, full of meaty material clues for the reader's delectation. *Castleford* presented critics with no conundrum over its quality. 'In *The Castleford Conundrum* Mr Connington goes to work like an accomplished chess player. The moves in the games his detectives are called on to play are a delight to watch,' raved the reviewer for the *Sunday Times*, adding that 'the clues would have rejoiced Mr. Holmes' heart.' For its part, the *Spectator* concurred in the *Sunday Times*' assessment of the novel's masterfully constructed plot: 'Few detective stories show such sound reasoning as that by which the Chief Constable brings the crime home to the culprit.' Additionally, E. C. Bentley, much admired himself as the author of the landmark detective novel *Trent's Last Case*, took time to praise Connington's purely literary virtues, noting: 'Mr Connington has never written better, or drawn characters more full of life.'

With *Tom Tiddler's Island* in 1933 Stewart produced a different sort of Connington, a criminal-gang mystery in the rather more breathless style of such hugely popular English thriller writers as Sapper, Sax Rohmer, John Buchan and Edgar Wallace (in violation of the strict detective fiction rules of Ronald Knox, there is even a secret passage in the novel). Detailing the startling discoveries made by a newlywed couple honeymooning on a remote Scottish island, *Tom Tiddler's Island* is an atmospheric and entertaining tale, though it is not as mentally stimulating for armchair sleuths as Stewart's true detective novels. The title, incidentally, refers to an ancient British children's game, 'Tom Tiddler's Ground', in which one child tries to hold a height against other children.

After his fictional Scottish excursion into thrillerdom, Stewart returned the next year to his English country-house roots with *The Ha-Ha Case* (1934), his last masterwork in this classicmystery setting (for elucidation of non-British readers, a ha-ha is a sunken wall, placed so as to delineate property boundaries while not obstructing views). Although *The Ha-Ha Case* is not set in Scotland, Stewart drew inspiration for the novel from a notorious Scottish true crime, the 1893 Ardlamont murder case. From the facts of the Ardlamont affair Stewart drew several of the key characters in *The Ha-Ha Case*, as well as the circumstances of the novel's murder (a shooting 'accident' while hunting), though he added complications that take the tale in a new direction.[6]

In newspaper reviews both Dorothy L. Sayers and 'Francis Iles' (crime novelist Anthony Berkeley Cox) highly praised this latest mystery by 'The Clever Mr Connington', as he was now dubbed on book jackets by his new English publisher, Hodder & Stoughton. Sayers particularly noted the effective characterisation in *The Ha-Ha Case*: 'There is no need to say that Mr Connington has given us a sound and interesting plot, very carefully and ingeniously worked out. In addition, there are the three portraits of the three brothers, cleverly and rather subtly characterised, of the [governess], and of Inspector Hinton, whose admirable qualities are counteracted by that besetting sin of the man who has made his own way: a jealousy of delegating responsibility.' The reviewer for the *Times Literary Supplement* detected signs that the sardonic Sir Clinton Driffield had begun mellowing with age: 'Those who have never really liked Sir Clinton's perhaps excessively soldierly manner will be surprised to find that he makes his discovery not only by the pure light of intelligence, but partly as a reward for amiability and tact, qualities

in which the Inspector [Hinton] was strikingly deficient.' This is true enough, although the classic Sir Clinton emerges a number of times in the novel, as in his subtly sarcastic recurrent backhanded praise of Inspector Hinton: 'He writes a first class report.'
Clinton Driffield returned the next year in the detective novel *In Whose Dim Shadow* (1935), a tale set in a recently erected English suburb, the denizens of which seem to have committed an impressive number of indiscretions, including sexual ones. The intriguing title of the British edition of the novel is drawn from a poem by the British historian Thomas Babington Macaulay: 'Those trees in whose dim shadow/The ghastly priest doth reign/The priest who slew the slayer/And shall himself be slain.' Stewart's puzzle plot in *In Whose Dim Shadow* is well clued and compelling, the kicker of a closing paragraph is a classic of its kind and, additionally, the author paints some excellent character portraits. I fully concur with the *Sunday Times*' assessment of the tale: 'Quiet domestic murder, full of the neatest detective points [. . .] These are not the detective's stock figures, but fully realised human beings.'[7]

Uncharacteristically for Stewart, nearly twenty months elapsed between the publication of *In Whose Dim Shadow* and his next book, *A Minor Operation* (1937). The reason for the author's delay in production was the onset in 1935–36 of the afflictions of cataracts and heart disease (Stewart ultimately succumbed to heart disease in 1947). Despite these grave health complications, Stewart in late 1936 was able to complete *A Minor Operation*, a first-rate Clinton Driffield story of murder and a most baffling disappearance. A *Times Literary Supplement* reviewer found that *A Minor Operation* treated the reader 'to exactly the right mixture of mystification and clue' and that, in addition to its impressive construction, the novel boasted 'character-drawing above the average' for a detective novel.

Alfred Stewart's final eight mysteries, which appeared between 1938 and 1947, the year of the author's death, are, on the whole, a somewhat weaker group of tales than the sixteen that appeared between 1926 and 1937, yet they are not without interest. In 1938 Stewart for the last time managed to publish two detective novels, *Truth Comes Limping* and *For Murder Will Speak* (also published as *Murder Will Speak*). The latter tale is much the superior of the two, having an interesting suburban setting and a bevy of female characters found to have motives when a contemptible philandering businessman meets with foul play. Sexual neurosis plays a major role in *For Murder Will Speak*, the ever-thorough Stewart obviously having made a study of the subject when writing the novel. The somewhat squeamish reviewer for *Scribner's Magazine* considered the subject matter of *For Murder Will Speak* 'rather unsavoury at times', yet this individual conceded that the novel nevertheless made 'first-class reading for those who enjoy a good puzzle intricately worked out'. 'Judge Lynch' in the *Saturday Review* apparently had no such moral reservations about the latest Clinton Driffield murder case, avowing simply of the novel: 'They don't come any better'.

Over the next couple of years Stewart again sent Sir Clinton Driffield temporarily packing, replacing him with a new series detective, a brash radio personality named Mark Brand, in *The Counsellor* (1939) and *The Four Defences* (1940). The better of these two novels is *The Four Defences*, which Stewart based on another notorious British true-crime case, the Alfred Rouse blazing-car murder. (Rouse is believed to have fabricated his death by murdering an unknown man, placing the dead man's body in his car and setting the car on fire, in the hope that the murdered man's body would be taken for his.) Though admittedly a thinly characterised academic exercise in ratiocination, Stewart's *Four Defences* surely is also one of the most complexly plotted Golden Age detective novels and should delight devotees of classical detection. Taking the Rouse blazing-car affair as his theme, Stewart composes from it a stunning set of diabolically ingenious criminal variations. 'This is in the cold-blooded category which [. . .] excites a crossword puzzle kind of interest,' the reviewer for the *Times Literary Supplement* acutely noted of the novel. 'Nothing in the Rouse case would prepare you for these complications upon complications [. . .] What they prove is that Mr Connington has the power of penetrating into the puzzle-corner of the brain. He leaves it dazedly wondering whether in the records of actual crime there can be any dark deed to equal this in its planned convolutions.'

Sir Clinton Driffield returned to action in the remaining four detective novels in the Connington oeuvre, *The Twenty-One Clues* (1941), *No Past is Dead* (1942), *Jack-in-the-Box* (1944) and *Commonsense is All You Need* (1947), all of which were written as Stewart's heart disease steadily worsened and reflect to some extent his diminishing physical and mental energy. Although *The Twenty-One Clues* was inspired by the notorious Hall-Mills double murder case – probably the most publicised murder case in the United States in the 1920s – and the American critic and novelist Anthony Boucher commended *Jack-in-the-Box*, I believe the best of these later mysteries is *No Past Is Dead*, which Stewart partly based on a bizarre French true-crime affair, the 1891 Achet-Lepine murder case.[8] Besides providing an interesting background for the tale, the ailing author managed some virtuoso plot twists, of the sort most associated today with that ingenious Golden Age Queen of Crime, Agatha Christie.

What Stewart with characteristic bluntness referred to as 'my complete crack-up' forced his retirement from Queen's University in 1944. 'I am afraid,' Stewart wrote a friend, the chemist and forensic scientist F. Gerald Tryhorn, in August 1946, eleven months before his death, 'that I shall never be much use again. Very stupidly, I tried for a session to combine a full course of lecturing with angina pectoris; and ended up by establishing that the two are immiscible.' He added that since retiring in 1944, he had been physically 'limited to my house, since even a fifty-yard crawl brings on the usual cramps'. Stewart completed his essay collection and a final novel before he died at his study desk in his Belfast home on 1 July 1947, at the age of sixty-six. When death came to the author he was busy at work, writing.

More than six decades after Alfred Walter Stewart's death, his J. J. Connington fiction is again available to a wider audience of classic-mystery fans, rather than strictly limited to a select company of rare-book collectors with deep pockets. This is fitting for an individual who was one of the finest writers of British genre fiction between the two world wars. 'Heaven forfend that you should imagine I take myself for anything out of the common in the tec yarn stuff,' Stewart once self-deprecatingly declared in a letter to Rupert Gould. Yet, as contemporary critics recognised, as a writer of detective and science fiction Stewart indeed was something out of the common. Now more modern readers can find this out for themselves. They have much good sleuthing in store.

1. For more on Street, Crofts and particularly Stewart, see Curtis Evans, *Masters of the 'Humdrum' Mystery: Cecil John Charles Street, Freeman Wills Crofts, Alfred Walter Stewart and the British Detective Novel, 1920–1961* (Jefferson, NC: McFarland, 2012). On the academic career of Alfred Walter Stewart, see his entry in *Oxford Dictionary of National Biography* (London and New York: Oxford University Press, 2004), vol. 52, 627–628.
2. The Gould-Stewart correspondence is discussed in considerable detail in *Masters of the 'Humdrum' Mystery*. For more on the life of the fascinating Rupert Thomas Gould, see Jonathan Betts, *Time Restored: The Harrison Timekeepers and R. T. Gould, the*

Man Who Knew (Almost) Everything (London and New York: Oxford University Press, 2006) and *Longitude,* the 2000 British film adaptation of Dava Sobel's book *Longitude: The True Story of a Lone Genius Who Solved the Greatest Scientific Problem of His Time* (London: Harper Collins, 1995), which details Gould's restoration of the marine chronometers built by in the eighteenth century by the clockmaker John Harrison.

3. Potential purchasers of *Murder in the Maze* should keep in mind that $2 in 1927 is worth over $26 today.
4. In a 1920 article in *The Strand Magazine,* Arthur Conan Doyle endorsed as real prank photographs of purported fairies taken by two English girls in the garden of a house in the village of Cottingley. In the aftermath of the Great War Doyle had become a fervent believer in Spiritualism and other paranormal phenomena. Especially embarrassing to Doyle's admirers today, he also published *The Coming of the Faeries* (1922), wherein he argued that these mystical creatures genuinely existed. 'When the spirits came in, the common sense oozed out,' Stewart once wrote bluntly to his friend Rupert Gould of the creator of Sherlock Holmes. Like Gould, however, Stewart had an intense interest in the subject of the Loch Ness Monster, believing that he, his wife and daughter had sighted a large marine creature of some sort in Loch Ness in 1935. A year earlier Gould had authored *The Loch Ness Monster and Others*, and it was this book that led Stewart, after he made his 'Nessie' sighting, to initiate correspondence with Gould.
5. A tontine is a financial arrangement wherein shareowners in a common fund receive annuities that increase in value with the death of each participant, with the entire amount of the fund going to the last survivor. The impetus that the tontine provided to the deadly creative imaginations of Golden Age mystery writers should be sufficiently obvious.
6. At Ardlamont, a large country estate in Argyll, Cecil Hambrough died from a gunshot wound while hunting. Cecil's tutor, Alfred John Monson, and another man, both of whom were out hunting with Cecil, claimed that Cecil had accidentally shot himself, but Monson was arrested and tried for Cecil's murder. The verdict delivered was 'not proven', but Monson was then – and is today – considered almost certain to have been guilty of the murder. On the Ardlamont case, see William Roughead, *Classic Crimes* (1951; repr., New York: New York Review Books Classics, 2000), 378–464.
7. For the genesis of the title, see Macaulay's 'The Battle of the Lake

Regillus', from his narrative poem collection *Lays of Ancient Rome*. In this poem Macaulay alludes to the ancient cult of Diana Nemorensis, which elevated its priests through trial by combat. Study of the practices of the Diana Nemorensis cult influenced Sir James George Frazer's cultural interpretation of religion in his most renowned work, *The Golden Bough: A Study in Magic and Religion*. As with *Tom Tiddler's Island* and *The Ha-Ha Case* the title *In Whose Dim Shadow* proved too esoteric for Connington's American publishers, Little, Brown and Co., who altered it to the more prosaic *The Tau Cross Mystery*.

8. Stewart analysed the Achet-Lepine case in detail in 'The Mystery of Chantelle', one of the best essays in his 1947 collection *Alias J. J. Connington*.

1 ADVISER IN GENERAL

MARK BRAND turned into the door of an Oxford Street office building, past the indicator-board which bore: "THE COUNSELLOR, *Second Floor,*" among the names of other concerns. He was a shade below middle height, wiry, quick-stepping, with a sparrow-like alertness; and his taste in fabrics favoured the louder varieties for his clothes. There was a hint of raffishness about him, a faint indefinable air of horsiness, though he seldom attended a race-meeting.

In his young days, his grandfather—a plain-spoken old gentleman who kept his carriage—had once glanced at him, grunted disapprovingly, and then declared: "That child looks like a stable-boy who'll never grow up into a coachman." And the family, accustomed to the awful dignity of the coachman caste, had agreed that Mark could never hope to reach that standard. This, however, proved of small importance; for Mark Brand, widely known as he was, had never appeared in the public eye. He was, to his host of admirers, only a disembodied voice.

Disdaining the lift, he ran upstairs with the swiftness of a terrier and reached the second floor opposite a door ornamented with a brass plate bearing the inscription: "THE COUNSELLOR. *No appointments.*" Along the corridor to the left was a plain door. Mark Brand opened this with a Yale key and let himself into his private office.

Though it was the smallest of the seven rooms in the suite, it was bright and airy; and the sparseness of the furnishing made it seem almost spacious. Three comfortable chairs, a Persian rug, a fire-proof safe, toilet fittings behind a curtain, a cupboard, a set of expanding bookshelves crammed with works of reference and other books, and a big roll-top desk: these were the main items. The desk had a telephone with a switchboard panel; and on the desk itself lay a small pile of neatly-docketed papers, and two wire trays.

Whistling softly to himself, Mark Brand hung up his oyster-grey felt hat and took the chair at the desk. He picked up the first set of documents from the pile and glanced at the typewritten slip which was clipped to them.

"*My employer is too familiar, but I can't afford to lose my job.*—PERPLEXED IVY."

This, supplied by the office staff, gave the gist of the letter to which it was fastened. Mark Brand flipped over the sheets of the epistle with a faint frown on his face.

"Better see what Sandra's got to say," he concluded, putting the documents into the right-hand wire tray and turning to the next set.

"*What about Urisk next week?*—PRESS-A-BET PETER. (N.B. Mr. Shalstone's opinion attached.)"

Mark Brand did not trouble to read the expert opinion on Urisk's form. All racing problems were in the hands of Mr. Shalstone, a University don known among his colleagues as the Student of Form, from his all-embracing knowledge of the proper handicaps for even the most obscure outsiders. It was his hobby. He boasted, perhaps truly, that he had never made a bet in his life; but he was not averse to drawing a liberal salary from The Counsellor, so long as his name was not disclosed. Press-a-bet Peter's inquiry joined that of Perplexed Ivy. Both had a wide human appeal, in the Counsellor's judgment. He picked up the next document.

" *When I sunbathe, I get a rash. But if I don't sunbathe, I am out of it.*—TROUBLED."

An almost superfluous note explained that the writer was " (female) " and added : " Doctor's opinion attached." This physician had once practised in the Harley Street neighbourhood, but had been struck off the Medical Register for reasons quite apart from his professional competence. He was now glad to put his experience at the disposal of The Counsellor for something much lower than his quondam fees.

Mark Brand pencilled : " *Send her the doctor's note* " on a blank space on the typewritten slip and tossed the documents into the left-hand tray. His public would not be thrilled by that subject.

" *Someone has palmed a bad pound note on me. What can I do with it ?*—CHEATED."

The Counsellor jotted down a memorandum : " *Ask him to send it to us for our museum,*" and dropped the papers into the left-hand tray.

" *My fiancé objects to my going alone on a cruise.*—ZENA."

This went into the right-hand tray on the strength of the epitome alone. That type of problem interested people, whether they went themselves on cruises or stayed at home. Also it was the kind of thing which lent itself to expansion into fields of wider application.

" *I have an inferiority complex which goes against me at the office.*—HARASSED CLERK."

" Poor devil ! " sympathised The Counsellor, as he read the letter. He put it into the right-hand tray, after scribbling a note : " *Write him a kind letter and enclose Leaflet D. 7.*"

" *My wife re-reads her late husband's love-letters.*—K.T."

"A polygon of a problem," mused The Counsellor, "so many sides to it."

He put the papers back for further consideration and continued to work his way down through the pile, sorting out the sheep from the goats, and occasionally making jottings on the typed slips. When his task was completed, he ran through the contents of the right-hand tray again, paying special attention to some of the letters. Then, for a time, he leaned back in his chair, pondering over the problems raised by his correspondents.

At twenty-two, Mark Brand had been left an orphan with no occupation except to look after a large fortune which he inherited from his father. He had tried spending his income in one way and another, but the process soon bored him.

"It's no good" he confided ruefully to a friend. "I can't spend even a mere £5,000 a year on myself and get direct personal enjoyment out of it. I'll have to look for a job. And I don't want to pile up more money. Stiff proposition."

A chance visit to America solved his problem. Listening to the WOR station on the wireless, he heard the talks of that peculiar genius who calls himself "*The Voice of Experience.*" Mark Brand made inquiries, learned something about the thousands of letters which flow in to V.O.E. daily, about the office staff which copes with them, about the books, the pamphlets, the questionnaires, and about the Charity Fund.

"This fellow's doing fine work," was Brand's conclusion. "We could do with something like it in Europe. Cost big money to start it. But I've got the money. And it must be great fun. I'll take it on. But he's got the best pseudonym possible. I'll have to think of something else."

And, from such musings, The Counsellor was born.

In one respect, Mark Brand possessed an essential gift for his self-chosen task. He had a perfect broadcasting voice: clear, expressive, and sympathetic. And he had also what his friends called "a most infernal curiosity," though he himself preferred to describe it as a deep interest in his fellow-creatures. The rest was merely a matter of spending money and building up a rapidly-increasing staff fit to cope with the ever-expanding demands of his rôle.

He "hired the air" for an hour each Sunday at Radio Ardennes, which formed his platform. When possible, his private plane took him over to the broadcasting studio; but when the weather made this impracticable, electrical recording served instead. Problems—social, financial, ethical, medical, legal and sporting—rained in upon him through his daily post. Those of most general interest he dealt with over the wireless, whilst the remainder were answered by letter. The demand for a sixpenny postal order with each query had hardly slackened the flood, and it served to keep the system practically solvent. The feat of which he was proudest was that once at least, like his prototype, he had prevented an impending suicide.

Begun in a modest way, The Counsellor's business had ramified and spread like a weed. Luckily for himself, Brand had a shrewd eye in picking his staff, and a talent for decentralisation which saved him from details except when he required them. His secretarial staff attended to his enormous correspondence, passing on to him only the few letters which had the wide human interest demanded in his broadcasts. In legal affairs, pensions, and insurance problems he was advised by an ex-solicitor of exceptional talent who had been struck off the rolls in circumstances which he scorned to explain. Financial matters were dealt with by another expert; but this was a field into which The Counsellor entered rarely and reluctantly. The Problem Department supplied solutions to cross-word puzzles and the like, week by week. Applicants for its assistance had to forward a shilling postal order instead of the usual sixpenny one. To balance that, the Advertisement Department charged nothing for its services, since its expenses were borne by the firms which sought publicity through it.

The Department on which The Counsellor looked with the kindest eye—as being the one most useful to him in his broadcasts—was known unofficially in the office as Cupid's Corner; and it was managed by a girl who had got engaged just before she was appointed to it. It was well understood that as soon as she married, her post would fall vacant; for, as The Counsellor said, the sympathetic touch was essential in that branch of his business.

After having considered the problems presented by his morning mail, The Counsellor extracted one document from the set and pressed a bell-push concealed under the edge of his desk. The door of the adjoining office opened and his private secretary appeared, notebook in hand.

"Morning, Sandra," The Counsellor greeted her, with his friendly smile. "No, no dictation just yet. I want your views on this, first."

He picked up Perplexed Ivy's epistle and flipped it across the desk.

"Glance through it, and see what you think."

Miss Rainham sat down and spread out the letter on her knee. She was chestnut-haired, clear-eyed, alert, and twenty-four. She looked her age, neither more nor less. People spoke of her as charming and unconsciously avoided such adjectives as capable, competent, and efficient. She merited them, but they did not express the more obvious side of her personality. Her good looks were sufficiently above the average to allow her to take them for granted, which perhaps had something to do with her charm.

"Well?" demanded The Counsellor, as she glanced up from the letter with a faint frown.

"Not a very nice case, is it?" retorted Miss Rainham. "The man seems to be worrying her badly, and she's got this invalid mother depending on her."

The Counsellor nodded.

" He'll chuck her out without a character, if he doesn't get what he wants ; and that would leave her and her mother stranded," he commented unnecessarily.

" I might see her," Sandra Rainham suggested tentatively.

" It's a well-written letter," The Counsellor said, critically. " You'd better see her. Don't bring her here. Take her to some teashop. You can pick her brains in no time, if she's what the letter looks like."

" And then ? " Sandra demanded. " No good seeing her, unless we can do something, is there ? "

" Trouble is, she'll need some sort of reference, to get another post. *If* she's all right, it's easy. Tell her to chuck her present job. We'll take her on here for a few weeks at the same screw. After that, she's got us behind her when she looks for other work. She can enclose circulars with letters, or something like that. But make it clear that we aren't an Old Age Pension."

" She might turn out to be efficient ; and we're going to lose two of our girls very shortly," Miss Rainham suggested.

" I remember that. Let me know in time to order the cutlery canteens."

A complete canteen of cutlery was The Counsellor's invariable wedding-present when any of his staff got married. These things were always useful and his method saved him the trouble of selection.

" No promises to this girl," he added with finality. " I'm not a charity."

The secretary smiled as she bent her head to jot down the girl's address. If Perplexed Ivy proved satisfactory during her probation, Sandra would see that she got a permanency. She had liked that letter.

" I'll see her and report," she said.

Sandra Rainham had been one of The Counsellor's

" finds " when he began to gather a staff. She was a distant relation, a third cousin once removed or something equally remote, left at her parents' death with just enough money to exist on and a fund of energy which demanded some useful outlet. The Counsellor had seen in this girl of twenty the sort of material he needed ; and after putting her through an expensive technical training, he had engaged her as his private secretary. Private secretary she remained in name ; but actually she and Wolfram Standish, The Counsellor's manager, jointly controlled the more mechanical side of the ever-expanding office work. Like The Counsellor himself, she was " interested in humanity " ; and in that office an interest in humanity implied an equal keenness in the working of the intricate system. It suited her. She satisfied The Counsellor who, though generally easy-going, was apt at times to develop inquisitiveness about details, which was his way of keeping his finger on the pulse of the business.

The Counsellor picked up the packet of documents from the right-hand tray, and at that signal Miss Rainham opened her notebook. This was the serious stage of The Counsellor's activities : the making of a rough draft of his next wireless talk from Radio Ardennes. He dictated slowly, with occasional pauses for thought, a shrewd and helpful series of answers to the selected letters, spiced with a dry humour which made his points tell. His style " on the air " was different from his normal snappy sentences, but it had an incisiveness of its own.

He had almost finished his dictation when an office-boy entered with a letter. As The Counsellor took it, he noted the broad vertical line on the envelope.

" Express Delivery ? Somebody in a hurry, apparently. Just wait a moment, Sandra."

He opened the envelope, drew out the letter, and glanced through it. Then, dismissing the boy, he turned to his secretary.

"Rum go, this. Have a look at it."

He pushed the letter across the desk to Sandra. She glanced at the heading: "THE RAVENSCOURT PRESS, Longstoke House, Grendon St. Giles," and her eyebrows lifted slightly as though in surprise. Then she began to read the letter itself.

9th September, 1938.

Dear Sir,

I venture to ask for your assistance, since you have facilities for getting in touch with people all up and down the country. As a guarantee of good faith I may mention that I am one of the experts employed by Mr. James Treverton, of the Ravenscourt Press; and I have his permission to approach you in this matter.

The facts are as follows. On 8th September, Miss Helen Treverton (Mr. Treverton's niece) set off in her car, intending to visit Dr. and Mrs. Trulock, who live a few miles away and who were giving a small garden party that afternoon. She did not return for dinner; and when inquiries were made, it was found that she had not gone to Dr. Trulock's house, as she had meant to do.

Up to the present, she has not returned home, and nothing has been heard of her. No message of any kind has been received from her. She seems to have disappeared completely.

I have Mr. Treverton's permission to ask you to help. Could you, in your broadcast next Sunday, ask if anyone has seen a brown Vauxhall 12 h.p. saloon, with the number EZ. 1113? Some of your numerous listeners may have happened to notice it. Your assistance may be invaluable.

Yours faithfully,

WALLACE WHITGIFT.

"Think it's a leg-pull?" demanded The Counsellor, with a shrewd glance at the girl's face as she finished her perusal. "We've had attempts before this, though they didn't come off."

Sandra shook her head.

"Hardly likely," she decided. "I'll ring up the Ravenscourt Press and get hold of Mr. Treverton, just to make sure. Funny. It was only last week that I bought one of these Ravenscourt reproductions."

"Good stuff, are they?" inquired The Counsellor. He had no interest in reproductions of the old masters, preferring to buy the work of the younger modern artists to whom sales meant encouragement.

"Amazingly good," Sandra assured him. "They beat anything else on the market when it comes to accurate reproduction of tints; and they've got some special paper as a basis which seems to help. Of course, they're not cheap. But they're worth the money to me."

She passed Wallace Whitgift's letter back to The Counsellor and added:

"If it's all right, I suppose you'll put it in the broadcast?"

"*If* it's all right," admitted The Counsellor. "But just ask a question, Sandra."

Miss Rainham smiled rather wearily. She knew that last phrase only too well, for it was one of The Counsellor's favourites.

"Well, what question?" she inquired.

"Why does Mr. Wallace Whitgift—who seems to be some sort of employee—butt into this business at all? Why didn't Uncle James write to us himself? Strange, eh?"

"That's three questions instead of one," Sandra pointed out. "I can guess the answers. First, Mr. Whitgift may be one of your fans. That would account for his turning to you. Second, Mr. Treverton may never have heard of you. Sorry, Mark, but it's a fact that quite a number of people don't know you exist. And if he never heard of you, he probably doesn't think you're likely to be of much use. So he lets Mr. Whitgift take the responsibility of raking you in. On that basis, the answer to your third question is: "Not at all." And, finally, Mr. W. is not just "a mere employee." He's a director of the Ravenscourt Press. Also, he's their expert in the actual reproduction processes. I know that from reading their catalogues."

"Doesn't account for his butting in like this," objected The Counsellor.

"Oh, well, just ask a question," Sandra parodied. "Is Wallace Whitgift keen on this girl, by any chance? If so, that might account for his zeal."

"I never butt into our Cupid's Corner Department," retorted The Counsellor with dignity. "Still, it's a rum start: total disappearance of a car with a young damsel inside. Cars get stolen, and girls disappear at times. But they don't usually vanish in pairs. A car's fairly identifiable; and when you add a girl to it, it becomes positively too conspicuous to grab easily."

"What makes you think she's a young damsel?" asked Sandra drily. "I've known nieces of forty-five and upwards."

"In that case, Wallace wouldn't be very keen on her, one might suppose. Have it one way or the other, but not both ways at once."

Miss Rainham became businesslike.

"I'll put through a trunk call and speak to Mr. Treverton," she proposed. "Then, if he makes no objection, you'll put this into the broadcast to-morrow?"

"Yes. No harm in that. And now I'll give you the rest of the stuff for it."

He resumed his dictation. When this was completed, Sandra Rainham closed her notebook and left the room. She came back again sooner than The Counsellor had expected.

"I managed to get through fairly quickly," she explained. "It's all right, apparently. The girl hasn't turned up yet. Mr. Treverton has no objection to your broadcast, so you can go ahead."

"He's worried, I suppose?" inquired The Counsellor.

"Not particularly, so far as I could make out," Sandra replied in a faintly puzzled tone. "It almost sounded as if he thought Mr. Whitgift was making too much of a fuss about the business. There was a suggestion of ' Let 'em alone, and they'll come home . . . ' about his tone ; as if a mislaid niece was a thing that might happen to anyone now and again. Even over the 'phone he doesn't sound a sympathetic character, somehow."

" How d'you mean, exactly ? "

" Well, he talks as if he were thinking of something else, all the time he's speaking. I can't get nearer than that. Nothing of the distracted relative about him."

" You think so ? Well, anyhow, we'll shove it into the broadcast. Just take this down, please."

He dictated a further note.

2 AT GRENDON ST. GILES

ON the following Monday morning, The Counsellor arrived punctually at his office and spent some time over matters of routine. But his heart did not seem to be in the business ; and when it was completed he turned from it with relief, and rang for Sandra Rainham.

" Broadcast all right ? " he demanded, as she entered the room.

It was one of her duties to listen to Radio Ardennes when he was speaking from the station and to supply him with any criticisms which occurred to her.

" Quite," she answered, " except that you're growing inclined to drop your voice at the end of sentences. You'd better watch that."

" Right ! By the way, have any wires or letters come in about that missing car ? "

Sandra shook her head.

" Nothing, so far. Monday's not usually a busy day for correspondence. Even if they write on Sunday, it doesn't get here till the afternoon, you know."

The Counsellor conceded this with a nod. Then he pushed the switch of his desk-telephone over to " RECORD DEPARTMENT " and picked up the transmitter.

" Records ? Go through the Sunday papers—yesterday's, I mean—and see if there's anything about a girl disappearing last week from Grendon St. Giles. Also, see if we've had any correspondents in that place."

The Counsellor was proud of his Record Department, and especially of its filing system. "Any fact in fifty seconds" was his boast about it, though this estimate was regarded as optimistic by Miss Rainham and others of the staff. On this occasion it was considerably under the mark. A girl cannot scan all the Sunday papers in fifty seconds. However, in a remarkably short time he got his answer. There was nothing in any of the Sunday papers about the disappearance; but in Grendon St. Giles there were two clients of The Counsellor. He picked up the notes which Records handed in.

"Our esteemed correspondents in Grendon St. Giles. Mrs. Sparrick. Anxious about her daughter's choice of a fiancé. Advised, with satisfactory results. Not much help there. Aha! Inspector Owen Pagnell of the local police. I remember that business. We helped him. Broadcast some message that couldn't well be put through official channels. He'll be handy, if he's got any sense of gratitude."

"Why all this interest?" demanded Sandra Rainham. "What's it got to do with you?"

"'I am a man, and nothing human can be foreign to me,'" quoted The Counsellor. "Aristotle said that, or was it Polybius?"

Miss Rainham had been as well educated as Mark Brand, and she had a better memory for quotations.

"Terence," she corrected acidly.

"Oh, well, it doesn't matter. Good man, whoever he was, I expect," averred The Counsellor, quite unabashed. "I've just been thinking of taking a hand in that affair about the girl. Helen Treverton, I mean. The one who disappeared last Thursday. I've often wanted to probe a mystery and all that sort of thing."

"You've been reading too many detective stories," Sandra decided, not without some basis for her judgment.

"Well, what else is there to read, nowadays?"

demanded The Counsellor, fretfully. "Everybody's doing it. I have to keep in touch with the Great Heart of the Public. It's essential to my work."

"I'd leave it alone, if I were you," said Miss Rainham in a decided tone.

"You don't sound encouraging, and that's a fact," complained The Counsellor. "If you feel like that, then we must find support elsewhere. We'll try Standish."

When The Counsellor began to build up his staff, he found his manager in his own circle. Wolfram Standish was a couple of years younger than Mark Brand, but they were old friends and suited each other. The manager's rather impassive face, cool manner, and slightly bored drawl made him a perfect foil for the volatility of his chief.

"This is how it is, Wolf," The Counsellor jerked out as Standish came into the room. And in a few illuminating phrases he laid the matter before his subordinate. Standish listened dispassionately. Then, when The Counsellor had finished, he took out his case and lit a cigarette.

"Well, what do you think of it?" Miss Rainham demanded, with some impatience.

Standish blew out his match, examined it carefully to see that the flame was extinguished, then pitched it into the wastepaper basket.

"I don't think anything," he began, and Sandra's face showed some relief until he continued leisurely, "He's made up his mind. What's the good of thinking?"

He paused, looked at his cigarette, and then added:

"It's just his 'satiable curtiosity' breaking out again."

Neither Miss Rainham nor Standish stood in any awe of their employer. They had known him when he was too young to expect reverence. Among themselves, The Counsellor was nicknamed The

Elephant's Child after the animal in *The Just So Stories*.

The Counsellor glanced from one to the other in feigned disappointment.

" You don't seem bubbling over with enthusiasm and desire to help the young master, and that's a fact," he commented.

" We'll bail you out when the police arrest you as a public nuisance," Standish promised. " That's always something."

" And his tall uncle, the Giraffe, spanked him with his hard, hard hoof ! " quoted The Counsellor, quite undepressed. " That means you," he added to Standish.

" ' And still he was full of ' satiable curtiosity,' " Sandra continued the quotation. " And that means *you*. Seriously, Mark, do you really mean to go down there as the complete detective ? "

" Absolutely," retorted The Counsellor. " I shall take with me all the necessaries. A hypodermic syringe, cocaine, a violin, a pound of shag, a Thorndyke research case, Sir Clinton Driffield's copy of Osborn's *Questioned Documents*, some of Mr. Fortune's intuitive capacity in my vest-pocket, and Lord Peter Wimsey's collection of jade—I can get that into a sack over my shoulder. . . ."

" I see," interjected Standish. " You're going down there disguised as a caddis-worm ? It's an idea, certainly."

" . . . and some of Poirot's little grey cells," The Counsellor concluded.

" That's a sound notion," Standish conceded. " It'll be just as well to have *some* brains with you."

Miss Rainham made an arresting gesture.

" You've forgotten the most important thing of all."

" Have I. What's it ? "

" A Watson, of course."

" Oh, that ? " said The Counsellor in a tone of relief. " That's provided for. That's it there."

With a jerk of his head, he indicated Standish. His subordinates exchanged a glance and then spoke in stage whispers.

"He really means to go?"

"Looks rather like it, doesn't it? Perhaps he'll waken up when he actually gets there."

"You'd better go with him, Wolf. He might get into trouble, in this state."

"Something in that. I can say his nurse let him fall on his head when he was in short clothes."

The Counsellor ignored this by-play.

"While you've been chattering, I've been thinking," he explained benignantly. "This is the plan. I'll go down to Grendon St. Giles to-day, to spy out the land. I hope to clear the matter up at once. If I have to stay overnight, I take rooms at the best hotel—just look it up in the A.A. book, Sandra, please. Wolf will mind the shop here, while I'm away. If I happen to need you, Sandra, I'll wire for you."

"Need *me?*" demanded Miss Rainham indignantly. "What for?"

"Delilah, or something in that line, perhaps," explained The Counsellor casually. "One never knows, beforehand. As to the next broadcast, I'll get it recorded so as to leave me free."

"Napoleonic!" Standish ejaculated in mock admiration. "What a grasp of detail. You're starting to-day, are you, Bonaparte?"

"As soon as I can get my car round."

Standish reflected for a moment and then began to whistle an air softly.

"What's that?" inquired The Counsellor.

Standish changed his whistle to song:

" 'Malbrouck s'en va-t-en guerre,
Mironton, mironton, mirontaine,
Malbrouck s'en va-t-en guerre,
Ne sait quand reviendra.'

It's what Napoleon whistled as he watched his troops

file over the river to the invasion of Russia," he explained. "It seems appropriate at this solemn moment."

"A bright and encouraging lot of helpers I have," said The Counsellor, disgustedly. "Throw yourself into the part, Watson. Now, Sandra, let's see that A.A. book. Heaven send there's a decent hotel."

"Grendon St. Giles isn't in the list," said Miss Rainham, with satisfaction in her tone. "There's no hotel there at all, so far as the A.A. goes. There may be a good-pull-up-for-carmen, perhaps."

"That being so, I shall probably return to town to-night," The Counsellor decided, glancing out of the window as he spoke. "I see my car below. The god will now get into the machine. Ta-ta!"

During the run down to Grendon St. Giles, The Counsellor put his coming business out of his mind. He had no doubts about a successful issue. With thousands of his wireless listeners to help him, the mere tracing of an easily-identifiable car was a dead certainty. But his audience would be interested in the hunt. It would be a good advertisement for his broadcasts. And, just possibly, there might be a story behind this girl's disappearance, something with the human touch in it. One must play the game, of course. It might not be the kind of thing for public use at all.

Grendon St. Giles, at the first glimpse, appeared as a little spire rising from among trees. On closer acquaintance, it turned out to be a pleasant little village, the cottage gardens bright with roses, a tiny village green with some spotless geese, a church with a lych-gate, and a tidily-kept inn. A glaring petrol-pump was the only jarring feature in sight.

The Counsellor picked up the speaking tube.

"Pull up at that pump," he directed his chauffeur. "Get a couple of gallons and ask the way to Longstoke House. Then go on there."

Longstoke House, it appeared, was a couple of miles

further along the road and just beyond an A.A. telephone-box. They turned into a gate. No lodge-keeper appeared, though the cottage was evidently inhabited. A short avenue led up to the main building ; and The Counsellor, who kept his eyes open, noted that the proprietor did not seem to spend much in upkeep. What had at one time been the park was now obviously let out as grazing-ground ; and the gardens, through part of which they ran as they neared the house, had been allowed to run to seed. The mansion itself, when they came to it, proved to be a gaunt affair in the Rural Italian style ; and its uncurtained windows reinforced the impression that the owner spent nothing on outward show. The whole place looked bleak and lifeless, except for the smoke rising from a chimney.

Telling his chauffeur to wait, The Counsellor got out and went up to the out-jutting portico of the main entrance. He had taken the precaution of wiring before he left London ; and when he asked for Mr. Whitgift he was shown into a room and asked to wait for a few moments. Mr. Whitgift, it seemed, was occupied.

Judging from the size of the mansion, The Counsellor inferred that originally this apartment had been a small morning-room ; but from the wholly feminine style of the furnishing it had evidently been converted into the modern equivalent of a boudoir. Its windows, unlike those in the front of the house, were curtained ; the colour scheme had been chosen by someone with a good eye ; and the furniture combined comfort with a certain artistry. It was obviously a room meant to be lived in. The only discord was struck by the ceiling, which had a heavy, old-fashioned decoration in stucco from the centre of which, in earlier days, a chandelier had evidently depended, for The Counsellor could see the closed end of an old gas-pipe in the middle of the design. Now the lighting was electric, by a standard lamp and a couple of pillar-lights on the mantelpiece.

The Counsellor had no time for a further survey, for the door opened and Whitgift appeared.

He was a big man, rather over six feet in height, with broad shoulders and a slow gait which somehow added to the impression of physical power. Instead of a jacket, he wore a white linen coat, as though he had just come from a workroom. He came forward with a pleasant smile showing even lines of very white teeth. A good mixer, The Counsellor decided at the first glance, a fellow who would get on equally well with men and women.

" Mr. Brand ? Well, I know you better than you know me, I guess. Your broadcasts, you know. It was very good indeed of you to give us your help in this awkward affair."

His face clouded at the last sentence as though it touched some sore spot in himself. Then he recovered himself almost immediately.

" Sit down, won't you ? Cigarette ? Or perhaps you'd rather smoke your own brand ? "

He took a box of cigarettes from a table near by, offered them to The Counsellor, picked out one for himself and lighted it before saying anything further. Meanwhile his eyes were evidently busy with Brand's outward appearance. It seemed to be not quite what he had expected.

" Any further news of Miss Treverton ? " The Counsellor asked, as soon as he got his cigarette alight.

Whitgift shook his head despondently.

"Not a sign of her. It's extraordinary. I can't make it out, you know. She was a level-headed girl, not the sort of girl to fly off the handle. Nothing freakish about her, I mean."

He went over to a writing-desk and came back with a framed enlargement of a snapshot which he handed to The Counsellor. It showed a girl in a sports coat stooping to pat a collie. She was looking towards the camera, and The Counsellor saw at a glance that she had an attractive face, with a frank smile and a dimple on each cheek. In the flesh, she must be pretty ; and, judging purely from the snapshot, The Counsellor put her down as a girl of character, dependable, and not at all likely to indulge in silly pranks.

" That's her collie with her, poor old Clyde," Whitgift explained. " He died less than a week ago. We found him out in the fields one morning, stiff. She was immensely fond of the beast, and I guess that's why she has the photo on her desk. I took it myself about six weeks back, the last one she had of him."

" She wasn't engaged, was she ? " asked The Counsellor, who had noted the ringless finger visible in the picture. " Nothing of that sort to account for her vanishing ? "

" No, she wasn't engaged," Whitgift answered with a reluctant sullenness in his tone which attracted The Counsellor's attention. " There was an American who was keen on her at one time, but nothing came of it that I know. Querrin, his name was, Howard Querrin. Not good enough for her, I thought, and probably she thought the same."

That sounded almost like a touch of jealousy, The Counsellor reflected. And not so unlikely, perhaps. Grendon St. Giles obviously offered little in the way of society. Whitgift must have seen a good deal of the girl, if she lived on the premises here. Add her attractiveness to the propinquity factor, and it wasn't unlikely that he might fall in love with her. If he had, then his obvious dislike of an intruding rival, in the form of this American, was intelligible. There might be something in Sandra Rainham's suggestion about the nature of Whitgift's interest in the case. But that was a side-issue. The Counsellor's present interest was in the facts of the disappearance.

" Was it her own car that she went off in ? " he asked.

Whitgift nodded.

" Yes, we've each got a car. Treverton has an old Ford, though he seldom uses it ; and I've got a car down at the lodge. I live there, you know."

The Counsellor reflected before putting his next question.

" What about money ? Could she lay her hands on enough to finance her for, say, a month away from home ? Without asking her uncle for it, I mean."

" Oh, yes, easily. Her father left her some capital, I believe. I know she put a fair sum into the Press when she came of age four or five years ago. We're all in it, if it comes to that, you see. I'm a director, as well as shareholder and expert, myself. Dividends are sub-microscopic, though. She had the rest of her capital, whatever it was, in other concerns which paid better, one hopes. I don't suppose she was rich, by any means ; but she had enough to go on with, I think. Enough for a girl living here, anyhow."

He pondered for a moment or two, then added reluctantly :

" I believe she and her uncle. . . . Well, there's been some faint friction because lately she talked of taking her cash out of this concern. But that's between ourselves, of course."

" I'd like to hear just how she came to disappear," said The Counsellor.

" I can tell you what I know myself, but that's not much. Last Thursday morning, I had to go into Grendon St. Giles on an errand. My own car was scuppered at the moment, something gone wrong with the pump ; and it was at the village garage getting fixed. That was a blazing day, you remember, and I didn't cotton to tramping four miles through it. Miss Treverton offered to take me in. She'd some things she wanted herself. . . . By Jove ! I never thought of that ! " he ejaculated. " It was your mentioning cash that brings it back. She called at the bank while I was doing my own bits of business."

He seemed impressed by this recollection.

" The bank could tell us how much she drew," he suggested.

" Banks don't babble about their customers' affairs," said The Counsellor, impatiently. " The counterfoil of her cheque book's all you want. Time enough for that. Go on with the story."

" All right," agreed Whitgift, though he seemed to keep the point at the back of his mind. " We came back here. She put her car into the garage because the sun was so hot that it would have been bad for the tyres to leave it standing about. Just as she was switching off, I happened to look at the petrol-gauge and saw her tank was empty, almost. We keep a stock of tins in the garage, just for that kind of emergency, so I pointed out the state of things and offered to fill up her tank for her while she went over to the house. I filled it full, and then came back here myself. That was before luncheon."

" Yes, yes," said The Counsellor. " Your point is that she started off in the afternoon with a full tank. I understand."

Whitgift nodded and continued :

" That afternoon, as I told you in my letter, some people Trulock were giving a kind of garden party, of sorts, and Miss Treverton was going to it. Treverton wasn't going ; he hates all that kind of thing. The Trulocks live about eight miles away and she was going over in her Vauxhall. As it happened, I'd had to go down to the lodge about three o'clock to get a document I'd left in another suit, and I met her with her car as I was coming up the avenue again. I stopped her and told her about having filled her tank, and I saw her glance at the gauge. We said a few sentences to each other, but I can't remember what they were—just commonplaces about the tennis-party, wishing her a good game, that sort of thing, you know. Finally she drove off, and that was the last I saw of her. That was almost exactly at three o'clock. I know that, because a bus passed the lodge gate while we were talking, and it's timed to reach Grendon St. Giles at five past three. That's the last I saw of her," he repeated.

Something in the tone of his voice betrayed an anxiety which hitherto he had apparently striven to keep under control.

"How was she dressed, then ?" demanded The Counsellor, more concerned to pick up information than to trouble about Whitgift's feelings.

"A light grey coat and skirt, but it's no good asking me what the material was. I know nothing about girls' clothes. She was driving over, dressed like that. But she was going to play tennis. She had her racquet in its press on the seat beside her, I noticed ; and she had an attaché case, too, with a tennis shirt and shorts and tennis shoes in it, I suppose. She meant to change when she got to the Trulocks. So I suppose, anyhow. There's quite a good court at the Trulocks' place, I'm told. I've never played on it, though. I'm not more than a nodding acquaintance of Trulock."

"And what happened after this ?" asked The Counsellor.

"Nothing. She didn't come home, that's all. I told you the rest in my letter, about my getting anxious and ringing up the Trulocks. She hadn't arrived there, they said. Apparently they took it that she'd got a headache or something like that and hadn't felt up to going over, and they expected that she'd ring up and explain later on. They'd had enough people there to make up their sets, so they hadn't bothered to ring her up and ask why she'd given them a miss."

"Yes, yes," said The Counsellor. "And when did you begin to get anxious about her ?"

"Not till about midnight," Whitgift explained. "I thought perhaps they'd got up a scratch dance or something and that she'd stayed on for that. It was a hot night, you remember, and I'd been sitting out in a camp-chair at the lodge, trying to get cool, so I knew she hadn't come home. Naturally I began to get a bit worried, so I came up here, got in with my latch-key, and rang up the Trulocks."

The Counsellor had a picture in his mind's eye of this big man sitting out in his garden in the gathering dusk, watching, watching for the return of that car, with anxiety growing as the clock crept on. Had Whitgift proposed to that girl and, despite a refusal, kept some hope alive of her changing her mind? Or was it that he hadn't enough money to make a proposal reasonable? That passing remark about the finances of the Ravenscourt Press might point in this direction. And that, too, might account for the jealousy in the matter of the American.

"Mr. Treverton hadn't become anxious when his niece failed to turn up?" asked The Counsellor.

"Apparently not," Whitgift confessed. "I woke him up when I got the message from the Trulocks, but he wasn't exactly grateful. He came to the door of his room and grumbled at being disturbed. The girl was old enough to look after herself, and that sort of thing. Between ourselves, you must remember that there had been that friction between him and Miss Treverton over the matter of the money she has in the business, and perhaps that didn't make him very sympathetic. He's . . . well . . . a little peculiar in money matters."

"Is he?" inquired The Counsellor, without apparent interest.

"He's a queer mixture," Whitgift declared. "Now, when we took over this house for our work, there was no current laid on. It had been empty for years; and the Grid hadn't reached out to here when it was last inhabited. What they'd used was acetylene gas. There's a generator in the stables. That was no good to us, of course, so the plant was scrapped and we got in the Grid current. But tearing out the old acetylene piping would have cost some money—not much—and

Treverton absolutely refused to spend a penny on that. You can see the piping still in place up there. And most people would have pulled down all this ghastly stucco ornamentation and made a plain plaster ceiling, just to get rid of these eyesores in every room. He wouldn't, although it could have been done cheap enough, and he's got an artistic eye which must make him gulp every time he sees one of these abominations. That looks as if he's mean, doesn't it ? Well, he isn't mean when it comes to the Press. We're a very small company working on on a mere mite of capital, and naturally we run up bills which we often can't pay. If we do, Treverton steps in, foots the bills out of his own pocket, and never thinks of charging that up to the company. A man who does that kind of thing isn't really mean, as you can see for yourself. It's simply that with him the Press comes first and foremost all the time, though he grudges money in every other direction."

"'Art's a rum job,'" quoted The Counsellor. "Turner said that, and he ought to know. And humanity's a rum crew. I said that, and I happen to know. When you mix 'em together, anything might happen. I'm not surprised."

He seemed to cogitate for a moment or two and then turned to a fresh line.

"Has Miss Treverton any other relations beyond her uncle ?"

"None that I ever heard of," Whitgift answered, after a moment's reflection.

The Counsellor did not pursue that subject. If anything had happened to the girl, and she died intestate, her uncle would get not only the money she had in the business, but the remainder of her capital as well. But this seemed pushing hypothesis over far.

His eye was caught by a picture on the wall, and he moved over to examine it.

"Monet's 'Corniche Road,' isn't it ?" he asked,

turning to Whitgift. "Is this one of your own productions?"

Whitgift nodded in confirmation.

"One of our most successful attempts," he explained with some pride. "The man in the street couldn't tell it from the original, I'm prepared to bet. An expert would, at a glance, though, if he was allowed to look at the canvas, for that dates it. It's done on canvas foundation, just to lend the last touch of verisimilitude," he added, with a smile. "And it cost me the devil and all of trouble to work out the process, I can tell you. We've been producing stuff in that line for a year or two, but it's too expensive, really, as a commercial large-scale product. I gave that copy to Miss Treverton. That's how it comes to be hanging here."

The Counsellor again examined the picture, this time with all his attention, peering into the detail of the reproduction.

"More than pretty good," he admitted. "Later on, I'd like to hear how you manage it, if you can tell me without giving away your trade secrets. But now I'd like to have a minute or two with Treverton, if he'll see me. There's a chance that I might be of some use in the matter of his niece. But I must make sure, first, that he won't object. After all, my methods are a bit public for some people's taste. Perhaps he mightn't care for them."

"Oh, he won't care, one way or the other," Whitgift assured him. "All he's really interested in is the Press. Something fresh in our method of reproduction would catch his fancy quicker than anything about Miss Treverton."

"If he proposes that I should boost his productions, I'll refer him to my advertising department," said The Counsellor, drily. "We have fixed rates for that kind of work."

"There's just one other thing," Whitgift added, after a momentary hesitation. "He and I haven't seen quite eye to eye on some points lately. Miss Treverton's disappearance is one of them. So if you don't mind, I'll just take you to him now and leave you together. You can say what you like all the better if I'm not there."

"You think so? Very good, then. All the same to me."

3 THE TROUBLES OF AN ART PUBLISHER

WHITGIFT led The Counsellor to a room even smaller than the one he had already seen. It looked out upon the garage; and originally it might have been a dressing-room, being only about fifteen feet by twenty. It was now furnished as an office, except for one big easy-chair drawn up near the fireplace. A mechanical upward glance assured The Counsellor that here also economy had prevailed over æsthetics, for the ceiling had a heavy stucco design like that in the other room and the original ugly marble mantelpiece had been left in place. The Counsellor found the room unpleasantly warm, and another glance showed him that all the windows were tightly closed, despite the heat.

"This is Mr. Brand, Treverton," Whitgift announced. "He wants a few words with you."

And with that he withdrew, leaving The Counsellor confronting across the desk a grey-haired, grey-moustached little man, every line in whose face betrayed a waspish temper.

"Brand? Brand?" said the little man, in a tone which seemed to translate his facial expression into sound. "Oh, yes. I remember, now. You're the person Whitgift told me about. You run a wireless station, or something. Well, what do you want with me? Be as brief as you can. I'm a busy man."

The Counsellor had seen too much of humanity to let bad manners ruffle him. He guessed how he could handle this peppery little creature. The less information he got, the more he would want; and relations might be established.

"I was asked to help in the matter of your niece's disappearance," he pointed out, taking a chair without invitation and sitting down to confront his unwilling host.

"Well, have you found her? No? I thought as much."

"I expect to hear something to-morrow, though."

"You do? You're on a wild goose chase, sir. You'll end by finding a . . . what is it? . . . a mare's nest. The girl's gone off on some prank or other. These modern girls are like that. No stability. You can't depend on 'em. And, let me tell you, when she chooses to come home again, she may not thank you for raising a hue-and-cry after her. That's your own affair; nothing to do with me, remember. I didn't invite you to poke your nose into her affairs. What have you done? Shouted her name over the whole country?"

"Oh, no. Merely asked if anyone had seen a car with the number EZ 1113. No harm in that, surely."

Treverton obviously racked his mind to find some cause for grievance, but apparently he could think of none on the spur of the moment.

"Oh, well," he said, with a rather contemptuous shrug, "if you think you're doing any good, let it go at that. No affair of mine. She's her own mistress. I'm not her keeper. Find the room hot?" he added, noting The Counsellor's obvious discomfort. "You're a fresh air fiend? I'm not. I was born with a chill in my blood. I could live in the Tropics and never feel it. In this infernal climate, I never feel decently warm, never. Draughts everywhere, no matter what one does to stop them."

He pointed to the door, and The Counsellor saw that it was fitted with draught-excluders.

"Difficult to avoid draughts in an old house," he commented. "But I suppose this place suits you for technical purposes. You use the bigger rooms for your machinery and so forth ? "

" Yes, that's so," Treverton grunted.

Whitgift had hinted that Treverton's mind was mainly occupied by the Ravenscourt Press and that everything else was subsidiary. The Counsellor saw his way clear, now that he had managed to touch on the subject.

" I noticed a reproduction of a Monet, downstairs," he explained. " I've seen the original in Amsterdam. Difficult to tell your copy from the original, I'd say, unless one had 'em side by side. My secretary praised your results to me the other day, but I'd no notion then that your things were as good as all that."

Evidently he had chosen the best line of approach. Treverton did not lose his rudeness, but his hackles seemed to subside under this unsubtle flattery.

" Good, you think ? What do *you* know about it, anyway ? But they are good, for all that. Too expensive for the ordinary buyer, though; for all he wants is a chromo of something by an Old Master to hang up and make him feel he's cultured. We're aiming at a different public. What's the use of reproducing Mona Lisa ? It's been done hundreds of times, hasn't it ? I'm doing things that aren't hackneyed. (That Monet was merely an experiment, not for sale). There's heaps of unhackneyed good stuff in the private collections. That's the line we are working."

" Perhaps you're right," confessed The Counsellor. " Personally, I buy things by the younger artists."

" Oh ? Interested in art, are you ? " said Treverton, with a more friendly note in his voice. " I thought you were just being silly-polite, at first. Have you anything good ? "

The Counsellor reeled off a short list of some things in his own collection.

" Nothing that would be any good to me," declared Treverton, bluntly. " Your taste's not mine."

The obvious implication was that The Counsellor's taste was far beneath his own.

"I suppose you need some experts?" inquired The Counsellor, who was always eager to pick up any information on things which might interest the public.

Treverton was now fairly launched on his hobby. He became quite communicative. Yes, he did employ experts. Whitgift, for instance. Treverton explained that originally he had intended to make his reproductions on paper; canvas was a later notion. Whitgift had come in as a paper-making expert. Then he'd taken a hand on the photographic side. Finally, when the canvas idea came up, he'd worked out a filling material to take the place of the preliminary coat of paint in actual painting. Useful fellow, one had to admit. And now he'd branched out again into experiments in the actual printing—a matter of reproducing as far as possible the brush strokes of the original, so far as they produced irregularities on the finished surface. Some modification of the old bichromate process with the raised pattern on the gelatine coming in. He'd got a small printing-press under lock and key in his workshop. No workman went near it. No use letting people know how these things were done until one was ready for the market oneself.

Then there was a chemist, Albury, with a laboratory on the premises. His job was to turn out dyes for staining the photographic plates to make them colour-sensitive in exactly the right degree required. One could buy dyes of the sort, of course, like neocyanin, but that wasn't good enough for the Ravenscourt Press. They often wanted something which diverged a shade from the purchasable dyes, and the only way was to synthesise something new and try it. So Albury had a busy time with his dyes and his spectrographs. Quite a good man in his line. Rather sullen and apt to take the bit in his teeth at times, though.

"Expensive? Of course it's expensive to run,"

Treverton admitted in answer to a feeler from The Counsellor. " It costs me a pretty penny, I can tell you."

Apparently The Counsellor had touched a sore spot by his question for after a momentary hesitation, Treverton produced his grievance.

" It's only a small company with a nominal capital. I finance it myself to a large extent, out of my own pocket. I pay the piper, so I call the tune. Albury's continually worrying me to turn out the ordinary kind of reproduction, the sort of thing you can sell by the hundred at anything up to a couple of guineas. It would put the Press on a paying basis, that's his continual cry. I suppose he wants dividends. I care nothing about dividends. What I want is to turn out the perfect reproduction. It's a matter of personal pride with me. I went into this line, aiming at that. And all the Albury's in creation won't turn me aside to pander to suburban tastes. It isn't only Albury. There's that niece of mine. She's on the same tack. And Whitgift, too, in another way. Not one of them with any ideas above cash. Not a dependable one in the lot. I almost lose my temper at times, and I'm the last man to do that in the ordinary way."

Apparently his outburst helped to soothe him. He worked himself into a state in which he was almost friendly to The Counsellor, who contented himself with listening and interjecting sympathetic noises at proper intervals.

" You're wasting your time over that niece of mine. What do you want to bother about her for ? "

The Counsellor's eyes twinkled.

" It's a matter of personal pride with me," he explained with a straight face. " You'll understand that. I've been asked for my help and I can't afford not to succeed, once I take up a thing of that sort."

" I see, I see. If you put it that way, I can see your point. I can't afford to fail either, in my field. Lose my self-respect if I turned aside from the line I've marked out. You understand? Not many people do. Well, what can I do for you?"

"Money's the root of all evil. St. Paul didn't say that, but never mind. Point is, did she take her cheque book with her when she went off?"

Treverton's little eyes inspected The Counsellor with more respect than before.

"You're smarter than you look," he admitted ungraciously. "I never thought of that. We'll go and see. She keeps it in a drawer of her writing-desk."

They descended to the room with the Monet reproduction. Treverton went straight to the writing-desk, pulled out one of the drawers, rummaged through the contents, and then turned round.

"No cheque book here," he reported.

He closed the drawer and began a systematic search through the desk, but drew blank in the end.

"Not there," he admitted. "She must have taken it with her. So she knew she was going before she left the house. Nobody takes a cheque book to a tennis party. Well, it doesn't worry me. She's her own mistress. I've nothing to do with her pranks."

"Did you question the servants?" asked The Counsellor. "She didn't leave any message with them?"

"Not that I heard. You can put it to them yourself if you like."

"If you don't mind," said The Counsellor.

Treverton rang the bell and summoned a housekeeper and a maid. Neither of them had been given any message by Miss Treverton before she went away. They were quite positive on that point. Treverton dismissed them.

"That doesn't get you much further," he pointed out, with ill-concealed satisfaction. "Anything else I can do for you?"

"Think there's a man in the case?" asked The Counsellor bluntly.

"How should I know? I'm not her father-confessor, you know. She's had cubs dangling after her at times. She's not unattractive in looks. That's her picture, over there, on the desk. There was an American, a year or two ago. They seemed to hit it off together. But he'd no money, so that was that. And Whitgift seems a bit struck. I see more than I'm meant to, at times. But all the glad eye was on his side. I could see that. Besides, he has no money either. I tried to get him to tide me over once, when expenses were heavy, but he'd absolutely nothing in hand. That was some years ago, of course; but he hasn't come into any fortune since, that I've heard about."

"It's as well this old bird doesn't know I've any spare cash," The Counsellor reflected. "If he suspected it, he'd be out to touch me for a monkey, in the interests of his Art."

He kept this idea to himself, however, and instead returned to Miss Treverton's affairs.

"You may have seen the letters she got. Any U.S.A. stamps on them?"

"You're thinking about that American, eh?" Treverton inferred. "Yes, I've seen an American letter now and again. One came for her about a fortnight ago, I remember."

"They still correspond, then? I'll bear that in mind."

Since the talk had passed from the subject of the Ravenscourt Press, Treverton had begun to show signs of fidgetiness; and now he had evidently no further interest in The Counsellor.

"That all you want to know?" he demanded. "If so, you'll excuse me. I'm a busy man."

"I'd like to have a word or two with Whitgift, before I go," The Counsellor explained.

"Very well. I'll send him here. Nothing else I can do? Then, good-bye. Sorry you're wasting your time. Still, it's your time. And your business. Good-bye."

He departed ungraciously. The Counsellor walked over and picked up the snapshot from the desk.

"It doesn't look a mercenary face, in spite of dear Uncle's views," he reflected.

In a few moments Whitgift reappeared.

"I hope you enjoyed your interview," he said, sardonically. "Did he succeed in touching you for funds—or perhaps I should say: Did he succeed in interesting you financially in the Press? No? He generally takes that line when he thinks there's a chance."

"Must be an expensive affair," The Counsellor commented.

"He'd sack the lot of us if he dared," confessed Whitgift philosophically. "But he can't. First, because we know too much. Second, because both my colleague Albury and I have contracts, which have three years still to run. He can't scrap either of us, otherwise he'd give us the push to-morrow and get in Chinese cheap labour in our shoes."

He gave The Counsellor a shrewd glance, and then continued:

"I shouldn't put any cash into this business, if I were in *your* shoes. Run on different lines, by different people, it might pay a dividend. But not so long as he's in charge. I'm being honest with you, because you've done me a good turn over this affair."

The Counsellor pulled a comic grimace.

"Don't count on gratitude for that tip," he cautioned Whitgift. "You haven't prevented me from losing any money in the concern."

"He hasn't an ingratiating manner, and that's a fact," Whitgift retorted with a cheerful grin. "But pass that. Did you learn anything about Miss Treverton from him?"

"Nothing very useful, except that she gets letters with U.S.A. stamps on them."

Whitgift's smile vanished.

"Yes, I believe she does," he confirmed. "She

still corresponds with that American, damn him."

"There's one thing I'd like to know," The Counsellor said carelessly. "You told me she took a tennis outfit with her in the car. Did you see it?"

"No, not the actual things. But I saw her attaché case on the seat beside her when she passed me; it's rather worn and has her initials on it, "H.T." She always uses it for her tennis things. And besides, she mentioned she was going to play tennis."

"That seems conclusive," admitted The Counsellor. "But does one usually need a cheque book at a tennis-party? Because it seems to be missing."

Whitgift knitted his brows at this information.

"It's gone, is it? You got old Treverton to hunt for it, I suppose? She keeps it always in that drawer there, but I didn't want to go ferreting among her private papers myself to make sure. I wonder. . . ."

For some reason, the news about the missing cheque-book seemed to have depressed him.

"Just a question," said The Counsellor, after a pause. "Was she a fast driver, in the ordinary way?"

Whitgift considered for a moment or two.

"No, nothing furious, so far as I've seen," he decided. "Call it a cruising speed of forty. That would come near it on the average. She was careful in built-up areas, always. I'd call her a good driver."

"Likely to get tired, easily?"

"No, not a bit. She was always in good condition, what with golf and tennis and walking. She wouldn't tire easily."

"Well, that's all for the moment," said The Counsellor, moving doorwards. "If any news of the car turns up, I'll let you know."

"Do all you can," urged Whitgift. "There's no use pretending; I'm damnably anxious about what's happened to her. Why should she dash off like this, at a moment's notice? She was her own mistress, as old Treverton's always saying. Nobody could hinder her going, if she wanted to, wherever she's gone. Then what's the point in clearing out like this, without a word to anyone and no luggage with her? I simply can't make it out."

He bit his lip as though in perplexity.

"I wonder now," said The Counsellor, using one of his clichés which irritated his subordinates.

4 THE TRACK OF EZ 1113

WHEN The Counsellor reached his office next morning, he found on his desk a small pile of six neatly-docketed letters: replies to the inquiry in his broadcast. Without glancing over them, he picked up his desk-telephone and summoned Sandra Rainham and Standish.

"Sit down," he directed, with a grin. "Not being Sherlock Holmes, I need a double allowance of Watsons."

Sandra took one of the arm-chairs; Standish seated himself on the edge of The Counsellor's desk.

"This is how it is," The Counsellor began.

He gave them a terse account of what he had seen and learned at Grendon St. Giles. Long practice in preparing his broadcasts had made him, when he chose, a master of précis-construction. Neither listener offered any comment; but at the end Standish nodded towards the papers on the desk.

"You offered a quid reward for any report of that car," he said to The Counsellor. "That's £6 you're out, up to the present. I've sent off the cheques."

The Counsellor picked up the papers and glanced at the dockets.

"Right! St. Neot's . . . Tuxford . . . Baldersby Gate . . . Temple Sowerby . . . Gretna . . . Crocketford," he said, reading the headings. "Well, it's plain sailing at the start. That car went right up the Great North Road, aiming for Carlisle. Just pass me the A.A. Road Book of Scotland, Wolf. Thanks."

He turned over the pages, consulted the maps, and then left the volume open on his desk.

"After Carlisle, it turned off through Gretna, Annan, and Dumfries. Crocketford's about ten miles west of Dumfries. And that's the last news of it. Now let's hear the details. Here's a letter from St. Neot's."

He picked up the top letter of the pile, unfolded it and read it aloud :

Sunday

Dear Sir,

If you want to know about a car with the number EZ. 1113, I can tell you, and I'll be glad of your one pound reward for these people took in eight gallons of petrol from my pump and gave me a bad pound note when they paid me. I can't afford to lose money this way, so I'll be glad if you'll forward your reward by return.

There were two people in the car. A girl in a grey dress with brown hair and a clean-shaven fair-haired fellow in grey flannels. It was him gave me the bad note, and he had an American accent or something like it. They had tea at the hotel here, near my garage. That would be about half-past five when they left, going towards Crosshall. I'll have the law on them if I can, for giving me bad money. Please send reward by return.

"He seems to have come out all square in the end," Standish commented. "What's he grumbling about ?"

The Counsellor paid no attention but picked up the next letter.

"Crosshall would bring them on to the Great North Road again," he pointed out. "Evidently they followed that up. This is from The Kirkcaldy Temperance Hotel, Tuxford. Just see what the A.A. Hotel List says about it, Sandra."

Miss Rainham picked up the green volume, turned to the page, and shook her head.

"Not listed. There's only one hotel given under Tuxford : a two-star one."

"Well, never mind just now," said The Counsellor. "This seems to be from the proprietress of the other place."

He again read aloud:

12th September

Sir,

I listened to your broadcast on Sunday. I always listen to your broadcasts. I've come to look on you as a real friend, though I've never seen you. You always say such sensible things and give silly girls such good advice. I've just been wondering why you want to know about this car with the number EZ. 1113, for I'm sure the young lady that was in it was quite a nice young lady, though it did seem to me queer her going about all alone with the gentleman and staying the night at hotels. But there was nothing wrong, I do assure you. They wrote their names in my book: Miss H. Treverton and Mr. H. Querrin of the U.S.A. I've copied his name from my book, to make sure I get it right, since it's a queer one.

They arrived here just about eight in the evening, last Thursday and wanted dinner, which wasn't quite convenient, but I gave them quite a nice little cold dinner and they didn't mind that, as she told me herself. She had only an attaché case for luggage, but it had her initials on it, H.T., and she had a tennis-racquet. He had two new suitcases with his initials on them too. I looked to see, because one never knows what sort of people may come in cars. But after dinner, I had a talk with her and when I found he was her half-brother and they wanted separate rooms, I knew it was all right. She was in a grey coat and skirt, with quite a fashionable hat, and he had dark grey flannels on. She told me her half-brother had spent some time in America, and I thought as much myself though really I mistook him for an Australian, having a brother out in Australia myself that I haven't seen for years.

They spent the night here, and slept very comfortably, as they said in the morning, and after they had breakfast, they went off again about nine o'clock. I overheard them say something about being over the Border that afternoon, so I suppose they were going to Scotland.

And before I stop, I'd like to thank you again for your broadcasts which I enjoy very much every Sunday. They are magnificent. I am glad indeed to have the privilege of helping you in this matter, for I am sure it is for some good purpose.

"Nice to be appreciated," confessed The Counsellor cheerfully. "I was afraid she'd spoil it all by reminding me of the reward. You sent it all right, Wolf ? "

" Of course," said Standish, wearily. " And what's the next article ? "

" Wait a bit, wait a bit," said The Counsellor, holding up his hand. " Just ask a question. Doncaster's only five miles or so from Tuxford. In their shoes, I'd have pushed on to there. Just look up Doncaster for hotels, Sandra."

" One three-star and three two-star ones," Miss Rainham reported after consulting the book.

" Just ask another question," Standish put in. " Isn't it possible that these people are hard up and want to do their trip on the cheap ? It seems possible. We're not all so flush as yourself, Mark."

" But this Querrin man ? " Miss Rainham interjected before The Counsellor could reply. " Is he her half-brother ? "

" Far from it," The Counsellor explained. " I learned at Grendon St. Giles that he's an American and once upon a time he seemed to be an aspirant for her hand. But perhaps I'd better give you the whole tale."

He amplified the information on this point which he had already given them.

" You say Mr. Whitgift saw that attaché case in the car as the girl drove away from the house," Miss Rainham said thoughtfully when The Counsellor had finished. " And evidently she had it with her at Tuxford, since the landlady mentions the initials. Well, she *may* have gone to bed in tennis shorts. But it doesn't sound likely to me. I'd bet that she had night things, a brush and comb, and so forth in that attaché case. Or else Mr. Querrin had them in his suit-cases. In either case, this affair had been planned beforehand and wasn't a spur-of-the-moment business."

" She may have bought these things *en route*," said Standish.

" Have it your way," said Miss Rainham, " and then explain why she went off at all like that. My idea makes sense, and that's always something."

"Well, then," retorted Standish, "explain why she poses as his half-sister, if they've gone off together by pre-arrangement."

"How could they have got married at that time in the afternoon," Sandra retorted. "It's after hours. Mark's impression was that she's a nice girl. And the initials on the luggage were different, so she couldn't pretend they were brother and sister, could she? I'm just pandering to your evil mind, Wolf. Besides, if you remember the tone of the landlady's letter, you'll see that the dear old soul wouldn't have had them under her roof at all, without some pretence of the sort."

"Granted," agreed Standish. "But in that case they could have gone on to Doncaster and found somebody less particular."

"I dare say," Sandra admitted impatiently. "Go on, Mark. Read the next one."

The Counsellor, who had listened only absent-mindedly to the argument, picked up the next letter.

"This is from Baldersby Gate," he explained. "It seems to be written by some infuriated female or other. If you'll stop arguing for a moment or two, I'll put you wise to the contents. Here goes."

Spreading out the letter on his desk he began to read:

Dear Sir,

If you are friends of the people in car No. EZ. 1113, then you can tell them from me that I've put the police on their track for killing my dog. They came through here between ten and eleven last Friday morning and ran right over the poor little thing, and if it wasn't done on purpose it looked more like that than an accident. When they pulled up after striking the poor little creature, I spoke to the woman who was driving the car and told her what a pet it was, and all she said was: "I'm not fond of dogs." Not a word about being sorry or anything, which was the least any human being could have done. And when I began to say some more about their carelessness, the man who was sitting beside her said: "Drive on, Helen," and she just drove away. But I took their number and went and complained at the police station, so they needn't think that they'll get off scot free, for they won't. I'll have the law on them for killing my dog, such a nice quiet pet it was, a springer spaniel that I'd had for years and I was so fond of it. I've written to the S.P.C.A. about it, too, because they could easily have helped the accident and it wasn't poor Brownie's fault, for a dog has as much right on the road as they have with their grand cars. I'll make them pay for it, though no money would ever pay me for the loss of my pet. So you just tell them that, if you know them.

"What a beastly thing to do!" Sandra said, hotly.

"Well, pass that for the moment," suggested The Counsellor. "We'll take the next dip in the lucky-bag. It comes from Temple Sowerby.

Respected Sir,

The car EZ.1113 you're looking for came to this hotel where I'm a waiter between one and two o'clock on Friday. The parties in it, a youngish man and a girl in grey who was a real good-looking piece, had lunch here. They made a rumpus about the wine-list, because we hadn't good enough drinks in stock for their taste, it seems, and when they got the best we had, they seemed to think they'd been given the vinegar bottle by mistake. They might have known we weren't the Carlton or the Ritz. They took in eight gallons of petrol before they went off.

I know I'm right about the car number, for I remember the EZ because I once had an Aunt Eliza, and I remember the 1113 because I have a habit of totting up the figures of the first car that comes here after one o'clock each day and if it tots up to 5, I put my money on No. 5 in the next race I bet on, and I remember the 1113 totted up to 6.

Please send me the one pound reward by return as I have an absolutely sure tip for a Thing that's bound to win at Warwick and I want to get my money on before the odds shorten.

"That's from The Nag's Tail Hotel," added The Counsellor. "Just look up Temple Sowerby, Sandra, and see what the A.A. says about it."

Sandra Rainham turned over the leaves of the Handbook rapidly.

"There's only a one-star hotel listed here—eight bedrooms—and it isn't The Nag's Tail."

"Then presumably our friend's right in saying that his hostelry could hardly be mistaken for the Ritz, if it's not on the list at all. But I like the way he stands up for his shop. Evidently he doesn't care to have its cellar despised. Wish him luck with his bet, I'm sure."

He paused, then added to Sandra:

"What's the next town further on? Penrith, isn't it?"

"Yes, 6½ miles further on."

"Just look up Penrith's hotel list."

"Two three-stars and one two-star," she reported.

"H'm! Let's see. Appleby's about six miles ahead of Temple Sowerby on the road, isn't it? Yes? What's it got in the hotel line?"

"A two-star and a one-star."

The Counsellor nodded without comment and picked up the next letter from the diminishing pile. As he did so, a curious expression passed over his face.

"Now after these dull details, we get a flash of romance," he explained. "It surprises me as much as it'll surprise you. It's from Gretna Green, no less."

Dear Sir,

Send your pound to me, at the above address. The car EZ. 1113 came here before four o'clock last Friday. The young chap and the girl on board it stood up before the anvil at the Old Blacksmith's Shop and got spliced in proper form. I was called in as a witness. The girl signed herself Treverdon or Treverton and the man's name began with a Q, which I noticed specially though I don't remember the rest of it. I remember the car number, because after the wedding, when they came out, he said something like: "Lucky number, isn't it, darling? Eleven and thirteen make 24—just your age." After that, they had tea and drove off along the Annan road.

P.S. please send the pound in a registered letter for fear it goes astray.

"'Curiouser and curiouser'," mused The Counsellor. "A lot of good confused thinking to be done on the data we're getting. But we'll take the facts first, before we start on theory. Here's the last of the batch. It's from an A.A. patrol."

Dear Sir,

At 5.40 p.m. on Friday, 9th Sept., I found the brown Vauxhall 12 h.p. mentioned in your Sunday broadcast standing about a mile east of Crocketford on the Dumfries road. The back tyre on the near side was flat. The young gentleman in the car had his arm in a sling and the young lady couldn't manage the brace to get the wheel off. I rendered the necessary assistance, and changed the wheel for them. They asked me some questions about the road to Stranraer. I gathered they were too late for the night boat to Ireland and would have to wait for the morning one instead. They said something about Moville, wherever that is, and being in time there, anyhow. They seemed in very high spirits, and I noticed the young lady wore a wedding-ring which seemed new, so perhaps that was why. They had a couple of suit-cases and an attaché case in the back seats of the car. When the wheel was changed, they drove on towards Crocketford and I saw no more of them of course. The foregoing is strictly confidential.

"Got his eyes and ears about him, that chap," commented The Counsellor. "H'm! Moville? That's in Donegal. But why Moville? . . . I have it! The Anchor Line boats stop, off Moville, to pick up and set down Irish passengers. That must be it. Or might be, anyhow."

He swung round on his two subordinates.

"Now, my dear Watsons, it seems to be your turn to take a hand. My throat's dry with all this reading. State your views."

"What I don't understand," said Sandra frankly, "is why this girl should have gone off like this, all in a hurry and with no notice, and got married in that beastly way at Gretna Green. It doesn't sound decent, to me."

"Well," said The Counsellor judiciously, "if they

wanted to catch the Anchor Line boat, perhaps they hadn't time down here, except by special licence. And special licences cost £25. Gretna Green may come cheaper. Besides, you've got to give reasons for wanting a special licence. And the Archbishop of Canterbury might not have approved of their reasons, whatever they were."

"What *I* don't understand," said Standish in his turn, "is how an English girl and an American could contract a valid marriage in this way at all. My people are Scottish, and I know definitely that you can't have a legal marriage unless at least one of the parties has his or her usual place of residence in Scotland, or has lived in Scotland for twenty-one days immediately preceding such a marriage. The first condition blocks out the girl; the second one blocks out this American, since he's been in England during part at least of the twenty-one days."

"You're sure of your facts?" demanded The Counsellor.

"Dead sure," retorted Standish. "I've won bets on it often with argumentative Englishmen who've never heard of Lord Brougham's Act."

"Of course one of them may have made a false declaration about the residence qualification," The Counsellor suggested.

"What good would that do? It wouldn't make it a legal marriage," Standish objected.

"Yes, but the girl might imagine that it was legal," Sandra Rainham put in.

"In which case Mr. Querrin would be a wrong 'un. Agreed," commented The Counsellor.

He pulled a jotting-pad towards him and made a note or two before continuing.

"Now let's ask a question or two. First, did she or did she not go off by pre-arrangement with Querrin? Second, why did they choose obscure hotels when better ones were to be found near at hand? And, third, the various incidents reported by some of our esteemed correspondents. Now, my dear Watsons, the meeting's open to hear your views on these points."

"Of course the thing must have been pre-arranged between her and this American," Standish said positively. "We know that she was corresponding with him. Probably that last letter she got from him was posted just before he left America and brought her the news that he was following it in the next liner. Most likely he turned up, unknown to the rest of the Longstoke House crew, and settled details with her. One meeting would do the trick. She took her cheque book with her. No one takes a cheque book to a tennis party. She knew she might need it in future. One can draw cheques in America even if one's bank is in England. And, finally, Querrin had two suitcases in the car *with his initials on them.* I can't imagine a young chap making a habit of taking a suitcase in each hand on all his walks abroad, even for exercise. Therefore, if he started out with these suitcases, he must have been waiting for the girl at some pre-arranged rendezvous. On the other hand, if he bought the suitcases and an outfit *en route,* after the girl picked him up, I'll bet he wouldn't have bothered to get his initials put on the cases. I know I shouldn't, if I'd been in his shoes."

"Let's keep to facts," begged The Counsellor. "What we really know is that Querrin and the girl were corresponding, which might mean no more than that they were friendly. As to the chequebook, all I told you was that it wasn't to be found in the place where she usually kept it. She may have shoved it into a drawer in her bedroom, for all I can tell. I'll admit that you may be right about the initials on his suitcases."

"Men do seem to prefer the long way round," Sandra commented in a faintly sardonic tone. "All this talk about chequebooks, and U.S.A. letters, and suitcases! Any woman would tell you that you can get your question answered if you find out one fact. Did she take her tennis things with her ? If she did, then she meant to go to the tennis party and she must have changed her mind on the spur of the moment. If she didn't, then she never intended to go near the tennis party, and she must have made other arrangements before she left Longstoke House. Simple, isn't it ? "

" Yes, but we don't know whether she took them or not," objected Standish. " All Whitgift saw was the old attaché case in the car."

Sandra threw up her hands in a pretty gesture of mock despair.

" Is there anything to hinder you from finding out ? " she asked in a blasé tone. " Get the housekeeper to go through her things and see if a pair of tennis shorts is missing. She's bound to know how many the girl had. Washing-lists are a great help."

" Something in that," The Counsellor admitted, making a jotting in his pocket-book. " And now, the second point : Why did they choose small hotels to stay at, when they were within easy distance of superior accommodation replete with hot-and-cold, lifts, lock-up garages, etc. ? "

" Because they were hard up, obviously," Standish declared contemptuously. " Anyone could tell you that."

" No," said The Counsellor firmly.

" Because they were on a sort of honeymoon trip and preferred quiet places," Sandra suggested. " Some people are built that way."

" *No,*" said The Counsellor again, with more emphasis.

He took out his cigarette-case and pushed it across the desk to each of the others. When the three cigarettes were lighted, he tapped on the desk to emphasise what he had to say.

" They weren't hard up, Wolf. I told you that Whitgift said the girl could easily lay her hands on enough money to finance herself for a month or so away from home. That meant she had it in current account. And behind that she had capital. Querrin must have had some money, too. They weren't hard up. Not to the extent of saving five bob on a night's lodging, anyhow. And your notion won't work either, Sandra, as you'll see in a moment or two."

" Well, then," Sandra countered, " perhaps the girl hadn't the clothes with her for evening in a big hotel."

" No good," said The Counsellor. " If you arrive in a car you can dress as you please at any hotel on the road. Besides, if it was a pre-arranged stunt, she could have got Querrin to pack an evening frock in one of his suitcases. Turn to the third point: the incidents on the road that we've heard of."

" Well, what are they ? " asked Sandra.

The Counsellor leaned back in his chair and ticked them off on his fingers as he produced them.

" First, they bought some petrol at St. Neots and the man found afterwards that they'd palmed a bad note on him. I lay no stress on that. Even the best of us gets landed with a bad note sometimes, and might pass it on quite innocently. You remember last week a gentleman " CHEATED " asked what he could do about it, in a similar case. By the way, did he send his note for our museum ? I suggested it in my reply to him, I remember."

" Oh, yes," Standish assured him. " It's framed and hung up in the Chamber of Horrors."

" Then take the next incident," The Counsellor went on, brushing aside Standish's further remarks. " At Baldersby Gate, they ran over a dog. To me, that's highly significant. In fact, that old lady's letter seems to contain the kernel of the whole affair. The next affair was at Temple Sowerby. They chose to stop at a pub that isn't on the A.A. list. Economy ? And yet they ordered the best bottle in the place, and grumbled because it wasn't good enough, grumbled hard enough to impress themselves firmly on the waiter's mind. And the night before, they'd chosen a temperance shop deliberately, when they could have got wine at another hotel in the place. What did they do at that T.T. place? The girl made friends with the landlady and thus stamped herself on the good dame's memory."

"Well, but, to judge from that landlady's letter, she was a nice old thing. And Helen Treverton was a taking-looking girl, from your description of her photograph. I don't see anything amiss in her chatting to the dame," Sandra objected.

"No more do I." said The Counsellor. "I'm just suggesting that it may have been done-a-purpose. Now we can pass the Gretna Green episode and get on to the final scene. They meet an A.A. patrol and stop him. And Querrin's arm is now in a sling, though so far as we know there was nothing wrong with him at Gretna, thirty miles or so back. What had happened to him in the meanwhile? What strikes me is that a man with an arm in a sling is just the sort of thing that one would notice, especially when the arm-in-a-sling is given as the reason for stopping the patrol."

"Well, what *did* happen to Querrin's arm?" demanded Standish.

"Nothing at all, I'll bet," said The Counsellor decidedly. "To my mind, the whole of these episodes had one object and one object only: to blaze the trail of car No. EZ 1113. And what's more, I'll bet that there were quite a lot of other incidents happened on that drive up the Great North Road which would be equally striking, only we haven't heard about them. Why do you find them going to small hotels instead of big ones? Because in a big hotel a guest is just one of a bunch; whereas in a small place he's an individual one can remember. It all hangs together, Wolf, if you've the eye to see it."

"And when you've seen it, what do you see?" asked Standish sarcastically.

"A damned queer affair," said The Counsellor.

"It's so queer that I'm going into it with both feet to see what I can kick up."

"Well, if I ever elope, preserve me from having you dashing in on top of it," said Standish, feelingly.

"Elope!" echoed The Counsellor with scorn. "The girl was her own mistress, as her uncle said. No one was trying to keep her from marrying Querrin, if she wanted to. Why all this secrecy, then? And all this on-the-spur-of-the-moment business. And a 'marriage' that isn't legal even by the liberal rules of your native land, Wolf. And where's car No. EZ 1113 gone finally? If those two are off to America by the Anchor Line, they must have mislaid it somewhere. The whole thing is a tissue of misfits. Can't you see that?"

"Well, take care that you don't come out a bigger fool than in you went, as Omar Khayyam said," warned Standish. "The odds look to me about 100 to 1 that you will. What do you propose as a first step towards paranoia?"

"Take my plane north at once. Saves time. There's an aerodrome at Carlisle. After that, we'll hire a car and go on by road."

"We?" queried Standish.

"I'm taking you," explained The Counsellor. "You speak the language. I never could burr my r's properly for Scots to understand me. We're going now. Get a move on."

5

LOCHAR MOSS

THE flight to the North did nothing to improve Standish's temper or reconcile him to what he regarded as a wholly futile expedition.

" 'Ay, now you are in Arden; the more fool you. When you were at home you were in a better place,' " he misquoted with some acerbity as they left the Carlisle aerodrome after seeing the plane into a hangar.

" 'But travellers must be content,' " continued The Counsellor. " Shakespeare, isn't it? The fellow who thought Delphi was an island and that Bohemia had a seaboard? Don't trust him on the subject of foreign travel, Wolf. But since you don't like this place, we'll try another as soon as we can hire a car."

The Counsellor had come well provided with money, and they had little difficulty in procuring a car at one of the garages of the town. A heavy deposit secured the absence of a chauffeur.

" I don't want anyone to have a nervous breakdown through wondering what we're up to," The Counsellor explained as he drove over the Eden and took the road to Gretna. " We're better alone."

Standish made no comment on this, and nothing further was said until they reached Gretna Green. The Counsellor had passed that way before, and drove straight to the Old Blacksmith's Shop, a long low whitewashed building bearing an A.A. plaque and, underneath, an inscription intimating that this was the Marriage Room. A notice-board at one end of the edifice indicated the location of a Free Car Park.

" You park the car and have a stroll round, Wolf,

while I invade this lair of Hymen," suggested The Counsellor.

Standish had not long to wait. In a short time The Counsellor returned.

"Quite a good sixpennyworth," he declared, as he stepped into the car again. "Historic coach, as used by Queen Adelaide; the famous old blacksmith's anvil over which marriages were and still are performed"; likewise a specimen of the old penny-farthing bicycle. Also one or two Repentance Stools, which may come in handy for those who marry in haste . . . A sinister touch, that. And a set of registers, which interested me most of all. I bought a series of picture postcards, too, for Sandra's benefit. It'll please her to know I thought of her."

"Did you get any information?" inquired Standish drily.

"The complete book of words. I took a copy. And here's the wording of the certificate, on one of these post-cards. Here you are! 'Howard Querrin from the Parish of Govan in the County of Glasgow, and Helen Treverton from the Parish of Grendon St. Giles, etc. being now both here present, and having declared to me that they are Single Persons, have now been married after the manner of the Laws of Scotland: As witness our hands at the Old Blacksmith's Shop, Gretna, this ninth day of September, 1938.' And then follow the signatures of the 'Parties', the Witnesses, and the Priest. So that's that."

"So Querrin made a false declaration about his residence, and the marriage is void under Lord Brougham's Act," Standish commented. "It's hard lines on the girl, if any doubts happen to arise. Did you make any inquiries about them?"

"They seem to have regarded it as a bit of a joke," The Counsellor reported. "The man kept his face straight, but the girl giggled once or twice during the ceremony, which apparently is not a prolonged one."

"Nerves, possibly," Standish suggested.

"You think so? There it was, anyhow. And now, I think, we'll follow the trail further. They took the Dumfries Road."

At first the road was almost level, but after Annan they began to climb to rather higher ground. At the top of the ascent, rather to Standish's surprise, The Counsellor pulled up the car and turned in his seat to examine the view.

"What's the point in stopping?"

"Just to look about me," The Counsellor explained. "I stayed hereabouts for a week or two on holiday when I was a cub. It's interesting to see it again."

Standish looked about him.

"What's that pocket Sahara down yonder?" he demanded. "The Solway Sands?"

"Yes," confirmed The Counsellor. "And if ever you come here and take a fancy to walking by the shore, better keep your eye open. That Firth's six miles wide at high tide, and only about a mile wide at the ebb. Incoming spring tides run up at eight or nine miles an hour with a roar you can hear miles away. Worth seeing. More like a flood than an ordinary tide. The sands are flat and get swallowed up at a devil of a rate. If you're caught far out on them, you have to run like hell for safety and you may not make it before the water catches you up. A nasty place. And just to make it a bit more difficult, you may blunder into a quicksand. There are plenty of them about."

"What's all this waste of heather and stuff below us?" inquired Standish.

"Lochar Moss," explained The Counsellor. "Just bog and heather most of the way from the coast to near Dumfries. I've been into it, looking for white heather. A god-forsaken tract. Dangerous, too, in the winter-time, some people told me. It's a rum place. They find sea-sand a bit below ground-level, and embedded in that are trees with their heads all pointing one way. Tradition says there was a forest there originally.

Then the sea broke in and tore up the trees, which accounts for their heads being all one way. Then the water retreated, and the Moss formed:

> ' First a wood, and then a sea.
> Now a moss, and e'er will be.'

So the country-folk say."

" It's pretty big."

" Big enough to have different names for districts of it. Down there, by the sea, you've got Longbridge Moor. Below us here is Ironhirst Moss. Round to the right is Racks Moss, and beyond that is Craigs Moss. There's another bit still further north. A nice dreary bit of work on the whole. One could murder a man out in it and unless he were missed by somebody and a search was made, he might lie there quite quietly for long enough. If you've seen enough, we'll toddle along."

They passed through Dumfries and drove on through rather featureless country. At last The Counsellor, after a glance at his milometer, pulled up again.

" It must have been hereabouts that the A.A. patrol came upon that car," he decided. " This is the end of the trail, so far as information goes."

" Well, what's your idea ? " asked Standish. " Build a cairn to mark the spot, and then go home again ? It seems all that's left to do."

The Counsellor consulted the dash-board clock.

" Stranraer's the next stop, I think," he determined. " We might get there for dinner, stay the night and make a few inquiries. No use stopping short in the last lap."

Standish shrugged his shoulders resignedly.

" Oh, just as you like," he agreed with a noticeable lack of enthusiasm.

" Then just dip into the A.A. Handbook—I put it in the cubby-hole in front of you—and see what hotels there are and especially what garages Stranraer boasts."

" Three two-star hotels and three garages," reported Standish.

" Oh, come," declared The Counsellor, " that'll be easy. I was afraid the place would be festering with them. We can do this on our heads. In fact, Wolf, I'm inclined to leave it entirely to you."

" Leave what ? "

" The necessary inquiries. I want to find car EZ 1113. The obvious thing is to ask about it at hotels and garages. You don't feel an urge ? "

" I do not," said Standish, decidedly.

" Feeling torpid ? " inquired The Counsellor anxiously. " A bit flat and sleepy ? It's the fresh air, probably. Well, then, I suppose I must do it myself."

But when they reached Stranraer and entered an hotel, The Counsellor had unexpected good luck. As he signed the visitors' register, he cast his eye over the pages and found : " 9th September, Mr. & Mrs. Howard Querrin " entered in a man's writing.

" Hello ! " he exclaimed, with a good imitation of surprise for the benefit of the clerk. " Mr. and Mrs. Querrin ? Are they still here, by any chance ? They're friends of mine. Here, Wolf, the Querrins landed here just ahead of us."

The clerk shook her head.

" No, they've gone," she explained. " They went off on the following day."

" Oh ? Pity, that," lamented The Counsellor. " Came in their car, I suppose ? "

Again the clerk shook her head.

" No, I remember them coming. They just walked in shortly after ten o'clock with their suitcases. They didn't garage a car, I'm quite sure of that."

" Mr. Querrin's arm in a sling ? " The Counsellor demanded.

" No," the clerk answered for the third time. " I remember him coming in with a suitcase in each hand and giving them to the porter."

"Ah! So that sprain can't have been serious," said The Counsellor with admirable readiness. "I suppose they made a bit of a fuss about rooms," he added, sympathetically. "They're too dashed particular, I always think."

"No, not here," the girl replied. "They had No. 19. It's quite a nice double room."

"I'll take it myself," announced The Counsellor, catching at the faint possibility that the couple might have left some traces behind them which had been overlooked by a housemaid. "If it satisfied them, it'll be good enough for us."

But again the girl shook her head.

"I'm afraid you can't have it, sir. It's occupied."

"Well, the two best single rooms you have," ordered The Counsellor, accepting defeat placidly. "And, by the way, can you give me a list of all the garages in the town? And then I'd like to use the 'phone."

After a minute or two, he got the list and rang up those which happened to be on the telephone. None of them had any information about Car No. EZ 1113.

"Well, we'll try the rest after breakfast to-morrow," he decided. "And the steamship office to see if they gave their names when they went aboard, though that's not likely. And now, Wolf, if you'll make yourself presentable, I'm quite ready for dinner."

An afterthought struck him and again he went to the reception desk.

"When did Mr. and Mrs. Querrin leave, can you tell me?"

"Just before seven o'clock on Saturday evening," the clerk replied, after consulting her books. "They didn't wait for dinner. I remember, now, that they must have gone to Castle Kennedy during the day. At least, they asked me about the grounds in the morning and how one got permission to visit the place."

"Thanks," said The Counsellor. "Could you let me look at Bradshaw for a moment?"

The girl handed him the timetables and he turned over the pages for a minute or two before giving the book back to her.

"If they left just before seven," he explained to Standish later, "it looks as if they were going to catch the Larne steamer which sails at 7.20 p.m. on Saturday. There's another boat at 6.5. a.m. but they obviously didn't get up early enough to catch that, so they filled in their day partly by visiting the Castle Kennedy estate. Next to Kew, it's supposed to be the best bit of landscape gardening in the country. But that doesn't exclude other possibilities. We'll know more to-morrow."

Next morning, leaving his unwilling assistant at the hotel, The Counsellor went out in search of further information. He was back sooner than Standish expected.

"'Curiouser and curiouser'," he declared on his return. "But not altogether unexpected by me. I've been to every garage in this place, and Car No. EZ 1113 hasn't been seen by any of them. Nor was it embarked on the Larne steamers. Nor yet is the name Querrin on the passenger lists on Saturday. Nor did anyone corresponding to their description stay at any other hotel in Stranraer on Saturday night."

"It's only a two-hour daylight crossing," Standish pointed out. "They'd just pay for their tickets. No one would ask their names unless they booked a berth; and they wouldn't do that. And now, what about it? Are you still bent on hunting down a pair of honeymooners and breaking into their privacy? That's bad taste, and none of your business, if you don't mind my saying so."

The Counsellor made a soothing gesture.

"You can keep your honeymooners, if such they be," he explained. "Though my impression is that a legal marriage usually precedes a honeymoon, in the ordinary way. I shan't disturb their transports. What I *do* want to know is what's become of Car No. EZ 1113. It's got no feelings to be ruffled if I intrude upon it."

"Well, cry for it in next Sunday's broadcast," suggested Standish.

"I shall, unless I can tree it sooner myself. It's always worth trying. Now, look here, Wolf. This is how it is."

The Counsellor spread out a map and took a notebook from his pocket.

"That car was last seen at Crocketford about 5.40 p.m. on Friday. Crocketford's 66 miles from Stranraer—say a couple of hours drive at the rate these people were averaging on the way up north. And yet, as I ascertained by scattering some largesse to a porter this morning they came here by a train which leaves Dumfries at 7.35 p.m. and comes into Stranraer at 10.3 p.m. My porter friend remembered the two suit-cases and the attaché case. Also the girl in the light coat and skirt. But they had no car concealed about their persons. Puzzle, find the car."

"Had a breakdown, perhaps, and couldn't wait for a repair since they had to get on to Moville to catch the Anchor Line there."

"And yet they wasted a day here, fooling about. It must have been a pretty extensive breakdown," commented The Counsellor. "If you're right, then EZ 1113 is in some garage along the line Crocketford to Stranraer, and we'll get news of it from Sunday's broadcast as you suggest. But there's another possibility. Suppose they abandoned it."

"Why should they?"

"Because," said The Counsellor with emphasis, "a car's easily traceable."

"'Ada had romantic notions,'" quoted Standish. "You seem to suffer from the same disease."

"I'm just exhausting the possibilities," declared

The Counsellor, unperturbed. " What we actually know is that they were at Crocketford at 5.40 p.m. and they joined the train that leaves Dumfries at 7.35 p.m. That gives them two hours to dispose of the car and join the train, doesn't it ? Now look at the map. If they went north of Crocketford into the hill-country round Loch Urr, it would take them further and further from the railway ; and how could they get back to the line in time ? That's out of the question. If they went south to find a lonely spot to leave the car, the Criffell massif's the only hope. But if they got their car into that, they'd have to get out again on their ten toes. It's almost roadless and they couldn't reckon on getting a lift from anyone. No good. Well, that leaves two possibilities. One is that they dumped EZ 1113 in a Solway quicksand. You can rule that out. Only the natives know where the quicksands are, and even then there's a lot of shifting about. And you'd need to know about the times of low tide. And you'd be miles away from the railway when you'd finished. So that leaves only one likely place that I can think of : Lochar Moss."

" Fantastic," was Standish's verdict.

" Watson," said The Counsellor severely, " this is not in your best vein. We'll now apply the time-factor. To get from Crocketford to the edge of Lochar Moss, you go back through Dumfries, and at Collin you take the Mouswald road. Crocketford to Mouswald is a matter of seventeen miles. Call that a thirty-five minute run, and you have them at Mouswald about 6.30 p.m., allowing a quarter of an hour for the A.A. man to change their wheel for them. Actually, it might have been a shade later."

" Why ? "

" Because when the A.A. man left them, he was under the impression they were going on to Stranraer. Suppose he went on towards Stranraer himself, they'd have to pass him and they can't have turned back without his noticing them. Suppose he went towards

Dumfries, again they'd have passed him and he'd have mentioned it in his letter. The only solution is that they turned off in Crocketford and went back by the secondary road through Milton and Lochfoot, which is a shade longer than the main road. Anyhow, they could reach the neighbourhood of Mouswald somewhere round about 6.40 at latest."

"Well, go on with the pretty story."

"The bother is that between the Mouswald road and Lochar Moss there's the railway, cutting through the edge of the Moss; and there aren't many places where you can get a car past the line. But there are one or two, judging by the map. A mile or so down one of these cul-de-sac tracks would land you well into the Moss and you could drive the car into the Moss itself, amongst the heather, and hide it fairly easily in some depression of the ground. Specially if you piled cut heather round the sides to screen it."

"It's possible," Standish admitted without enthusiasm.

"That leaves the pair to walk back to the road. Allow a quarter of an hour each way, including hiding the car. They'd dump the luggage where they left the main road, so as not to be laden with it on the way back. Once on the road again, they'd have no difficulty in getting a lift either on a bus or on a passing car. Having to catch a train would be excuse enough, especially if a pretty girl made it. That gives them time enough to get into Dumfries and catch the 7.35. And we know they did catch the 7.35 somehow."

"So you think EZ 1113 is somewhere in Lochar Moss? Like looking for a needle in a haystack to find it, then, if you ask me."

"Not from a plane, perhaps," The Counsellor pointed out. "They'd camouflage the car against people on ground level. I'll bet they didn't think of covering the roof. Anyhow, I'm going to have a look. So back we go to Carlisle, Wolf. It's just over a hundred miles. We can get there in time to have a try before dark."

"You'll find nothing. Pure waste of time, if you ask me," said Standish discouragingly.

"You think so? Well, we'll have a dash at it, anyhow."

As it turned out, Standish was wrong. In fact it was he who, from the plane, caught the first glimpse of shining metal amid the waste of heather, roughly in the position which The Counsellor had suggested as likely. Flying over the spot, they were able to recognise the brown roof of the missing car.

"Fantastic!" said The Counsellor, with heavy irony, as he turned the plane towards Carlisle again. "Now we take our car and visit that mare's nest. It'll be an experience for you, Wolf, seeing a mare's nest. Almost as good as hearing a true cock and bull story."

A little over two hours later, they had found their way into the Moss and come upon the hidden car. Just as The Counsellor had inferred, it had been run off the track into the heather; and though care had evidently been taken to conceal its passage by choosing the best route, they found it without much difficulty, standing in a slight depression and stacked about with cut heather so that even at a short distance it was unnoticeable.

The Counsellor could not resist a final flourish.

"Temple Sowerby to Crocketford, 67 miles," he said. "Crocketford to here, say twenty. Eighty-seven miles. Call it three gallons. They took in eight gallons at Temple Sowerby, which must have filled the tank. There ought to be between five and six gallons in hand now. Observe the triumph of brains, Wolf."

He opened the door of EZ 1113, switched on the ignition, and pointed to the petrol gauge.

"Something gone wrong with the works," said

Standish with a grin. "The tank's bung full, by the gauge."

The Counsellor stared at the dial in some dismay. He hated to find himself mistaken.

"Not so brisk," he objected. "Just take something and sound the tank, Wolf. I'll bet it isn't full."

Standish obeyed and, much to his disgust, found that The Counsellor was right. The tank was no more than two-thirds full at the most.

"These gauges sometimes strike work," he commented.

The Counsellor seemed to pay no attention. He was giving the car a minute examination, evidently in hopes of finding something important; but apparently he discovered nothing that interested him. Diving into the driver's door pocket, he fished out a driving-licence. "Helen Treverton" he read when he had opened the booklet.

"It's hers, all right," he vouchsafed to Standish.

He considered for a few moments.

"No use leaving this car here to stand the weather. We'll leave word at one of the Annan garages for them to send out and bring it in. Let's see."

He slipped into the driving seat, worked the self-starter, and assured himself that the engine was intact.

"Right! We can't do any more here. Let's get back to Carlisle. Too late to fly to London to-night. I hate night flying. We'll start early to-morrow, if you can get out of bed as soon as there's light enough, Wolf."

They stopped at Annan on the way back and gave the necessary directions about salvaging the car.

"And when it comes in," directed The Counsellor, "just take a look at the petrol gauge. And wire me what's wrong with it. Here's my card. Charge expenses to me. Want a deposit? How much?"

He counted out some notes, got into his car, and drove off towards Carlisle.

"That's a rum business," he said thoughtfully. "I said it was rum at the start. Now it seems rummer than ever. That tale about Moville, for instance. They'd have been just as quick to go direct to Glasgow and catch the liner before she started, instead of wasting time going round by Stranraer and Larne and Moville."

He paused for a moment or two, then continued:

"There's a train leaving Stranraer for Glasgow at 7.13 p.m. They left their hotel at about 7 p.m. In time to catch *either* the Larne steamer or that train. Well, let's leave that for the moment. One point's clear. They'd plenty of spare cash."

"Why?" demanded Standish.

"Because if they'd been hard up, they could have sold EZ 1113, of course, and they didn't. They preferred to leave it hidden in a bog. If you don't see there's something rum in that, then you need medical attention."

"Something in that," admitted Standish. "I don't see myself throwing away anything up to a hundred quid's worth of car."

"That's your Scots blood, perhaps. Anyhow, this Anglo-American alliance took a different line."

"Well, you've tried your hand on this business, Mark, and all you've got out of it isn't much, so far. Take my advice and drop it."

"Always discouraging," said The Counsellor cheerfully. "Why, it's just getting interesting."

"What's your next idea, then? Count me out, anyhow."

"Go back six squares and start afresh," said The Counsellor, obviously undepressed. "To-morrow I shall go down to Grendon St. Giles again and fish out some more information. The original premises don't seem to have been broad enough to reason from. I'll look up our friend Inspector Pagnell. . . ."

"Now, look here, Mark," interrupted Standish rather crossly, "it's over the score to go stirring up the police in this affair and putting them on the track of these two. That kind of thing simply isn't done—you know that well enough."

"I'm not going to do that," protested The Counsellor. "I'm just going to have a nice little gossip about local conditions. No harm in that, is there? And I'm going to send round to Somerset House, where they keep wills and all that sort of thing. No harm in that, is there? They welcome inquiries there, if you pay a small fee. And I may get in touch with the Anchor Line, too. Quite the busy little bee, in fact, flitting from flower to flower to collect the honey of information."

"But *why?*" asked Standish, irritably. "It's no affair of yours."

"Why?" echoed The Counsellor soberly. "Because I don't want to see any harm come to that girl, Wolf. That's why. I liked the look of her, in that snapshot I saw. And from what I've seen, I'm beginning to be damnably worried about her. So now you know. And will you kindly keep quiet for a while. I want to think."

Standish was surprised to see the expression on his face.

6 THE LOCAL SITUATION

NEXT morning, Standish found that The Counsellor meant to let no grass grow under his feet. He was roused at an early hour, given a minimum time for breakfast, hurried to the flying-ground, and embarked on the plane with the least possible delay. When they reached London, The Counsellor's car was waiting at the aerodrome.

"You can go to the office," The Counsellor curtly informed Standish, handing over a paper as he spoke. "I'll be back later on. Here are the directions about some things you're to do."

He gave an order to his chauffeur and the car drove off, leaving Standish to find a taxi for himself.

On reaching Grendon St. Giles, The Counsellor directed his chauffeur to stop before the local police station. As he got out of the car all signs of haste and worry left his face. He walked into the station and inquired for Inspector Pagnell, offering his card as he did so. He had two kinds of visiting-card: a private one, and another which emphasised the fact that he was The Counsellor. It was one of the latter which he handed over to the constable. By good luck, Inspector Pagnell was on the premises; and apparently the card was sufficient to draw him from whatever work was occupying him at the moment. In a couple of minutes he came into the room: a big burly man with red hair and a faintly cynical expression about his lips. He walked with a slow, heavy tread; but the deliberation of his movements seemed out of keeping with the alertness of his eyes, which took in his visitor's figure with one comprehensive glance. Apparently the loudness of The Counsellor's tweeds made some impression on him. It seemed as though he had been prepared for something more distinguished in appearance and less striking in attire.

The Counsellor gave him no time to bring his new impressions to a focus.

"Inspector Pagnell? Glad to have been able to give you a little assistance, a month or two ago. Hope you'll be able to do me a good turn now. This is how it is."

The inspector pushed forward a chair and invited The Counsellor to sit down. He himself leaned against the edge of a desk, examined The Counsellor again, and then, unexpectedly, took the lead in the conversation.

"I heard your broadcast last Sunday, sir. Did you get any answers about that car?"

"I did," The Counsellor admitted. "But what do you know about that car?"

"I've seen it every day for months, nearly," the inspector deigned to explain. "Miss Treverton's car. I knew that from the number, straight off. And what set you asking for it, if I may ask?"

"Somebody asked me to broadcast about it," said The Counsellor cautiously. He glanced at his watch. "It's about lunch time. Come and have a bite with me at the inn down the street. The atmosphere here's too official for a quiet chat," he added with a smile.

"If you can wait ten minutes, sir, I'll join you there," the inspector agreed.

He had seen the expensive car at the door and argued that the lunch would not be stinted. Inspector Pagnell liked his food and was a sound trencherman.

"Right! I'll go along and order it," The Counsellor decided. "Come as soon as you can."

He went out, gave his chauffeur orders to fend for himself, and by the time the inspector appeared at the inn, everything was ready for him. The Counsellor had gauged his man accurately; and during luncheon he kept the conversation at a minimum, allowing his guest ample time to devote himself to his meal.

"Coffee here, or in the other room?" he said at last. "We'll try the other room. It's quieter."

When they got their coffee, The Counsellor, having now established contact with the more human side of the inspector, approached his real objective.

"This isn't official," he began. "All I want's some general information about the neighbours and neighbourhood. I pitched on you not because you are in the police, but simply because you're the only knowledgeable person in the place that I've had dealings with. And nothing between us is for official use. Understand?"

"Oh, quite so," Pagnell agreed. "Did you get any news of the car. We've had no word of it being stolen, or anything."

"I've had it traced," The Counsellor admitted, "and after we've had our chat I'm going along to Longstoke House to report about it. What sort of person is Miss Treverton, by the way?"

"A very nice young lady," said the inspector approvingly. "Always got a nice smile when I come across her accidental-like. Very pleasant and friendly. But no gush about her. She keeps herself to herself, if you see what I mean. Quite popular in the village. Helps sometimes at charity affairs and all that kind of thing."

"A sociable kind of girl?" asked The Counsellor. "She's got friends round about here, I suppose?"

"Oh, plenty. She plays golf and tennis and bridge, and you need company for all of them. She's got some money of her own, too, they say. She lives with an uncle. He runs a picture-factory or something at Longstoke House."

"I've heard something about it," admitted The Counsellor. "Does it need a big staff—apart from the actual workmen, I mean."

"A few," the inspector said, evidently going over the list in his mind. "There's Whitgift to begin with. He lives in the lodge at the gate. And there's a man Albury, a bit of a boor, he is, from anything I've seen of him. And there's a sharpset little chap called Barrington. There's another—Dibdin's his name—but he's only here once in a way. He doesn't live about here. A kind of commercial traveller for them, or something, perhaps. But how do they come to interest you, sir?" he inquired with a faint air of suspicion, as if he feared he might be saying too much.

"Pure curiosity," admitted The Counsellor, frankly. "In my line, you know, one never knows when a little local knowledge may turn out to be useful. Next time you're in London, Inspector, just drop in at my offices and you'll begin to see that everything's useful some time or other."

"Well, you certainly did give me a hand," Pagnell confessed.

"What kind of a countryside is this?" demanded The Counsellor, evading further questionings. "Nice people about? I've heard of one family . . . what's their name? . . . Mulock or Hurlock or something that sounds like that."

"Trulock's what you mean, I expect, sir. Dr. Trulock. He's not what you'd call a native here. He took Fairlawns furnished, in the spring—that's a place with a big garden a few miles along the road, past Longstoke House. He's a medical but he doesn't practice. Retired, I gather, though he's only in the forties. Handsome man, grey-haired, always very pleasant when I run across him, and sociable. Gives tennis-parties quite a lot, mostly for the young people hereabouts. A kindly sort of man, too. He paid for a treat to some kids at an orphan home, the other day. Hired a bus to take them to the Fair we had last week and stood each of them half-a-crown for the shows. Very decent of him, I thought. His wife's quite young—under thirty, I'd say. They've got two kids, about four or five, with a nannie to look after them, one of the kind that wears a special uniform to show she's out of the ordinary run. She's been on holiday lately, but I see she's back again now."

"Anyone else of interest ?" asked The Counsellor.

"There's the vicar, of course. A fine old gentleman, and if you're interested in the history of the place he's the man for you, sir. It's his hobby. He's spent twenty years digging into all the family records he could get his hands on round about here, and he'll talk yards about it, if you give him a start. Not my line exactly ; I'm more interested in things that haven't been dead fifty years."

"Anybody else worth noticing ?"

The inspector slapped his knee as though he had just remembered something which should not be passed over.

"And if I wasn't almost forgetting that !" he exclaimed. "If it's out-of-the-way things you're looking for, we've got one for you here. What do you say to a monkery ; you know, the sort of place people retire to, to be out of the swim ? Only, this is a sort of mixed monkery and nunnery, male and female. The vicar doesn't much care about it, I gather. Opposition show, perhaps, is the way he may look at it. I've seen a nasty look in his eye when he called it a something-or-other . . . a thellemy, I think . . . whatever that is."

"Theleme," suggested The Counsellor.

"That's it !" confirmed the inspector. "This thing's run by some silly sort of society, I gather.

They took Grendon Manor, an old house up Fairlawns way, this summer. They call it The Abode of Light. Some new fancy religion, perhaps. I don't know. They don't make themselves a nuisance, and that's all that concerns me. Not liked about the village, though, because they don't buy much. Everything comes from some Stores in London. That doesn't make for popularity, as you can guess, sir. There's a good deal of nasty gossip and hints about this and hints about that amongst the local people, mostly invented, I expect."

"Not running a Hell-Fire Club, are they?"

"I'm not quite sure what a Hell-Fire Club is, sir," admitted the inspector, cautiously. "I see them playing tennis on Sunday, but that's not supposed to be much in the hell-fire line nowadays. You'd better ask the vicar about that side of it. Not that he's ever been inside the gate, so far as I know."

"It seems a quiet enough countryside," The Counsellor commented. "I suppose you have fairs, and that sort of thing occasionally?"

"Fairs? Oh, yes, we have 'em. There was one last week in Byward's Field, at Little Saltern, a bit beyond Fairlawns where Dr. Trulock lives. They had a circus, and a lot of side-shows, and some fellow brought an old plane and gave them five minutes in the air for five bob. Did quite a good trade, he did, from what I saw. But not with me. I didn't much like the look of his machine. However, he got off with no accidents, and that's always something. Called himself "The Great Foscari" to catch the public. His real name's Nat Rabbit, which is perhaps why he uses the other. No one has much faith in rabbits, cricketing or other."

"When was this fair?" inquired The Counsellor, without much interest. "What days, I mean."

"Wednesday to Saturday. I had to put some of my men on extra duty at it. These things bring a lot of sharks about the place, always : three-card men and what not."

"I expect so," said The Counsellor, sympathetically.

"And now, sir," said the inspector, unexpectedly, "perhaps you'll give me a bit of news in return. There's been a bit of gossiping about the village about Miss Treverton. The Longstoke House maids started it, most likely. They say she's cleared out at a moment's notice. It's no affair for the police, you understand? No one's given us any official news. But what with that, and your broadcast about her car, one can't help putting two and two together and wondering what the total is. I hope it's all right. I wouldn't like to see any harm come to Miss Treverton. She's too nice a young lady for that."

He looked earnestly at The Counsellor's face, and The Counsellor had to do some quick thinking before he answered.

"All I can tell you is that she went off in her car on Thursday afternoon. The car's in a garage at Annan, up in Scotland. We traced it there. But where she is, I don't know. What makes you think there might be anything amiss ?"

Inspector Pagnell rubbed his nose as though in some perplexity before he answered :

"There's nothing amiss, that I know of. I'm just giving you the common talk when I say that she and her uncle didn't get on well together. I was just wondering. They may have had a row, and she found the place too hot for her. That's not unlikely. He's a sharp-tempered old man, not easy to get on with. Well, they say she's got money enough for her wants ; and that's always something. Still. . . ."

"I know nothing about where or why she went off," The Counsellor hastened to assure him with a frankness which carried conviction.

"But you'd like to find out," said the inspector, shrewdly. "I'm not such a fool as all that, sir.

I can make four out of two pairs as well as the next man, and I could see you were fishing for information. And you broadcast about that car of hers. That makes the four, and it means you're interested in her, some ways. Well, it's no affair of mine officially, as I told you. But if it does veer towards the official side, you can count on me. I wouldn't like to see any harm come to her, just as I said. A real nice young lady. . . . You're going on to Longstoke House, you said? Just you see what that uncle of hers has got to say about it."

"I shall, if I can," said The Counsellor. "In fact, I'll go now."

He rose from his chair.

"Just to avoid misconceptions, Inspector," he added with a grin, "I've never met Miss Treverton in my life. So don't be getting any romantic notions into your mind. See?"

"I see, sir," admitted Pagnell. "I shan't make one and one into a pair, if that's what you're afraid of."

He glanced at his watch.

"And now it's time I was back at work. Good afternoon, sir, and thanks for the lunch. And if things turn out so as I can be useful, I'll be quite glad to help, you understand?"

The Counsellor paid his bill, recalled his chauffeur, and went on to Longstoke House. This time he inquired for Treverton; and after some delay, the crusty old gentleman appeared.

"Well, what is it?" he demanded crossly as he recognised The Counsellor. "I suppose you've come to say you haven't found out anything. Just what I expected. Now, I've no time to waste on busy-bodies. What d'you want?"

"I've found the car EZ 1113," explained The Counsellor, quietly. "It's in a garage at Annan, just across the Border."

"Oh, you have, have you?" said Treverton,

evidently taken aback by the news. " Well, what next ? "

" I suppose you'd better send for it," suggested The Counsellor. " It's costing so much per day while it lies up there," he added with a faint touch of malice.

" What's that to me ? " asked Treverton angrily. " It's not my car. I've nothing to do with it. I'm not responsible for garage charges on it. They can send the bill to my niece if they want their money. No business of mine."

" No, I see your point. Now for another matter. Are you interested in what's happened to your niece ? I notice you don't ask about her."

The implied rebuke did nothing to soothe Treverton.

" She's gone off on some wild-goose chase, I suppose," he growled. " No business of mine. She's her own mistress—can do what she likes."

" It looks as if she'd gone off with a friend of yours, one Querrin," The Counsellor explained. " Does that interest you ? "

" Querrin ? That American ? Gone off with him ? How d'you know that ? " demanded Treverton with a trace of uneasiness in his tone and manner.

" Well, two people giving the names of Querrin and Miss Treverton went up the Great North Road in EZ 1113 last week. And they went through a form of marriage at the Blacksmith's Shop at Gretna Green on Friday."

" The devil they did ! "

" The proceedings were illegal," added The Counsellor.

" No proper marriage, you mean ? That man's diddled her, eh ? And what do you expect me to do ? Throw a fit, for your amusement ? I'm not going to. She's a fool, that girl. She always was a fool, without any idea of her own interests. And now she's gone and landed herself. Well, what am I to do about it ? She's of age, isn't she ? I'm not her guardian. If she's made a fool of herself, it's her own look-out. I wash my hands of the matter—entirely."

"You won't give me any assistance in going further in the matter then?"

"Not if it means wasting my valuable time. I'm not interested."

"The police might be, if I dropped them a word," said The Counsellor smoothly. "They're beginning to prick up their ears already, I may tell you."

Treverton's mouth worked as though he were about to break out into a storm of words. Then, by an obvious effort, he regained his temper.

"Well, what is it you want? I've no wish for a public scandal—on my own account, purely. And I suppose there's been some hankey-pankey in this marriage business which might let the police push themselves in if they were incited to do it—by *you*."

"All I want is a talk with your housekeeper."

"Ah! A little gossip below stairs, eh?" sneered Treverton. "Have it if you like. More suitable company for you than I am, I suspect. Very well, I'll ring for her."

He did so; and when the woman appeared, he made a gesture of introduction towards The Counsellor.

"Give this gentleman any information he wants," he said, regaining some manners in presence of the servant. Then, with a nod to The Counsellor, he added: "I'll wish you good day. I've other things to do."

When Treverton had left the room, The Counsellor turned to the housekeeper, a rosy-faced woman of fifty-odd who evidently did not favour modern methods of make-up. With considerable tact, he managed to elicit that she was rather worried by Helen Treverton's disappearance. Yes, she admitted, she had even said a word or two about it in the village. Everyone there liked Miss Treverton, so naturally they were interested. It wasn't ill-tongued gossip at all. But there was no denying that the whole business was puzzling. No one could make head or tail of it, her going off like that.

"You're sure she did go off on the spur of the moment?" asked The Counsellor. "She didn't take any things with her?"

"I'm as sure as sure about that," retorted the housekeeper. "When she didn't come back, I got to worrying over it, and one night I couldn't sleep, I was that anxious about it all. We were all so fond of her, you see? She was always so thoughtful for other people. One of the last things she did was to arrange for us to go to the Fair, if we wanted to. Offered to take us over in her car, to save us any walking, though the buses pass the foot of the avenue. That was the kind of thing she was always doing. So when I was worrying and worrying about her I thinks to myself: '*Did* she take any night-things or anything with her, without us knowing it?' And I got up and crept down to her room, there and then, just to feel sure about it in my mind. And I went through her things. Everything was there: all her brushes and things on her dressing-table, her nightie, her dressing-jacket, all her clothes, except the grey coat and skirt I saw her go off in and her tennis-things that she took with her to play in at the party. It worries me a lot, for she wasn't the kind of girl to go off all unprepared like that. If she'd meant to go, arranged it beforehand I mean, she'd have had every thing packed hours before, for she was always ready in plenty of time for anything of that sort. No, I can't see her dashing off without anything, the way she did. It doesn't fit with her character, if you understand what I mean."

"And she hasn't written to anyone?"

"No, and that makes it all the queerer," the housekeeper declared. "When she went away any time, she always used to send us a picture post-card to show us what the place was like. She treated us like as if we were friends, as well as servants, though none of us would have presumed on that, not for anything. But this time, not a card's come to any of us. And she hasn't written to Mr. Treverton either, or I'd have recognised her writing on the envelope. It's very worrying."

"She used to get letters from America, I think?" hazarded The Counsellor.

"She did. One of them came just a few days back. I know who they were from, for he had a habit of writing his name and address on the envelope. A foreign kind of habit, I suppose. It was Mr. Querrin that was writing to her."

"You knew him?" asked the Counsellor.

"Well, I've seen him when he came to call often, when he was staying over here. A good-looking young gentleman and it was plain enough he was struck with Miss Treverton, though it didn't seem to come to anything at the time, though he's kept on writing since he went back home."

"They weren't engaged then?"

"I never see her wearing a ring on that finger, I can say that."

"But some people get engaged without publishing it, don't they?"

"I'd call that underhand myself," said the housekeeper decidedly. "There's nothing to be ashamed about if you get engaged. And Miss Treverton was the last girl in the world to do anything underhand, the very last. If she'd got engaged, she'd have said so, I'm sure."

"Nobody else on the horizon?" queried The Counsellor.

The housekeeper hesitated, evidently in doubt whether she should commit herself or not. At last she made up her mind.

"There was one of the staff here would have liked her," she admitted reluctantly. "Mentioning no names, of course. But anyone with half an eye could see how it was with him. He'd no chance at all. Not half good enough for her, to my way of thinking, so it was all for the best, really."

Whitgift, obviously, The Counsellor surmised from what he himself had already gathered.

" Do *you* know anything about where she's gone ? " demanded the housekeeper, anxiously.

" Afraid I don't," The Counsellor confessed. " But from what you say about her, she's not likely to leave you in the dark much longer. Just one more question. Do you know if she carried her driving-licence in the car always ? "

" I couldn't say about always, but I know she often had it in the door-pocket next the driving seat. Once or twice she's sent me out to fetch things from that pocket, little odds and ends that she's bought in the village and so on, and I do remember seeing her licence and her insurance form when I was hunting through the pocket for the bit of ribbon or whatever it was she'd forgotten to bring into the house with her."

" She was going to a tennis party at the house of some people Trulock on the day she went away, wasn't she ? What sort of people are they ? "

" Oh, very nice." Evidently the housekeeper was one of those people who have the good fortune never to meet anyone who isn't " nice " or " very nice ". " They were very fond of Miss Treverton. She liked children and she used to bring their two over here and give them picnics in the garden. And Dr. and Mrs. Trulock were often here to play tennis. Mrs. Trulock isn't much older than Miss Treverton—a matter of three or four years or so—so they got on together very well. They're both terribly cut up about Miss Treverton going off like this, for in a kind of a way they seem to feel responsible for it, seeing she was going to their tennis party that afternoon. They ring up every day and ask if there's any news, most anxious about it they are."

The Counsellor, fearing that he might be given more information than he wanted if he lingered, bade the housekeeper good day and went out to his car. Just before parting, he asked if Whitgift was on the premises, and was told that he was occupied.

"It's one of his busy spells," the housekeeper explained. "There's times when he shuts himself up behind locked doors in that workshop of his, and it's as much as your life's worth to disturb him. So unless you're wanting him very particular, I don't think I'd bother him to-day. He always leaves strict orders that he's not to be interrupted."

"Oh, don't trouble him, then," The Counsellor said, indifferently. "I've really nothing to say to him."

"It was him that was the last of us to see Miss Treverton, sir, but likely he's told you about that," the housekeeper went on. "I heard her car go off down the avenue and just then I found I wanted to ask her about some little thing or other, and when Mr. Whitgift came in, a minute or two later, I asked him—just to make sure—if he'd seen her driving out. And sure enough she'd passed him in the avenue. I didn't ask him any more, for he was in a hurry to get to that room of his and get on with his work. He's a hard worker, is Mr. Whitgift. I heard his machinery turning and him walking about the best part of the afternoon after that."

The Counsellor nodded indifferently and was turning away when an idea crossed his mind and he put a final question:

"Was Mr. Treverton a friend of the Trulocks, or were they only friends of Miss Treverton?"

"Mr. Treverton took very little to do with them," the housekeeper explained. "You see, they were more of an age with Miss Treverton. A bit young for Mr. Treverton; and besides, he's not very sociable; he doesn't care much about going about and seeing people and having them to the house here. He never bothered about Dr. and Mrs. Trulock when they came to pay Miss Treverton a visit, hardly ever looked near them. And when they ring up now, they just ask me if I've any news about Miss Treverton and don't bother him at all."

7 THE BOARD OF DIRECTORS

THE housekeeper's answer cleared one difficulty out of The Counsellor's path. He had been casting about for some method of forcing himself on Dr. Trulock without seeming to do so. Now the way seemed open. If he posed as a friend of Treverton, anxious for information, it was most unlikely that Trulock would think of asking Treverton about him. Treverton's bad manners and worse temper would be sufficient deterrents to a mere acquaintance such as Trulock obviously was.

This time, The Counsellor presented his private card. He had no wish at the moment to disclose his profession. He was shown into a pleasant drawing-room with a french window opening on a terrace below which was a tennis court. Knowing that the house was merely rented furnished, The Counsellor wasted no time in drawing any inferences from his surroundings; and in a minute or two Dr. Trulock came into the room.

He was one of those men who make an immediate good impression. The Counsellor put him at forty; for his prematurely-grey hair had the curious effect of making him seem young rather than old, and his only lines were the crow's-feet at the eye-corners. He had humorous blue eyes and a pleasant smile. His figure, in his grey flannels, was well-filled-out without suggesting stoutness, and he moved with a light step. As he entered, he glanced at the card in his hand as if to refresh his memory.

" Mr. . . . Brand ? Well, we're strangers, but that's

no reason why we shouldn't get better acquainted. Sit you down."

He offered a silver box with cigarettes to his visitor, and fitted one into a long holder with a gold and a silver band. When they got their cigarettes alight, he gave The Counsellor a shrewd glance and waited for him to make the next move.

"I've just been calling at Longstoke House," The Counsellor volunteered. "Treverton told me about his niece's disappearance. You know Treverton, I suppose? Difficult to get a plain tale out of him. (I've known him long enough to say that). So his story left me a bit puzzled, and a shade worried about the girl. I thought, perhaps, you'd be able to throw some light on the business and relieve my mind about her. She'd arranged to come over here for tennis? And she hasn't turned up since? A curious business."

He ended with just the right note of perplexity in his voice. To his relief, Dr. Trulock seemed to accept him as an old friend of the family. The grey brows knitted slightly; two vertical lines appeared between them; and the mouth-corners drooped a little, as though The Counsellor had broached a subject which caused anxiety.

"It's worrying," Trulock admitted. "It's very worrying. My wife's very uneasy about it, and naturally enough, for she was very fond of Helen Treverton. And the fact that Helen was due here that afternoon makes us both feel. . . . Well, not responsible, exactly, but. . . . You know what I mean," he ended, giving up the attempt to find the precise words for it.

"They've had no word of her, up to this afternoon," said The Counsellor. "Now this occurs to me. Was that party of yours arranged long before, or was it a scratch affair got up by 'phone at the last moment?"

"It was quite an informal affair," Trulock explained. "Just a few friends who often come here for tennis. It's an understood thing that we're at home on

Thursday afternoons, and people drop in without invitation if they feel inclined. If they don't care to come, they'd stay away and we don't expect them to notify us. So naturally we didn't pay any attention when Miss Treverton didn't turn up. We'd a dozen or more people that afternoon, quite enough to make up all the sets we needed. So she wasn't missed as she might have been if it had been a formally-arranged affair."

He was interrupted by the entrance of a young woman whom The Counsellor guessed was Mrs. Trulock. She was a shade under average height, fair-haired, good-looking, and evidently an artist in make-up. She hesitated for a moment on the threshold and then, in response to a glance from Trulock, came forward into the room.

"This is Mr. Brand, Meriel," explained Trulock. "He's a friend of the Trevertons and naturally he's anxious about Miss Treverton."

Mrs. Trulock acknowledged the introduction with a friendly smile.

"It's dreadfully worrying," she said, while an expression of disquietude flitted over her face. "I don't know what to make of it. I'm very fond of Helen, you know, Mr. Brand, and I can't bear to think of anything happening to her. And it *is* such an incomprehensible business, no matter how you look at it."

"Mr. Trulock's just been telling me that your tennis-party was an informal affair. No invitations, just come if you can," said The Counsellor. "I suppose your guests just drifted in, so to speak. You didn't receive them individually?"

"Oh, no. They all knew their way about the premises. If any of them wanted to change into tennis things, they knew what bedrooms to go to without asking anyone; and they just joined the rest of us in the garden when it suited them. We run a sort of Liberty Hall in that matter."

The Counsellor considered for a moment or two.

"It doesn't get us much further, but suppose this happened," he suggested. "She would arrive and walk into the house without any maid seeing her. Suppose she turned sick suddenly. She might have gone to some room to lie down for a while. She was enough at home here to do that without making any fuss or ringing for a maid?"

"Oh, yes," Mrs. Trulock admitted at once. "That's just possible. But the whole house is open to our guests. They wander all over the place. Someone would have come across her and told us she wasn't well. My husband's a doctor, you know, and he'd have been called at once if anyone had found her in that state."

"I'm merely putting it as possible, not probable," said The Counsellor with a deprecatory gesture. "Then she might have pulled herself together and slipped away without anyone noticing her."

"That doesn't get us much further forward, does it?" asked Dr. Trulock. "You've still got to explain what happened to her when she went away. Why didn't she go straight home, if she wasn't well? No, I'll give you my theory for what it's worth. Amnesia's the only explanation."

"Sudden loss of memory, you mean?" said The Counsellor thoughtfully. "I hadn't hit on that idea, I confess, but now you've suggested it, the thing's possible. Let's see. Your notion is that she left home in her car, meaning to come here. . . . By the way, are you sure that she did intend to come here that afternoon?"

"Oh, quite," Mrs. Trulock broke in. "She promised to come, at the beginning of the week. And on Thursday morning I ran across her in the bank at Grendon St. Giles and asked if she was coming that afternoon, and she said she'd be here. So unless she changed her mind suddenly, she did mean to come."

"Then Dr. Trulock's view is that she left home in

her car, lost her memory completely *en route*, and drove off into the unknown somewhere. But in that case surely she'll come to her senses in due course and come back home again ?"

"You never can tell how long these attacks may last," Trulock answered rather gloomily. "Sometimes they last for years. I'm no expert in that field but it's all mixed up with dual personalities and things of that kind. For all we can tell, she may have settled down into a completely fresh existence and forgotten everything about her past life."

"Oh, don't talk like that, Joe," his wife protested nervously. "It makes my flesh creep to think that anything of that sort could have happened to Helen."

"Well, it's possible, my dear, though not probable, as Mr. Brand says. The thing's incomprehensible on any normal basis, so far as I can see, from what we knew of the girl."

"Well, she may have gone off with somebody," Meriel Trulock suggested. "That's not probable either, but it's more probable than these horrors of yours. I'm certain of one thing. She didn't come here. It's quite impossible that she could have come, without someone noticing her. Everyone knew her quite well."

The Counsellor nodded, as though conceding this. When he spoke again, he seemed to have dismissed the main subject.

"Got some curious neighbours, Dr. Trulock, haven't you ?"

Trulock frowned as the question was put. Obviously he caught The Counsellor's meaning at once and apparently Pagnell's "monkery" was not much to his taste.

"Oh, that crew!" he said contemptuously. "It's amazing how some people will swallow any kind of Mumbo-Jumbo business. We've no dealings with them, I can assure you."

"I wish they hadn't come here," his wife added

vehemently. " I know nothing about them, really, but one hears stories about them. And when one has children, one doesn't want neighbours of that sort. Luckily Hugo and Inez are too young to understand anything they hear; and I've warned Nannie not to encourage any questions about the place, if they did happen to ask. I wish they'd chosen some other spot to settle down in."

" I shouldn't worry," Trulock said. " One can't swallow all one hears. My impression is that they're just a pack of fools looking for a fresh sensation or two."

Evidently, The Counsellor reflected, he had secured all the information he was likely to get from the Trulocks; and he took his leave. As he walked out to his car, he passed two children—the young Trulocks, he surmised—in charge of a fair-haired nurse. She wore a light-blue uniform with a conspicuous badge embroidered on it, apparently an indication of some special training institution. At the first glance, something faintly familiar about her appearance struck The Counsellor; but when he looked again, he failed to recognise the girl. Closer inspection seemed to dispel the idea that he had ever seen her before. A little puzzled by this, he got into his car and ordered the chauffeur to take him back to his office.

He reached it shortly before closing-time, went up to his room, and summoned Sandra Rainham and Standish. Then, from the Records Department he obtained a medical directory and an Ordnance map of the Grendon St. Giles district.

" This is how it is," he began, addressing his two assistants. " You were quite right, Sandra. I inquired from the housekeeper at Longstoke House about that girl's clothes. She went off with her tennis-things and no other spares of any sort. So that pins it down to an unpremeditated bolt, I think. She was popular amongst the people round about. There's one exception—her uncle. He seems to be suffering badly from some grievance or other against her. Not that that matters much, really. He's a cross-grained old brute at the best, I judge, with no good word for anyone. Then I went on to the Trulock's place: Fairlawns. The man's a medical. Let's look him up."

He turned over the pages of the medical directory for a second or two, then read an entry.

"Qualified, London University, 1920. No distinctions of any sort. Five years in a Welsh practice. Went to South America after that. Then came home again, apparently, with enough cash to drop practice. At least, he isn't practising now, I gathered. The oldest kid's not more than five. Probably he married when he came back here, for his wife's obviously English. Not much in that."

He closed the book.

"Affable cove, I found him, with a steady eye and a trick of hunting in his vest-pocket for something that isn't there. They're both a bit upset over the girl's disappearance, naturally. It's pretty plain that she never got the length of Fairlawns, that afternoon. I didn't leak any information over them, just posed as a friend of the family. But Trulock had a theory for the case: amnesia—loss of memory. He suggested that she'd just driven off in her car and might not wake up into normal life again for months."

"Rubbish!" interjected Standish. "That wouldn't account for Master Querrin being with her."

"Why not?" Sandra broke in in her turn. "Suppose her memory of the last few months was blotted out. That wouldn't cover the time when she knew him before. She may have driven to meet him, quite mechanically, and then her mind would take up round about when she last saw him, and they may have gone off together on the spur of the moment."

"Pigs might fly," commented Standish, acidly.

"Well, pigs *could* fly, nowadays, if anyone bothered to take them up in a plane," Sandra retorted.

"No good," was The Counsellor's verdict. "Possible, of course, Sandra; but then most things are possible except three-sided squares and a few odds and ends of that kind. It doesn't sound probable which is the main thing, so far as I'm concerned. Let's get down to something more like brass tacks."

He unfolded the Ordnance map on the desk before him and took up a pencil.

"Here's Grendon St. Giles," he explained, pointing to it on the map, while the others bent over to examine the lie of the land. "Two miles out, you come to Longstoke House on the right. Three miles further on, a road goes off to the left towards the village of Witton Underhill, about two miles away. Then a couple of miles further along, you come to another road branching off to the right. That leads to the Great North Road, and EZ 1113 may have gone that way. Half a mile further on, another road branches to the right and leads to Amblesham village, a mile off the road. Then a mile further on, on the left hand, you come to Grendon Manor. That's a big gaunt-looking shop with an avenue approach, and it seems to be the headquarters of some fancy religion or other. A quarter of a mile on, on the other side of the road, is Fairlawns, the Trulocks' place, where the Treverton girl was supposed to be going that afternoon. A mile past Fairlawns, you come to Little Salten village cross-roads. Down here, to the left, is a piece of ground where they hold fairs. It seems they had one running on the day that girl disappeared. You know the thing: circuses, sideshows, shooting-galleries, swing-boats, and so forth. They even had somebody with an old plane offering five-bob flights. I see there's a pub marked there, nice and handy for the thirsty pleasure-seekers. If you turn at the cross-roads, you can get on to the Great North Road, but it's a longer way than if you turned off earlier."

"Wooded country, to some extent," commented

Standish. "The road seems to run through spinneys here and there. Is there much traffic?"

"Not much, so far as I saw in passing," explained The Counsellor. "It's mostly pasture country. There's a bus service that runs once an hour along the route, each way. So they told me at the hotel I stopped at for luncheon. But it's off the main routes altogether, as you can see from the map."

"Well, what's your point?" demanded Sandra, who had little interest in rural geography.

"Somewhere along that track, this man Querrin must have been waiting with his suitcases ready packed," The Counsellor pointed out. "Question is, where did she pick him up?"

"Assuming that she did pick him up on that stretch," objected Standish. "She may have picked him up after she left that road and turned towards the Great North Road."

"In that case, speculation's fruitless," said The Counsellor, "so let's not suppose it. My point is that no man burdened with a couple of suit-cases is likely to walk a step further than he has to. To get on to that stretch of road, he must have come by car or by bus or he must have had only a short distance to walk. Amblesham and Witton Underhill are one mile and two miles off the road, so if he walked from either of them, he'd stop at the turn-off from the main road in either case; and I doubt if any man in his senses would tote a suit-case for a mile if he could find any other way of doing it. So we come to buses and taxis. Make a note, Sandra, to put an inquiry about this into the next broadcast. No name, of course. Just the usual reward to any busman or taxi-driver who picked up a gentleman with two suit-cases in that part of the county. And for information as to where he set the man down, of course. That finishes the map. Now what about your affairs, Wolf?"

"The stuff from Somerset House? It's here,"

Standish explained, producing some papers from his pocket. "To start with, here's the Memorandum of Association of the Ravenscourt Press. . . ."

"Skip that," ordered The Counsellor. "Or, no, give us the list of subscribers. Just note them for me, Sandra, in case I need a separate copy. Go on, Wolf."

"James Treverton, Longstoke House, etc., gentleman, 500 shares; Wallace Whitgift, same address, printer, one share; John Albury, Elm Villa, Grendon St. Giles, etc., chemist, one share; Frederick Barrington, 19, Partington Square, London, W.1.—that's their London depot—clerk, one share; Harold Dibdin, same address, clerk, one share; Jenny Lydbrook, 11, Shrewsbury Street, Grendon St. Giles, typist, one share; Doreen Wickwood, 7, Blackthorn Lane, Grendon St. Giles, typist, one share. Total 506 shares, with the necessary seven subscribers."

"Treverton and his staff, evidently. Part of his staff, anyway. Now what about the shareholders?"

"Capital, £12,000, divided as follows: James Treverton, £6,098; Helen Treverton, £3,000; Whitgift, £1,200; Albury, £1,000; Barrington, £500; Dibdin, £200; and Jenny Lydbrook and Doreen Wickwood hold a £1 share each. Treverton's Managing Director. Whitgift's a second Director. Barrington's the Secretary. Want the bankers, auditors, and so on?"

The Counsellor shook his head.

"No Preference Shares? No?" he asked. "And did you see a copy of the balance sheet?"

"Never paid a dividend," Standish volunteered. "Losses every year, running from £500 or so up to £900 at the peak. That Press seems to be a philanthropic institution for supplying the public with something it won't pay for."

"Not much wonder if the investors on the staff are grumbling, then. Whitgift told me the thing could be made to pay well enough if it were run on better lines. But old man Treverton holds a majority of the shares, so I suppose he can call the tune unless they could fake a liquidation. Mad as a hatter, he seems to be, wherever his Press is concerned," said The Counsellor, taking out his cigarette case.

"And what do you make out of all this stuff?" demanded Sandra rather impatiently.

"Some idea of Miss Treverton's financial status," answered The Counsellor. "She's no pauper, that's one thing clear. She's got £3,000 locked up in this dud non-dividend-paying show, and beyond that she's got capital enough to bring her in sufficient income to live on. I heard a rumour that she wanted to take her money out of this affair and it's led to friction between her and her dear uncle. I don't wonder. £3,000 is always £3,000. They'd have to buy her out or let the shares go to the public, if she insisted. And my impression is that Treverton would simply hate that. He wants no fresh discontented shareholders asking about dividends. There's trouble enough in that line for him already. By the way, Wolf, did you notice in the prospectus whether they had any borrowing powers?"

"There's a provision for that," Standish said.

"When did they hold their last general meeting?" asked The Counsellor incuriously.

"June 27th, 1937," said Standish, after consulting his notes.

"And now it's September 15th, 1938." He counted the months over on his fingers in an undertone. "They'll have to buck up if they want to get their next meeting within the statutory fifteen months. Well, that's their affair. I don't suppose they're going to declare a dividend this time either, so they won't be unduly excited."

Miss Rainham evidently felt that the time had come for plain speaking.

"After all this fuss, Mark, you've really discovered nothing about that affair. You've poked your nose into it against our advice, and possibly caused some annoyance to that girl, for all you can tell. But you're no nearer finding out where she is than you were at the start."

The Counsellor examined the tip of his cigarette with great earnestness. A faint, transitory smile flitted across his face before he defended himself.

" I know where she *isn't*, and that's always something, Sandra. And I know where she *wasn't*, too, and that's something more. Wait till the replies to the next broadcast come in. Then we'll talk a bit more about it."

" You might ring up the Anchor Line and find out whether she and Querrin are aboard that liner," Standish suggested. " Shall I do it ? "

" Certainly, if you like to spend the money. But not my money, Wolf. No, not my money. I'm not bothering about certainties. And that reminds me of an old country wife I once came across who had a still more aged husband. The old boy sat about a good deal—he was past work. I asked the old lady what he did with himself. " Oh, he just sits there, thumpin' and thumpin' at the thinkin'.' That's the line for you, Wolf. Just you go ' thumpin' and thumpin' at the thinkin',' and perhaps you'll see what I saw a while ago. It's interesting."

8 EXIT TREVERTON

ON Sunday, from Radio Ardennes, The Counsellor sent out his S.O.S. to bus-drivers and taxi-men, asking about a gentleman burdened with two suitcases. Monday brought no response. When he went to his office on Tuesday, he rang for Sandra Rainham.

" Any answers to that S.O.S. this morning ? " he demanded, when she came into the room with no documents in her hand.

Sandra shook her head.

" Nothing, so far," she declared. " I've just been through the morning mail."

" Looks as if we'd drawn blank," The Counsellor commented in a disappointed tone. " And yet I'd hoped for better luck. A quid usually draws 'em. It begins to look as if Master Querrin must have toted his suitcases with his own fair hands to wherever she met him."

" You can't very well put out a broadcast asking for information about anyone seen carrying two suitcases," said Sandra. " It's not such an uncommon sight as all that. You'd be flooded out with demands for your reward."

" That's so," admitted The Counsellor, ruefully.

" Wolf will laugh," Sandra pointed out, gently.

" And you, too, no doubt," snapped The Counsellor.

" No, not exactly," she admitted. " That abandoned car sticks in my throat."

" I don't wonder," said The Counsellor, ambiguously, " I can't swallow it myself. But since Wolf's not among those present, I'll admit that I may have to revise some of my ideas."

" For instance ? "

"Well," said The Counsellor, rather fretfully, " we've drawn blank in the Story of the Young Man with Two Suitcases. But is it a snick that he had those suitcases with him when the girl picked him up ? The first we hear of suitcases is at Tuxford. But before that, those two must have passed through Stamford, Grantham, and Newark—all sizeable towns. Any of them could have furnished passing travellers with two suitcases and equipment enough for a couple of nights in hotels. They were new suitcases, remember. But against that, there's the fact that they had his initials on them. That wasn't necessary and it would have meant waiting while the lettering was put on. And the time-schedule doesn't indicate that they wasted any time on any of those three places. So there you are—and where are you ? "

Before Sandra could offer any comments, the telephone buzzer sounded at The Counsellor's elbow. He picked up the receiver and began a conversation with someone unknown. His own contribution to it conveyed nothing to Sandra, for it consisted merely of monosyllables indicative of surprise, acquiescence, dubiety, tolerance, and eagerness. At last he put down the instrument and turned to his secretary, with the air of one who is sure of making his effect.

" Well, *that* puts the cat among the pigeons," he announced.

" Does it ? All I heard was 'Yes' and 'Well' and others like them. I'm not a mind-reader. Don't be so mysterious, Mark. You're no good at it."

The Counsellor ignored this.

" That," he said with dignity, " was my old friend Inspector Pagnell asking for my assistance."

" He did that once before," said Sandra, rather exasperated by this procrastination. " Whose tail-wagger's missing this time ? "

" Treverton's suicided," said The Counsellor, concisely.

"What! Killed himself?" ejaculated Sandra, completely taken by surprise. "Are you sure?"

"As sure as Death," said The Counsellor seriously. "He didn't put in an appearance at breakfast this morning. When they went to knock him up, his room was empty. Bed unslept in. No sign of him anywhere. They hunted about until at last someone thought of looking to see if his car was in the garage. They found him in the garage, dead. The usual thing: garage doors shut and the car engine been running. Carbon monoxide poisoning."

"It may have been an accident," Sandra objected, since she did not like the idea of suicide.

"Pagnell doesn't seem to think so."

"And why did the inspector ring you up?"

"Apparently he thinks I know more than I cared to tell him the other day, and he's clutching at any straw that might help him for the inquest. As a matter of fact, I've got an idea or two. But they're so cloudy that I wouldn't care to put them down in black and white," said The Counsellor cautiously.

"Are you connecting this suicide with that girl's disappearance in any way?" Sandra demanded, as the thought occurred to her.

"Everything's connected with everything else," said The Counsellor instructively. "I shouldn't wonder if that was true in this case."

"Oh, don't be an ass, Mark," exclaimed Sandra sharply. "It's too serious a thing to be funny about. Think of that poor man, dead."

"You never knew him. And I didn't like him," pointed out The Counsellor. "What I'm really worried about is that girl, I may tell you. There's something serious afoot, Sandra. I'm not getting above myself," he added seriously, "but here have I been rousing the countryside from Radio Ardennes, and generally showing that I'm poking my nose into this affair of that girl—and now we get this suicide. A bit sinister, that. Have I, in some way, made things too hot for Treverton? It almost looks like it, doesn't it?"

"Well, both Wolf and I told you to leave it alone at the start," Sandra reminded him. "I only hope, Mark, that you haven't let yourself in for sackcloth and ashes."

"That's as it may be," The Counsellor retorted. "Never judge a tale till you've heard the end of it, Sandra. And if I have to repent, there's always one advantage: I know where to buy a repentance stool. They keep 'em at Gretna."

"You're a brute," said Sandra. "All you're really thinking about is how to gratify your 'satiable curtiosity.'"

"We'll let it go at that, then. Meanwhile, duty calls. Or at least Inspector Pagnell does. Just 'phone for my car. I'll be ready by the time it comes. You and Wolf can keep shop here while I'm away. If I'm wanted, try the Grendon St. Giles police station."

"It would serve you right if they locked you up there. You've got no finer feelings, Mark, I know; but you needn't show it so plainly."

The Counsellor dismissed her and busied himself with some routine matters until his car arrived. When he reached Grendon St. Giles, Inspector Pagnell was waiting for him at the Police Station.

"Now I'm going to make a note of what you say," the inspector warned him as he showed him into an unoccupied room. "That's just a matter of routine, of course, sir; it doesn't mean I've any suspicions of *you*."

"Right!" The Counsellor assured him. "But you see, Inspector, one of us has got to start the play. And that's going to be you. And I shan't take any notes. So you can put your paper away for the moment."

"I don't quite see it that way, sir," said the inspector, rather coldly.

"But I don't see it any other way," declared The

Counsellor. "You want to hear what I know that bears on this business. How the deuce do I know what bears on it until I've heard your story? My way's the quicker of the two. Stands to reason."

Inspector Pagnell was no fool. He realised the force of The Counsellor's argument. He realised also that he had no power to extract any information whatever, if The Counsellor turned obstinate. After a few moment's consideration, he gave in gracefully.

"Very well, sir. I'll be frank with you and I expect you to play the game by me in return."

"Right!" agreed The Counsellor, beaming. "Now we understand each other, and we'll get on like a house on fire. Start in. I'm listening."

Pagnell produced a notebook which he consulted occasionally during his narrative. Having flattened it out on the table before him, he began.

"Last night, Treverton had his dinner as usual. He dined alone, of course, since his niece isn't here. He puts on a dinner-jacket always, and he did so last night. After dinner he generally goes to his study or office or whatever you call it."

"I know the place," interjected The Counsellor to save explanation.

"He went up there last night. It seems that sometimes, when he doesn't want to be disturbed, he locks his study door; and then no one is allowed to bother him."

"Like sporting his oak," elucidated The Counsellor. "Quite so. Go on."

"At about ten o'clock, his housekeeper, Mrs. Yerbury, had a question to ask him about some household affair; and she went up to the study and tried the handle gently as she usually does. The door was locked, so she came away again without trying to attract his attention, as is her usual custom in such cases. She could ask him her question at breakfast time, she explained to me. When I pressed her, she said she heard nothing in the room—I mean no movements or that kind of thing. He was evidently sitting down either at his desk or in an armchair. Asleep, perhaps. I gather from his housekeeper that she suspected he didn't always work after dinner. Took a nap, instead."

"No proof that he was in the room at all, then?"

"Not from her, but I've got it elsewhere," Pagnell explained. "At about eleven o'clock, the maid came back up the avenue. She'd been having her evening out. She happened to notice the lighted-up window of the study. Nothing remarkable in that seeing that it was the only lighted window on the front of the house at the time. This girl—her name's Florence Etham—kept her eye on the window as she came up towards the house. You know how one tends to look at any light in a dark night, a sort of home-and-friends feeling. Well, while she was looking up, she saw a shadow cross the blinds. They're light holland, and take shadows sharply; and she's quite positive that the shadow she saw was Treverton's. All the rest of the men about that place are big fellows. Treverton was on the small side and he walked with a sort of strut that was unmistakable. You've seen him yourself."

The Counsellor nodded.

"I'm quite satisfied about that bit of evidence," Pagnell continued. "So that establishes that he was in his room with the door locked at about 11 p.m. That's quite normal. He never went to bed before midnight as a usual thing. The maid went in by the back-door of the house, had a chat with the housekeeper for a few minutes, and then they went upstairs together to bed. They're both quick and sound sleepers, they tell me, and that finishes their evidence about last night's doings."

"Seems quite all right," commented The Counsellor. "Go on."

"Now we come to breakfast time," continued the

inspector. "It seems the maid knocks on Treverton's door in the morning but as a rule he never bothered to reply. She knocked as usual and wasn't surprised to get no answer. She went along to the study, which she usually tidies up before breakfast. The door was open and the place was empty. Nothing unusual, you see. She cleared out the ashtrays and so forth, pulled up the blinds—there were no curtains—and opened the windows to air the place. What are you smiling at, sir?"

"No curtains," explained The Counsellor. "That's all of a piece with Treverton's economical methods, you know."

"They give him the name for being a bit near," the inspector confirmed. "But to go on with the story. Treverton didn't show up in the breakfast room, which was a bit unusual, for generally he's like a bit of clockwork. They didn't think anything of it until an hour went past. Then the housekeeper took it into her head he might be ill, so she went up and hammered on his bedroom door. No reply. More hammering. Nothing doing. So at last she decided to push open the door, and she put her head in. She got a bit of a start, she says, when she found the bed hadn't been slept in, and his pyjamas were where they'd been left the night before."

"Sensation!" said The Counsellor. "And what did they do next?"

"They didn't know what to do, and I don't much blame 'em," said Pagnell. "After all, an old gent might go for a morning stroll, though it wasn't much in Treverton's line, apparently. So they just talked it over between them and decided to wait till some stronger character turned up to take responsibility. Whitgift, who lives at the lodge, was due fairly soon; so they made up their minds to wait till he arrived and see what he made of it."

"Sensible enough," commented The Counsellor. "I expect they were a bit afraid of making a bloomer of some sort. Treverton's temper was none of the best."

"Quite so. They said as much to me," confirmed Pagnell. "When Whitgift put in an appearance, they explained matters to him. It was all a bit unusual, considering Treverton's regular habits, you understand. Anyhow, Whitgift seems to have acted much as you or I might have done. He collected some of the staff and started to search the grounds. He didn't know what to make of it all, but he thought that was as useful a thing to do as he could think of. Perhaps, he said, the old boy had gone wandering out in the dark and broken a leg or something, though midnight strolls weren't much in his character, I gathered."

"No," declared The Counsellor, "from what I saw of him, fresh air wasn't much in his line, especially chilly night air. That doesn't sound a bit likely. Still, I suppose they felt they had to do something to show zeal."

"They found nothing," Pagnell continued. "Then one of them—it was Albury, so far as I can make out—suggested that perhaps Treverton had gone off in his old car and got stuck somewhere. That sounded likely enough—the car sticking, I mean—for it was a shabby old crock. So off they went to the garage to see if the car was amissing as well. And when they opened the side door, there was the car O.K. They found more than the car. Treverton was lying on the floor by the side-door to the garage. The car engine wasn't running—I found later on that the tank had gone dry—but the place was full up with exhaust gases. The stink warned them, luckily; but one of them rushed in and hauled Treverton out into the open air, and then they swung the doors wide to clear the choke-gas out of the place. Incidentally"—Pagnell added sardonically—"they destroyed any evidence we might have got from the position of the body. One of them, I admit, had enough wit to notice that the radiator was warm."

" Half a jiff," interrupted The Counsellor. " You talk about a side door to that garage. Let's get the lie of the land clear."

" It's an old coach-house converted into a garage," Pagnell explained. " It must have been built to take two carriages side by side with a couple of big double doors, cheek by jowl, to let in the vehicles. These doors are fastened by bolts on the inside and they open outwards, of course. You take your car in and bolt the door from the inside. Obviously you can't get out that way. So there's a small door at the back of the garage, in the side wall just about level with the bonnet of the car. That door leads into another room in the building, which may have been the original harness-room. It's now filled up with all sorts of odds and ends decrepit garden tools, old garden hose, and a big cylinder and fittings which were once part of the old acetylene plant that used to light the house, before they got current in. It's just a lumber-room, and through it you pass out by another door into the yard. To get your car out, you pass in this way and then unbolt the big doors to open a way for your motor. Most people would have modernised the place a bit, put on a ' roll-top ' pattern door or at any rate one that slid on rollers. But Treverton grudged the expense, they tell me. He had the name for being a bit ' near ' in some things."

" Sure it was suicide and not accident ? " asked The Counsellor doubtfully. " Some people, you know, are fools enough to stay in a garage with the engine running. The engine had been running ? "

" Ran till the tank went dry," Pagnell assured him. " The radiator was faintly warm when I got there. Besides the ignition key was turned on."

" Right ! " said The Counsellor, apparently satisfied.

" Now here's the rum bit," the inspector continued, with a satisfied smile. " When they came to look about, once the fumes had cleared off, they found a foot-pump attached to the tyre of the off front wheel. I've taken the pressure of that tyre, and it was pretty low. So he must have started pumping it up when he came in. Likely he felt it was down, while he was out in the car."

"Looks more than ever like an accident through sheer carelessness," said The Counsellor. "I was just wondering how he came to be knocked out if he was in the place only for the minute or so needed to fix the door and get to the other exit. But if he was working a foot-pump, of course, he'd be breathing deeper than usual owing to the exertion. He didn't look in good condition when I saw him."

"Very nice," admitted Pagnell with an air of suppressed triumph. "But the light in the garage was switched off, and the car lamps were off as well. Do you usually pump up a tyre in the dark, by preference, sir, when light's available?"

"Moonlight?" suggested The Counsellor.

"No good, sir. The place has no windows, except a tiny one and it faces the wrong way to catch any moonlight. Besides, it was a cloudy night. But here's the clincher, sir. We know Treverton was pretty 'near'. He never spent or wasted a penny if he could help it. Now is it likely that a man of that sort would leave his engine running—wasting petrol—while he pumped up a tyre. No! You can take it from me that this foot-pump business was all my eye, just planned by him to make it look like an accident. He may have had an anti-suicide clause in his insurance policy."

"Wonder where his money goes," mused The Counsellor. "His niece is the only relation I've heard about."

The inspector made a jotting in his notebook.

"Something in that, perhaps, sir. I'll see his solicitors and get a look at his life policy and his will. Nothing like being thorough, is there? But I've no doubt it's suicide. I gathered from a hint that Albury dropped that this picture business wasn't doing too well. He may have been in financial trouble, for all we know."

"It's a limited company," said The Counsellor, doubtfully. "But he may have had financial bothers apart from that. Whitgift gave me a hint that pointed that way. Well, let's call it suicide. And now, I suppose, you want to know about Miss Treverton's disappearance?"

"If you please, sir."

"Well, this is how it is," The Counsellor began. "It's a longish tale, so I'll just give you the gist of it. Miss Treverton went off at three o'clock last Thursday afternoon. She had a grey coat and skirt on, and in her car was an attaché case containing tennis things. She probably had her racquet with her, but no one can speak to that. She was going to play tennis at the Trulocks. She didn't turn up at Fairlawns. But her car, No. EZ 1113, was next seen at St. Neot's. She was then accompanied by a young man. They took in some petrol there, after having tea, and they paid with a bad pound note. Just keep that note in your mind, Inspector. This pair—the girl in the grey coat and skirt and the young man—were next heard of at Tuxford. There's a two-star A.A. hotel in Tuxford but they didn't go there. Nor did they go on to Doncaster, where they could have got a choice of hotels even if the racing did happen to be on at that time. No, they picked out a very small temperance hotel in Tuxford. Note that point, Mr. Pagnell. They unloaded two suitcases from the car along with the attaché case containing Miss Treverton's tennis things. The suitcases were new and initialled H.Q. The attaché case, as one might expect, had H.T. on it, Miss Treverton's initials. They had dinner at this temperance shop, and stayed the night there, occupying different rooms. The girl had a long chat with the landlady and left a marked impression. Note that, also. They left next morning, and their next appearance was at Baldersby Gate about noon. The girl was driving, and she ran over a pet dog. The owner of the dog says it looked like being done on purpose, and when she tackled the girl about it, all she got was: 'I'm not fond of dogs.' That's another point to note."

"If there's going to be more of them, I'll jot 'em down," interrupted the inspector. "Let's see. Bad pound note . . . poor hotel (temperance) . . . accident to dog. . . ."

"And the strange young man and the two suitcases," amplified The Counsellor. "Now I'll go on. At Temple Sowerby they stopped for lunch. They could have gone to a one-star A.A. hotel, but apparently they went to one that isn't on the A.A. list. They could have been in Carlisle in half an hour at the rate they were driving, and there they could have had a choice of larger hotels. Or they could have stopped at a three-star hotel in Greta Bridge, earlier on the road. But no, they chose this very minor pub. And then, mark this, Inspector, they made the devil's own fuss because the best wine the place kept wasn't good enough for their palates."

The inspector made another jotting and then looked up, waiting for The Counsellor to continue.

"The next stop was—now for Romance, Inspector—at Gretna Green where they were made man and wife over the famous anvil in the Old Blacksmith's Shop, quite in the best tradition. They gave the names of Howard Querrin and Helen Treverton, but unfortunately the marriage didn't conform to the present laws of Scotland, as Mr. Querrin hadn't the necessary residence qualification."

The inspector pricked up his ears.

"Sounds like some White Slavery dodge," he surmised uncomfortably. "I wouldn't like to see anything of that sort happen to so nice a young lady as Miss Treverton. You're sure of your facts sir?"

"Dead sure," The Counsellor affirmed. "I've

seen the register myself and read the entry. Took a copy of it, in fact."

"And who's this man Querrin?" demanded the inspector. "I've a notion I remember that name . . . Querrin . . . Querrin? . . . Oh, yes, now I've got it. There was an American, name of Querrin, was in this neighbourhood a while back; and he was often about Longstoke House. Is that him?"

"Let me finish the story first," The Counsellor suggested. "They left Gretna Green and pushed off on the road to Stranraer. About six o'clock that evening, they hailed an A.A. patrol near Crocketford and got him to change a wheel for them. The man in the car had his arm in a sling, which accounted for his needing help. They happened to say something about Moville, which he picked up."

"Moville? Isn't there some darky song about Old Moville, sir?"

"I daresay," agreed The Counsellor, "but the Moville I think they meant was the one in Donegal. The Anchor Line boats lie off there to pick up and set down passengers from or to Ireland."

"Ah! Now I see where it's leading," declared the inspector. "I remember there's a service to Ireland *via* Stranraer. I see, I see."

"Do you?" said The Counsellor, innocently. "That's nice. Well, the young couple turned up in Stranraer *by train* at about 10 p.m. They stayed the night at an hotel—sharing a room this time, which would be all right for a properly-married couple—and they left on the following evening in time to catch either the Irish mail-boat or a train to Glasgow. And they left their car, EZ 1113, hidden in a small wilderness called Lochar Moss. And to get to Lochar Moss from the place they met the A.A. patrol, they had to go back some thirty miles of the road they'd already traversed. There it is, inspector. All in plain sight, I think, if you'll just put your brains on to it. I've given you the tips as I went along."

Inspector Pagnell apparently set his brains to work for a minute or more, as his face betrayed. But evidently he thought it would be easier to take a short cut to the solution by asking The Counsellor for his version.

" Well, sir, I'll save time by giving it up and taking what you've got to say about it."

The Counsellor grinned without dignity.

" Put it in four words, Inspector. Laying a false trail. Look at what I've given you. The first thing you hear is that they pass a bad pound note. Isn't that likely to get them well kept in mind ? Of course it is. Then in Tuxford, they don't go to an ordinary hotel. Not they. They pick out a little temperance shop, and the girl takes care to stamp herself well into the memory of the landlady. Why choose that particular pull up ? Because a guest in a tiny little hotel gets more notice than in a bigger place. Then next morning they run over a pet dog, with the girl driving. And when she's given a bit of the owner's mind, all she says is : 'I'm not fond of dogs.' Just put your brain to work there, Inspector. You can't miss it."

" But she *was* fond of dogs," Pagnell protested. " Why she had a dog of her own, sir, a collie ; and when it died the other day she was terrible cut up about it, I know."

" I'd seen a snapshot of her with her collie. That's what made me sit up and take notice. Why, man, it stares you in the face. That girl in the car wasn't Miss Treverton at all. It was another girl, dressed in the same kind of get-up—grey coat and skirt."

The inspector sat up in his chair, taken aback by this suggestion.

" It doesn't sound over likely," he objected. " After all, it was her car."

" Well, let's continue the tale, if you're not convinced," retorted The Counsellor. " At Temple Sowerby, they deliberately choose a small pub to stop at for lunch. Why? Because they're more likely to be noticed there than in a bigger place such as they could have found in Greta Bridge or Carlisle. And to impress themselves on the staff, they kick up a dust about the wine. A couple who were quite content to stop at a temperance place for dinner the night before! It simply screams at you, Inspector."

"It does fit in with your notion, sir, I'll admit," confessed Pagnell, becoming convinced in spite of himself.

"Then they go on to Gretna and go through a form of marriage. That leaves a permanent record in the register kept at the Blacksmith's Shop. Another dodge to leave a trail behind them, obviously. After that, they take the trouble to make themselves conspicuous again. The man puts his arm in an improvised sling—to make himself the more noticeable and to give an excuse for stopping the A.A. scout. I don't suppose that tyre was punctured at all. I expect they simply slacked off the valve and let some air out. Anyhow, they waited till someone came along to help. They were lucky in an A.A. scout turning up, but anyone would have done for their purposes. And they were careful to talk loud about their next arrangements—Stranraer, Moville."

"You're almost convincing me," Pagnell admitted. "But why did they leave their car in this place . . . what's its name . . . Lochar Moss?"

"Because they wanted to be rid of it without leaving traces. A car's much too easily identifiable. They might have shoved it into a garage. Admitted. But people sailing for America don't shove their car into the nearest garage and leave it. That would have made the Moville stuff look a bit thin when the car was brought to light. Nor could they risk trying to sell it. That might have led to inquiries about their bona fides. So they had to 'lose' it, and well back on the road. Hence Lochar Moss. And once they landed at Stranraer, all they had to do was to vanish, eaving the impression that they'd taken the boat to Larne. Whereas, I believe, they really took the train to Glasgow. Anyhow, so far as I'm concerned, they've gone into the unknown. Now, does that help you much ? "

" It just makes things worse," the inspector grumbled. " That is, if all this has any connection with Treverton's suicide at all. Why did he do himself in ? Do you think he was mixed up in his niece's disappearance, sir ? "

" I don't know, but I can find out," answered The Counsellor, using one of his repertoire of clichés. " I've a vague glimmering of an idea, Inspector. Too thin yet to talk about. Still, from what I *do* know already, I'm inclined to back the notion that Treverton's death and her vanishing aren't independent affairs. There's a link between them, somewhere."

" You think Miss Treverton's been kidnapped ? At least, that's what I took you to be driving at."

" I leave it to you," said The Counsellor. " I'm practically certain the girl in the car wasn't Miss Treverton. Therefore Miss Treverton must have left that car somewhere after she set off from home and before she got to Fairlawns. After that, the car was taken away by two people who took great care to leave clues *en route* to give the impression that Miss Treverton had gone out of the country. Well, I don't think she went that way."

" My point is," said the inspector doggedly, " was Treverton himself mixed up in this abduction ? Had he any motive for getting his niece out of the way, temporarily or permanently ? And did something go wrong with the works, so that he found himself in the devil of a tight corner, and had to suicide ? That would fit the two affairs together, since you're looking for a connection between them."

" Something in that, perhaps," admitted The Counsellor. " That is, provided you can prove he was mixed up in the abduction, find his motive, and discover why he suicided. Otherwise, I can't see any definite proof of a connection between the two affairs myself, for the moment."

"Well, I believe there's a connection, and I'm going to find it," declared Pagnell decidedly.

"I know where I'd start, if it were my job," said The Counsellor with equal decision in his tone.

"And where, then?" demanded the inspector, clutching at the suggestion, since he himself had no clear idea of how to begin.

"I'd get that dog of Miss Treverton's dug up and have the spectrum of its blood examined by an expert," explained The Counsellor. "Whether he'd find much after this delay I can't say. But I'd ask him to see if he could spot the absorption spectrum produced by the presence of carbon monoxide."

"I see what you're after," said Pagnell, after a few seconds consideration. "You mean that Treverton had a preliminary canter with that dog, just to see if he could be sure of finishing himself comfortably with the exhaust gases in the garage?"

"No, I don't mean anything of the sort," retorted The Counsellor. "The dog died a day or two before Miss Treverton disappeared, didn't it? Well, in that case, why rehearse a suicide at all, just then? If you're anxious, I can suggest another reason for the dog's death. Suppose Miss Treverton had taken it along with her in the car to that tennis party? It might have been a nuisance to the person who got hold of her, mightn't it?"

"So you think it was destroyed to prevent it protecting her?"

"Don't bother to speculate till we've got something to go on," said The Counsellor impatiently. "Find out about its blood, first of all. And another thing, Inspector. Would you ring up the housekeeper at Longstoke house, now, and ask if Miss Treverton used to take that dog with her to tennis-parties. It's not likely but. . . . Yes, just ask her if the Fairlawns children got on well with the beast. Do it now."

The inspector left the room and returned in a few minutes.

"You seem to have hit it," he admitted. "The housekeeper says the Trulock kids fairly doted on the beast. They loved playing with it when they came over to Longstoke House, and Miss Treverton always took it to Fairlawns whenever she went there, for their amusement. She didn't take it to other places. No one wants dogs at tennis parties."

"That seems a bit suggestive," The Counsellor admitted. "But I'd rather have more facts about that dog before I waste time over it. You get it dug up, Inspector. And, if I may suggest something, I'd do that at dead of night, without informing the town crier. See?"

"I see," said Pagnell with a portentous nod.

9 THE AMERICAN

ON the day after his interview with Inspector Pagnell, The Counsellor felt an unwonted disinclination for the work of his office. He decided that it would be early enough if he dropped in there after luncheon. Part of the morning he spent in poring over ordnance maps, but this proved to be time wasted. Yet he could not shake himself free from the Treverton problem. He had a feeling that the solution was just round the corner and that it would emerge if only he kept his attention fixed on the subject. But it stubbornly eluded him, try as he might. At last, about half-past two, he decided to go to his office.

Hearing of his arrival, Sandra Rainham came into his private room with a sheaf of papers in her hand; but he waved them aside impatiently.

"Fix them yourself," he ordered. "I'll get Wolf now, and give you both the stop press news on the Treverton mystery."

"Has that poor man really committed suicide?" asked Sandra.

"Dead, for a ducat. Shakespeare." The Counsellor assured her.

"I think you're simply beastly," Sandra retorted. "It's not decent, to talk like that about a thing of that sort."

"Well, I didn't like him," declared The Counsellor, defensively. "And, what's more you wouldn't have liked him either, if you'd met him. Besides, surely he knew what was best for him. No need for you to voice an opinion about the rights or wrongs of the case. Ah! Wolf," he added, as Standish came into the room, "Sandra wants to know all about the Treverton business, so I thought you'd better hear it too."

"Very kind of you," said Standish, ironically. "That means you feel you must talk about it to somebody, so Sandra and I suffer. Well, go on. I'm not a bit interested, really; but I'll try to make the right noises."

Quite undamped, The Counsellor rapidly outlined the tale of Treverton's death as he had heard it from Inspector Pagnell.

"And that's how it is," he concluded.

"Oh!" said Standish.

"Oh?" said The Counsellor with a touch of petulance in his tone. "What d'you mean by saying 'Oh!'"

"One of the appropriate noises," Standish explained. "One can do a lot with 'Oh', according to intonation, you know."

"Oh, you can, can you?" said The Counsellor, giving an unconscious illustration of Standish's contention. "And what does this particular 'Oh' mean?"

"Expanding it by Humpty-Dumpty's method, it means I think this Treverton case is an excellent thing to leave alone, Mark. This flood of detective fiction's gone to your head, evidently, and that's a bad symptom. About as bad as a rush of brains to the feet."

"I'm going on with it," said The Counsellor, doggedly.

"Well, I rather agree with Wolf," Sandra declared. "It's all very well to use the wireless to trace missing people. That's useful work, in a way. But, once suicide comes in, I think it's time for you to drop it, Mark. I do indeed."

The Counsellor glanced at her with a foxy smile.

"Ah, wait till you take a hand in the game yourself, Sandra. Then you'll feel the fascination of it."

"*I* take a hand ? I like that ! What do you think I'm going to do in a business of that sort ?"

"I offered you a job as Delilah before, but you didn't seem to bite," complained The Counsellor. "I don't mind changing the spelling to suit you. You're going to be Dalilah the Crafty, out of the *Arabian Nights*." He changed his tone, and added gravely, "This is serious, Sandra. There's something damned fishy about this whole affair, and so long as that girl's missing, it's every decent person's business to lend a hand. I'm not fooling."

"Oh, if you put it like that . . ." Sandra answered, reluctantly.

"I do. I'll tell you afterwards what I want you to do. It's all straight and above-board, really. Still, it'll need tact, and I can't do it myself. Nor can Wolf."

Sandra considered for a moment or two.

"If you really believe that girl's been kidnapped, of course, I don't mind lending a hand."

"I hope it's no worse than kidnapping," The Counsellor retorted, soberly. "This suicide has jarred me up more than I wanted. It doesn't look too well, all round."

He put his hand into his pocket and drew out a copy of the last balance sheet of the Ravenscourt Press which he had got typed out. He put it down on the desk before him and placed his finger on one item.

"*Sundry creditors*— £2,573 14s. 9d.," he read. "One of them should be Treverton, for I heard that he helped to finance the show out of his own pocket when it got into deep water at times. But why not have put his name down in black and white ? And who are the rest of the Sundries ? I'd like to know, just as a matter of curiosity."

Before either of his companions had time to put a question, a typist brought in a card. The Counsellor read it with raised eyebrows, flicked it across the table to Sandra, and ordered the typist to show the visitor in at once. Standish, leaning over Sandra's shoulder, read the name on the card : "Mr. HOWARD QUERRIN", and his brows also lifted in surprise. The Counsellor made a quick gesture commanding : "Leave this to me"; and all three of them turned towards the door as the visitor was announced.

Sandra Rainham was no mean judge of men, and it was with some surprise that she found her first impression of Howard Querrin was favourable. He was obviously what she called 'the best type of American', a young man with a frank eye, a rather humorous mouth, a lean face, and a reserved manner which was wholly free from shyness; the sort of person, in fact, who looked as if he could be trusted in a tight corner. This did not fit in at all with Sandra's preconceptions of the Querrin who had lured away a girl and cheated her with a sham marriage ceremony.

Querrin wasted no time in preliminary talk. He glanced at the trio, picked out The Counsellor, and addressed him :

"Mr. Mark Brand? I thought so. Inspector Pagnell sent me on to you. So here I am. I want to hear your story about Miss Treverton."

"Miss Rainham. Mr. Standish," explained The Counsellor by way of introduction. "They're colleagues of mine. Friends, too. You can speak freely in front of them, Mr. Querrin. Mr. Standish gave me some assistance"—he threw Standish an ironical glance—"in tracing Miss Treverton's car."

Querrin acknowledged the introductions.

"I quite understand," he went on. "but I came here to listen to you, not to talk. What's happened to Miss Treverton; that's what I want to know."

His eye wandered over The Counsellor's tweeds and then fixed itself on Brand's face with a steady gaze of expectation.

"Wait a minute," said The Counsellor cautiously. "It's easy to come in here with a visiting card and say: 'I'm Mr. Querrin.' But how do I know you're the right Mr. Querrin? Anyone can get a card printed."

"You're talking sense," Querrin admitted, putting his hand into his pocket. "Here's a passport—I landed yesterday. Here are a couple of letters with my address in the States on them. If that's not enough, my banker can identify me personally."

He was obviously impatient to get to business, but it was plain that he recognised the reasonableness of The Counsellor's precautions.

"Right!" said The Counsellor. "You want to know what's happened to Miss Treverton. I don't know. But I'm trying to find out. What I *do* know, I'll tell you. This is how it is."

His broadcasting experience had made The Counsellor a master of succinct narrative; and his account of the episode was concise without the omission of any relevant detail. Querrin listened to the whole of it without interrupting with a single question, though Sandra guessed that this must have entailed considerable self-restraint.

"As I landed yesterday, it's plain that this other Querrin wasn't me," he pointed out when The Counsellor had finished. "I suppose you took him for me. Quite natural if you did."

"I did, at the start," The Counsellor admitted frankly. "But when I began to see that the girl in the car wasn't Miss Treverton, I had my doubts as to whether her friend was the genuine article either. Now we know both of them are frauds. But where do you come in, Mr. Querrin, if I may ask?"

Querrin hesitated for a moment or two. Then he made up his mind.

"This isn't a time for beating about the bush," he said. "I'll give you the straight of it. I was over here in the fall of 1936. I came across Miss Treverton then. We . . . liked each other. But my folk had lost their money in the Wall Street crash when I was a youngster. I hadn't anything to offer a girl, financially. Besides, she'd some money and I don't believe in that kind of marriage. So . . . well, we understood each other, more or less. No engagement. I went off to make good if I could. Meanwhile, we wrote to each other regularly. I've managed to make good. Been lucky in some things. I told her so in my letters. Then I wrote saying I was sailing, and would arrive yesterday. She should have got that letter last week."

"She did, I believe," interjected The Counsellor.

"Well, of course she must have known what was bringing me over. She could have cabled to stop me if she didn't want me. Now I land here; and, the first thing, I go up to Longstoke House. Everything's upside down there. My girl's vanished and old Treverton's suicided. They referred me to this Inspector Pagnell. The housekeeper did that. I saw him. He gave me a rambling sort of yarn. I could make neither head nor tale of it. In fact, I didn't believe half of it, because it didn't sound the least like Miss Treverton. But perhaps I wasn't in the best of form for taking things in just then. The news I'd got at Longstoke House was enough to knock one off one's perch. I expect I was a bit dazed by it. Anyhow, this Inspector Pagnell must have felt his tale wanted independent confirmation if it was to get across. So he sent me on to you. I'm cooler now. Not so stunned, anyhow. And I've taken in what you've told me. But it doesn't seem to make sense. You say you haven't got any further than what you've told me?"

Sandra could see that under a mask of self-control, Querrin was all on wires. The Counsellor pushed a box of cigarettes across his desk and the American, evidently glad to have some mechanical operation to perform, chose a cigarette and, after a gesture asking her permission, lighted it. As he did so, she could see that his fingers were unsteady.

"You know more about Miss Treverton and her uncle than we do," said The Counsellor. "I thought you might throw some light on the affair. But don't say anything now, if you'd rather not. I can guess the kind of shock you've had. If you'd rather think over things for a bit. . . ."

Querrin shook his head decidedly.

"No, you can have it now, if there's any question you want to put. No use wasting time, is there?"

Again his anxiety broke through the mask.

"Why should anyone want to get hold of her? That's what I don't understand. But if anyone's laid a finger on her, they'll pay for it. I promise you that."

The Counsellor evidently thought the best treatment was coolness.

"Ever hear of some people called Trulock?" he asked.

Querrin shook his head.

"Never heard of them."

"Or a man called Whitgift?"

"Whitgift? Oh, yes. One of Treverton's experts? Yes, I remember him. Surly sort of beggar . . . I may as well put the cards on the table. I'd reason to believe that he'd some aspirations . . . so I gathered from one or two things that Helen—Miss Treverton—dropped casually. I didn't cut him out, you understand? He simply wasn't in it and wouldn't have been in it even if I'd never turned up. Not her type, or anywhere near it. I saw him this morning. Very cut up about this business, obviously. In fact, I liked him better after a talk with him than I did before. No jealousy about him now. He seemed a bit that way in the old days, which is understandable enough. But this morning we seemed to be both in the same boat. Worried about her, I mean. He was very decent."

"Know a man Albury?" queried The Counsellor.

"Another of the experts? Yes, knew him by sight,

but not much more. Surly beggar. Not a taking personality. But that's all I know about him."

"Now here's something that's been worrying me," The Counsellor said, leaning forward over the desk. "We know Miss Treverton was a shareholder in the Ravenscourt Press to the tune of £3,000. That earned no dividends, but she had some sort of income. Have you any notion of what other capital she had?"

"No figures," Querrin explained, "but I had a notion she had four or five hundred a year—pounds, I mean—from somewhere. It's a guess, but she must have had something like that."

"In Trustee Stocks that would be round about £10,000 capital," mused The Counsellor.

A thought seemed to cross his mind.

"In this correspondence between you and Miss Treverton, did she ever say anything about her financial affairs? The merest hint of anything?"

Querrin reflected for almost a minute before answering.

"I've a hazy idea that once or twice she did mention something, something about her uncle trying to get her to lend him some money to tide that Press of his over a bad spot. I never referred to that when I replied. Finance, you see, was a sore point with me in the state of the case. I couldn't advise her to lend the money, not knowing anything about the business. And if I advised her not to . . . well, you see how it was? It might have looked as if I was interested in her money affairs, since I hoped to marry her. I left it alone. But I certainly remember clearly enough now, that about his trying to borrow from her."

"Was she a business-like girl?" asked The Counsellor.

"Meaning did she keep accounts of her finances? No, she wasn't likely to, from what I know of her. A bit careless, in that line, I'd say."

"Trustful? Not likely to run to a lawyer about money affairs?"

"I can't see her doing that," said Querrin with the first sign of a smile that had crossed his face.

"What about her uncle?" asked The Counsellor. "Was he much of a business man? I may as well say I'm not impressed by his dealings with that Press of his."

"Well, he's dead," Querrin said, rather shamefacedly. "I don't like to say anything against him. And I didn't know much anyhow. But I wouldn't call him a genius in the money-market. That's just an impression, mind, and I'm not running him down in saying it. Some men are built that way."

The Counsellor switched over to a fresh line.

"When you were here in 1936, you saw something of them together. What sort of terms were they on?"

"Meaning did they get on together? Yes. So far as I saw. They seemed on quite good terms. Not all over each other, in any way. But quite happy together. She used to chaff him, and he seemed rather to like it. See what I mean?"

"I see," said The Counsellor, in a tone which suggested that he had seen more than the others had.

He pondered for a while before he spoke again.

"Well, Mr. Querrin, I'm not going to bluff. We've come to what may be a dead end, so far as my resources go. But if you can see any way for us to lend a hand, you can count on us. I mean it. Perhaps when you've got over this shock a bit, something may occur to you. It's been a bad business for you, anyone can guess that. And I wish I was able to tell you I had the key in my hands. But I haven't."

Querrin got up from his chair with all the reluctance of a disappointed man.

"Well, I'd hoped for something more than that," he confessed frankly, with a smile which was a little awry. "You were so cute in tracking that car of hers. I was sure you'd got something more up your sleeve. But if you haven't, why, you haven't. I'm downright grateful for you doing as much as you have done. But I want my girl back " . . . his voice shook slightly despite his effort at control . . . " and I suppose it's up to me to do something for her myself, now."

" Where are you going ? " asked The Counsellor. " Give us your address in case something turns up."

" I've booked a room at The Black Bull in Grendon St. Giles," Querrin explained. " Not much point in staying there, perhaps. Still, I want to go through this business, and that seems the best place to start. Thanks, again, sir. If anything does turn up. . . . "

" We'll let you know immediately," The Counsellor assured him.

And with that cold comfort, Querrin took his leave.

" What do you think of him ? " demanded The Counsellor, swinging round on Sandra.

" He's nice. And I am so sorry for him. He kept himself in hand, but one could see that he's completely dazed by having this sprung on him. Going up there to meet that girl after all this separation and finding she'd vanished. The bottom must have dropped out of his world when he got that facer. You'll have to do *something*, Mark. I can see his face still . . . as if it were frozen, or something like that."

" A change in the wind, evidently," said The Counsellor, with a smirk of satisfaction. " I seem to remember some people doing their best to persuade me to drop this business. And that wasn't so long ago, either. *Souvent femme varie.* And what about you, Wolf ? "

" He seems a decent sort. Useful in a tight corner, by the look of him. I admit you've scored, Mark. Let it go at that. If we can help, then let's help. But I'm damned if I see how we *can* help. And that's a fact."

The Counsellor had no modesty in his triumphs.

" Try the old prescription, Wolf. Go on ' thumpin' and thumpin' at the thinkin'.' It pays in the end.

I've no particular use for you at the moment, so you can get on with your thumping. But let's have no more of this defeatist talk, if you please. Don't distract the Great Brain from its purpose by the puny criticisms of minor intellects. That means you. And the proof is that you don't even know what the next obvious step is. Do you?"

"No, I'm damned if I do," confessed Standish with rueful frankness.

"Saved, then, so far as that goes," said The Counsellor graciously. "For you certainly don't seem to know." He turned to Sandra. "Now it's up to you to make yourself useful. Any objections to playing Dalilah *now?* Quite a respectable job, my dear. Nothing to do with luring beery old men into corners or anything of that kind. Say Yes or No smartly."

"Yes, certainly," said Sandra immediately. "I begin to think that perhaps there's something in you as a 'tec, after all, Mark. I was a bit of an ass to discourage you. There! Are his injured feelings soothed? That's nice. Now what am I expected to do?"

The Counsellor rummaged among his papers and extracted a copy of the Memorandum of Association of the Ravenscourt Press.

"Here we are," he announced. "Jenny Lydbrook, 11, Shrewsbury Street, Grendon St. Giles, typist, one share. Likewise Doreen Wickwood, 7, Blackthorn Lane, Grendon St. Giles, one share. Each of them now holds a £1 share in the company. Your job, Dalilah, is to go down there and buy one of these two shares for me. Give my private address, of course."

"What price am I to go to?" Sandra inquired in a businesslike tone.

"Anything up to £100. If they hold out for more, 'phone me. And, remember, until you've got a firm promise, my name doesn't come in. In fact, it had better not come in until the actual transfer. Now, you, Wolf, will get Sandra the cash and a blank transfer to take down with her. If she pulls this off, she'll bring that back to you, signed, and you'll hustle like blazes to see that the transfer of the share is registered in the shortest possible time. That clear ? "

" As a direction, yes," Standish admitted. " As a move in the game, no."

" Capablanca and Alekhin don't take their pawns into their confidence " explained The Counsellor with an air. " They move them. Get a move on, both of you."

" Getting a bit worked up, isn't he ? " said Standish in a stage aside to Sandra. " Needs a sedative. Quinine or bromide, which do you think ? "

" Both, in big doses," said Sandra. " You can't pose with us, Mark. Come off that perch and tell us all about it."

But The Counsellor evidently preferred to tantalise them a little.

" When you want to keep a secret, begin by keeping it under your own hat," he declared, sententiously. " I don't see why I should do all the thinking for the firm. Though, I suppose," he added kindly, " it's not your fault. No doubt you do your best with the means you have. Well, I'll give you a hint. Helen Treverton and her uncle were the biggest shareholders in that company. They're both off the map, the uncle permanently. And this happens just before the annual meeting of the company. If they're not present, they can't vote. And the remaining shareholders can do what they like, according to the agenda. I'm just a shade interested in what they do. Hence I buy myself a seat at that meeting."

" Rubbish ! " said Standish, acidly. " Who'd want to get control of a two-penny-halfpenny £12,000 company that's never yet paid a dividend ? "

" It's never paid a dividend because of the lines it's been run on," rejoined The Counsellor. " But on sounder lines, it might pay quite well. So Whitgift said. I may see something for my money after all."

"Live in hope," advised Standish, ironically.

"Very well," said The Counsellor, "if you don't like the swings, try the roundabouts. Why did Treverton suicide so soon after his niece vanished? It wasn't a broken heart at her loss. That was pretty clear from what I saw of him."

"H'm! I see what you're driving at," Standish declared. "You think he was mixed up somehow in her disappearance? Something's gone wrong that he can't face up to, so he takes the short way out?"

"You don't think the girl's dead, Wolf!" exclaimed Sandra as the inner meaning of Standish's suggestion dawned on her. "That would be too horrible." She appealed to The Counsellor. "*You* don't think that, do you, Mark?"

"Blest if I know," admitted The Counsellor, dropping pretence and speaking gravely. "All I do know is that the sooner we get on her track, the better. I've been worried all along, but neither of you would take it seriously. Put it at the lowest, I can't see that girl disappearing voluntarily. We know from Querrin that she was expecting him this week. They were keen on each other. Obviously he was coming across to fix things up and perhaps take her off to the States almost immediately. No girl would leave him in this fix of her own accord, unless she was a rank wrong 'un. And everything points the other way. No, there's no sense in it unless she was made to disappear, and disappear unexpectedly. She didn't reach the Trulocks. I'm fairly convinced of that. And I'm fairly sure, too, that she wasn't taken far away. It's possible she was, of course. She could have been gagged and taken anywhere in a closed van, I admit. But we can't follow that up, whereas we can investigate in the Grendon St. Giles neighbourhood.

"So we'll:

'Do the work that's nearest,
Though it's dull at whiles,"

as Carlyle says."

"Kingsley," Sandra corrected mechanically.

"Well, he cribbed it from Carlyle, or *vice versa.* I know I'm right about that, anyhow," declared The Counsellor testily. "Where was I? Oh, yes. We'll comb out Grendon St. Giles to begin with. Do you remember what was on in that district on the day the girl disappeared? A country fair, of sorts. Well, what's a country fair? A collection of gypsy vans, side-shows, merry-go-rounds, and what not. And they disperse afterwards, don't they? Get a girl into one of these vans and you might trundle her anywhere, and nobody'd ask a question. That's one possibility. I don't say it's right."

"Neither do I," agreed Standish, ironically. "I'm with you there, Mark. And what do you propose to do?"

"Go down and see my good friend the inspector, again, to-morrow," explained The Counsellor. "About a dog," he added.

Sandra did not, of course, see the underlying meaning of the phrase.

"Really, Mark, cheap jokes are a bit out of place, I think. Can't you be serious?"

"It's a good joke, it you could only see it," retorted The Counsellor. "But enough of this foolery, as you say, Sandra. Let's get down to brass tacks. It's past banking hours, so Wolf will give you thirty fivers out of the safe, if it holds as much. You'll go down to Grendon St. Giles and put up at The Black Bull, in case you have to spend a day or two over your Dalilahing. That reminds me, if you see me about, kindly look the other way. We shan't be on nodding terms, for the moment. And that reminds me further, we had better warn Querrin not to know you either. Wolf, you can fix that either by a wire or on the 'phone if you can get him at that inn. If he's out, you'd better wire him to ring you up and speak to him over the 'phone. No use giving too much away even to the telegraph clerk there. I may have to stay at The Black Bull myself, but there's no harm in Querrin knowing me on sight. It's only the connection between Sandra and me that must be kept dark till this deals through and we've got that share. You can start first thing to-morrow, Sandra. Your car's O.K., not getting decarbonised or anything?"

Sandra shook her head.

"No, it's on hand. But I think I'll start to-night. I hate the idea of losing a moment, now that things have got to this stage."

"Your part's quite straightforward," The Counsellor assured her. "It just needs a bit of tact."

10 THE TREVERTON BEQUEST

"DID a Mr. Querrin pay you a call, sir ?" demanded Inspector Pagnell when The Counsellor presented himself at the police station in Grendon St. Giles, next forenoon.

"He did," admitted The Counsellor. "I suppose he told his tale of woe ? Then that saves me going over it. Did you verify his tale in any way ?"

"No," admitted the inspector in a surprised tone. "He seemed all right."

"Well, I did," explained The Counsellor. "Just to be on the safe side—since we've two Querrins on our hands—I rang up the shipping people. It's O.K. A Howard Querrin *did* arrive from America on Tuesday. So the gentleman with the two suitcases wasn't *that* one, anyhow. By the way, there's no word about him touring the country with his suitcases. We've had nothing in reply to that last broadcast on the point."

"I've got a few fresh points myself," explained Pagnell, evidently pleased to let The Counsellor see he had not been idle. "First of all, we've got the results of the P.M. on Treverton's body. There's nothing mysterious about it. No poison in the stomach, no suspicious marks anywhere on the body, nothing but a plain case of carbon monoxide poisoning."

"That settles the 'How ?' of his death," admitted The Counsellor. "But it's the 'Why ?' that's worrying me."

"Well, while I'm on the subject of expert evidence, I'll give you another bit," volunteered Pagnell. "I got that dog dug up, as you suggested. I don't know how you came to think of that, sir, but it was quite worth the trouble. It was a bit 'gone' by this time, naturally, after being buried all this time. But the surgeon took some trouble over it with a spectroscope thing and what not; and he's quite definite that it died of carbon monoxide poisoning also. I still think the killing of that dog was a preliminary canter, just to see if a car running in the garage would make the place fatal. There's no other real explanation. And of course, if Treverton had suicide in his mind, he wouldn't leave the dog's body in the garage for anyone to find. He must have carted it out into the fields and left it there, after he'd finished it. There was nothing to show how it died. I've made inquiries, and no one suggested examining it when it was found. They all say that Miss Treverton would never have had her pet cut open just out of curiosity. She was grieved enough at losing it."

"Probably you know best," admitted The Counsellor. "Still, it's always something to know what killed the beast. Anything else that's fresh?"

"This next bit isn't public yet," said the inspector, cautiously. "But it's bound to come out when they apply for probate, so there's no harm in telling it to you now. I went to see Treverton's solicitor. He made something of a fuss at first, but I got over his professional scruples before long, and got a look at Treverton's will."

"Yes?" said The Counsellor, with a certain eagerness.

"If you're looking there for your 'Why?', you'll need to try again, sir," explained Pagnell, with a touch of complacency. "He's left half his money for the purpose of keeping this Ravenscourt Press afloat, and the other half goes to some artistic society, The British Association of Sign-Painters or some title like that. Anyhow, it's a perfectly genuine, old-established, respectable affair with high aims about helping Art along the road one way or another. So unless you can imagine that they've put Treverton out of the way for the sake of his money, there's no motive behind that will. It don't seem likely, to me."

"What about the half of the estate that goes to help the Press?" asked The Counsellor.

"Lord bless you! There's nothing to be got out of that. It's to be in the hands of trustees—that solicitor's one of 'em—and nobody could touch the money in a month of Sundays, except for the purposes laid down in the will. And, after all, it don't look as if it would amount to a fortune, anyway."

"No?"

"No! Nor even as much as it might have been. Most of it was in an insurance policy on his life. I got that looked up. There's a suicide clause in it. *Felo de se* barred. That may have been why he tried to stage his death to look like an accident. It may come off yet. After all, that's a matter for the coroner's jury to settle in their wisdom. They've met and viewed the body; but our coroner thought he'd best adjourn for some evidence he hasn't got yet. If they bring it in as an accident I suppose the insurance company will pay up. Otherwise they won't."

"Did anyone outside know about the purport of his will?" inquired The Counsellor.

"I asked about that," said Pagnell. "Unless he talked about it himself, there was no way for anyone to find out. And from what the solicitor said, Treverton wasn't the kind of man who would talk about his will."

"Then if he didn't, no one could expect to inherit. And if he did, they'd know they weren't going to inherit," commented The Counsellor. "Evidently you're right, Inspector. There's no motive in that will. By the way, I take it that you're now *officially* interested in Miss Treverton's disappearance, since it links on to Treverton's death?"

"Yes, I am," said Pagnell. "But that doesn't

seem to get me any further. The only thing I've definitely established is that the fake Querrin with the two suitcases didn't stay at an inn or cottage in my district before the day of the disappearance. And he didn't reach here by any train or bus on that day, either."

"Then he must have stayed with a friend, or come in a car, or arrived in an aeroplane," suggested The Counsellor. "There must have been plenty of cars about, with this fair going on. And didn't you say there was an aeroplane doing stunts at five bob a hop?"

"There was," the inspector confirmed. "But it was busy at the fair all day. It didn't bring anyone from a distance."

"A small affair, was it?"

"It just held the pilot and one passenger, sir."

"And it was busy all the afternoon, taking people for flights?"

"Right on till about sunset, sir, I remember. After that, it was parked for the night in the field, because there was no shed big enough to house it."

"What sort of person is this Nat Rabbit—that's the name of the fellow who was running it, isn't it?"

"Nat Rabbit? I've nothing against him. Young fellow. Under thirty, I'd say. As a matter of fact, he's engaged to a girl in the village here, and the only thing her people have against him is that he won't settle down to a fixed job with sure pay. He prefers this sort of chancy way of picking up a living, although he could draw quite a decent screw as a mechanic. Independent nature, as he calls it. Wants to be his own master instead of drawing a weekly wage. That kind of a man, if you understand me, sir."

"That seems quite O.K.," admitted The Counsellor.

Pagnell evidently thought it was time to take the initiative in the conversation.

"What's your view of things?" he demanded. "Treverton's past helping; but there's Miss Treverton still amissing, and I'm fair worried about her, sir. I don't like it."

"Neither do I," The Counsellor admitted. "But you know as much as I do, Inspector, in that affair. I've been quite frank with you. But I'll tell you one thing that isn't evidence. I've got a hunch, suspicion, inkling, or whatever you like to call it, that she's not gone very far away. I haven't a spark of evidence to prove it. I just feel it in my bones, somehow. Put that alongside the fact that the fake Querrin appears here suddenly from nowhere. Doesn't it suggest that some resident in this district is providing facilities?"

"You're thinking of Dr. Trulock, may be?" suggested Pagnell. "I've gone into that already. I got a list of all the people who were at Fairlawns that afternoon, and I've questioned every one of them, separately. Their evidence covers the whole time, one way or another, and it's impossible that Miss Treverton ever came near Fairlawns during that tennis-party. The drive to the front door's in view of the tennis courts, and from the place where the non-players sit to watch the sets you look right at the front door. Nobody saw her arrive; nobody saw her leave; and nobody saw her car at any time during the afternoon, if she'd parked it on the drive. No, sir, I've put everybody through that mill, the Trulocks themselves, the maids, every visitor that was there; and you can take it from me she never turned up. There was one girl who specially wanted to see her about a dress pattern or something like that, and she was on the alert to get hold of her and was a bit put out when she didn't come. So there was one witness had a definite interest in looking for her. No, she never came near Fairlawns that afternoon. That's beyond any doubt. Besides, the Trulock kids were looking out for her specially because they were fond of her. They wouldn't have missed her, even if the grown-ups had. I questioned them, too, and they hadn't seen her."

"No? Then can you suggest any other house where she might have been taken? You couldn't get a search-warrant, I suppose? Not on the evidence, seeing there isn't any."

"No, I couldn't wangle that, sir. No magistrate would look at it, without definite information."

"So I supposed. And if you drew blank, there'd be the devil to pay. An Englishman's house is his castle, and all that kind of thing, though it doesn't apply to the men who come to read the meters or the wireless-pirate hunter, apparently. You might disguise yourself as a gas-man or an electrician and get in that way."

"I might," said the inspector sourly. "But if she's been kidnapped by anyone, I don't just see them tying her up to the gas-meter; so I don't see how I'd find her, even if I did get into the house."

"Something in that," The Counsellor admitted. "Well, the resources of civilisation are not exhausted, as Gladstone said in 1866—or some other year. We must think of something else."

"What's worrying me, sir, isn't kidnapping, but something worse. Kidnapping's all very well in thrillers. But when it comes to real life, how're you going to persuade a girl like Miss Treverton to go off with anyone? And when they've got her, how're they going to keep her secure? There's servants, for one thing, about the house. They'd see something and talk about it, for sure. No, what I'm afraid of is her being dead and buried by this time. But then you come back to a motive; and I'm blest if I can see any. Why should anyone want to kidnap her? Fine-looking girl, I admit. But you simply can't swallow any White Slave racket in such a case. You can't drag a protesting girl about the countryside, you know."

"I could think of ways," objected The Counsellor.

" But I agree with you, Inspector. It doesn't sound likely. Well, time's getting on. I'll let you know if anything fresh turns up."

After leaving the inspector, The Counsellor glanced at his watch and found it was near luncheon time. He strolled along the street to the Black Bull Inn and entered the dining-room. Querrin was at one of the tables; and The Counsellor, with a nod of recognition, drew out the second chair and sat down. Except for themselves and a waiter, the room was empty. The Counsellor gave his orders and waited until the waiter had gone out of the room.

" Anything fresh ? " he inquired in a low tone.

Querrin shook his head.

" Nothing. I'm getting damnably worried," he admitted with a frown. " That inspector doesn't seem to get a move on. He just looks wise and does nothing, so far as I can see. Somebody ought to ginger him up."

" Our police haven't quite so free a hand as your ones in America," The Counsellor pointed out, not without an ulterior object. " For instance, suppose he wanted to search some house where he suspected Miss Treverton might be detained. He can't do that without swearing information before a magistrate and getting a warrant for whatever he does. Even so, he might not get his warrant if the magistrate wasn't satisfied. If he acted without a warrant, he'd be a common burglar, more or less."

" Well, I don't know exactly how it stands in the States, but I call that damned silly," said Querrin. " You might as well blow a trumpet at the gate and warn them to conceal all suspicious articles."

" Oh, you don't need to apply for the warrant publicly," The Counsellor explained. " Still, I admit there are cases where the procedure is a bit hampering. What's really wanted," he added slyly, " is an unofficial person who wouldn't bother about a warrant but just go and see for himself and take the consequences."

" D'you mean that ? " demanded Querrin with a cock of his eyebrows. " Have you got any special place in your mind ? I wouldn't mind taking a risk myself, in this case, if it would do the least bit of good."

This was what The Counsellor had been angling for, but he showed no sign.

" I've nothing in view," he admitted. " But if anything does turn up, I'll drop you a hint. But, remember, if you get nabbed, you take your medicine without squealing. I'm not going to be dragged into it—not at any price. That's understood ? "

" Of course," Querrin acquiesced. " This is my affair, not yours. By the way, I got your message. Miss Rainham's here. Is she on the same game ? "

" No, not exactly," parried The Counsellor. " She's doing a bit of work for me. You've seen her ? "

" At breakfast. She went out shortly afterwards."

The return of the waiter interrupted their conversation, and The Counsellor switched the talk to indifferent subjects, as though he were speaking to a chance acquaintance. As they were finishing their meal, Sandra Rainham came into the room and took her place at another table. Behind the back of Querrin and the waiter, she gave The Counsellor a glance which, supplemented by a faint gesture told him that so far she had not been successful in her efforts. The Counsellor, making an excuse to Querrin, pulled out a loose-leaf notebook and scribbed a short message on it. He paid his bill with two notes and, while the waiter left the room to get change, he stepped over and dropped the note on the table before Sandra, retiring again to his own chair before the waiter returned. Sandra read the message, stowed it in her bag, and gave The Counsellor a glance to show that she had understood. Querrin was obviously curious about this by-play, but he asked no questions.

11

THE TROUBLES OF A TYPIST

SANDRA RAINHAM did not return to the office until well on in the forenoon of the following day. When she arrived, The Counsellor and Standish were in conference in Brand's private office, but she had no hesitation in interrupting them.

" Sorry to break into the pow-wow," she apologised, as she shut the door behind her " but I expect you want to hear the results, Mark."

" Right, first guess," confirmed The Counsellor. " What about it ? "

" Here's your transfer, just to set your mind at ease."

Sandra produced the paper and handed it to The Counsellor, who passed it over to Standish.

" Get it registered immediately, Wolf. Time's getting short. Yes, Sandra ? "

" Will you have it short and snappy, or long and detailed ? "

" Make it as short as you can, but keep in all the details," said The Counsellor, with the air of one making a just decision. " All the important details," he added hastily, as he saw a gleam of mischief in Sandra's eye.

" Very well. This is how it is," she began, borrowing one of The Counsellor's favourite openings. " I didn't see myself going down there and simply asking one of these girls point-blank to sell her share. Too crude, that, for my taste ; and apt to cause chatter. Besides, I wanted an excuse for a general look-round. You and Wolf have been busy in the clue-hunting business, and I didn't see why I should be left out in the cold. So I cast about for a suitable disguise. It's quite simple. You just take a few of your visiting cards to a jobbing printer and get him to put the name of a good newspaper in the south-west corner. Then you sharpen some pencils at both ends and buy a note-book. And that converts you into the best kind of lady journalist on the hunt for copy, and gives you a free hand in asking all sorts of inquisitive questions which might be resented if you were a private person."

"Not so bad," commented Standish. "Dishonest, of course; but one gets that way, in an office like this."

"I went down to the Black Bull and took a room for the night. As soon as I arrived, I interviewed the landlady and left her under the impression that I was the latest thing from Fleet Street. You know what these little places are? My profession would be all over the village before a hen could scratch twice."

"The rural touch," commented The Counsellor. "Getting the atmosphere. Go on."

"I went up to Longstoke House, sent in my card, and asked for Mr. Albury. You'd seen the Whitgift man, so I thought I might begin with someone else. I saw him. He's a big man with an eye for a smartly-dressed girl. An uncomfortable eye. Too much of the strip-tease act about it altogether, for my liking. I disliked him on sight, but that had nothing to do with the matter in hand. I explained that naturally Fleet Street was horrified at Mr. Treverton's demise—yes, I said demise—and was burning for a few anecdotes about his life and character. I also said a word or two in praise of the products of the Ravenscourt Press—it's lucky I know something about them and could talk coherently on the subject. Then, after a little, I asked him if he could throw any light on Treverton's death. No, he couldn't. He'd no theories about it at all. Mind a complete blank on the subject, it seemed. As for anecdotes of the deceased's career, he couldn't remember any, except one about a row he had had with him, which wasn't very interesting. All I gathered was that they didn't hit it off together, and of course Treverton was always in the wrong. There's no *de mortuis nil nisi bonum* nonsense about Mr. Albury. So then, casually, I asked a question about Miss Treverton, and got more from the same tap. She thought a deal too much of herself, it seems, and so on. I gathered, vaguely, that she'd given Mr. Albury a downright good snubbing, at one time or other, and he hadn't liked it. Take him over all, I didn't care for Mr. Albury. He wanted to stand me a lunch, but I excused myself—courteously but firmly."

"So then?" prompted The Counsellor.

"So then I asked for Mr. Whitgift. You've seen him yourself, Mark; but for Wolf's benefit I'll say that he's not quite 'it', but he's got some manners and a nice smile. He gave me some notes which might have been useful if I'd been a journalist, and they put Treverton in a rather better light than Albury did. Whitgift set all the bad temper and so on down to nerves, overwork, worry, and some financial trouble. He wouldn't say it straight out, but it was plain enough that he thought the man had worried himself into a bad state of mind, and the suicide happened when he was a bit unstrung. As an instance of how things had been banking up lately, he mentioned Treverton's quarrelling with his niece. Before that, they had got on very smoothly, but within the last few months they seemed to have got on each other's nerves, for some reason or other. It was only on that subject that he had a hard word to say about Treverton. You were quite right, Mark. He seems to have more than a fancy for that girl. He couldn't conceal it, even when talking to a journalist; it leaked out all over. So I asked what he thought had happened to her. Oh, she'd gone off with that American, of course. Driven from home by the Wicked Uncle.

And no wonder, considering the home atmosphere in recent days. And so on, all given off with an expression as if he were chewing a pickle while he spoke. Finally, I asked to see Mr. Barrington. But Mr. Barrington was out, apparently. However, I managed to interview the housekeeper, a nice old thing."

"You seem to have been full of zeal," commented Standish ironically. "By that time you'd fairly covered your trail. If I hadn't seen that transfer, I'd conclude that you completely lost yourself in the journalist and forgot all about the real business."

"Wet blankets don't damp me," retorted Sandra. "I scorn 'em. Well, I interviewed this Mrs. Yerbury. She took me into that room you saw, Mark, the one with the stucco ceiling and the Monet reproduction. She wanted to show me a portrait of Miss Treverton, on the desk there. I think I could make a friend of that girl. She looks the right kind. And this old Mrs. Yerbury couldn't say too much in her favour."

"She gave me the same harangue," interjected The Counsellor. "Skip it."

"Well, it seems she's completely bemused about the girl's disappearance, simply can't make head or tail of it. Miss T. was the last person to do anything underhand; and I gather that runaway matches come under that heading in Mrs. Yerbury's opinion. So she just opens her eyes wide, lifts her eyebrows, and makes nothing of it, except that she does hope nothing's happened to the poor young lady. I gathered that no one has bothered to tell her about your finding EZ 1113, so I kept quiet about that myself. No use disturbing the poor old thing further, was there?"

"Anything more?" demanded The Counsellor.

"Lots. As I'd gathered already, the girl and her uncle got on quite well with each other until quite recently. Then something seems to have gone askew. The old lady shied at putting it into words, but she spelt it M-O-N-E-Y for me, apparently thinking that this might put eavesdroppers off the scent. Then I switched to Mr. T. Apparently this 'working after dinner' business was something of a fraud. At least, I elicited that more often than not he simply went up to his study or office or whatever it was to have a good nap and forget his troubles. And at last she did say something that caught my attention."

"Sensation!" interjected Standish.

"Not just quite exactly, so to speak. So calm yourself, Wolf. Still, it's interesting. You remember that she went up to the study after dinner, the night that Treverton finished himself? Mark got that from Pagnell. But Pagnell didn't mention—perhaps he didn't know—that when the maid went up to tidy the study next morning she noticed that the key was on the *outside* of the door. So he must have transferred it from the inside to the outside just as he was going down to finish himself in the garage; because Mrs. Yerbury found him locked in the study when she went up about ten o'clock at night. I can't think why he should do that; but there it is, quite definite."

"Well, pass that," said The Counsellor after a moment's reflection. "What next?"

"I asked if I could see Miss Wickwood, the senior typist. After a bit, she turned up. She isn't exactly a dream of beauty, poor thing. Sallow, with lank hair, too long in the spine and too short in the leg. She somehow reminded me of a lizard in the back view. And the front view's mostly tortoiseshell specs. But by a merciful compensation of Providence, she seems to think a lot of herself and her looks. And she's got a most suspicious mind. In fact, she nearly penetrated my disguise, confound her! Instead of my questioning her, it was the other way about. She wanted to know where my office was—luckily I remembered that all right. Did I get well paid? (That with a look at my clothes which suggested depths of infamy in the way I supplemented my modest screw). Was I a 'feature writer' (whatever that is) or just a reporter?

And so on and so forth, before I could get a word in edgewise, with a sort of sniff at every answer I gave her. A most irritating female, altogether. I hadn't spoken to her for two minutes before I realised that it was no good trying any games with her in the matter of her share. She'd have suspected something at once, if I'd tried that on. So I left it at that, and went after anything else of interest. I'd no difficulty in getting her to talk about the men about the place. She's a typical repressed spinster. Mr. Treverton had been quite a good boss, a bit hasty in temper at times, of course, but easy to get on with, really. Mr. Whitgift was " a very nice gentleman and very clever." I got a vague impression that she associated him with Mendelssohn and Wagner, bridesmaids and bouquets. Fallen for him, completely, in fact. But ' he keeps himself to himself', apparently. Albury hasn't got her approval. ' I'm always telling Miss Lydbrook that a girl can't be too careful with gentlemen.' And so on. Very dull. However, she brisked up when I mentioned Miss Treverton. ' One of these quiet ones. Looks as if butter wouldn't melt in her mouth. But we know what we know.' She hadn't been a bit surprised by Miss T.'s disappearance. ' She's treated poor Mr. Whitgift cruel, I think. If she didn't want him, she shouldn't have kept him hanging around her skirts like she did, and her with another man after her all the time.' Jealousy, of course, poor creature. As to the disappearance, ' those that live longest will hear most ' about it ; but nothing would surprise *her* when it all came out. As for Querrin, she hadn't liked what she saw of him, but then she never did like foreigners of any description. One had to be very careful, what with White Slavers and so forth going about looking for young good-looking girls. (She'll never see 35 again.) But if girls got into strangers' clutches, well, that was their own look-out and no one could pity them, could they ? I'll cut out the rest."

She took a cigarette from The Counsellor's box and lit it before continuing.

"Then I got her on to Barrington. He's the accountant of the show, it seems. And from him she wandered back, by some association of ideas to the finances of Treverton and his niece. It was all a bit confused and mixed up with verbal dabs at Miss Treverton, but the gist of it was that Miss T. for a long time had been lending money to her uncle, and he'd been using these loans to keep the Press solvent—or at least nominally in debt to himself. You remember the size of the item 'Sundry creditors'? I didn't gather how this woman had nosed the thing out, but she was that kind of person and I believe she had solid grounds for what she said. You must remember she detested Miss T. and was all out to find anything against her. So by her way of it, the row between niece and uncle was owing to Miss T. demanding her money back, and her uncle being put in a tight corner on that account. 'And now he's gone, poor gentleman, fair driven to it by his own flesh and blood; and she's next of kin and gets everything he had.'"

"Mostly bad debts, apparently," commented Standish. "She didn't suggest that Miss Treverton murdered him to get her claws on *them*, did she?"

"Not exactly. But she quoted Whitgift—as Gospel—that the Press could be made to pay if it were run on sensible lines. 'And of course Miss T. knew that, well enough, for she'd heard him tell her so, herself.'"

"That fits in well enough," The Counsellor conceded. "Anything else?"

"Not from her," Sandra admitted. "I got tired of her pretty soon. Then I went off to lunch at the Black Bull. I saw Mr. Querrin there, along with a funny-looking little man in loud tweeds. He reminded me strongly of you, Mark, but I didn't give him a second glance."

"You seemed a bit down in the mouth at lunch," said The Counsellor, "so I gathered you hadn't made much of things up to that point. Hence my note."

"Telling me to offer the typist a job, in case she felt she'd be in awkward hole at Longstoke House after she'd sold the share? I saw the point of that. But I didn't see the bit about this Abode of Light affair. Was that just some more of your 'satiable curtiosity?"

"More or less," admitted The Counsellor. "Go on."

"Well, I didn't think it advisable to go back to Longstoke House a second time and ask to see the Lydbrook girl, especially with the chance of the Wickwood specimen butting into our conversation. So I filled in the afternoon by loafing about the hotel, talking to the landlady, and in a run out to the Trulocks' place to have a look at it and this Abode of Light at Grendon Manor. I tried to get into the Abode of Light, but they don't want journalists on the premises, it seems. Inhospitable beasts! There was a tough-looking fellow at the lodge to stop all cars. Mine was one of them. There's no getting past him on the nod, I found. Even the glad eye fails. An implacable Cerberus, that. I didn't like the look of him."

"I never thought much of you as Dalilah, myself," commented Standish. "It's nice to be justified in one's judgment."

"Circe and Judith would have failed with that fellow," Sandra protested. "He'd got his orders and that was that. So I went back to Grendon St. Giles and filled in time somehow until the Lydbrook girl came off duty. Then I dropped in on her at her diggings in the village. I'd taken the precaution of getting her address from old Mrs. Yerbury. She turned out to be a different brand from her colleague: a nice little girl with a mop of fair hair, and quite good-looking. So I got out my note-book and pencils and interviewed her on a strictly journalistic footing to start with. She was a bit timid at first. Mr. Treverton was 'quite nice' to her. Mr. Whitgift was 'very clever, of course.' Miss Treverton was 'just a real dear, and she wished her the best of luck, whatever it was.' But she'd no ideas whatever as to anything, not a glimmer, even. She just didn't understand what could be behind it all. I think that was quite genuine. So gradually my journalistic side faded out and I started to be a friend of the family, so to speak. And then it came out that she wasn't at all happy in her job there. This Albury person had been a nuisance to her. He'd been very friendly and taken her to London to one or two shows. She loves London, it seems. But the last time, he almost managed to make her miss her last train back at night. And he'd dropped hints about taking her to some place 'where one could have a real good time. Something out of the common.' Altogether his attentions had been plainer than pleasant. So for a while she's been feeling that Longstoke House isn't exactly a home from home, with him about her skirts continually."

"Decent little girl, then?" queried The Counsellor.

"Oh, quite," Sandra declared. "A bit younger than her years, perhaps; but that's the worst one can say about her. Well, after talking of this and that for a while, I said I knew of a good post in London, interesting work, a good screw, and nice people—you needn't blush. She's dying to get to London. But, unfortunately, the Wickwood woman had been talking to her about me, quite slanderously, and suggesting that I was a White Slave agent. Me! Anyhow, she'd warned this poor little thing against the wiles of flashily-dressed females; and I had my work cut out for me to soothe suspicion. Very awkward, too, since I was actually sailing under false colours and couldn't put my real cards on the table. However, I gave her my banker's name and asked her to write to him about me; and I also quoted this office in support. And I mentioned one or two other references. So she began to nibble a bit."

"Then I pointed out to her that she'd probably lose her job at Longstoke House in any case, because the Ravenscourt Press seemed to be in a bad way financially. Evidently she'd heard rumours of the sort, for that waked her up a trifle. So then I asked her if she had any shares in the conern. Of course she had one. And that led on to talking about her leaving and the awkwardness of having any connection with the affair after she went. And, finally, I offered to take the share off her hands at a reasonable premium. She'd need a fresh outfit for her new job, etc. So at last she parted with it for £30, after I'd made it clear that I was buying it on behalf of someone else and wouldn't personally be out of pocket over it. I told you she's a decent little kid."

"Meaning that she wouldn't rob you, but had no objections to robbing a stranger," commented Standish.

"Well, what of it? Most people are like that," defended Sandra. Then I asked her about the date of the next Annual Meeting of the Company. It's to be held at Longstoke House, Mark, next Monday, the 26th, at 5.30 p.m."

"At 5.30 p.m.?" echoed The Counsellor. "That's an odd time for a business meeting. Oh, I see. They're all employed on the Press, so they probably found it convenient to have it just after working hours. But they certainly seem to have left it till the very last day that's legal. Well, presumably they know their own business best."

"Very likely," said Sandra, drily. "Do you want the rest of my story? It's mostly mere gossip, picked up from your new employée and the landlady of the Black Bull. This Abode of Light that you put me on to. It seems a rum affair, Mark. I can't make out what it's all about. The landlady shook her head over it and said it was a queer business with a lot of queer folk mixed up in it. But the plain truth was that she knew nothing at first-hand and gave me only village tittle-tattle. Something about a new religion, it sounded like. But they don't welcome casual converts. Witness my reception at the gate of Grendon Manor. No, it's apparently a high-class affair, with a service—if it is a service—once a week or so, which draws a lot of strangers in motor-cars. No local proselytes need apply and the services are strictly private, though they seem to be attended by quite a biggish circle. I asked what kind of cars brought them. Mostly Rolls and that class of thing, so evidently the faithful are not sworn to poverty, at any rate."

"Sounds like some new sensation for wealthy dizzards," commented Standish. "Somebody may be making a good thing out of it."

"It'll sound a bit shady, if you wait for the rest of the tale," Sandra assured him. "I got this bit from your new typist, Mark. It seems that one night she happened to be passing the gate of Grendon Manor. Several cars of the luxury brand had passed her as she walked along, with one or two people in each, but never a chauffeur amongst them. (She's really not unobservant, you see.) As she came up to the gate, a car stopped there, and the lodge-keeper came out to open the gates. There seemed to be some sort of identification business going on, before the lodge-keeper would let them through. Then, when he did open the gates, Miss Lydbrook was 'fairly staggered' to see the driver of the car and his passenger haul out black silk masks and put them on before they drove into the avenue."

"Annual Meeting of the Ancient and Amalgamated Penguins, eh?" interjected Standish. "I suppose they said: 'Quonk!' or something, as a password. It sounds childish to me. But there are a lot of apes wearing clothes in this world."

"Might be the Black Mass or something of the sort," The Counsellor reflected. "I got the impression from Trulock that they were a bit off the rails. Modern Hell-Fire Club, possibly. In that case one can see why they have to be identified at the gates and also why they mask themselves afterwards. It may be a very select affair which makes it unsafe for one member to be able to recognise another member in the outside world. The point that interests me is that it's a close corporation, and no outsider's welcomed either at the meetings or at any other time. Witness Sandra's experience. We'll think about it later on. Now that finishes my business for the moment, so you two can run away and work for your livings."

When Sandra and Standish had left his room, The Counsellor took up his desk telephone and switched over to his Record Office.

"Records? I've some recollection that we once had an application from the Leonardo Society—the big picture people, reproductions of the Old Masters, and so on. You know who I mean? Look it up, please and tell me what we did for them."

Within a few minutes, Records had the information. Some plates had gone astray, left in a train by an employee; and The Counsellor had been instrumental in recovering them by means of a broadcast appeal.

The Counsellor glanced at the slip of paper, took up his telephone directory, and dialled a number.

"Give me the manager, please."

He introduced himself and found his listener ready to repay the kindness in the matter of the plates.

"This is it," explained The Counsellor. "In strict confidence, I want to know what's the present value of The Ravenscourt Press if it came into the market just now. . . . Oh, just a round figure, within a thousand or two. . . . Yes, of course, it's a poor spec. as it stands, but on a business footing. . . . Then you'll ring me up later and let me know what you think? . . . Oh, naturally. Quite confidential—and the same to you, of course. . . . Yes, yes, just a round figure, and no responsibility on your side. I'm interested, that's all."

After thanking the manager, he hung up his receiver. "That bit of bread seems to have returned satisfactorily from the waters," he commented to himself. "Nice obliging chap, their manager. And I suppose we did save them a lot of bother over these plates."

12 THE ANNUAL GENERAL MEETING

THE Ravenscourt Press boasted no special Board Room at Longstoke House; and The Counsellor found that the Annual General Meeting of the Company was being held in what was obviously the Trevertons' dining-room. Some extension leaves had been put into the table for the occasion, and chairs had been drawn up, each with a blotting-pad and some paper before it.

Whitgift was in the chair at the head of the table; and beside him, with an open minute-book, was a small, hungry-looking man whom The Counsellor assumed to be Barrington, the Company's Secretary and Accountant. On Whitgift's right sat an alert-looking, sharp-eyed man, dressed with more care than his colleagues; and opposite Whitgift, at the foot of the table, was a heavily-built common-looking personage, whom The Counsellor tentatively identified as Albury, the chemist of the concern. The girl between Albury and Barrington was obviously Miss Wickwood the typist; and The Counsellor could not help congratulating Sandra Rainham on the aptness with which she had hit off the characteristics of that repressed virgin.

Whitgift glanced up as The Counsellor entered the room, and gave him a non-committal nod of recognition.

"This is our new shareholder: Mr. Brand," he explained to the others in a neutral tone.

It was plain enough to The Counsellor that they needed no enlightenment. Obviously his intrusion into the Company had been thoroughly discussed before the meeting; and from their demeanour he gathered that they were puzzled to know what he meant by it. He walked over and took the vacant chair on Albury's left, opposite Miss Wickwood, who favoured him with a supercilious stare through her tortoiseshell spectacles. Apparently his loud tweeds jarred upon her, for she gave a faint sniff as she turned away again.

Whitgift wasted no time, but began the business of the meeting as soon as The Counsellor had taken his seat.

"With your approval, we'll take as read: the notice convening the meeting, the directors' report, the accounts, and the report of the auditor. They've been circulated to you beforehand. You got copies, I think?" he added, turning to The Counsellor, who nodded in confirmation.

"Since our last meeting, as you know," Whitgift continued, "we have lost my co-director, Mr. James Treverton, by a sad accident. Will someone move that the Secretary be instructed to send an expression of our sympathy to his relatives?"

"I have much pleasure in moving that," said Miss Wickwood, importantly.

"I second," said Albury, concisely.

"No dissent?" asked Whitgift formally. "Then the Secretary will draw up a letter and send it. That brings me to another matter. By the death of Mr. Treverton, we are short of a director, since we need two directors. Next to Mr. Treverton, Miss Treverton is the largest shareholder in the Company; but I do not think she would wish to act nor can we get in touch with her at the moment to ascertain her views. After her and myself, Mr. Albury has the largest holding."

"I move that Mr. Albury be appointed in place of Mr. Treverton," said The Counsellor, with a glance at his neighbour.

"I second that," Dibdin said, indifferently.

"Any other nomination?" inquired the chairman. "No? Then Mr. Albury becomes a director. Now I turn to the balance sheet which you have in your hands. I do not think you would wish me to go through the various items in detail. We have had another difficult year and there is no question of declaring a dividend. Our sales, I am sorry to say, have not expanded to any extent, but there has been no notable decrease in the volume of our business, which is something to be thankful for. We are just able to carry on. Frankly, I see no prospect of any improvement so long as the policy of the Company remains what it has been in the past. I mean that so long as we limit ourselves to catering for the select few, we cannot expect to extend our business much beyond its present limits."

"Hear, hear!" interjected Dibdin with obvious approval.

"We shall have an opportunity of discussing future policy in a moment," Whitgift continued. "Meanwhile, I beg formally to move the adoption of the report and the balance-sheet for the year."

"I second that," said Miss Wickwood, with the air of someone performing a feat.

"Any amendment?" inquired Whitgift, with a glance at The Counsellor. "No? Then I declare the motion carried—unanimously."

Dibdin tapped the table by way of applause, but no one else seemed to regard the occasion as one for rejoicing.

Hitherto, Whitgift had spoken in a purely formal tone, as though conducting a mere routine. Now, in opening a fresh subject, he allowed more interest to appear in his voice.

"I come to the next item on the agenda. The Secretary has received a letter making an offer to purchase our Company, stock and goodwill, trade mark and patents included. I think it will be convenient if we take this as read, while the Secretary hands round a copy of it to each of you, so that you can examine the details."

There was a rustle of paper as Barrington dealt out some typed sheets, and then followed an interval of silence as the shareholders perused the documents. Albury seemed perturbed by its tenor, and it was he who first made a comment.

"I see this is signed by Messrs. Spurstowe & Hague. Who are they, do you know?"

"A firm of solicitors. Quite a good firm," Whitgift informed him briefly.

"I see they're acting for unnamed clients," Albury pursued. "Have you any information about the clients themselves?"

Whitgift shook his head impatiently.

"I see that they're prepared to take over all this Company's contracts," Albury continued. "That includes the contracts which the company has with myself and yourself, does it?"

"It says 'all contracts' in the letter," Whitgift pointed out. "That would obviously include ours. They couldn't turn us out except by compensating us for loss of salary during the period over which our contracts still run."

"I see they're prepared to pay £4,000 for the business—lock, stock, and barrel," Albury went on. "That's only thirty per cent. of the original capital."

"Considering that the original capital has never paid a dividend I should say we're lucky to get an offer of £4,000 for the business," Whitgift declared.

Dibdin had listened to this interchange with a dissatisfied expression on his face. Now in his turn he put his criticism.

"Mr. Whitgift and Mr. Albury have contracts running for some years yet," he pointed out. "But what about the rest of us? I can be thrown out at a month's notice; and Mr. Barrington and Miss Wickwood are in the same boat. I admit that we've never seen a dividend from start to finish, but we've managed to make the turn-over pay our salaries, anyhow. If we accept this offer, it may mean the key of the street for the three of us at the end of the month, coupled with the loss of two-thirds of the capital we put in at the start. I think we ought to get a better offer than that. What do you say, Barrington ?"

"I'm always open to a better offer," Barrington admitted. "Whether you'll get it or not, is a matter of opinion. But there'd be no harm in trying."

Miss Wickwood had been studying Whitgift's face intently as if in an effort to grasp his personal position. Apparently she thought she knew it, for she said in her thin little voice :

"I'm in favour of accepting the offer."

"Your capital loss would be thirteen and fourpence," said Dibdin acidly. "Ours are a bit bigger, if you don't mind my pointing it out."

Miss Wickwood glared at him through her tortoise-shell spectacles but did not consider him worth answering, apparently. None of them, The Counsellor noted, seemed to have given a thought to how the matter might affect Helen Treverton, who was now the principal shareholder.

"Well, there it is," Dibdin pointed out. "It's in the interest of all of us to get that offer made bigger. Also, in the case of three of us, there's the matter of terms of employment. What do you think about it ?" he demanded, swinging round in his seat to look at The Counsellor.

"I quite agree with you. In fact, I'm prepared to make you a better offer than this £4,000."

The Counsellor glanced round the table as he spoke, trying to read the expressions on the faces before him. Whitgift was obviously surprised by this intervention, but whether he was pleased or otherwise, it was hard to tell. Dibdin's astonishment was evidently mixed with some relief at the prospect of better terms.

Barrington showed no detectable emotion. Miss Wickwood, apparently annoyed by this new proposal which stultified her last move, regarded The Counsellor with unmistakable distaste. Albury leaned his elbows on the table and turned to The Counsellor.

"Are we to take it that this offer of yours would be in the same terms as those here"—he tapped the typescript before him with his finger—"except that its puts a bigger figure than £4,000 as the purchase-price? And what would be the figure?"

"The terms would be the same," The Counsellor assured him. "As for the figure, say £6,000. That gives you back fifty per cent. of your capital; and I think you're lucky to get it. I daresay some arrangement could be made to satisfy the reasonable difficulties of Mr. Dibdin and Mr. Barrington. I have an idea of making a change in the general policy—if this deal goes through—which might turn the Company into a paying concern. . . ."

"Tapping a different stratum of purchasers?" interjected Dibdin.

"Exactly," The Counsellor assured him. "And, naturally, since you, for instance, Mr. Dibdin, have had a hand in keeping the present Company afloat under discouraging conditions, it would be only fair to let you share in any future prosperity. That's a matter for further consideration. There's no question of rushing you into a decision. If anyone cares to move that we meet again in three months, after you've had time to thrash the thing out, I shall be quite satisfied."

"Then I move that a Special Meeting be called for that purpose this day three months," said Dibdin, "and that in the meanwhile the Secretary be instructed to inquire further into the offer received from Messrs. Spurstowe & Hague as well as this offer from Mr. Brand."

"I second that," said Albury.

"Any amendment?" asked the chairman. "None?

Then we'll take a formal show of hands. Thank you. The motion is carried. And I think we have to thank Mr. Brand for his offer."

"I think that concludes our business?" responded The Counsellor. "But I'd like to move a hearty vote of thanks to the chairman, directors, and the staff for their services."

"You'll have to second it yourself, then," Albury pointed out with heavy humour. "All the rest of us are included in the staff, and we can't go passing votes of thanks to ourselves. We're not such a mutual admiration society as all that," he added, with no attempt to conceal a cynical expression.

"No seconder?" inquired Whitgift, glancing round the table. "Then perhaps Mr. Brand will withdraw his motion."

"Oh, certainly," agreed The Counsellor, with a smile.

"That concludes our business," Whitgift intimated.

Miss Wickwood threw a final glance of dislike at The Counsellor, pushed back her chair, rose, and left the room. As she went, The Counsellor realised how apt Sandra had been in describing her back view as lizard-like. Dibdin followed her, giving The Counsellor a parting smile as he passed. Albury remained in his seat, his brows knit, as though he were cogitating over something. Whitgift, after a few words to the Secretary, came round to where The Counsellor sat, and, bending over him, demanded in an undertone:

"Any news yet?"

"Nothing to report," The Counsellor declared, when he grasped that Whitgift was asking for news of Miss Treverton.

"That American fellow—Querrin—has turned up here," Whitgift continued. "He says he knows nothing about her disappearance. In fact, he's badly cut up about it. . . ."

"She's put him in the freezer, too, has she?" interrupted Albury, who had evidently been listening.

"Well, well! I wonder who she's got in tow with next?"

Whitgift gave him an angry look, but Albury seemed quite unperturbed.

"She's 'off with the raggle-taggle gypsies, O!' if you ask me. Or one of 'em, anyhow. I shouldn't worry your heads over her, if I were in your shoes. 'She's her own mistress', as old Treverton used to say. Or somebody else's, perhaps. Can't a girl have a fling without half the countryside poking their noses into her affairs? Have a heart, Whitgift."

This was so intentionally provocative that The Counsellor wondered how Whitgift would take it. Apparently he decided to ignore it, though The Counsellor could see a slight movement at the hinge of the jaw which spoke of clenched teeth.

"How are you getting back to town?" he asked The Counsellor, as though he had not heard Albury's remarks.

"I sent my chauffeur down to The Black Bull to get something to eat," The Counsellor explained. "I suppose I can ring him up from here?"

"Oh, yes," Whitgift volunteered. "I'll do it for you, if you like. Going now?"

"Wait a moment," Albury broke in. "I want a word or two with Mr. Brand before he goes. You can spare the time? It won't take long. I just want to hear a bit more about this offer of yours. Come along to old Treverton's den. We can be private there," he added with obvious intention.

Whitgift hesitated for a moment, as though in doubt as to the course he should take. Then he shook hands with The Counsellor and went round the table to where Barrington was collecting his papers.

"Well, come along," suggested Albury, rising lumberingly from his seat. "I thought that'd scare him off. This is between us two. I don't want him butting in."

13 EUTHANASIA

ALBURY led the way to Treverton's little office, and, with a brusque gesture, invited The Counsellor to take a seat. He himself leaned against the mantelpiece ; pulled out a briar pipe much burned on one side through frequent lighting at Bunsen flames ; and charged it leisurely from his pouch. During this process he said not a word, but examined The Counsellor's appearance with a minuteness which bordered on rudeness. Not to be outdone, The Counsellor drew out his case and lit a cigarette, giving his new associate stare for stare.

" I talk best when I'm smoking," Albury explained at last when his pipe was well alight. " And, to come to the point at once, what's this little game of yours, Mr. Brand ? "

" Little game ? I don't quite get you," retorted The Counsellor disingenuously.

" Put it in words of one syllable," said Albury. " Do you mean to buy the Press, or is it just a kid ? I'd like to know."

" Yes, I do mean it," answered The Counsellor. " I'd a notion I'd made that clear enough already."

" Think you can make it pay ? " asked Albury bluntly.

" Not on present lines, certainly," replied The Counsellor with a smile.

" You're right there. Second question. Are you a business man, or a second art-maniac like Treverton ? Meaning, are you out for the dibs or are you going to run the thing as a mere hobby ? "

"In this matter, I'm out for the dibs, as you concisely put it."

"Well, thank God, that sounds like commonsense," said Albury. "The way this show has been run in past years would make angels weep. You and I are going to get on together, Mr. Brand."

"The deal's not closed yet," pointed out The Counsellor. "You don't happen to know the names of Spurstowe and Hague's clients?"

Albury shook his head.

"I don't. Nor does Barrington. Whitgift may; but he and I don't happen to be on confidential terms, as p'raps you noticed. I've tried to put a line on that Wickwood doll. She eats out of his hand. But I got nothing for my pains, and I don't think she knows anything either."

He paused for a moment, and then continued slowly:

"I've been wondering if Treverton's niece isn't at the back of it. That's just possible. Look here. She's got £3,000 locked up in shares. Beyond that, I've some grounds for saying that Treverton borrowed money from her to keep the show afloat in bad years. If you look in the balance-sheet, you'll find a biggish item: 'Sundry Creditors.' She was one of them and Treverton was another—for money lent to the Company. Now, just lately, she and the old man began to get across each other. To me, that spells cash, for there was no other reason that I can see. This Yank was in the offing, you know. That meant she'd want her money to earn dividends, instead of being locked up in old Treverton's hobby. And if she took her money out, it meant B-U-S-T for the Treverton policy, for no one else would put cash into the thing on the old terms. Hence the rows."

"Your idea looks like throwing good money after bad," commented The Counsellor. "She has £3,000 locked up already in shares You say she's prepared to pay over £4,000 more, making £7,000 in all embarked in a derelict concern."

"You're not such a goop as all that, if I'm any judge," said Albury, shaking his pipe-stem at The Counsellor. "You've offered £6,000 for this show, which means you think it's worth that at least. So the fair Helen, if she got it, could sell it for £6,000 after sinking £7,000 in it. That leaves her only £1,000 to the bad, instead of being £3,000 and more, out of pocket as she is at present. And the show might be worth a deal more than £6,000 if it were run on sound lines. It might pay her to leave her money in it. By the way, did you notice the date on that letter of Spurstowe & Hague?"

"September 12th," said The Counsellor, who had a memory for some details.

"Yes, September 12th. That was it. And that was just a day or two after she disappeared, wasn't it? Don't you see how that fits in? When old Treverton got wind of this manœuvre, he'd have spotted her hand in it and given her hell, if she'd been handy. He was that kind of man. But she dished that by disappearing just before this letter. She's cleared out with no address and done the thing through this lawyer-firm, so that her name doesn't appear."

"No good," said The Counsellor, decisively. "Treverton held the majority of the shares. He could block the acceptance of the offer at any meeting."

"On the face of it, yes," Albury agreed. "But you've forgotten something. The Company's insolvent, really; and if one of the Sundry Creditors chose to turn nasty, it would go bankrupt. Then it would be Carey Street and the Official Receiver, and a forced sale to anyone who offered, see? Oh, that's all right, you take it from me. And another thing. Here's this Yank turned up just at the critical moment. He's a business man, I'm told, able to advise her. Naturally she'd want him on the spot to help her to negotiate. And of course he's not going to give away her address. He doesn't want Treverton butting in."

"No good," reiterated The Counsellor. "If your

ideas were right, there's nothing to hinder her coming forward now. Treverton's out of it all for good."

"Perhaps she hasn't heard of his death," objected Albury.

"She can't have missed it," said The Counsellor. "There was quite a long obituary notice in *The Times*."

"She never read *The Times*," said Albury, scornfully. "She wasn't a highbrow. I don't read *The Times* myself."

Suddenly he seemed to recollect that he had been neglecting hospitality. He got up, went across the room to a cupboard, and looked at the contents. Finally he produced a syphon, decanter, and glasses.

"Have a drink?" he invited. "There's no whisky. Brandy was old Treverton's tipple, so a B. and S. is the best I can offer you."

Without awaiting an answer, he poured out a liberal three fingers into each glass and splashed in some soda-water. The Counsellor accepted the drink and, being rather thirsty, took a draught. Albury contented himself with a mere sip before putting down his tumbler.

"Who does the actual photographing of these pictures you reproduce?" asked The Counsellor, following up an idea which had suggested itself to him some time before this.

"I do that," explained Albury. "Whitgift's the head bummaroo of our printing department, he looks after some of the photographic side as well. You see, in such a miserable little firm, each of us has to do a bit more than his share, whether he likes it or not. I'm a chemist, nominally, and my real job's in trying out new dyes for colour-sensitive plates and for colour-screens, but actually I do part of the technical side of the photography. And a lot of odd jobs as well."

"Dibdin's sales manager, I gathered; and Barrington keeps the books?"

"That's so. Dibdin's done not badly in pushing sales for us. You'd find him worth keeping on, if you take over the show and launch out a bit. He's quite sound."

"And Whitgift?"

"Whitgift and I don't love each other much, as I said before. I thought he might have a finger in this business of Spurstowe & Hague, at first. He let slip a word or two once, that made me suspicious on that score. A bit eager to have us snap at the offer when it came in. We talked it over amongst ourselves, you know: Treverton and the rest of us. And Treverton had a strong suspicion that Whitgift had managed to interest some outsiders and raise capital somehow. That made him damned annoyed, needless to say. But most likely he got on to a mare's nest there. Anyhow, I've no desire to see Whitgift at the head of things here. He'd do his level best to get me the push; you can count on that."

Before The Counsellor could make any comment on this, there came a knock to interrupt them. The maid, Florence Etham, appeared at the door and spoke to Albury.

"There's someone wanting to speak to you on the 'phone, sir."

Albury rose with a look of annoyance.

"I'll have to go along to the 'phone," he explained. "We've no extensions in this place. Old Treverton was too mean to stand the extra expense of putting them in. It's a damned nuisance having to rush along to the instrument every time one wants to talk. I'll be back in a minute or two. Just stay where you are."

He went out, closing the door behind him.

Left to his own devices, The Counsellor cast about him for amusement until Albury returned. There was a large bookcase containing a miscellaneous assortment of works upon Art, and after scanning the shelves he took down a ponderous copiously-illustrated tome and, returning to his seat, began to examine the pictures in it. But in a few minutes his interest slackened and he let the book lie on his knee. He tried to concentrate upon the relations between the various shareholders in the Company, but found that his thoughts persisted in wandering. Then he became conscious of a slight headache. He sipped some of the brandy in his glass, but now it seemed to have a peculiar taste which he had not noticed before. Then a wave of nausea swept over him, leaving him dizzy. With an effort, he pulled himself together, and the sight of the brandy-decanter, suggested an idea.

"That must be poisonous stuff of old Treverton's . . . Poisonous. . . Brandy doesn't take me like this. . . ."

Another spasm of nausea shook him, and with it came a terrifying suspicion :

"That stuff's been doped. . . . They've tried to knock me out. . . . Must pull myself together somehow. . . ."

Easier said than done. He attempted to rise from his chair, but all his muscles seemed to have gone slack. The blood began to throb in his ears, accentuating his headache ; and he had more and more difficulty in thinking lucidly. Drowsiness crept over him ; and he was sinking into sleep when with a final effort of will, he forced himself to his feet.

"The door. . . . Get out. . . . Call for help. . . ."

He moved door-ward, swaying and staggering, with waves of nausea shaking him as he went ; and it was only by repeating disjointed commands to himself that he was able to walk at all. Stretching out his hand, he gripped the door-handle, turned it, and pulled. The door remained fast. He began to feel breathless.

"Locked outside . . . fresh air . . . window . . ." he impressed on himself.

He tried to call out, but found he had no voice left.

"Bell. . . ."

A few stumbling steps took him to the bell-push which he pressed in passing.

" Mustn't fall down . . ." he muttered. " Never get up again if I do, in this state. . . ."

He staggered against the desk, striking his ankle-bone heavily on the wood ; and this shock roused him slightly. Then, with his head reeling, he floundered to the nearest window and tried to throw up the old-fashioned sash. It resisted, and he abandoned his attempt. Then, with a final gathering of mental and physical concentration, he put his shoulder to the panes and drove out the glass, sinking to his knees after this supreme effort. A high wind was blowing outside, and through the broken panes came a vivifying rush of cold fresh air.

Only semi-conscious now, The Counsellor heard faintly the sound of someone knocking on the door, excited voices, and then the door flew open and someone hurried into the room. He heard a cry: " Keep back ! Out of the way there, at the door ! " Then he was picked up like a child and carried out into the corridor. In a last flicker of consciousness he saw the horrified faces of Mrs. Yerbury and the maid as he was carried past them.

It was a very shaken Counsellor who awoke to find himself stretched on a bed in a shabby little bedroom. He lifted his head for a moment and found himself gazing at his own reflection in the mirror on the dressing-table beyond the foot of the bed. Then he found that Mrs. Yerbury was beside him.

" That was a terrible attack you had, sir," she said sympathetically, as she saw that he had waked up. " Are you subject to these fits, though I'm sure I hope not. When we heard you ringing the bell like that, Florence and me rushed up at once, but we couldn't get in, for the door was locked fast and we never noticed the key in it ; and then Florence let out a scream that brought Mr. Whitgift a-running, and lucky it was that he happened to be working in his room and heard her. He got in, just pushed us aside and told us to get out of way while he carried you out and brought you in here, which is Mr. Treverton's room, poor man. Are you feeling better now? We're just going to get the doctor. I told Florence to go and ring him up."

"You can cancel that, now," ordered The Counsellor. "I know what's the matter with me. Don't worry. It's all right. But you might ring up my chauffeur at The Black Bull, please. Now, at once."

"Will you not have the doctor, sir?" pleaded Mrs. Yerbury in obvious distress. "Surely you'd be the better to see someone after an attack like that. Is it epilepsy, sir? I once knew somebody with an epileptic relation, and a terrible trial he was to her, poor thing. Fits is terrible afflictions, no matter what kind they are."

The Counsellor lay back and closed his eyes, feeling deadly sick.

"Ring up my chauffeur," he repeated. "Tell him to put my car in the garage here and then come up to me. Quick, please."

The effort of saying this exhausted him for the moment, and he lay back on the pillow.

"Well, I'm sure a doctor's more what you need, sir," Mrs. Yerbury insisted.

"I know what's wrong with me," declared The Counsellor. "Run to the 'phone. And then come back and sit with me, please, until my chauffeur turns up. Go now, please."

"But . . ."

"Oh, do as I tell you," said The Counsellor. "I've something in my car that'll put me right. Quick, now."

This put things in a fresh light to Mrs. Yerbury, and she hurried off at once.

"I'll be back in a moment, sir," she assured him as she turned at the door.

In going out, she blundered into Whitgift who had come to inquire about The Counsellor's condition. He sat down on the chair by the bed side and began in a sympathetic tone:

" By Jove, you've given us a fright, I can tell you, Mr. Brand. I thought you were a goner, by the look of you. Lucky I was on the premises, for these two women were less than no use. They went into mild hysterics with excitement. Feeling better now, I hope ? "

" A shade," said The Counsellor with a not very successful attempt to smile. " Don't worry. It's an old trouble of mine that sometimes bothers me."

Whitgift evidently had more tact than the housekeeper, for at this hint he refrained from further questions on the subject.

" Care for a spot of brandy to pull you together ? " he asked.

The Counsellor shook his head feebly.

" No, no brandy, thanks. How long was I unconscious ? "

Whitgift glanced at his watch.

" Matter of five minutes, or so, I'd say. But you were pretty groggy when you came to, so I thought the best thing was to let you alone. It's half an hour or more since you had your trouble. The doctor may be here any minute. He was out on his round when we rang him up, but they were to get in touch with him."

" I won't see any damned doctor," declared The Counsellor peevishly. " I know what's wrong with me better than any G.P. I'm not going to be poked and prodded about by some ignorant sawbones. I mean it ! I know what's best for me. All I want is to get back to town again, and quicker than that."

In a minute or two, Mrs. Yerbury came back to announce that The Counsellor's chauffeur was on his way up. With the housekeeper's return, The Counsellor seemed to have lost any desire for conversation ; and Whitgift, after a word or two of sympathy, left him in her charge. Ten minutes later, the chauffeur was ushered in.

" Just leave us for a minute," The Counsellor asked Mrs. Yerbury.

When she had left the room, he beckoned to the chauffeur to bend over the bed, and whispered something in his ear.

" Very good, sir. I'll see to that."

The chauffeur left the bedroom and Mrs. Yerbury returned to find The Counsellor making a rather dizzy attempt to walk about the room.

" I must have dropped it when that turn came on," he said, half to himself. " Mrs. Yerbury, would you mind giving me your arm ? I want to see if I can find something I've lost. It may be in Mr. Treverton's office."

She helped him along the corridor, and in the office they found Whitgift.

" I've lost an important paper," The Counsellor explained. " I think it may have slipped out of my pocket when I came down on the floor."

He glanced rather dazedly hither and thither, casting his eyes over the floor, the windows, even the ceiling, as if slightly bemused still.

" Not here," he confessed at last. " You'll let me have it if you come across it ? A blue foolscap sheet. Thanks. Now I think I'll go down to my car. My man was to bring it round to the door. Sorry to have given you all this bother. No choice of mine, I assure you."

When his car had passed out of the avenue gate, he picked up the speaking-tube and gave a fresh order to the driver :

" Stop at the police station and bring the inspector out to the car."

In a few minutes the car drew up, and fortunately Pagnell was on the premises. Evidently the chauffeur had said something to him about The Counsellor's attack, for he came out, looking rather concerned.

" Get in," said The Counsellor, opening the car door. " This is urgent and I'm in no state to hang about.

I want to get home. I'll send my man back with you after that. But you've got to come now. I've got a damned good 'attempted murder' case for you."

The inspector did not even pause to get his hat. He stepped into the car, which drove off at once Londonward.

14 THE CONTROL OF THE COMPANY

BY morning, practically all traces of indisposition had passed off, and The Counsellor went down to his office as usual. When Sandra and Standish came into his room in answer to his summons, they found an unwontedly grim and hard-mouthed Counsellor awaiting them.

"You look a bit under the weather," commented Standish, critically. "Sat up too late last night, playing Musical Chairs, or what?"

"Yes," admitted The Counsellor, "with Death playing zig-a-zig-a-zag on his violin, the way he does in the *Danse Macabre*. Amusing experience, but it leaves the deuce and all of a headache after it."

"A bit strange in his manner," said Standish to Sandra. "Trying to be mysterious, and obscure, and cryptic, and allusive, and all that sort of thing. Tongue furred, most likely, too. You impress us both, Mark, which counts two points to you. Now spit it out, will you?"

"This is it," said The Counsellor. "And for your kind remarks, I'll just give you the tale as it comes and you'll get the zig-a-zig-a-zag bit in its proper place but not before. You remember that the Annual General Meeting of Treverton's company was fixed for last night? I went down to it. This is what happened there."

He outlined the course of the meeting, briefly but accurately.

"What on earth do you want to buy a concern like

that, for ?" demanded Standish. "From all we've heard, it's a pure dud."

"I don't particularly want to buy it. I hope I won't have to buy it at all. You'll see my point later. But let's get on. After the meeting, there was some chat which made it plain that Albury and Whitgift aren't on happy terms. Then Albury, having shaken off Whitgift, invited me to have a private talk with him in Treverton's little office. We went there. Did I ever tell you that Treverton was an anti-fresh-air fiend? Draught-excluders and all similar fittings *ad lib*. That has its bearing on the tale."

Throwing away the remains of his cigarette, he took a fresh one from the box beside him and lit it.

"I don't remember very clearly what Albury had to say to me. A rather greasy fellow, I judge, with a sharp eye to the main chance. I imagine he thought he was ingratiating himself with me with a view to the future, if I took over the company. But that's by the way. After a few minutes, he produced a decanter from a cupboard and offered me a drink. Some stuff of Treverton's, he informed me. Brandy's not my special line in connoisseurship, but that stuff did no credit to Treverton's taste. Very good for reviving a cart-horse after an exhausting day, I don't doubt. But I happened to be thirsty just then, and I took a good pull at it. Then the maid came with a message to say that Albury was wanted on the 'phone. So he left me to amuse myself till he got back. I haven't seen him since. I picked up a book from the shelves, to pass the time, and sat down to wait for him. Then I began to feel queerish. And I got queerer: dizzy, sick, a bit bemused in the brain department, and most damnably tired. . . ."

"He'd doped you?" interrupted Standish.

"Wait a moment," Sandra broke in. "You say this was some of old Mr. Treverton's brandy? Suppose it had been doped for him by someone. Then this

Albury man might have given it to you without knowing there was anything wrong with it."

"Well, leave the dope question aside for the moment," said The Counsellor, rather impatiently. "My symptoms were a dashed sight more interesting to me at that moment. My ears began to buzz and I felt a bit breathless. That screwed me up—and it took some screwing—to get out of my chair and go to the door. I thought fresh air was what I wanted. So I turned the handle. By that time I was fairly muzzy; but even so I can remember the jump it gave me when I found the door was locked on the outside. And, naturally, when I couldn't get out, I felt more choky than ever. So I rang the bell and staggered over to the window, meaning to open it. But it was fast, too, immovable. So I just put my shoulder through a pane or two and then I collapsed."

Sandra's face showed her feelings, but Standish refused to take The Counsellor too seriously. He had suffered in the past.

"Well, you're here," he pointed out, "so evidently you didn't die. That's most satisfactory. Now go on from where you awoke with the sawbones and fair-haired nurse by your bedside."

"There's a bit comes in before that," corrected The Counsellor with a faint grin. "Just as I collapsed, the door opened and Whitgift shot out of a sort of general meeting on the door-mat. He picked me up and carried me into old Treverton's bedroom hard by, where I awoke later to find Mrs. Yerbury watching over me. You remember the old housekeeper?" he added, turning to Sandra.

"Yes, a nice old thing."

"Well, the nice old thing had got it into her head that I'd had a fit, or something; and it seemed advisable not to disabuse her of that notion until I'd pulled myself together a bit and could think clearly. So I encouraged her illusions. And when Whitgift came in to see how I was getting along, I let him think so, too. They wanted to call in the local sawbones, but I barred that. I was beginning to feel a bit better, by then. and I was clear enough in the head to know that the less I talked, the better, especially to a body-snatcher. You see, I'd caught a glimpse of myself in a mirror, and I'd got a nice pinky complexion that would have done for a beauty-specialist's advertisement."

"That *must* have given you a start," admitted Standish, making a pretence of inspecting The Counsellor's rather leathery and weatherbeaten face. "Like the old lady in the rhyme: 'Oh, dearie, dearie me, this is none of I', I suppose."

"Thereabouts," agreed The Counsellor, unperturbed. "But to continue. I got them to 'phone up for my car. I'd sent Picton to get his tea in Grendon St. Giles while the meeting was on. I made them direct him to come up to Longstoke House and put my car in the garage till I felt fit to get home. Then he was to come up and see me. I gave Mrs. Yerbury the impression that I had some medicine in the car, specially in case of such fits coming on; and Picton would get it for me when he came. When he turned up, I gave him some directions privately, and ordered him to bring the car to the front door. Then, when he'd gone, I suddenly discovered that I'd lost a valuable paper out of my pocket. . . ."

"So they'd been giving you a fan, had they? while you were dead to the world. Was it a fiver or a tenner?" Standish inquired.

"It was imaginary," retorted The Counsellor. "But I managed to stagger up and look for it in Treverton's office."

"Well, I think you might have had more sense," said Sandra, severely. "You might have over-strained your heart, or anything. Why couldn't you wait for the doctor they'd sent for?"

"Because he might have spotted what my trouble was, and I didn't think that advisable," The Counsellor explained. " Much better to leave somebody guessing. I mean the person who tried to do me in. Left as it was, he couldn't be sure that I suspected his little effort. For all he could tell, his attempt might have brought on some real tendency to fits on my part, in which case I'd never guess that he'd been up to any game. But if a medico had blundered in and diagnosed the real affair, then my criminal friend would have known at once that things were getting warm for him. See that ? "

" Please drop all this mystery-business, Mark," Sandra begged. " Tell us the plain story, please. It's really worrying to hear about things like this."

" Very well," The Counsellor agreed. " Note, first of all, that this affair took place in Treverton's office. Whether that brandy was doped or not is beyond proof at present. I didn't get the chance to grab the decanter after my collapse; and if the liquor was doped, I'm prepared to bet that by this time it's been poured away and replaced by innocuous stuff. But as a matter of fact, I'm not worrying much about that part of the stunt. What I want you to note is that when I tried to get out, I found the door locked on the outside. Now compare that with the Treverton affair, Sandra. Remember that old Mrs. Yerbury noticed, the morning after Treverton died, that the key of that little office was on the *outside* of the door."

" Yes, so she told me," Sandra confirmed. " So you think. . . ."

" Wrong word. I don't ' think ', because I happen to know," said The Counsellor triumphantly. " Take it from me, Treverton didn't die in that garage at all. He died in his office, just as I'd have done if I hadn't been lucky. I knew that as soon as I saw the pinkness of my skin in that bedroom looking-glass after I woke up again."

" What's that got to do with it ? " asked Standish, with a shade more respect in his tone.

" This is where thoroughness comes in, you see,"

explained The Counsellor with no concealment of his self-satisfaction. "When I heard about Treverton's so-called suicide, my curiosity was aroused. . . ."

"It would be," commented Sandra. "Trust it to waken up on the slightest excuse."

"Well, it waked up to some purpose," retorted The Counsellor. "One of the symptoms of carbon monoxide poisoning is that the blood goes pinkish; so I found by reading up the matter. And the sensations I had in that room tallied pretty closely with a bad dose of carbon monoxide. And remember Treverton's anti-fresh-air notions, which made his office pretty well air-tight. It's not a big room. Say twenty by fifteen feet and perhaps twelve or fourteen feet high to the ceiling. Call it a cubic content of roughly 4,000 cubic feet. Now the forensic medicine experts say that about 2 per cent. of carbon monoxide in the air will produce fatal effects in a very short time. Two per cent. of 4,000 cubic feet is 80 cubic feet; so if 80 cubic feet of carbon monoxide got into that room, the gas would be at a fatal concentration or thereabouts, according to the best authorities that I read."

"But how could they get it in without your seeing it done?" demanded Standish. "You're not altogether an owl, Mark, I'll say that for you. And where could they manufacture the stuff? You didn't see any charcoal stove about, I take it?"

"Oh, no. The room was quite O.K. But I keep my eyes open, you know, Wolf. And when I pulled myself together, I gave these orders about Picton putting my car into the garage when he arrived. Then when he turned up, I gave him private instructions to go back to the garage, ostensibly to bring the car round to the front door. Actually I told him to put his hand on the radiator of Treverton's old car if it was still in the garage. It was. He did. And he found the radiator warm."

"Oh, now I begin to see," Standish admitted.

" Of course there's a lot of carbon monoxide in a motor's exhaust gases. . . ."

" Anything up to 6 per cent., according to the authorities," amplified The Counsellor, beaming. " No trouble in getting plenty of it, you see."

" But how did it get up to the office ? " queried Sandra. " You say the door and the windows were all tight shut. They couldn't have laid a pipe. . . ."

" It wasn't needed," The Counsellor pointed out. " There was a pipe all ready for them. Probably you didn't notice it, Sandra, as you're not interested in mechanical and scientific things generally ; but that house was originally lit by acetylene gas. The gas-plant was in part of the old stables, next door to the present garage. What's more, Pagnell mentioned to me that in the gas-plant room a lot of old odds and ends had been stored, including some hose-pipe. And there's a door between the garage and the room where the gas-plant is. So to get carbon monoxide pumped into the office, all you need do is to start up a car in the garage, clip a hose-pipe on to the end of the exhaust, fill up the old gas-reservoir with the exhaust gases, and then flood the stuff through the old acetylene piping. Quite neat."

" The acetylene piping's still in place, is it ? although they've gone over to electric light," said Standish. " Are you sure ? I'd have thought they'd have taken it out when they put the current in."

" Treverton was too stingy to face the expense of that. It would have meant a lot of re-plastering in the walls."

" But then the poison gas from the reservoir must have got into every room in the house," objected Standish.

The Counsellor shook his head.

" No," he explained. " On my first visit, I noticed the end of the acetylene piping in the ceiling of Miss Treverton's room ; but the end was pinched where they'd cut it off short. Same in Treverton's office.

But when I crawled back into Treverton's office in search of my lost and imaginary paper I had a look at the fitting. Somebody had been busy in the meanwhile and had prised the piping open again. You'd never notice it unless you'd looked specially. But there it was. So one could flood that room, and that room only, with the stuff from the gas-reservoir"

"Quite neat, as you say," Standish admitted. "But exhaust gases stink a bit. Why didn't you recognise the smell when the stuff began to pour in on top of you?"

"The answer to that is 'not beyond conjecture'," The Counsellor pointed out. "I'm sorry I wasn't in a fit state to make any investigations after my knock-out. I'd like to have done so, just to have sound evidence; but I simply wasn't up to it. Still, I think one can take it that whoever tried to do me in was a fairly sharp artist. The reservoir would act as a kind of washing-plant and the water in it would take out some of the stink; but I suspect that some kind of charcoal absorbing filter was shunted into the circuit as well, to make sure. A thing of the sort would be easy to fake up. So that the stuff that came down the old piping would be a pretty pure mixture of air and carbon monoxide. And carbon monoxide itself is quite odourless, and couldn't be spotted by scent. Certainly I never noticed anything when I got landed with the thing."

He threw away the stub of his cigarette and took a fresh one from the box at his elbow. When he had lighted it, he resumed.

"Now we come to the dog. Ah! Forgotten the dog, have you? It belonged to Miss Treverton and it was found dead out in the fields shortly before she disappeared. Well, as I see things, the dog's death was a preliminary canter for the Treverton affair. Picton tells me that the garage at Longstoke House just holds two cars and no more. Call it twenty feet by twenty, and perhaps ten feet high. That's about

4,000 cubic feet, which is just about the size of Treverton's office. So by shoving the dog into the garage with a car-engine running, X—the criminal, whoever it is—could get a rough idea of how long the engine had to run before the carbon monoxide of the exhaust would reach a fatal concentration in a space roughly the same as Treverton's office. That was just to make sure of the facts. And that explains the dog, I think."

"You're really quite clever, Mark," Sandra confessed frankly. "I didn't think you'd make much of a success as a 'tec, but I'm changing my ideas."

"Put the bouquets in the wash-hand basin," directed The Counsellor solemnly. "And send them to the hospital, later on. Now need I underline the rest of the details? Obviously Treverton was killed by carbon monoxide in his office and his body was carried round to the garage afterwards. The killer, X, whoever it was, could easily lift the corpse out of the office window and take it into the garage, which is just opposite. Then the faking with the foot-pump, etc., was child's play. And, by the way, I forgot to mention that in my search for my imaginary paper I had a look at the office windows. They'd been fixed with little wedges so that they wouldn't open—a job that could be done in a couple of minutes by X, if he were in a hurry. A thoughtful cove, evidently. Not to be under-rated, by any means."

"But who *is* X?" demanded Sandra, evidently now quite ready to believe that The Counsellor had a complete solution up his sleeve.

"I don't know, but I can find out," said The Counsellor, using one of his favourite clichés. "And I'm going to find out."

"But why did they bother about you?" questioned Standish. "You aren't in the cast at all, except as a super."

"That point has not entirely escaped me," said The Counsellor with heavy irony. "In fact, I've thought over it a good deal, Wolf. One thing's plain. I became of interest to X, whoever he is, only after I'd butted in and made an offer to buy the company."

"But what on earth did you want to buy it for at all?" demanded Sandra. "It's not a line you know anything about, and it's not even a paying concern."

"I'm not sure that I want to buy it," explained The Counsellor. "But what I did want to do was to prevent this gang disposing of the company without consulting Miss Treverton, who's the principal shareholder now. She wasn't at the meeting, of course. And these fellows were calmly preparing to sell out on terms that would have involved her in a heavy loss. So I nipped in with my offer and held up the whole affair for a month or so. That gives her time to reappear and look after her rights—if she ever does reappear," he added sombrely.

"And so they tried to knock you out?" said Standish incredulously. "It doesn't sound likely. In fact, it makes bosh to me. Who's going to commit murder for the sake of a derelict company? You're barking up the wrong tree, Mark."

"May be. But if it's not that, then why try to knock me out at all?"

"Perhaps because you've interested yourself in Miss Treverton," suggested Sandra.

"But it was Whitgift—one of the crew—who dragged me in at the start," objected The Counsellor. "That won't fit, Sandra. No, this is it, as I see it. Somebody is very anxious to get control of that company. Now it's not because the thing's a little gold mine. Even at the very best under energetic management, it won't pay anything remarkable in the way of dividends. So I believe, anyhow. And yet somebody wants it badly. Why?"

"Don't ask me," said Standish.

"I shan't. I'll tell you, instead. As a straight proposition, the thing's a poor affair. But suppose you bent it a bit? Turned it into a crooked concern.

And suppose that crookery made it a gold mine. Here's a notion. I don't say it's true, but it might fit the case. Sandra told us these Ravenscourt Press reproductions were the best on the market. I've examined one of them, pretty carefully. Short of a close and careful scrutiny, you couldn't tell them from the originals. Now most of their work is in the reproduction of rather out-of-the-way pictures, the lesser-known good stuff. They generally keep off the beaten track. That means they go to private collections to do their photographing, mainly."

"That's true enough," Sandra confirmed.

"I had it from Treverton himself. Well, then. Suppose I'm the company's photographer. I go by permission to a private collection and I see a nice little picture, worth a fair amount, hung well up out of range for close inspection. I ask to have it brought down and I photograph it for reproduction. The reproduction's made, and care's taken to make it absolutely like the original in every way, even to the canvas foundation. Then I say: 'Sorry! This hasn't been a success. Mind if we photograph it again and have a second shot?' The owner's not likely to object, since he's already given permission for the reproduction. So down I go again, and by hook or crook I substitute my reproduction for the original and take the original away with me. The reproduction's hung up again, and it's a hundred to one that any specialist will turn up in the next few years wanting to see that picture particularly. Who else is going to give it attention? Nobody, so far as I can see. And meanwhile I can sell the original on the quiet to some collector who's prepared to ask no awkward questions. At the worst, what I sell him is an unknown replica."

"Devilish ingenious," Standish admitted. "But could it be done?"

"I don't know, but I can find out," retorted The Counsellor. "All we need do is to make a list of these reproductions and send a real expert down to look at the pictures in the collections. That can easily be fixed up to look innocent enough. You're writing a book on the subject, Sandra, if we happen to need you as an excuse. And if we find one wrong 'un amongst them, then we'll know why somebody's so eager to get hold of this company—which controls that particular method of reproduction, with its faked canvas and all the rest of it."

"Might be something in that," admitted Standish, judicially. "Go on."

"I may be wrong in details," The Counsellor confessed frankly, "but it needs some scheme of that sort in the background to account for the three things we know about: the girl's disappearance, Treverton's death and the attempt on me. The girl's removal served a double purpose. First, it left Treverton alone at Longstoke House at night except for the servants, who have orders not to disturb him in the evenings. That made it easier to contrive his removal since his body had to be transferred from the office to the garage without anyone seeing what was being done. Second, after Treverton's death, Miss Treverton was the only shareholder big enough to outvote the others combined, so by removing her they made sure they could carry through this sale which they seem so keen on. Treverton was killed, obviously, because he would never voluntarily have allowed control to go out of his hands. And they tried to knock me out because I threatened their scheme by making an offer for the company."

"You're assuming Treverton was honest," objected Standish. "It's on the cards that he wasn't. He may have had a hand in the substitution game all along, for all you know. In that case, they must have done him in simply to concentrate the winnings in fewer hands."

"My impression was that he was honest," declared The Counsellor. "In fact, I thought he had a bee in his bonnet about the honest side of the concern; and that would have been quite unnecessary if he'd been drawing illicit profits."

"Except that he may have taken a pride in his work," commented Standish, "whether he was running a side-line or not. But go on with your yarn, Mark. You haven't told us what happened after you got away safely."

"I'm not sure I did the right thing," The Counsellor confessed rather dubiously. "But I wasn't in a good state for clear thinking. you know. And I was damned mad with the swine who tried to knock me out. So I stopped the car in Grendon St. Giles and had a chat with Inspector Pagnell. In fact, feeling so rotten, I brought him along to town with me, because I couldn't hang about there any longer. I wanted to get home and see my doctor as soon as I could. So I gave Pagnell all the news I had and then packed him back to Grendon St. Giles under Picton's care. An hour or two of delay didn't matter much; for I'm sure all their murder-plant was cleared away even before I recovered consciousness, so there would have been nothing for Pagnell to find, even if he'd gone straight up to Longstoke House as soon as I reported to him. They could dismantle the whole caboodle in a couple of minutes. I didn't think it worth while to go to the garage myself, before leaving, because I was sure there'd be nothing to see by that time."

"If you had," suggested Sandra, "most likely they'd have knocked you on the head, or something, and told Picton that you'd had another fit."

"Quite likely, being the resourceful coves they seem to be," The Counsellor agreed. "But to continue. Pagnell rang me up this morning to report progress. He and a couple of constables went up to Longstoke House during the night, and had a good look round the garage. Pagnell doesn't seem to mind a little technical burglary in the cause of justice. Everything was ship-shape by that time, of course. The old hose was back amongst the other odds and ends and the acetylene gas reservoir was empty. Nothing left to show what game had been played—except one point. The petrol tank of Treverton's old car was a quarter full. Now, if you remember, Pagnell examined that tank after Treverton's death ; and then it was bone-dry because the engine had gone on working until the petrol ran short, that time. So someone must have put more petrol into it in preparation for doing me in. That gives independent corroboration to Picton's evidence about finding the radiator hot when I sent him to the garage."

"Useful enough," commented Standish.

"Next morning, bright and early, Pagnell dropped in on Albury at his place in Grendon St. Giles and asked a few questions. Albury had his tale pat. Someone had rung him up on the 'phone while he was talking to me the night before. The sad news was that a fire had broken out in his lodgings in the village, and would he please go along at once. What he could have done in the matter, I don't know. But by his tale, he had some valuable chemicals at his digs., and off he bolted at once to rescue his lares and penates, without bothering to let me know. He got down to the village and it didn't take him long to learn that the 'phone call had been a hoax. There was no fire in sight when he got to his digs. Seeing that, or rather not seeing that, he didn't bother to go in, nor did he bother to ask any questions. He remembered that he'd left me in the air, waiting for him. So he came back and found I'd just left ; and he learned about my fit.

"Pagnell asked him if anyone had seen him in the village. He didn't think so. He'd just walked to the corner of his street, looked along at his digs., seen no sign of any fire, and tumbled to it that he'd been hoaxed. So he says. Pagnell asked who would want to hoax him, whereupon he said something about doing some business with me which it might pay somebody to interrupt. Pagnell checked up the times, and Albury's story might have been true, assuming that he'd walked both ways. Apparently he doesn't use a car to get from his digs. to Longstoke House and back. There's a bus service that suits him. But of course there wasn't a bus handy to take him that night. It was the wrong time. So he tramped it, by his account. He could hardly have borrowed Whitgift's car, considering the terms they were on."

"So, as far as that goes, he may never have left the Longstoke House grounds?" queried Standish.

"So far as that goes," agreed The Counsellor.

"So any of the gang may have been responsible for trying to do you in?"

"So far as I can see, yes."

"What are you going to do next?" demanded Sandra. "You can't let that sort of thing go on. So long as you leave that offer of yours standing, there's a motive for getting rid of you, Mark. You must write at once and withdraw it. At once. Then they'll have no reason for doing any more against you. Dictate it now, and I'll see it goes off by the next post. Or will you wire?"

A glance at The Counsellor showed her that she was wasting her breath. That obstinate lower jaw had come forward, and both she and Standish knew the symptom only too well.

"Withdraw it?" asked The Counsellor contemptuously. "And let them play Old Harry with Helen Treverton's affairs? If that's your idea of knight-errantry, Tennyson could have learned a lot from you, Sandra. I'm not worrying about my own safety."

He took his hand from his jacket pocket and put a wicked-looking automatic on the table. Among other curious accomplishments, accurate pistol-shooting was one of The Counsellor's attainments.

"No," he went on, in an anxious tone, "I can look

after myself. But I *am* damnably worried about that girl. She's probably dead by this time; they don't seem to stick at much. But there's an off-chance that she's still above ground and we've got to act on that basis. And no one seems to have the foggiest notion what's become of her. Our friend Querrin has been combing that place on the chance of a clue, but so far he's picked up nothing. But she's got to be found, if she's alive; and quick, too, though I'm not a bit hopeful. They're an ingenious crew. . . ."

He broke off and pondered for a full minute.

"How the devil did they get her away at the start? That's what beats me."

"Stopped her car and held her up," suggested Standish.

The Counsellor shook his head impatiently.

"Would any girl, *alone in a car*, stop for anyone? After all these hold-ups on the road? Not if she'd any sense."

"I certainly wouldn't, myself," Sandra admitted.

"They may have faked an accident," suggested Standish. "Poor injured man in the ditch and frantic friend yelling for help."

"May be," conceded The Counsellor. "But it might not have come off. And my impression of these people is that they'd want to make a sure thing of it with no chance of any hitch. Your idea doesn't allow for the probability that she wouldn't waste time in stopping but would drive straight on, hell-for-leather, to fetch assistance as soon as she could."

"Well, that's all a minor issue," Standish pointed out. "Question is, what do you propose to do now?"

"I've settled *that* already," declared The Counsellor rather unexpectedly. "'That which hath wings shall tell the matter.' Ecclesiastes wrote that."

"Did he so?" retorted Standish. "Then I wish he'd taken pains to be a bit clearer. It means nothing to me."

"Candour for candour," said The Counsellor. "And seeing it's only you, Wolf, I don't mind admitting I've been kicking myself for a fool because I didn't think of it sooner. Homer nods at times, and even I myself have my dull moments. But not so dull as yours, when you set about it. You have me there."

"It sounds like English," said Standish in mock perplexity. "Shakespeare used those very words, every one of 'em. But they made sense when he used them. When you use them, Mark, they sound just like an unnecessary noise. Try 'em in a different order, or something, will you?"

"*Carpe diem.* See Horace," replied The Counsellor, rather obscurely. "'Now's the time and now's the hour' for me to revisit Grendon St. Giles. Friends will please accept this, the only, intimation."

"I do wish you wouldn't make jokes like that, Mark," protested Sandra uneasily. "They don't sound nice. I don't like to think of you going back to that place after what happened to you yesterday. Why can't you leave it to the police?"

The Counsellor shook his head firmly, picked up his pistol from the desk and replaced it in his pocket.

15 THAT WHICH HATH WINGS

THOUGH The Counsellor had made a show of confidence in his new idea when speaking to Sandra and Standish, he frankly admitted in his own mind that it was a long shot and might well miss the target completely. Still, anything was worth trying, he reflected as he drove down to Grendon St. Giles. Before leaving London, he had rung up Pagnell to say that he was coming ; and the inspector was there to greet him when he reached the police station.

" I hope you're none the worse for that business yesterday, sir," he began. " You look all right."

" Quite O.K.," The Counsellor confirmed. " Now look here, Inspector. Considering my sufferings and all that, I think I'm entitled to take a hand in the game on your side. If we pool our information, we're likely to get ahead quicker than by operating independently. And, whether you take me in or not, I'm out to get square with whoever played that trick on me last night. It's only human nature. Is there any way of giving me some legal status ? Special constable, or something of the sort ? "

Pagnell rubbed the side of his nose with a doubtful air.

" A bit difficult, sir. Being an inspector, I could make a requisition to have you appointed under the Special Constables Order of 1923. But the actual appointment lies with two of our local Justices of the Peace. And if I got them persuaded about it, then notice of the thing has to go to the Secretary of State and the Lord Lieutenant of the County. It would be difficult. . . ."

"Not worth the bother, eh? I quite agree. All I wanted was the advantage of an official status if I have to question people. I'll just have to rely on my charm of manner to wile news out of 'em. But I suppose that if I fail, I can drop you a hint and then you can apply the official thumbscrews to the patient."

"Well, I think it would be better, so, sir," Pagnell confirmed, not without grasping the fact that this placed him in a much stronger position *vis-à-vis* his volunteer colleague. "Besides, it'll perhaps be handy to have you nosing out things unofficially in some cases."

"Obviously," agreed The Counsellor, rather too heartily for the inspector's taste. "Well, let's begin immediately. You remember telling me a while ago that there was some sort of a Fair held in Byward's Field, close to Little Salten village? That Fair was running on the day Miss Treverton disappeared, wasn't it?"

"It was," the inspector confirmed, after a moment's reflection. "Are you connecting the two?"

"There was a circus, wasn't there? And a lot of sideshows?" pursued The Counsellor, omitting to answer the question. "Vans, and caravans, and all that sort of thing?"

"That's so," said Pagnell. "I think I see what you're driving at, sir. One could hide a girl in one of these vans and whisk her off without anybody knowing. There's perhaps something in that."

"Perhaps," agreed The Counsellor. "Worth looking into? Well, I want to get in touch with a man who might have seen something. You mentioned something about an old plane that somebody brought over to give the citizenry a chance of growing air-minded at five bob a hop. What was the fellow's name?"

"That's an idea!" ejaculated Pagnell with some enthusiasm. "Now I never thought of that. Of course, being up in the air, he'd be able to see a lot that people on the ground might not notice. Some of these vans were parked off by themselves, away from the shows, and a girl might have been hustled into one of them without the crowd guessing anything out of the common was going on. The steam organ of the roundabout made enough row to drown any small disturbance. But from the air, a man might notice it. . . ."

"And think the girl was drunk, eh? So he'd never mention it except by chance, afterwards. Now where's this fellow to be found? What's his name?"

"On his hand-bills, he's The Great Foscari," explained the inspector. "Real name: Nat Rabbit. As to where he's to be found, that's not difficult, sir. As it happens, he's sparking one of the girls in the village, and he comes here whenever he's not doing his show at some fair or other. He's in the village to-day; I saw him in the street this morning. I'll just come along with you. . . ."

"No, you won't," said The Counsellor with so much firmness that the inspector glanced at him in surprise. "Unofficial interviews first, Inspector, if you please. Then you can go along with the thumb screws if you like. If you butt in at the start, he may think you're after him for something and shut up. And if he does, you've no power to make him unlock his jaw. Let me try my hand first of all. What's his address?"

Pagnell was quick enough to see the soundness of The Counsellor's reasoning, and he gave way with as much good grace as he could.

"I see your point, sir. But of course it's understood that you tell me anything you find out? Otherwise. . . ."

"I never let a friend down," retorted The Counsellor with some asperity. "You'll hear all there is to hear. Don't be afraid."

"Oh, well, in that case. . . . He's lodging with old Mrs. Trout in Malkin Lane. It's the third turn on the right, as you go out of the station door, sir. The cottage is on the right-hand side as you go down the lane; and it's got a little wooden porch, so you can't mistake it."

At Mrs. Trout's, The Counsellor had a further stroke of luck, as he found Ned Rabbit in the cottage. Rabbit proved to be a tight-lipped man with eyes set just a shade too closely together; and The Counsellor's knowledge of humanity suggested that any information would probably have to be paid for. Mr. Rabbit looked the sort of person who would give nothing for nothing, and be glad to do so.

"I'm told you were giving a flying exhibition at Little Salten about a fortnight ago," The Counsellor began.

Ned Rabbit nodded curtly without opening his mouth, but his eyes searched The Counsellor's features suspiciously.

"Remember anything about the passengers you took up?" queried The Counsellor.

Rabbit pondered over this before replying, as if he suspected some hidden trap.

"I might, if I was pushed," he admitted, while his face asked, as plainly as print, the subsidiary question: "What is there in it for me?"

"Could you write down a list of them for the afternoon of Thursday?"

"I might, if it was made worth my while."

"Call it a quid," said The Counsellor, producing a note.

"Not enough," objected Rabbit.

"Quite enough," said The Counsellor firmly. He had no intention of acting as a gold-mine to Mr. Rabbit. "You charge a bob a minute for your flights. That's twenty minutes worth in front of you. Get started, or the deal's off."

Rabbit's shrewd glance at The Counsellor's face

evidently convinced him that he was running a risk of losing the money.

"All right," he agreed. "Wait till I think of the names."

The Counsellor put a notebook and pencil on the table.

"Your list will be checked up," he said, casually, and was amused to see Rabbit's face fall a little.

Rabbit picked up the pencil and, with intervals for thought, produced a list of half-a-dozen names.

"That's all the lot I can think of," he said when he had finished. "I took up more than that, but I didn't know their names. These ones come from this place, so I knew them by headmark."

"Very good," said The Counsellor, taking back his notebook.

He reflected that Rabbit was apparently playing fair; and if more names were required, Radio Ardennes would probably elicit a further list if necessary.

"You're an experienced flier?" he went on. "That means you can look about while you're up. Did you notice anything that struck you while you were in the air that afternoon?"

"A bargain's a bargain," Rabbit pointed out with an avaricious grin. "You've had your quid's worth. If you want more, you've got to pay more. Call it another quid, mister, and we won't quarrel."

The Counsellor took out his notecase again and extracted a second note. He reflected that so long as Rabbit imagined he was getting the best of the deal, he would probably give honest information.

"There you are," he said. "Now did you notice anything that struck you?"

"Sweet damn all," retorted Rabbit, with a cackling laugh. "That's six-and-eightpence a word, mister. Any more at the same rate?"

The Counsellor took his defeat with a smile.

"Oh, then, you're no further use to me," he said, picking up his hat. "I thought you might have been able to confirm something; but since you can't, you can't. My time's valuable, like yours. Ta-ta."

"Here, hold on a mo'," cried Rabbit, seeing his gold mine petering out. "Not so fast, you. Gimme some notion of what you're after, and perhaps we'll get to something. Make it another quid and I'll do what I can for you."

The Counsellor smiled bleakly, having now got his man into the position towards which he had been manœuvring.

"I trusted you to start with; now you trust me," he explained. "Payment by results is the new scheme. Or else . . . nothing doing."

Rabbit took fright at the inflexibility of The Counsellor's attitude.

"Oh, all right, *all* right," he assured Brand. "I see your point, mister, and I'm sure I can trust you to be straight over it. What is it you're wanting to know?"

"You could see over the fair-ground from the air?"

"Except what was just below me."

"Notice anything in the way of horse-play going on at any time? Anybody being hustled, or anything of that sort?"

"I did see a copper taking a drunk man off the field, once. Is that it?"

"What time was that?"

"Search me! I saw it, that's all I can remember."

"You could see the road between here and Little Salten, could you?"

Rabbit nodded, his little eyes fixed on The Counsellor's face as if trying to read there what information was required.

"And the village here? And the grounds of Grendon Manor?"

"Nothing much in the village; I wasn't high enough. Nor in the Manor grounds, 'cause of the trees in them. I saw the Manor, of course."

"And the roads? Anything you remember on them? Much traffic on account of the Fair?"

"No, not over much. People with cars don't go to that kind of show, mister."

"And you noticed nothing on the roads? You must be damned unobservant," commented The Counsellor, as though he himself already knew something.

That little flick put Rabbit on his mettle, since he saw the chance of further largesse receding.

"Hold on, mister, hold on!" he protested. "Gimme time to think. I'm trying to do the right thing by you. Lemme see, now."

He pondered for a few moments, evidently determined to dig out from his memory something which would justify a further claim. Then his face brightened.

"Yes, now you jog me up, I do remember one thing," he resumed. Once I saw a car coming along the road towards me, a . . . lemme think . . . yes, a browny car with the sunshine roof open. No good asking me the make. Looking down on it from up there I couldn't see the shape of the bonnet. But it was browny-red or reddish-brown; reddish-brown comes nearest to it."

"Thrilling," said The Counsellor, contemptuously. "That will come to about twopence, for value received."

"Ah, but hold on a bit, hold on a bit," protested Rabbit, seeing The Counsellor's hand stretch out to pick up his hat. "That's not it all, mister. This car stopped and a girl got out of it. I remember it now. She got out and went to lift the bonnet. Something had gone wrong with the works. She hadn't barely begun to fiddle, when she stopped. Then she put down the bonnet again and looked up and down the road. Just then along came one of old Radnor's buses which had been behind the car a bit. You can't mistake them, painted mustard and black like a wasp. The girl stepped out and signalled the bus to pull up. And then I had to turn and go back to the Fair ground as my passenger's five bob's-worth was up. So that was all I saw."

He glanced swiftly at The Counsellor, attempting to discover how much interest his tale had roused.

"*That's* nothing very exciting," commented The Counsellor, hiding his acute interest completely. "And, even if it were, how do I know you're not making this up? Where exactly did this car stop? Are you ready for that?"

"I'm not making it up," protested Rabbit, eagerly. "I'll tell you just where it happened exactly. There's a hayfield on the south side of the road there, and that car stopped almost dead in line with the hedge on the Little Salten side of the field. You know where the road goes off to Witton Underhill, mister? Well, that hayfield's a bit nearer Grendon Manor and before you come to the road that leads off on the far side to join the Great North Road. I could take you to it, the very spot."

"You needn't bother," said The Counsellor, dampingly. "Did you see anything else? I mean something worth talking about?"

Rabbit scratched his head despairingly, trying to recollect any further items of information.

"There was some sort of a party going on at that house Fairlawns, now I remember," he said at last. "Playing tennis in the garden, a lot of them. Seven or eight cars standing in the drive."

"What time did you see that?" demanded The Counsellor, with a show of eagerness.

Rabbit shook his head despondently.

"Any time in the afternoon. I can't remember exactly when I was looking at them."

"See anything that struck you particularly," demanded The Counsellor.

"No, nothing much, except one couple hugging behind a bit of hedge. But that might happen to anyone," he admitted glumly.

"You didn't recognise them?"

"Not me."

The Counsellor fingered his notecase.

"That's worth not more than ten bob," he said judicially.

"Make it a quid, mister. Times are hard."

"It's charity at that, but here you are."

"What d'you expect to get out of all that?" demanded Rabbit, as he stowed the note in his vest-pocket.

"My charge is a quid per question answered," said The Counsellor. "How many would you like to ask?"

"None at that rate," said Rabbit hastily. "I can stifle my curiosity."

"Then we're finished? Very good. Bye-bye."

The Counsellor strolled back to the police station, deep in thought, with his eyes on the ground. Pagnell was waiting for him.

"Got anything fresh, sir?" he inquired.

"I think so," returned The Counsellor, and he proceeded to keep his promise to the inspector by retailing the gist of what he had heard from Rabbit.

"Now," he concluded, "if you've got half an hour to spare, Inspector, come along with me and give me a hand in hunting for something."

Picton was waiting with the car outside the police station. The Counsellor invited Pagnell to get in.

"Take the Little Salten road," he instructed the chauffeur, "and slow down as soon as you pass that A.A. signpost: 'To Witton Underhill.' It's about five miles on."

"What are you going to hunt for, sir?" inquired Pagnell as the car started. "I suppose you're banking on it being Miss Treverton's car that Rabbit saw stopping by the roadside that afternoon. But that's a fortnight back, and more. Any tracks or things of that sort will have gone, long ago."

"I'm not bothering about tracks," explained The Counsellor. "I'm looking for something more substantial. This is it, Inspector. I don't know if I told you about it before, but when I found that car EZ 1113 dumped in Lochar Moss, I examined the petrol gauge. It showed the tank bung-full. But when we examined the tank itself, it was half empty. My acute brain at once inferred that the gauge was out of action—jammed at the point where it indicated a full tank. That little fact I pigeon-holed, because it seemed a bit queer. See it now ? "

" I can't say I do, yet, sir," Pagnell confessed.

" Then go back to when Miss Treverton started out from Longstoke House that afternoon she disappeared. She gets into the car and switches on. The gauge shows that the tank's full, if she bothers to look at it. If she doesn't look at it, she must have had a pretty good idea that she'd enough petrol on board to take her to Fairlawns anyhow. But before she got more than four miles, the car stopped. *Teste* The Great Foscari, alias Nat Rabbit, who saw it stop and noticed the girl getting out. She opened the bonnet and probably looked at the carburettor. It was, I'm prepared to bet, bone dry."

" Wait a minute," interrupted Pagnell. " I think I see it, sir. You mean that somebody jammed her gauge and siphoned off all the petrol from her tank, just leaving enough to get her a mile or two along the road ? "

" That's it, more or less," The Counsellor admitted. " Now you see, Inspector, that covers one possible snag in the kidnapping business. It made dead sure that she couldn't escape by jamming down her accelerator and driving away, as she would normally have done if anyone tried to hold her up. That was a point that puzzled me at first in the whole business."

" Still, I don't see what you're expecting to find, sir, after all this time."

" Try again, then. The car EZ 1113 didn't stay by the roadside that afternoon. The next we hear of it is at St. Neot's. It took in eight gallons of petrol at

St. Neot's, which means that its tank must have been pretty low when it got there. It's just a bit over fifty miles from this stopping-place to St. Neot's—say two gallons of petrol, roughly. Therefore, after the car EZ 1113 stopped on the road here with a bone-dry tank, somebody must have put in more petrol. And the amount put in must have been a couple of gallons, which is one tin. There's no word in the later history of EZ 1113 about that empty petrol tin. Therefore—though it's a long shot—I'm inclined to think that it was chucked away behind the hedge after the tank was replenished from it."

"I guess you may be right," admitted the inspector. "She had no tin in the car when she started, and since they were trying to pretend that she had gone off with Querrin, they wouldn't want to drag an unexplained tin about with them in case someone mentioned it. It seems sound. And so it's this tin you're going to look for?"

"Yes. And as it might be an important bit of evidence, I've brought you along to find it or see it found. Well, there's the A.A. signpost. Now we slow down and look for a hayfield on the left. It ought to be close by. . . . There it is. . . . A bit further on, Picton. . . . Pull up!"

The car halted at the spot which Rabbit had described to The Counsellor, and all three got out.

"If Rabbit's description was all right—and it seems to have been—then that tin—if it exists—should be in behind one of these hedges," said The Counsellor. "There's not much cover on the hayfield side," he commented, after glancing over the low hedge, "so we'll try the other side of the road first."

It was Inspector Pagnell who eventually unearthed the empty tin in the middle of a thicket of nettles; and when he did so, he regarded The Counsellor with enhanced respect.

"That was a good shot of yours, sir," he confessed. "I never imagined there *was* any tin—except in your imagination. But here it is, sure enough, and quite empty, too."

He gave it a rap with his knuckles to confirm this.

"And now, sir, what's your idea of the next move?" he demanded, swinging the tin by its handle.

"I forget the name of the man," said The Counsellor. "Who is it that owns a fleet of buses about here? They're painted like wasps."

"That'll be Radnor's buses," said the inspector.

"Radnor! That's the man. The name slipped my memory for the moment," The Counsellor confessed. "Well, I don't think we can do better than look him up, if he's to be found handy. Where does he hang out, Inspector?"

"In Stoke Alderbrook, his headquarters are, sir. That's about fifteen miles back on the road, past Grendon St. Giles."

"Well, we'll pay him a state visit now. Hop aboard, Inspector. Don't forget the exhibit. This time you can come along and give an air of respectability to the proceedings. But you'd better let me do the questioning."

16 THE ROYAL DEFIANCE EXPRESS SERVICE

WHEN they reached Stoke Alderbrook, Pagnell directed Picton down the side street in which Radnor's premises were situated. The establishment was larger than The Counsellor had expected. Along the façade of the garage ran a large inscription: THE ROYAL DEFIANCE EXPRESS SERVICE; and, in smaller lettering: *H. Radnor, Proprietor*. The proprietor, it seemed, was on the premises; and the inspector's official status gained them immediate admittance to his office. H. Radnor proved to be a quiet, keen-faced man who regarded them rather distrustfully as they entered.

"Well, Inspector? I hope none of my drivers has got into trouble with your people. They've reported nothing of the sort."

"Oh, no, nothing of the sort," the inspector assured him.

Radnor's face lightened at this.

"Then what can I do for you?" he inquired in a less official and more friendly tone.

"This is Mr. Brand," explained the inspector, tactfully leaving The Counsellor's status undefined. "He's making some inquiries, and he thinks you may be able to help, perhaps."

Radnor glanced at The Counsellor. He had never come across any high police officials and had no idea how they dressed; but apparently The Counsellor's garish tweeds surprised him a little. He made no comment, however, and it seemed that he was prepared to accept The Counsellor, tweeds and all, on the strength of Pagnell's introduction.

"Yes?" he said, leaving The Counsellor to explain himself.

"This is it," began The Counsellor, nothing loth. "First of all, I've nothing against your service—no complaints of any kind. That clear? Good. I simply want to ask a question or two about your buses. You run 'em all over the district, don't you?"

"We have a number of routes in operation," Radnor confirmed, "and we hope to open one or two new ones when we can get delivery of extra buses."

"You run to schedule, of course?"

"Of course," agreed Radnor, with a faint smile.

"And your men keep to time, I suppose?"

"They're expected to."

"Any means of checking that?" asked The Counsellor.

"They keep time-sheets," Radnor explained.

"Ah, splendid. I think you run a service which passes through Grendon St. Giles and Little Salten. Have you a time-table of that route handy, by any chance?"

Radnor pulled open a drawer in his desk, produced a pink pamphlet and handed it across to The Counsellor.

"You'll find it on page 3," he pointed out.

The Counsellor opened the flimsy pages and scanned the data on the third one.

"You run a forty-five minute service on that route in the afternoon, I see. Going out from here, a bus passes Grendon St. Giles at 2.50 p.m., then another at 3.35 p.m., and another at 4.20 p.m. And on the inward route, they leave Little Salten at 2.0 p.m., 2.45, and 3.30 p.m. I see you allow twenty minutes for the run between the two places."

He reflected for a moment, his lips moving silently as if he were making a calculation. Then he looked up at Radnor.

" Then, on this basis, none of your buses was on the road from Grendon St. Giles to Little Salten between 3.10 p.m. and 3.30 p.m. ? "

" That's quite correct," confirmed Radnor, who evidently knew his timetable by heart.

" Ah ! Would it surprise you to learn that one of your buses *was* on that stretch of road about ten past three; that is, at the time your outward-bound bus had just reached Little Salten and your inward bus had passed Grendon St. Giles and was on the road to your garage here ? "

" It would surprise me very much," retorted Radnor, with more than a tinge of incredulity in his voice. " That is, if I believed it. When was this supposed to happen ? "

" On the 8th," The Counsellor declared.

" We'll look into this," said Radnor.

He rang a bell and, when his typist appeared, he ordered her to bring the necessary time-sheets. She returned with them in a minute or two and then, after dismissing her, he spread them out on his desk so that The Counsellor and the inspector could check them.

" There, you see," he pointed out, putting his finger on the relevant information. " Both these buses ran quite on time over that stretch. No reports of anything amiss. What do you say to that ? "

" Nothing," admitted The Counsellor. " Except that your sheets don't tell the whole story. Could I see your men who were on these two buses ? "

Radnor evidently had his whole business at his finger-ends. He glanced at his watch.

" As it happens, the driver and conductor of the outward-bound bus are on the premises at the moment, just waiting to go out. You'll have to be quick with them, if you want to question them. We can't have delays, you know."

He seemed to search his memory for a moment and then added:

"You're in luck, Mr. Brand. As it happens, the driver of the other bus—the 2.45 from Little Salten—twisted his ankle a bit and has to lie off for a day or two. He's doing odds and ends of work in the garage to-day, to fill in time; so I can get him up here for you if you wish."

"If you would be so good," said The Counsellor.

Radnor gave the necessary directions, and the driver and conductor were brought into the office. The Counsellor knew that he had no time to spare in their case, so he went straight to the point.

"I just want you to answer a question or two. It'll be worth your while," he explained. "You were on the bus that left Grendon St. Giles at 2.50 p.m. on Thursday, the 8th?"

"Yes, sir," said the driver.

The conductor, evidently a slower-minded person, nodded a second after his colleague had answered.

"Did you see anything out of the way between Grendon St. Giles and Little Salten? Any signs of an accident, car in distress, or anything of that sort?"

"No, sir," answered the driver immediately.

The conductor again confirmed this with a nod.

"Much traffic on that trip?"

"No, sir, not that I recall. There never is much. Sometimes we don't see a car for ten miles."

"You're quite sure you know the day I'm speaking about?"

"Quite sure, sir. I had my young niece aboard that trip, going to the Fair at Little Salten. That's how I can be sure."

"And you?" asked The Counsellor, turning to the conductor.

"I remember that, too. I know his niece and I remember passing a word or two with her while I took the fares."

"Thanks. That's all."

The Counsellor produced some coins from his pocket and Radnor dismissed his employees.

"I may say one thing," he pointed out when the door had closed. "My men are all decent chaps. They don't lie. You can take what they told you as sound."

"Right!" said The Counsellor, who had believed the men. "And what about this third chap, now?"

Radnor summoned the remaining witness, who limped into the room with a certain reluctance. He was a gloomy-looking, blackavised individual; and as he entered he cast an uneasy glance at the inspector, whom he evidently knew by sight. Pagnell interpreted the look and thought it well to put the man more at his ease.

"I've nothing against you in the way of motoring offences," he explained, briefly. "This gentleman wants to ask you a question or two."

"You drive the bus which leaves Little Salten at 2.45 p.m., coming this way, don't you?" demanded The Counsellor, without giving the man time to raise any objections.

"I drive it every day, barring a time like this when I'm off with something," the man agreed.

"Can you remember the afternoon of the 8th? A Thursday. There was a Fair on at Little Salten," The Counsellor asked.

The driver shook his head.

"Too far back, unless it's something special."

"You'd remember anything special? Anything out of the way that you saw on the road: an accident, a car in distress, a traction-engine, anything of that sort."

"Yes, I expect I would."

"Well, can you remember seeing anything that took your attention?"

The man reflected for several seconds, then shook his head decidedly.

"Nix."

"You didn't pick up a girl dressed in grey, say

round about where the road to Witton Underhill branches off ? "

" No, I'd remember that. I remember the day you're speaking about, now."

" Good ! And you saw no car by the wayside, during your run ? No ? Right ! It wasn't likely you would. I just want to make sure. That's all, thank you."

He dismissed the driver with a gratuity which did not escape Pagnell's eye.

" If we could be as free with our tips as you are," the inspector commented with a trace of envy, " we'd often get our information a bit quicker than we do."

The Counsellor gave him a grin in response before turning to Radnor.

" That disposes of your regular service, Mr. Radnor. But don't you occasionally take on what one might call outside work ? I see on the front of your time-table that you offer your buses for dances, club outings, picnics, football parties, and so on. Had you any of your buses out for that kind of thing on the 8th ? "

Radnor reflected for a moment and then consulted some papers in his desk.

" I had, as it happens," he explained. " One of them took a party of children to the Fair that day—in the afternoon, too."

" Was that Dr. Trulock's treat ? " inquired The Counsellor, with an amused glance in the inspector's direction.

Pagnell pricked up his ears at the question. Evidently he was much impressed by The Counsellor's memory for trifling details, since Brand had got his information about the orphanage treat from the inspector himself in the most casual way.

" It was Dr. Trulock's treat, as you say," Radnor confirmed.

" Ah ! I'd like some particulars, if you have them

handy. Could you tell me when your bus reached the Fair ground at Little Salten ? "

" I can do that," Radnor assured him, consulting a paper. " It was booked to arrive at the Fair ground at 2.30 p.m. That was a special point in the order, for some reason or other."

" Oh, then it had gone over the route long before 3 p.m.," interjected the inspector. " Nothing much in that, I'm afraid, sir," he added to The Counsellor.

" One can never tell," retorted The Counsellor, working off one of his clichés. " Have you the name of the man who drove that bus ? " he asked, turning to Radnor.

" Oh, yes," said the proprietor, " Reuben Speke, his name is. But I can do better for you than that. It just happens that he'll be on the premises now, waiting to go out with his usual bus. I'll have him up. He's due out in a quarter of an hour," he added warningly.

Reuben Speke proved to be a hearty-looking, burly personage with a ready smile.

" Anything I can do for you, sir . . . " he said, when the matter had been explained to him briefly.

The inspector, something of a cynic where men were concerned, inferred that Speke had learned in the garage that generous treatment might be expected from The Counsellor.

" You ran some of these Orphanage children out to the Fair at Little Salten on the 8th, didn't you ? " asked The Counsellor. " Just tell us exactly what you did—all the details you can think of."

Speke had evidently determined to give The Counsellor good value for his money.

" It was the *Ramillies* I had given me to take out that afternoon," he explained. " All our buses—as perhaps Mr. Radnor here has told you—are named after battleships. At the garage here, I got aboard and I had my old woman with me and three of my kids." He turned to Radnor with just a shade of misgiving in his expression. " Did Dr. Trulock tell you about that, sir ? "

Radnor shook his head.

" Well, it was quite all right, sir, really. Dr. Trulock came to the garage the day before and left a note addressed to the driver of the bus that was taking his treat to Little Salten. That was me, of course, though he didn't know my name. He said—leastways, he put it in the letter, and I've got it at home somewhere still, if so be you'd want to see it—He wrote, anyhow, that there wouldn't be enough orphans for to fill up all the seats in the bus, and if the driver—which was me, of course—cared to take four of his friends along with him, children for choice, then he'd look on them as his guests—same as the orphans—and stand 'em the drive. I took it that was all right sir," he added, turning a rather doubtful eye to Radnor.

" Quite all right," the proprietor admitted. " Dr. Trulock hired the bus. It's all the same to me who he put into the seats. It was his affair."

" That's how I took it, sir," declared Speke. " So I took my party aboard at the garage—which shows I'd no hole-and-corner ideas about the business but was doing it quite open-like—and I drove round to the Orphanage. All the little kiddies was there, ready, with their clothes brushed and their shoes shined, looking as good as gold. So I got them aboard with a nurse, or a keeper or whatever they call 'em, as well to look after 'em. And some of 'em needed it, though it was all high spirits really and no real mischief in 'em."

" Had you a conductor with you ? " demanded The Counsellor.

" No, not on a trip like that," explained Speke. " There's no fares to collect. It's all paid for at the office."

" Right ! Go on," said The Counsellor.

" Then I drove straight out to the Fair ground, sir."

"See anything that caught your attention by the roadside? Anything out of the ordinary, I mean: gypsy vans, stranded cars, or anything of that kind?"

"Not a thing, sir. One of the pore little kiddies got a bit car-sick, but nothing to hurt. That was the only trouble."

"Good! You reached the Fair ground O.K. When was that?"

"That was 2.26 p.m., sir. I'd been warned I must be there by 2.30 p.m. at latest. I know the reason for that. Just as I came along the by-road to the Fair ground, I saw a car behind me in my driving-mirror. It pulled up alongside me at the Fair ground and out got Dr. Trulock. He came up to me, and he says: "Look here, driver, did you bring some of your little friends along, same as I suggested?' 'Yes, sir,' says I, 'and very kind it was of you for to think of it.' And I was going to call up the kiddies for to make them thank him, but he stopped me and, says he: 'How many have you?' Says I: 'Four, my missus and three kids.' 'Splendid!' says he, quite pleased-like, for he's a real good sort as anyone can see with half an eye. 'Now,' says he, 'I'm standing these here orphans their seats at the circus. It starts at three o'clock. And I'll be glad to do the same for your lot, too, if you and your missus will go in with them. And if you can give a hand with the orphans as well, I'm sure their overseer will be grateful. Had any bother with them on the way up?' he asks.

"So I says, that was very kind of him and we'd all enjoy the show, for I'm not too old yet myself to laugh at a clown. So he handed me the dibs to pay the entry for the lot—my lot, that is, for he'd squared up with the woman in charge of the orphans beforehand, I gathered. And I took my ignition key out and put it in my vest pocket and went off with my wife and kiddies to have a look round the place before going into the circus at three.

" We went in and saw the show. It lasted for an hour and a half altogether. Then I came out, and we went round the booths a bit and had a try at the shooting-gallery and a plunk at the cocoanut shy and a few other things, until it was time to think of going home again. Oh, and we had our photos took by one of these fellows who take you when you ain't looking in the street with a sort of cinema camera kind of thing. And not badly they turned out, either."

The Counsellor suddenly seemed to prick up his ears.

" Where was this photographer posted ? " he interrupted.

" Just at the gate, taking the people as they came in," Speke explained.

" How many entrances are there to the ground ? " asked The Counsellor.

" Just the one. But I was going to tell you a funny thing. I was dead sure I'd taken out my ignition key and put it in my pocket. But when it came to half-past five and we were due to start, the orphans all come a-trooping up, and my wife and I took a hand in helping them aboard the bus, and at last we got them all stowed and I went round to my seat and felt in my pocket. No key ! I was a bit flummoxed, I can tell you ! And then I looked at the dashboard, and there it was, stuck in the hole. I must have forgot to take it out, after all. And yet I could have sworn. . . . But I suppose the orphans must have flustered me or something. Anyway, there it was, and everything right. So we got away all right and landed the orphans home on schedule time, very pleased with their treat, I suppose, but a bit tired and apt to be peevish, as my wife told me afterwards. Is there anything else you'd like to know, sir ? Time's getting on and I'm due out shortly."

" Just one point," said The Counsellor. " You got your photos taken by this cinema expert. He gave you a card with his address on it, as they usually do ? Remember that address ? "

"I do, sir. His name's John Yabsley—that's apt to stick in one's mind, isn't it?—and his shop's here, in Acre Lane, with his name over the door, on the right-hand side, going down. I went there to get the photos myself."

"Then I needn't keep you longer, Mr. Speke," said The Counsellor. "Thanks for your help."

Speke retired beaming, and again the inspector sighed enviously at the munificence of the reward.

"Quite worth the money," said The Counsellor, who had caught the inspector's expression with the tail of his eye. "And now, Mr. Radnor, we're all busy people, so I mustn't waste any more of your time. Thanks for giving us your help. If I can ever do anything for you in my own line, let me know."

And he solemnly presented Radnor with one of his professional visiting cards.

"What do you want with this photographic fellow, sir?" asked Pagnell as they came out of the garage. "I follow you up to a point, but I don't see where he comes in, I don't mind admitting."

"I want to see the negatives of the pictures he took that day," explained The Counsellor. "Come along. It may be worth while. Or, again it may not," he added judicially. "One can but try."

They had no difficulty in finding Yabsley's shop in Acre Lane, for the front of it was decorated with showcases containing an assortment of portraits and groups. The Counsellor, after a cursory inspection of them, guessed that Mr. Yabsley did not cater for the neighbouring county families.

"What's Early Closing Day in this town?" he asked the inspector. "Thursday, is it? Yes? Ah, that accounts for it. Evidently Mr. Yabsley had to shut his shop here that afternoon and decided to make a little on the side by taking his grinding-machine to the Fair. Zeal! Let me do the talking, please."

A little bell clanged as they opened the shop door, and they found themselves amid a further array of camera products. In a few seconds, a little man with tinted glasses on his nose entered by another door.

"What can I do for you?" he asked politely in a high treble voice which seemed likely to rise to a squeak at times.

"I want to buy a dozen copies of one of your photographs," The Counsellor explained.

"Number, please?" inquired the photographer. "I mean the number of the photograph in my series," he added, fearing that The Counsellor might misunderstand him. "With a large output like mine"—he almost visibly swelled with pride—"a System is essential. Every negative is numbered and stored in proper sequence. I can put my hand on any required picture at a moment's notice. Efficiency, the keynote of a business like this."

The Counsellor valiantly repressed a smile. He hardly knew whether to take this as bluff or as conceit.

"Trouble is, you see," he explained, "I don't know the number. I lost your card with the number on it. It was given to me by a friend," he added. "It's not my own photograph I want."

This evidently reassured Yabsley. He had been examining The Counsellor's tweeds with increasing doubt. No one, having photographed material of that character, could have forgotten the wearer for some weeks at least. And, naturally, he had not been able to recall taking any such photograph.

"I see," he admitted, dubiously, as he realised that in this particular case his beloved System was of no assistance. "Then. . . ."

"I can tell you something to put you on the track, though," The Counsellor interrupted. "This photo was taken at the Little Salten Fair on the 8th, round about three o'clock."

The inspector's face showed that he had only a faint glimmering of The Counsellor's purpose. Yabsley, on the other hand, beamed with pleasure, as he found that his System could meet even this emergency.

"I think we can do something with that information," he volunteered, "I think we can . . ."

"The quickest way would be to let me see the negatives," suggested The Counsellor. "I'll know the thing when I see it."

"That we can do, that we can do," declared Yabsley. "Let me see . . . September 8th, about 3 p.m. Just a moment, please."

He opened a drawer and pulled out a fat loose-leaf pocket-book.

"September . . . 8th. Here we are," he exclaimed, opening the book and glancing over the pages. "A great thing, a System. Invaluable. I note down time and place opposite each number, you see? So there can be no mistake, of course. Unnecessary trouble, some of my colleagues tell me. What do you want that for, they say, when you've got the number of the film? System, I say, System. What's worth doing, is worth doing well. And here comes your order to prove it. Let me see . . . 2.45 p.m. I took No. 6423 then. Would you care to start at 2.45 p.m.? Or earlier, if necessary. No trouble, I assure you. Only too glad to be of service. . . . A dozen copies, you said? I'll just make a note of that. One moment. . . ."

He made a jotting and then turned to a row of film albums on a shelf.

"No. 6423 . . ." he ran his finger along the backs and pulled down the album he required. "Here it is . . . and," he flicked over the leaves, "here is what we want. One would be lost without a System in this business."

He withdrew the film and fished for a moment in another drawer.

"A piece of opal glass," he explained. "If you lay the film on it and hold it up to the window, you'll be able to make out the picture, I think. That is, if you are accustomed to negatives."

"I am," The Counsellor assured him, picking up the film and glancing at it. "No, I'm afraid this isn't it. Sorry to give you trouble."

One by one, Yabsley handed out his negatives for inspection, but at each of them The Counsellor shook his head. At last, one fell under his scrutiny which extracted from him an ejaculation of satisfaction.

"This is the goods," he said, turning it up to the light so that Pagnell could examine it in his turn.

The inspector was not an amateur photographer, so that negatives were unfamiliar to him; but he recognised some object in the background of the picture which bore a pattern of black-and-white vertical stripes. Evidently this was what The Counsellor had hunted for.

"As a test of your System," The Counsellor said with a smile, turning to Yabsley, "could you tell me at what time you actually took this particular snap?"

Yabsley took back the negative, read off the number on it, consulted his loose-leaf book, and then—

"I took that at 2.53 p.m." he announced with a note of triumph.

"Quite sure? You'd swear to it?" asked The Counsellor in a tone between jest and earnest.

"I'd swear to it any day," said the photographer emphatically. "And what's more, my notes would prove it to anyone. System, that's the real secret. Do a thing well, and you don't need to worry about it afterwards."

"I wish *I* had a well-ordered mind," said The Counsellor. "Now, let's see, here's my card,"—he produced one with his private address on it—"and you might send me half a dozen copies as soon as it's convenient. How much will that be, including postage? . . . Ah, thanks. I'd better pay now, since you don't know me."

He paid over the sum demanded and then, with a few more words in compliment to the System, he left the shop, followed by Pagnell.

"Well, sir," the inspector pointed out as they walked up the lane together, "I get a glimmering of what you're after. But you promised to put your cards on the table with me, you remember. I'd like to know just exactly how you look at it."

"That's only honest," admitted The Counsellor. "I'll tell you just what I think about it."

When he had finished, Pagnell shook his head dubiously.

"It would take a professional dipper to manage that trick," he objected. "It'd be beyond an amateur."

"Think so?" asked The Counsellor with a grin. "Well, there's nothing like evidence. I do a bit of parlour-magic myself, sometimes. Here's your fountain-pen, Inspector. Likewise your notebook. Can you tell me how I got them?"

Pagnell laughed at the hit and then turned on his companion with mock ferocity.

"I could charge you with larceny, for that."

"Don't try your bluffing with me," retorted The Counsellor, with a twinkling eye. "The essence of larceny is intent to deprive the owner permanently of his goods. You've got them back, haven't you? And I gave them to you freely, didn't I? Then it's not larceny. See?"

"You know a bit too much, sir, one way and another," the inspector declared, as though rather vexed at the failure of his joke. "But as to this notion of yours, I'd like to have a think before I'd care to take steps in the matter. It's clever; it's ingenious, I'll admit. But still. . . ."

"Think it over," advised The Counsellor.

A thought seemed to strike him and he continued in a slightly different tone.

"By the way, Inspector, was old Treverton a

member of the A.A.? Had he a badge on his car, do you remember?"

Pagnell shook his head decidedly.

"No, he hadn't. He never spent a penny that he could avoid, and he wasn't much of a motorist. Miss Treverton, she had the badge. And Whitgift had one on his car, I remember. But not Treverton, I'm dead sure of that."

17 THE ADVENTURES OF A BUS

WHEN he summoned Sandra Rainham and Standish to consultation on the following morning, they gathered at once from his manner that The Counsellor was in good spirits. He pushed his box of cigarettes forward as they came in.

"Sit down, my dear Watsons. Take a cigarette, do. They're the sort I keep for visitors, you know. And now, with your kind attention, I'll clear up this business—or part of it, at any rate," he added cautiously.

"Seems very pleased with himself," Standish commented as he reached over and took a cigarette.

"You've found the girl?" exclaimed Sandra, impulsively. "Oh! Good! I'm so glad!"

"Am I telling this story, or are you?" demanded The Counsellor, testily. "Let me do things decently and in proper order, will you? All you need say is: 'Wonderful!' and 'Amazing!' and so on, at proper intervals. I'll do the rest without assistance."

"Wonderful!" said Standish, obligingly.

The Counsellor ignored this.

"I shall now explain Helen Treverton's disappearance," he said with dignity. "But perhaps, Wolf, you've taken my advice about thumpin' and thumpin' at the thinkin', and have got a solution yourself? No? Somehow, I thought not. Well, this is how it is. As I told you before, Miss Treverton had an invitation to go to a tennis party at Dr. Trulock's on the afternoon of her disappearance. She got out her car after luncheon, put her attaché case on the seat beside her, and went off. I know the exact time she left, because it was just after a bus passed the lodge gate, going towards Grendon St. Giles—two miles away. That bus was on time. It's due at Grendon St. Giles at 3.05 p.m. Therefore it passed the lodge just about 3 p.m."

"How do you know that?" asked Sandra. "About the bus, I mean."

"Whitgift saw it pass when he was talking to the girl on the avenue," explained The Counsellor. "I proceed. Four miles up the road, Miss Treverton's car stopped. She got out of it and opened the bonnet."

"Second sight, you've got?" interjected Standish. "Amazing!"

"Brains," retorted The Counsellor. "When you want to know a thing the best method is to ask. Brains come in when you pick out the right person to ask. I picked out the right person. He's called The Great Foscari."

"Nobody would trust a man with a name like that," objected Standish. "Nobody with brains, that is."

"Call him Nat Rabbit, then, if you find it more convincing," said The Counsellor agreeably. "He owns a debilitated plane, I may say; and if you like to risk your neck at five bob a shot, he'll accommodate you. He was accommodating the more temerarious of the autochtones—good word, that!—at a Fair which was held at Little Salten on that afternoon and on succeeding days. During one of his aerial gambados, he made the observations I'm summarising; but he didn't see the end of the story, unfortunately."

The Counsellor picked out a cigarette and lit it deliberately before proceeding.

"The next thing that happened was the arrival of a bus, coming from the Grendon St. Giles direction. Seeing the car in distress, the bus-driver kindly stopped to give assistance. . . ."

"Did he?" interjected Standish sceptically. "Oh,

well, you said the Treverton girl was pretty. Perhaps even bus-drivers have feelings. Still, seeing they're usually running to a time-schedule. . . ."

"I am telling you what happened, Wolf. No doubt you have your own reasons for knowing it didn't happen. But there it is. That bus did stop. It's a conspicuous kind of bus, painted wasp-pattern in black and yellow. No one could mistake it. Now the curious thing is that no such bus should have been on that particular stretch of road at that particular time. I checked that. As I told you, a homeward-bound bus of that fleet passed the Longstoke House lodge gates at 3 p.m.; and an outward bound bus had left Grendon St. Giles at 2.50 p.m. on the way to Little Salten, so it was ahead of Miss Treverton's car. As it's a forty-five minute service, no bus of that fleet should have been there at all. I interviewed the proprietor of The Royal Defiance Express Service which runs these wasp-patterned juggernauts. Also various drivers in his employ. So that's that."

"'Curiouser and curiouser'," said Sandra impatiently, as The Counsellor made a pause for effect. "Get on with the story, Mark."

"Hold on a moment," interrupted Standish, as The Counsellor was about to speak. "How did. . . .?"

"Let me do things decently and in proper order," repeated The Counsellor. "I'm telling a plain tale just now. Questions afterwards. Now we take up a fresh thread. It seems that somebody—Dr. Trulock, as a matter of fact—very decently offered the children in some orphanage at Stoke Alderbrook a treat. He hired a bus from The Royal Defiance Express Service to take these kids to the Fair, and he stood them seats at the circus as well."

"Oh, so it was *that* bus that stopped, was it?" asked Sandra. "It would be apart from the regular service, of course."

"That bus reached the Fair ground at 2.26 p.m. in time for the kiddies to go into the circus at the

2.45 p.m. performance," said The Counsellor, mildly. "So it passed over that stretch of road ahead of the 2.50 bus from Grendon St. Giles, which in turn was ahead of Miss Treverton's car."

"Oh!"

"I proceed. The driver of that bus had, by permission, brought his wife and—I gather—a selection of his family with him. They accompanied the orphans to the circus performance, after parking the bus in a corner of the Fair ground. The driver—a perfectly reliable man, according to his employer—took away the ignition key with him. Like to make any remarks, Wolf?"

Standish shook his head.

"Now all that's fair, square and above board," The Counsellor pointed out. "The first bit of funny business was when the driver went back to his car and found the ignition key in its place instead of in his pocket."

"But how did it get there?" demanded Sandra.

"Just what my friend Inspector Pagnell asked," said The Counsellor. "But I convinced him easily."

"How?"

"By picking his pocket as an illustration," explained The Counsellor. "Obviously someone did the same for the bus-driver, and so got hold of his ignition key. After that, of course, there was a bit of a risky passage in driving the bus away from the Fair ground. But all the uniform these chaps wear is a common brand of cap; and as the Royal Defiance fleet is a pretty big one, an unknown driver wouldn't attract attention particularly. And I take it that they had a faked conductor as well, with cash-bag complete. Anyhow, they got the bus away safely enough."

"Is this guess-work?" asked Standish. "It sounds a bit like it."

"No, I can prove that bit," retorted The Counsellor with a twinkle of satisfaction in his eye. "Not to keep you in the fidgets any longer, I'll tell you how I did that. I learned that, that afternoon, a photographer fellow had planted himself at the gate of the grounds and was doing a bit of trade with a turn-the-handle camera, recording the dials of any burgesses who seemed likely to part with a tanner. I interviewed him and made an excuse to see all the negatives he took from a quarter to three onwards. The citizenry's physogs didn't interest me; but I hoped that perhaps the handle had been turning when that bus went out of the Fair ground. It was a long shot, but it came off. In a photograph taken at 2.53 p.m., the waspy bus appeared in the background, driving off. Unfortunately the photo did not show either the driver or the conductor, so I can't identify them. But there's no doubt that bus left the Fair ground at 2.53, when it ought to have been in the park."

"Hold on a jiff," interrupted Standish. "When was the bus leaving Grendon St. Giles at 2.50 p.m. likely to reach Little Salten?"

"It's timed for 3.10 at Little Salten," explained The Counsellor. "Your point is that the bus from the Fair ground, leaving at 2.53, would meet the regular bus somewhere on the road between Grendon St. Giles and Little Salten?"

"Exactly," agreed Standish, "and the driver of the regular bus would notice it, seeing that it was one of his own fleet and had no business to be there just then."

"Well, he didn't notice it," The Counsellor pointed out. "So that means it wasn't there to meet him. There's a road from the Fair ground which leads straight to the Little Salten cross roads; but there's also another one which strikes the Grendon St. Giles—Little Salten road about a quarter of a mile nearer Grendon St. Giles than the cross roads. The bus from the Fair ground could take that road and wait in it until the regular bus passed along. Then it could nip out and go all out for Grendon St. Giles with no chance of meeting anything. See?"

"But in any case it would meet Miss Treverton's car

coming up to Little Salten," objected Standish. " Buses don't usually take a run down a road for a bit and then turn back. And by your tale, this bus came up *behind* her before it stopped."

" There are such things as side roads," The Counsellor pointed out. " I'm merely guessing here; but obviously you can hide a bus in a side road, wait till a car passes on the main road, and then come out and follow the car back along the main road. There's a road that goes off to Witton Underhill which would serve; but if they couldn't get that length in the time, there are other lanes leading off to farms by the wayside which would fill the bill well enough."

" That's assuming that the fellows on the bus knew that her car would break down on that stretch of road. And what's more, they must have had a rough idea of just whereabouts it was likely to stop."

" Just so," The Counsellor agreed. " They knew her car was going to run out of petrol just there or thereabouts."

" Guessing again?" asked Standish, caustically.

" No, facts in support," retorted The Counsellor, placidly. " But we come to them later. I proceed. As I told you, my friend The Great Foscari saw the next scene: where the bus came up and stopped beside Miss Treverton's car. Now, Sandra, I put it to you. Suppose you have an engagement at your friend's house up the road. Your car sticks for want of petrol. A bus comes up in the nick of time, going your way. What would you do?"

" Lock my car and leave it, and take the bus to my friend's gate. Then later on, come back in his car with some petrol. That's what I'd do."

" Quite so. And I expect that was what Miss Treverton did. The only point is that she'd take her attaché case and racquet with her. But I can imagine the bus-conductor being a bit officious and taking them from her hand while she was busy locking up her car—helpful fellow. Anyhow, they got left behind, accidental done-o'-purpose like. And so you have this bus, with her aboard, bowling up the road towards Little Salten and going, I've no doubt, lickety-split. Helen Treverton would have no suspicion of anything wrong unless the bus passed the Trulock's house without stopping. If it had gone past, she might be inclined to make a fuss and no fuss was wanted, just then on the open road. So I'm inclined to think that the rest of the game was played out before the bus reached the Trulock's place, Fairlawns, at all."

"Two men could easily have overpowered her; and if they stopped the bus, both the driver and the conductor could have lent a hand," Standish admitted.

"And any cars that came along at that moment—as they might have done—would have passed by on the other side, like the priest and the Levite? Not with any rough-and-tumble business going on, surely," objected The Counsellor. "No, Wolf, I don't think they even threatened her with a pistol on the public highway. If I'd been in charge of a job of that sort, I'd have aimed to take the girl by surprise. And I guess the fellow who planned this was quite clever enough to do the same. We'll leave an open *fracas* as a last resort. But in the meanwhile, as the old novelists used to say, what has become of EZ 1113? I'll tell you."

With an obvious pleasure in leaving his hearers in suspense, The Counsellor turned to this fresh thread.

"As soon as the bus had teuf-teuffed off, two figures appeared from the neighbouring landscape. One was a girl dressed in grey. The other was a young fellow in grey flannels, carrying a petrol tin. They had been in retirement behind a hedge, probably, further down the road, and had watched EZ 1113 go past; but they had kept out of sight until Miss Treverton had been enticed into the bus. The young man poured his two gallons of petrol into the tank of EZ 1113. . . ."

"But the car doors were locked," objected Standish.

"You make me tired, Wolf," The Counsellor protested. " Heaps of people leave their door keys in the cubby-hole or the door-pockets of their cars. No doubt Helen Treverton did the same. And any friend of yours could go out to your car while it's lying at his front-door during one of your visits, get your key, take a squeeze of it, and file a blank to match. Of course these people had a duplicate of her key. Give them credit for some brains, do."

" Oh, very well," grunted Standish vexedly. " Go on."

" These two car-snatchers then got aboard EZ 1113 and drove off towards St. Neot's," The Counsellor continued. " But before doing so, they pitched the empty petrol tin behind the hedge, whence it was recovered yesterday by a man of infinite-resource-and-sagacity. . . ."

" Mr. Henry Albert Bivvens, A.B., I presume," interjected Sandra. " I had the feeling, all along, that it was a whale story."

" You have the name wrong," The Counsellor corrected her with dignity. " It was Mark Brand who had the infinite-resource-and-sagacity in this particular affair. Alone he did it. But to proceed. By the time EZ 1113 reached St. Neot's—as an examination of the map will show—its petrol tank was almost dry ; so it was able to take in eight gallons of petrol there, and then start on the job of leaving a false trail up to Stranraer. There the man and the girl faded out of the picture. Most likely they returned to their normal haunts after that."

" Yes, yes," said Sandra, impatiently. " But what happened to Helen Treverton ? That's the only important thing."

" I don't know ; but I can find out," declared The Counsellor. " And in the meantime I can make a guess at it. This is the guess. So long as the bus was on the high road, Miss Treverton would have no suspicion. Why should she ? She's in a bus belonging to a well-known local service. But suppose the bus swings abruptly off the main road. She'll want to know why, and there may be a rumpus. Now if that bus simply swung down a side-road, her kidnappers aren't any better off in the way of privacy. A car may come along a side-road at any moment and interrupt their little game. So, on the face of it, side-roads would be no use to them. They must have turned off along the road to some house or other, where they could get her under cover. But in his search for the pseudo-Querrin man, Pagnell made inquiries about most places in the neighbourhood and found nothing suspicious, and she certainly never got to Trulock's. So that leaves us with the possibility that Grendon Manor, a quarter of a mile from Fairlawns, might have been used. It's got a nice big avenue into which a bus could swing off the road. And, from all we've heard, it's got a rummyish kind of reputation. So I plump for Grendon Manor as being the likeliest place for the finish of that part of the game. As I said, that's only a guess."

"There might be something in it," Standish conceded grudgingly. "After all, the further they ran that recognisable bus, the more trail they were leaving for anyone to follow up. And they had to get the bus back to the Fair ground before the real driver came out of the circus performance, or the fat would be in the fire. That limited their available time, obviously. I'll admit that your guess does fit the case, Mark, though it's far from proved."

"And, suppose all that stuff *were* true," Sandra objected. "How could they prevent the girl making some sort of attempt to get away? Or raising a row of some sort?"

The Counsellor shrugged his shoulders impatiently. "Suppose you were the girl. Suppose you were stripped to the skin and put into a room with no furniture bar a plank bed. Suppose you were efficiently gagged and your hands tied behind your back. How would you propose to get away or raise a racket? Especially if you were told that you'd be lammed with a rubber truncheon if you showed any enterprise. It's easy enough to fix that side of it."

He rubbed his chin hard with thumb and forefinger, a sure symptom that he was perturbed.

"It's not that that bothers me," he went on. "This is it. Either that girl's dead already, or else they mean to let her loose again eventually. There's no third course. And how they propose to let her loose after this, I simply can't see. They couldn't expect her to keep quiet, once she was out of their grip. That's what's worrying me, Sandra. Remember what happened to Treverton."

"What beats me is the motive behind all this," Standish confessed. "There must be a gold-mine somewhere. What about that notion of yours, Mark, about a substitution of pictures?"

"I've communicated with some of the private galleries," The Counsellor explained. "The ones which seem likeliest for a game of that sort to come off successfully. We ought to hear shortly if any hanky-panky of that kind's been tried."

He looked at his watch and seemed to shake off his depression.

"I've fixed an appointment with Querrin," he explained. "You two had better clear out. I must see him alone."

Sandra gave The Counsellor a sharp glance.

"You're not going to run any more risks, are you, Mark?" she demanded with an anxious note in her voice. "You've done more than enough in that line already. Wolf and I agree there. Don't do it. Please, don't. It's an affair for the police, not for you, now."

"The police can't do everything. But make your mind easy, Sandra. I've asked Querrin to call because he's been collecting some information for me," said The Counsellor, telling only half the truth. "Also, it's only fair to give him the latest tips in the business. After all, it's his girl. . . ."

The desk-telephone rang and The Counsellor picked up the receiver.

" This is Whitgift," he explained to Sandra. Then to the girl at the office switchboard he ordered, " Put him through."

For some minutes The Counsellor spoke over the wire to Grendon St. Giles, but Sandra and Standish paid little attention to what they heard, knowing that he would explain afterwards. At last he hung up his receiver.

" That was Whitgift. Poor devil, he seems in a bad way over that girl's disappearance."

" I suppose he's very fond of her in spite of having no chance," said Sandra sympathetically.

" He's damnably anxious, and that's a fact," The Counsellor admitted. " Wants to know if we've picked up anything that gives a gleam of hope."

" Did you tell him—about the kidnapping, I mean ? " asked Sandra.

The Counsellor gave her an impish glance.

" Oh, dear no ! As you reminded me just now, most opportunely, it's a police affair. We mustn't interfere. By no means. So I referred him to my good friend Pagnell for further news."

" I think you're a perfect beast, Mark ! Why couldn't you tell him what you've found out ? The police didn't find it, so there's no reason why you shouldn't tell him."

" I suppose not," admitted The Counsellor. " Still, it's much better to have one person giving out information instead of a whole gang babbling about different details. And Inspector Pagnell's the man to say what can or cannot be made public without hampering his future work. I like Pagnell. Decent chap. He'll tell Whitgift all that's necessary."

A typist brought in a card at this moment.

" Send him in, please," said The Counsellor, after glancing at it. " And now, clear out, you people. Oh, Wolf, you might ring up Pagnell and warn him that Whitgift will be applying to him. No use letting him be taken unawares on the spur of the moment. Say I leave it all to him."

When Querrin entered the room, The Counsellor wasted no time in formal greetings.

"Got it?" he asked, abruptly.

Querrin nodded.

"Yes, this Hell-Fire Club, as you call it, meets on Wednesdays, generally. Spend the night at the Manor. That's picked up from three different sources. It seems sound enough."

"Wednesday, that's to-night," mused The Counsellor. "H'm! Sure you didn't rouse any suspicion by your inquiries?"

"Absolutely none. I took mighty good care of that."

"The inspector's tip agrees with yours," The Counsellor admitted. "That's enough to go on. I asked him to find out on his side, just to get an extra line on it. Now, Querrin, this is serious. Are you fit for a bit of law-breaking? I hope to put it through quietly. But there's always a risk. And if we get caught out, the police will have to act against us, whether they like it or not. What about it?"

"Anything you like, short of murder," said Querrin, shutting his teeth.

"Right! Then this is it. . . ."

18 THE CHILDREN OF LIGHT

IT was not until well after luncheon time that The Counsellor put in an appearance at his office on the following day.

"You look as if you'd been up all night, Mark," Sandra commented when she saw him. "What have you been doing with yourself?"

"Joining the Children of Light in one of their sprees," growled The Counsellor, who looked headachy. "We've all been hearing the chimes at midnight: Wolf, Querrin, and myself. Wolf had the easiest part of it."

"He doesn't look as bad as you do, certainly," Sandra admitted, glancing at Standish as he came into the room. "But do you mean you went down there without saying a word to me about it? That's not playing fair, Mark. Suppose you hadn't turned up to-day, I'd have been sure something had gone far wrong. And you've no right to take risks of that sort. Remember what happened to you at Longstoke House. You ought to leave it to the police, you and Wolf."

"The police can't do everything," said The Counsellor crossly. "They did all that was required in this affair. That is, turned a blind eye on our proceedings. Feeling brisk, Wolf?"

"Bit sleepy, that's all."

"Oh, get on with your story," interrupted Sandra. "Have you found that girl?"

"No, we haven't," admitted The Counsellor, rubbing his brow with his hand as if trying to dispel his headache. "I'll tell you about it, but don't try to be funny. My head's too sore. What Querrin feels like, I can't say. He got different treatment, and I haven't had time to ring him up this morning."

"Go on," said Standish. "Querrin's troubles are his own affair. Let's hear what happened."

The Counsellor turned to Sandra.

"Last night, the three of us, Querrin in my car and Wolf in his own, went down to Grendon St. Giles. I'd seen to it that the police would not be a nuisance to us. We left the cars on the road near the Manor gate. We also left Wolf there. His job was to flicker a flashlight when a car arrived at the gate and there was no other car in sight. Querrin and I didn't go near the gate, but got into the grounds over a wall and planted ourselves amongst the trees of the avenue up to the Manor, at a point out of sight of both the lodge and the house. We were both in evening dress and masked up to the eyes. That's the uniform of the Children of Light on business, as you'll recall."

"Querrin looked the bigger villain of the two," Standish explained to Sandra. "He's three inches taller. Otherwise, they were much of a muchness."

"When you're quite finished . . ." said The Counsellor. "Well, this was it, as I saw the business. If you remember, the dear Children are stopped at the gate by the lodge-keeper, and they don't put on their masks until he's given them the once-over and passed them as sound. There may be some password, for all I know. I wasn't going to take the risk of that. So Querrin and I got in quietly behind that bar. We waited while two or three cars went up the avenue. Then Wolf gave us a flicker, and we knew that the next car hadn't anything following immediately behind it to interrupt our proceedings. When it came along, Querrin stepped out into the avenue and did the windmill act to induce it to stop. As it did so, I stepped smartly alongside and shoved an equaliser through the window—I'd counted on the window being open, the the lodge-keeper had to have it open to talk to the driver. As it happened, there were two fellows in the car, which saved us stopping a second one.

" Well, they showed no fight. If they had, they'd have got an ammonia douche which would have kept 'em quiet. Querrin came up with a second pistol—ammonia, really, though it looked like an automatic—and before you could say Raminogrobis, we had them out of the car and neatly tied up among the trees. Also gagged. In fact, off the board. Querrin's a useful fellow with his wits about him."

" Suppose it had been a girl in the car ? " interrupted Sandra.

" Then we'd have warned her politely about some bits of broken glass further up the avenue and waited for a likelier victim. No rough stuff with girls. We'd arranged that. Quite the little gentlemen. We nipped into the car, drove up to the front door, parked in a handy spot, and so gave the complete illusion of two Children of Light arriving quite normally.

" Well, it seems that all the check-up is done at the gate, as I'd hoped. The front door was opened by a man-servant. He asked no questions, never blenched at the masks, and showed us into a big room on the ground floor. There was a fair blaze of light in it, about half the number of lamps would have been enough. But what hit my eye at once was the painting of the walls. 'Member the way they used to fix up ships in the war—dazzle-painting, they called it ? This was just like that. Great random streaks of vivid colours spread from floor to ceiling, breaking off and interlacing in the wildest way. I thought some paulo-post-futurist had got on the loose. And the ceiling was just the same, a weird entanglement of bands and arabesques. Striking's not the word for it, especially in that blaze of illumination. And tubs of hot-house flowers had been brought in and scattered around the walls, just to mix up the tints a bit more. Even the wineglasses stacked on trays on a table at one end of the room were coloured red and green.

Very strong on colours, these folk. You'll see why, by-and-by.

"Well, it was a rum den, and not a bit what I'd expected. Nor were the company, either. As a meeting of a Hell-fire Club, it was disappointing at the first glance. Some thirty or forty people, all masked. Half a dozen couples dancing to the air from a softly-played wireless. The rest of the crew sitting about on divans, arm-chairs, or cushions, or standing around on the floor. Most of 'em seemed self-isolated. No truck with their neighbours.

"No one seemed to bother about us. If there was an M.C., he didn't exert himself. Querrin and I drifted over to a couple of arm-chairs and sat down. When we'd done so, I began to wish we'd chosen better, for there was a tub of tropical plants on each side of us and the fragrance palled considerably, before long. Too late to think of changing, then; and it came in handy eventually.

"One or two late-comers arrived. It all seemed damned dull, and I began to wonder when Hell was going to break loose. Nothing to do but stare at the company. Mighty little to be made out of the men; short coats and black ties don't give you much to take hold on. The women—about fifty per cent. of the gathering—offered more to the eye, in spite of the masks. Some of them were just girls; others were past their first youth; and there was one withered old beldame leaning on a stick. The couples dancing seemed to know each other, but on the whole the gang didn't seem eager to extend their circle of acquaintance. Not much doing in the *camaraderie* line.

"I was getting bored, so I looked about to see if one could smoke. And then I got one identification. When I called on Trulock, I noticed he used an extra long cigarette-holder, about six inches long with one gold and one silver band round it. And a grey-haired chap in a mask had one exactly the same. I kept my eye on him without seeming to do so, and I noticed he had Trulock's trick of putting both thumbs and forefingers into his waistcoat pockets, as if he were hunting for a key or something. So that was that! Then I had a further look round, and I noticed a big clumsy fellow crossing the floor, walking a bit hen-toed with his right foot, if you see what I mean. . . ."

"I know," interjected Sandra. "I noticed that in somebody—Albury, it was, wasn't it?"

"Albury, as you say," confirmed The Counsellor, rather annoyed to have his thunder stolen in this way. "There was no mistaking him. So that was two of them spotted. But it ended there. I could make neither head nor tail of the rest.

"A last arrival seemed to bring the company up to full strength. Everybody brisked up a bit, and I could see one or two of them glancing at their watches and turning their heads towards the table with the trays and glasses. Evidently the show was due to start; and from the charged glasses, I inferred that it was dope of some sort they were waiting for. Two kinds of dope, possibly, since they had glasses of two different tints. We'd have to go light on anything of that sort, Querrin and I, lest we got laid out.

"Querrin, luckily, knew the Morse code. Picked it up, like me, from short wave wireless work. So I communicated with him. . . ."

"How?" asked Standish. "Did you wag iddy-umpty with your heads? A bit apt to be noticed, that."

"This way."

The Counsellor rested his elbows on his chair-arms, clenched his left fist and brought his right hand over it, so that his right-hand fingers lay in the spaces between his left-hand knuckles.

"Now, if you move your right finger up and down a fraction of an inch," he pointed out, "it looks just as if you were a bit impatient and fidgety. And, properly done, it's not visible to anyone except people sitting next you. That's how. So I gave him the tip to go slow on the drinks and also to choose the colour of glass that I didn't take myself, so that if there were two brands of dope, each of us would get his own and we could compare notes afterwards.

"We'd just finished this by-play when the door opened and the man-servant came in. He walked over to the table, lifted one of the trays, and went round the nearest guests with it. I noticed that they took care to choose glasses of particular colours, so I was pretty certain the drinks weren't all alike. When he came to us, I took a green glass and Querrin helped himself to a red one. I had a look round to see how one drank, but apparently you could sip it or gulp it as you fancied. So Querrin and I sipped once or twice, and then—taking care no one saw us—we got rid of the rest into the tubs beside us. Just as well we'd picked such convenient chairs. After a bit, the man-servant went to and fro, collecting the empty glasses. Then he left the room.

"I didn't feel anything amiss from the stuff I swallowed. Querrin told me afterwards that his throat went a bit dry and he felt thirsty. Also, I happened to notice, his pupils expanded a bit, so he'd evidently drawn some mydriatic stuff from the pool."

"Atropine? Belladonna? Something of that sort?" queried Standish.

"Something of that sort," The Counsellor concurred. "But to proceed. I'd taken particular note of one or two people who'd gone in for a red glass and a couple or so of the green glass lot. When the stuff began to act, the two effects were different. My job was easy enough. All I had to do was to sit still and stare at vacancy. But the crew that drank from the red glasses—most of the couples on the floor favoured that tipple, I'd noticed—had a livelier bit of work. The dancing got quicker and quicker, quite out of time with the music. Then some of the lot who'd been sitting around, got up and started *pas seuls* which looked like a can-can flavoured with a bit of invention. Even when they didn't dance, some of them, didn't seem able to sit still, but got up and wandered about the floor, paying no attention to their neighbours. The doctor seemed to be one of my gang, for he sat tight, looking cool and collected behind his mask and glancing about as if he were taking a professional interest in the show.

" By and by, the effects of the dope took another turn. I noticed one chap sitting with clenched hands and elbows bent, making sawing motions as if he was playing pully-haul with the two ends of a rope running over a sheave. At the same time he was glaring in front of him intently. These antics beat me, for a bit; then I saw he thought he was driving a car. And with that tip to guide me, I spotted what was behind some other stunts that were going on. One fellow was practising putting—and with fair success, too, to judge by the number of times he took his imaginary ball out of the invisible hole. Another beggar was running up a gigantic break on a billiards-table that nobody could see but himself. And so on.

" By this time the dancing had become a bit—well, I spare your blushes, Sandra—a bit unseemly. They were talking incoherently at the top of their voices and laughing in a mad kind of way. Then one couple broke away from the rest, and the man hurried the girl out of the room. Another pair followed them, and another. I could hear the shrieks of laughter growing fainter and then the noises of doors being slammed on the floor above. Soon most of the dancers, and some of the others, had gone. Querrin had got up and was wandering about the floor, imitating the others who'd taken his brand of dope. By and by, when I looked for him, he'd vanished. That didn't worry me. I knew he'd gone easy on the stuff and we'd arranged to operate independently if necessary. I simply sat tight with the more sober section of the mob and waited to see what would happen.

" When it came, it was marvellous. That stuff is

all the goods and nothing less. And I'd taken a very mild snort. What the full-dose crew experienced must have been a foretaste of heaven. First of all, a sort of care-free gladness seemed to ooze into me coupled with a mental acuteness and physical fitness. . . . No, it's no good trying to describe it to you. . . . I can't find the words for it. Then illusions started and simply flowed over me so quick that I couldn't keep track of them. Colours! That was what the dazzle-painting was for, I suppose, to give the initial kick-off. But one soon got far beyond that. I never saw such tints as the ones that drifted up before me: brilliant, they were, and with a delicacy and variety that's beyond description. It was like living in a kaleidoscope. The ordinary world, as one remembered it, was grey and dead by comparison. I saw spheres and cubes changing size and flowing with iridescent colours, networks of gold and silver, weird arabesque lacework in pure light, landscapes with sunsets and dawns, with trees and plants like nothing on earth. And fabulous monsters, too, painted like the rest, and fairly glowing with splendour. . . . And it affected my ears, too. I heard tinklings away in the distance, organ notes of a new sort, and plucked harp-strings. . . ."

The Counsellor paused, evidently trying to find fitting words. Then abruptly he gave it up.

"Like being landed on another planet where our rules don't apply and where everything's pleasant beyond describing. Not a shadow of fear anywhere, even when a griffin swoops down and lands at your feet. One just watches the play of iridescent colours on its wings and scales. . . . It's no wonder these people call themselves the Children of Light. The other dope, the stuff in the red glasses, may be exciting enough, to judge by its results; but I wouldn't have missed my experience for a good deal, I can tell you. Marvellous, wonderful, fascinating—lump all the adjectives you like together and still they wouldn't come up to it. Perfumes, too, finer than any rose-garden.

And new. Like nothing that ever entered your nostrils in this life."

He paused for a moment as if brooding over the recollection. Then a thought seemed to strike him.

"By the way, Wolf, did you manage your share of the show all right?"

Standish nodded complacently.

"Oh, yes. I waited in my car for an hour or two. Then I got over the wall and poked about a bit till I found your two friends, still trussed up and pretty sick. It was a chilly evening. Of course I had a mask on, as you advised. Before cutting them loose, I gave 'em a few words according to plan. Told 'em someone'd played a practical joke on 'em and damned lucky for them, too. There'd been a police raid on the Manor, and the Children of Light were 'for it' most distinctly. Some very rummy things had been found, very funny indeed. It would be a nasty scandal when it came out. They got the wind up badly, I could see. What were they to do? Well, my advice was to cut their sticks across country and not go near the lodge. Police patrol was down there, ready to lift anyone who appeared. One of them had some wits left. "But our car will be up at the door. They'll get its number and trace us by that!" So I said: "I don't know how you're fitted out for lying, but one can always have one's car stolen by somebody and taken to a place one knows nothing about, can't one?" That fetched 'em. They were all for a clean pair of heels. So I cut 'em loose and showed 'em the easiest place to get over the wall. And then I wandered down to my own car and came home according to directions. Nothing further to report."

"Right!" said The Counsellor approvingly. "Now I'll cut the rest of the illusions and continue the tale. Querrin came back into the room, after a while, but naturally we took no notice of each other. All the green drink crew were still sitting or lying about, evidently in Paradise. The one I was most afraid of was Trulock; but I could see he'd got his dose and wasn't likely to bother about mere earthly affairs for a while. I was still a bit under the influence, but it was wearing off. Querrin seemed to be a bit queer, but fairly in control of himself. Since neither of us had swallowed anything like a full dose, we were bound to come right quicker than the whole-hoggers. The only question was how long would it be before we were fit to drive a car. There was nothing to do but wait.

"It was hours, as I found afterwards from my watch. But I didn't regret it. I was so interested in seeing that world of illusion getting thinner and thinner, and the real world getting solider and solider about me again as the effects died down. I forgot to tell you that when Querrin came back, he seemed to me like an angel of light as he walked across the room: all flowing colours, with a many-tinted aura round about him; and all the time I knew he was just a man in a short coat and black tie. It was damnably confusing, in some ways.

"It was getting on towards dawn before the crew about me gave any signs of waking up. What happened to the couples upstairs I've no idea. None of them showed up again before we left. We watched the symptoms of our neighbours and copied them when we decided it was time to wake up. One couldn't see their faces, but when they got to their feet they looked damned tired. We let two or three of them leave the room before us. Luckily Trulock must have stood himself a stiffish dose. He was still under the influence when I got up to go. Albury I didn't see.

"We found our appropriated car where we'd parked it and drove off. There were no formalities at the gate. The lodge-keeper didn't even show up. Then we came to my car, standing by the roadside and I shifted over into it, leaving Querrin to drive the one we'd snatched. We thought it best to drive it to the address on the Insurance Certificate that we found in the door-pocket. No use leaving the car by the road-side and raising trouble. We left it a few doors away from its proper home, Up West somewhere. Then I took Querrin aboard and buzzed off to my abode.

" It wasn't breakfast time, but we didn't feel eager for breakfast anyhow. What I wanted was Querrin's tale. I'd difficulty in getting it out of him. His memory was muzzy, more than a bit, and I could only get fragments of his doings. You'll see the point of that in a minute.

" Remember, none of us has seen Helen Treverton. So we might have passed her in the street, if she had her face turned away, since that snapshot's all we know of her looks. But Querrin knew her well enough. Now here's what he told me. He took a few sips of the stuff in the red glasses, and after a short time he began to feel rummy. Some impulse to get up and move about the room came over him. He couldn't sit still. So he got up and began to wander round. Like me, he'd given the company the once-over when he came into the place and he'd seen no one he recognised, not even Trulock or Albury. Which shows he's not a very keen observer ; note that. Now he began to take a bit more interest. And suddenly, amongst the girls dancing, he noticed one that struck him. He couldn't see her face for the mask, of course ; but she had the same build and figure as Helen Treverton ; and the more he stared at her, the surer he grew that it was Helen. She was at the far end of the room, near the door, when he noticed her ; and before he could go up to her, she and her partner cleared out. He pushed his way to the door and followed them ; but by that time they must have run upstairs, for he heard a door slam on the floor above. He bolted upstairs after them, three at a time, and found himself in a long corridor with doors on each side, some open, some shut. And each door had a Yale lock on it, which isn't so very usual. He tried the first closed door he came to, but the Yale was on. Inside he heard a girl laughing fit to split. But there was a good deal of laughing going on, in other rooms as well, and he didn't see what to do next. So he sat down on the floor—evidently he was quite bemused by then—and he got so interested in a lot of fish that swam past him in shoals that he clean forgot everything else. So he sat there, so he says, trying to count the fish as they went by, and losing count, and getting more and more depressed because it was most important to get the total right. . . . And that's all he seems to remember for quite a while. By and by, he sobered up a bit and, having forgotten all about the Treverton girl at the moment, he wandered downstairs again and came back into the reception room. Nobody bothered about him. Grendon Manor, it seems, has Liberty Hall for its other name on these nights. But that's all I could get out of him, try as I would. He remembered his fish illusion better than anything else, so far as I could see. Real events had got washed out of his memory except in scraps."

"Was it Helen Treverton, do you think?" interjected Sandra.

"I don't know, but I can find out," retorted The Counsellor with a headachy smile. "But I've a strong suspicion it wasn't. My point is that he didn't recognise her till he was well under the drug and fit to see fish and all the rest of it. That girl's picture's in his mind all the time, since he's in love with her. Once the drug sapped his normal control, he might see her in the first girl that came along. No, I don't believe Helen Treverton was in that show last night. But now that my brain's growing a shade clearer, one or two things do strike me."

"Well, what are they? Quick!" said Sandra, whose interest was almost entirely concentrated on Helen Treverton's fate.

"First," said The Counsellor, laboriously ticking off his points on his fingers, "you remember I looked up Trulock in the Medical Directory and found he'd spent some years in South America before he settled down at Fairlawns? Note that, then. Second, some girl personated Helen Treverton on that trip to Stranraer. She wouldn't need to be her double, since she hadn't to pass the test of meeting anyone who actually knew Helen Treverton. But she must have been near enough in looks so that the people we interviewed would give us a description of her which would fit the real girl. That's sound, isn't it? Third, Querrin, when sober, didn't identify his fiancée in any of the girls who were there last night. But when he got a bit doped, he saw someone whom he mistook for Helen Treverton. Chances are, it's the same girl, and she does look a bit like Helen Treverton. Fourth, when I was at Fairlawns, I saw a girl who reminded me of somebody, but I couldn't think who it was she resembled. Now I've got the key, I see it. She was a bit like Helen Treverton, and her attitude when she stooped down to one of the kids was much the same as Helen Treverton's attitude in that snapshot I'd seen showing her bending over her dog and looking up at the camera. It's no cert., but I'd bet fair odds that Trulock's nannie was the girl who drove EZ 1113 up to Gretna Green. Fifth—making a straight flush—that nannie was reported to be on holiday at the time Helen Treverton vanished. So Pagnell told me. So she was off the local map just at the time that impersonation occurred. Sixth, Trulock was the philanthropist who financed that orphan treat and stood the bus-driver a seat at the circus. And that made it possible to get the bus away, as you remember. Seventh, it was the Trulocks who asked Helen Treverton over that afternoon to their tennis party, which ensured that she and her car would be on the road just where and when they were wanted. That's enough to go on with, I think. Things are narrowing down a bit. In fact, they're coming to a point."

Standish had apparently kept The Counsellor's items in his memory.

"Trulock was in South America," he commented.

" And you and Querrin got doped with some rummy drugs last night. South America teems with them; and I think I can put a name to the one you drew in the gamble: peyotl. I read about it, once, somewhere."

" Peyotl it was," confirmed The Counsellor. " I rang up a specialist in drugs after breakfast this morning, and he sent me round a book about them. It comes from a cactus, *anhalonium lewinii*. It's got as many names as a Royalty or a criminal. Mescal's one of them."

" What was the other drug, the one Mr. Querrin took? " asked Sandra.

" Ah! That's a rank bad 'un," said The Counsellor gravely, picking up a book which lay on his desk. " I'll read you a bit about it."

He opened the volume at a mark and began to read:

" ' If only a small quantity of the plant is given to a person, his mind is depraved and deluded to such a degree that anything can be done in his presence without fear of his remembering it on the following day. . . . You can do what you like with him, he notices nothing, understands nothing, and knows nothing about it on the next day. . . . By means of this drug one can do as one pleases with women and obtain anything from them. That is why I believe there is no more noxious plant in the world, and none whereby such evil things can be accomplished in a natural manner.' That's an indictment of it, isn't it? Ugh! Makes one feel sickish to think about it."

He put the book down on his desk again.

" So that's why Querrin was a bit mixed in his souvenirs this morning," said Standish. " And he got only a fraction of a full dose. You seem to have identified it all right. And it's pretty plain that Trulock is running a dope club of sorts at the Manor. Probably he brought a supply of the peyotl stuff with him from South America when he came back. I begin to see things clearer. You say there were about forty people present at last night's binge; and they meet once a week. Ten quid would be a cheap price to some people for a jag of that sort. Call it ten quid per skull per meeting. It comes to £20,000 a year; and Trulock must be doing pretty well out of it. Naturally, in a stunt of that sort, the less the members know about each other, the better. Hence the masks, I suppose. Just in case of blackmail amongst themselves, eh?"

"Quite likely," agreed The Counsellor. "Trulock's the only person—bar the gatekeeper, perhaps—who need know the identities of his . . . patients."

"And Helen Treverton's being kept in that beastly house?" said Sandra. "If I'd been there, instead of you two. . . ."

The bell of the desk-telephone interrupted her. The Counsellor picked up the receiver.

"Yes? O.K. . . ."

There was a long message from the other end of the wire. Then The Counsellor said: "Right!" and put the instrument back on its stand.

"Here's the stop press news from Pagnell," he said, turning to his assistants. "A fire broke out in Grendon Manor this morning. Two people hurt. Our friend Pagnell is a smart lad. There's a clause in the Public Health Act or somewhere, which authorises constables to enter burning buildings and do anything necessary to protect life and property, without getting the owner's permission. He took advantage of that and made a thorough search of the premises from top to bottom. Helen Treverton wasn't there. He's sure of that."

"Oh!" said Sandra, much cast down.

"How did the fire start?" demanded the practical Standish.

"In one of the bedrooms—probably from a smouldering cigarette thrown down in a waste-paper basket. The injured couple had been occupying the bedroom. Doped, I expect, and didn't realise what was happening."

"Who were they?"

"Male and female, that's all I learned from Pagnell."

"And what are you going to do?"

"This is Thursday," The Counsellor pointed out. "I'm going to clear the decks as far as possible for next Sunday's broadcast, just in case we're pressed for time later on. Business first."

"Well, you *are* a cold-blooded beast!" said Sandra, hotly. "Mark! Can't you do something to help that poor girl, instead of talking about your broadcast?"

"We must keep faith with our listeners," said The Counsellor, mildly. "I was going to tell you something more, but we'll not waste time over details, since you don't wish it, Sandra. See your way through the business, Wolf?"

"Can't say I do," Standish admitted. "I'd have bet big money that the girl was being kept at the Manor."

"Well, go on thumpin' and thumpin' at the thinkin'," was The Counsellor's advice. "*Nil desperandum*, you know. And if you want a little reading to pass the time when you're not thinking, I recommend Poe's essay on Maelzel's Chess Player. Most suggestive work, that, especially for those too stupid to see beyond their nose-points. Try it! And in the meanwhile, kindly arrange for the loan of a small epidiascope. You know, the thing they use in lectures to show solid specimens instead of lantern slides. Hire it, or get it somehow. Also a screen for same."

Standish glanced at Sandra rather doubtfully.

"Think he's still under that dope?" he asked in a stage whisper. "It doesn't make sense to me."

"Oh, it's just a brain-flash," confessed The Counsellor. "I may be on the wrong track altogether. But get the thing, anyhow; and as quick as you can, or quicker. Meanwhile, I'll have a look through our museum. We may have to fill out the broadcast a bit, and a few minutes chat about some of our specimens might interest people. We haven't worked that stunt yet. And get me a pair of dividers, too," he added with a smile at some undisclosed jest of his own. "Fine ones. And get me Picton on the 'phone. I think I'll send him up to St. Neot's, later on."

19 THE STALKING-HORSE

"SO that's over," said The Counsellor, as the car reached Grendon St. Giles and slowed down in the High Street. "You've got your search-warrant, Inspector."

"I hope it's all right," retorted Pagnell, with a shade of discomfort in his tone. "Awkward, if we've got the wrong sow by the ear, sir, after you making that sworn declaration."

"Let by-gones be by-gones," suggested The Counsellor hastily. "By the way, did you make these inquiries about the source of that telephone call, the one that robbed me of the pleasure of Albury's society that evening they tried to do me in?"

"Yes, I did," the inspector returned. "There was a call, right enough, to Longstoke House at that time; and it came from the A.A. telephone box just at the foot of the avenue. That's funny."

"Most amusing!" snapped The Counsellor. "Hear me laugh: Ha! Ha! Well, at least I can swear that Albury didn't send it from the A.A. box, since he was with me just then."

The big seven-seater drew up in front of the police station, where Querrin was waiting for them along with three uniformed constables and a man in plain clothes. The Counsellor turned to his chauffeur.

"Amuse yourself in the village, for a while, Picton," he directed. "I'll drive myself. We'll pick you up on the way back. The car will hold the rest of us with a seat apiece," he added to the inspector. "I'll take Mr. Querrin beside me, and the rest of you have room enough behind. Any last words ? "

Pagnell shook his head.

" No, it's all fixed, sir. Davis "—he nodded towards the man in plain clothes—" he goes round to the back-door, pretending to peddle sundries to the maids. Then Croom and I ring the front-door bell. You and Mr. Querrin have to get into the shrubbery alongside that ground-floor window with the blinds down. The other constables remain in reserve. Once we start, no one's to be allowed off the premises. That's as far as we can foresee things."

" The doctor ? " queried The Counsellor.

" All arranged for," Pagnell assured him. " He'll be there on time."

" Right ! Then off we go," said The Counsellor, cheerfully, as he slid into the driving-seat and started his engine. " Now we shan't be long."

Nor were they, for The Counsellor was a fast driver. They took the Little Salten road, and in less than fifteen minutes the big car was pulled up close to the gate of Fairlawns, under a hedge which concealed it from the house windows. Constable Davis got out, with a shabby little leather case in his hand, and walked up the drive.

" Give him time to get busy," said the inspector, glancing at his watch. Then after a few minutes he added : " Now Croom and I go. You and Mr. Querrin. . . .? "

" Cut up through the trees," explained The Counsellor. " I've been over the ground early this morning, before anyone was awake. There's a gap we can scramble through. We'll be there when we're wanted. But remember to clear your throat and talk loud when you get into that room."

The inspector nodded assent and set off with his uniformed satellite up the drive. Two minutes later, Querrin and The Counsellor made their way along the road, found the gap, and entered the grounds.

At the front door the inspector demanded to see Trulock and he and the constable were shown into a sitting-room while the maid went in search of the doctor. In a few minutes he appeared and greeted the inspector genially.

"Glad to do anything I can for you, Inspector. What's the trouble to-day?"

Pagnell feigned a slight embarrassment.

"Well, sir, I expect it's all right, really. But information's been laid with us in the matter of the Dangerous Drugs Act, and we've got to look into the point, just as a matter of routine. Nothing in it, I expect, sir."

"The Dangerous Drugs Act?" echoed Trulock, with an air in which relief seemed to be blended with something else. "That's morphine, heroin, and things of that sort. Well, I have a stock of morphia, if that's what you're after. Why not? I'm a qualified medical man. I don't practise, nowadays, but I have a dispensary of sorts and I keep morphia for emergencies. Somebody's been pulling your leg, Inspector, I'm afraid," he added with a smile.

"Coca leaves and Indian hemp come under the D.D.A. also," said the Inspector.

"Indian hemp?" queried the doctor, as though quizzing Pagnell. "That's a pretty vague term, isn't it?"

"'The expression "Indian hemp" means the dried flowering or fruiting tops of the pistillate plant known as *cannabis sativa*, from which the resin has not been extracted, by whatever name such tops are called,'" quoted the inspector triumphantly. He had memorised that definition from the Act with some care and was glad he had done so.

Dr. Trulock laughed unaffectedly.

"That's a mouthful," he commented. "But suppose you saw the stuff itself, would the definition help you? I mean, would you recognise these 'tops' if you came across them without a label attached? Come, now,

Inspector, Honest Indian, without the hemp. Could you swear to them?"

"Well, I might. Or I might not," said Pagnell with an air of great caution. "But I daresay an expert could tell me, if I put it to him."

Dr. Trulock suddenly changed his tone.

"This is all rubbish, you know, Inspector," he said sharply. "Who gave you this tale?"

"It was what we call 'information received,'" said the inspector, freezing up in his turn. "I'm sorry, sir, but we've got to act on it. You see, I've got a search-warrant."

"Oh, you have, have you?" answered the doctor. He showed no signs of being taken aback. He dipped his fingers and thumbs into his waistcoat pockets in his habitual manner and fumbled idly for a moment or two, as though his thoughts were on other things.

"Let's see your warrant," he said at last.

Pagnell produced it. The doctor glanced over it, but the inspector could see he was paying it but little attention. Then, apparently, Trulock reached a solution of the problem which had been puzzling him.

"Very well," he said, coolly enough. "I'll put no difficulties in your way; though I'd like to say just what I think of these goings-on. Come along to my dispensary and you can hunt for yourself. You're welcome to anything you can find."

He led the way along a passage towards the back of the house and ushered them into a small room fitted with shelving, a chemical work-bench, and some apparatus-racks.

"I do a bit of research at times," Trulock explained, with a nod towards a series of glass utensils perched on sand-baths and heated by bunsen burners.

"And what are these, sir?" asked the inspector, professing a civil interest.

The doctor seemed to have got over his temporary annoyance.

"Soxhlet extractors, they call them," he explained.

" Suppose you want to extract quinine from Peruvian bark. You fill up this little papier-mâché container with the bark, and put alcohol or chloroform into the bulb at the bottom of the apparatus. Then you heat. The liquid boils up, gets condensed at the top of the apparatus, filters down through the chamber containing the bark, and so extracts your quinine. Then a siphon works and tips the solution back into the bulb below. From there, the pure liquid boils up again, but the quinine doesn't come away with it ; and the process goes on again. It's a method of using the same quantity of alcohol time after time, and extracting so much of the quinine each time ; which is cheaper than using a big amount of alcohol in a single extraction."

" I see," said the inspector. Then, as a thought struck him, he added, " And what have you got in these papier-mâché containers this time ? "

" Oh, just some plant or other," Trulock said in a careless tone which did not carry conviction to the inspector's ears.

" Some plant or other," he echoed suspiciously. " What kind of plant, may I ask ? "

Trulock gave him a sharp glance.

" Is that casual curiosity ? " he asked " Or are you putting an official question to me ? "

" I'm asking officially," retorted the inspector, making no attempt to hide his suspicions.

" Then I don't need to reply," Trulock rejoined. " I'm not bound to incriminate myself, as you know."

" That's correct," admitted Pagnell. " But I'm bound to search for anything that comes under the D.D.A. I'll come across the thing, sooner or later, when we begin to hunt."

Trulock seemed to ponder over this for a good many seconds. Then he appeared to make up his mind on some definite course.

" Well, I suppose you're bound to nose it out eventually," he admitted. " I may as well save you trouble and avoid having my stuff turned upside down in your search. Look here!"

He pulled out a long drawer and motioned to the inspector to examine the contents. Pagnell stooped over the drawer and found it full of lumps of some vegetable matter, roughly circular in form and about an inch in diameter. They were covered with yellowish matted hairs and the summit of each disc was a thick cushion, dirty-white in tint. The inspector picked out one and examined it inexpertly.

"Indian hemp?" he asked with a sardonic smile.

"I told you I'd make no admissions," Trulock reminded him. "If you say it's Indian hemp, I'm not going to deny it."

"You're taking this rather lightly, doctor," said the inspector. "Remember, under the D.D.A. the maximum penalty's £1,000 fine *and* ten years penal servitude. There's nothing in that to be funny about. Now another thing. Do you admit that you've been making extracts or tinctures from these things by means of these Soxhlet extractors there?"

The reference to the penalties seemed to have sobered Trulock.

"Well, I've admitted that already," he conceded in a much more serious tone, "so I don't see what use it would be to withdraw that statement. Let it go."

The inspector pulled out a notebook and made a few jottings in it before saying anything further. Then he produced a large envelope from his pocket and shovelled a handful of the lumps into it, after which he handed the packet over to the constable.

"Taking samples?" inquired Trulock.

"Just so," said the inspector. "Part of the routine."

"And now, are you going to arrest me or what?"

"We haven't come to that yet," explained the inspector. "I've got to make a search of the premises."

"But you've found the stuff," objected the doctor. "What's the good of wasting time?"

"It's part of the routine," said the inspector, with more than a hint of obstinacy in his tone.

The doctor seemed to recognise the ring of decision in Pagnell's voice, for he made no further objection but followed the two officials into the hall. The inspector halted for a moment, as though to get his bearings, and then advanced towards a door. Trulock pushed past him and stood on the threshold, barring the way.

"You can't go in there!" he said in a low voice, but with unmistakable earnestness. "I've got a patient in there, one of the two who got so badly burned at the Manor the other day. She mustn't be disturbed on any account. Understand that. I won't be responsible for anything if you burst in there and give her a shock."

"Come along here," said the inspector, with a complete change of manner.

He took Trulock by the shoulder and forced him into the adjacent sitting-room, where they stood confronting each other. The inspector looked his captive up and down with a certain angry contempt before he spoke again.

"Now, look here, doctor. Let's have no more of this foolery. You thought you were too clever for a simple country policeman, but you were too clever by half. You trotted out these dried vegetables, and you thought you'd diddled me into believing they were"—he bowed ironically—"'the dried flowering or fruiting tops of the pistillate plant known as *cannabis sativa*.' And then, when you were had up in our country police court and the stuff was produced, you'd have brought a botanist to swear that they weren't hemp at all, but things called mescal buttons, the tops of the *anhalonium Lewinii*, which don't come under the D.D.A. And you were grinning to yourself in prospect over the laugh you'd have when the case against you fell apart. But we're not so simple as all that. I've been up to London to get put wise. And I've seen specimens of Indian hemp. And what's more, I've made myself acquainted with the appearance of mescal buttons, so I recognised them at once, as soon as you showed me them in that drawer. *Now* have a good laugh at the joke, doctor. It's worth it."

The constable at least agreed with him, for he hurriedly stifled a guffaw, and then became the very image of duty.

The inspector put out his forefinger and laid it on the breast of the doctor's jacket. The very gentleness of the gesture made the menace of his attitude unmistakable.

"I'll quote you another section of the D.D.A.," he went on. "'If any person wilfully delays or obstructs any person in the exercise of his powers under this section . . . he shall be guilty of an offence against this Act.' I'm exercising my powers in searching these premises. If you delay or obstruct me in the slightest . . . Well, ten years penal is a fair sentence, let alone a £1,000 fine. And just note that you can get that whether you've got a grain of dangerous drug on the premises or not! I tell you straight that if you so much as lift a finger to hinder me now, I'll arrest you on the spot, and I'll not make it easy for you when you're on trial. Understand?"

Dr. Trulock caught the inspector's eye, flinched, and turned away his head. The sudden reversal of their positions seemed to have taken the heart out of him.

"Do as you like, then," he said, tonelessly. "But you'll find a patient in that room and I ask you to be careful of her. I give you my word of honour there are no dangerous drugs in that room, and you must take the full responsibility of any harm you do."

"I'll take the risk," said the inspector, bluntly, as he walked out into the hall.

He glanced at his watch to make sure that the Counsellor and Querrin would be in their place; then very gently he opened the door of the darkened bedroom and switched on the light. His glance went to the window, and he saw the curtains waving gently.

"Thank the Lord that all these doctors are fresh-air fiends," he reflected. "The window's open wide."

Trulock had followed him into the bedroom, the constable close on his heels. The inspector moved over to the side of the bed in which a form was lying, heavily bandaged about the head. The eyes were open but they seemed to take no note of the entry of the trio into the room.

The inspector coughed loudly and then, turning to Trulock, demanded in a loud voice:

"Who is she?"

Before Trulock could answer, an even louder voice sounded from outside the window:

"Helen! Helen!! Are you there? It's Howard, here. Wake up, dear!"

The inspector, his eyes on the muffled form beside him, saw a movement in response to the cry. For a moment the eyes examined him and then, as though in disappointment, the lids closed. But what he saw had been quite enough to satisfy him. He turned to Trulock.

"So that's how it is," he said softly, echoing one of The Counsellor's clichés. "You're going to have a lot to answer for, it seems." Then he added to the constable: "Take him next door and see he tries no tricks."

When Trulock had gone, the inspector went the window and held a short conversation with the two men outside. Then he switched off the light and left the room, closing the door gently behind him. At the front door he found a fresh visitor, an alert, keen-faced man, with an air of decision about him.

"Come in, Dr. Westhorpe," the inspector greeted the new arrival. "You're exactly on time—thanks. Your patient's in that room there," he nodded towards the closed door. "You know what's wanted. Can we give you any help?"

"I've brought a nurse with me," Dr. Westhorpe

explained, with a gesture towards his car, which was standing in the sweep before the front door. "We needn't waste any time."

Pagnell saluted the nurse as she came up; and she followed the doctor into the bedroom. When the door had closed behind them, Pagnell went out on to the front steps and summoned Querrin and The Counsellor.

"Nothing to do now but wait," he explained. "It shouldn't take long till we're certain."

"Where's this scoundrel Trulock?" demanded Querrin, between his teeth.

"Under my protection, for the moment," the inspector replied, with a certain stiffness. "I know just how you feel, Mr. Querrin, and I don't say I don't sympathise—unofficially. But we want nothing in the way of a rough house. Not with an invalid next door."

The last sentence had more effect on Querrin than the rest.

"Quite right, Inspector," he agreed, with obvious regret.

To be on the safe side, the inspector descended the steps and began to pace up and down the gravel sweep, inviting the others with a gesture to join him.

"Next question is," he pointed out, "what's to be done with this patient of Dr. Westhorpe's? She can't be left here, if she's fit to be moved. That's plain enough."

"It depends on what she's fit for," suggested The Counsellor. "If she can stand being taken away in an ambulance, perhaps the best thing would be to remove her to my house in town. There's any amount of room there. I can put you up as well, Querrin, if you like. And we can get in a couple of nurses to look after her. And Miss Rainham would come in useful if anything had to be done. It would be more home-like than a nursing home, once she can get about again. And Westhorpe's my own doctor—first-rate man—so he'd be on tap at any time we needed him."

" She can't go back to Longstoke House, and that's a fact," the inspector pointed out.

" It's damned decent of you," Querrin hastened to add. " I don't know how to thank you. Nothing could be better."

" Right ! " said The Counsellor, hurriedly. " Then that's fixed, if she can be moved."

The inspector felt it advisable to keep the conversation going, to distract Querrin's thoughts from reprisals. He turned to The Counsellor with a question.

" You haven't told me, sir, how you got on with your inquiries about these pictures. The possibility of substitution, I mean."

" I've only had information from two places," The Counsellor explained. " There's hardly been time yet to get a full set of facts. But in these two cases the results are negative. No substitution either tried or accomplished. It looks as if I'd been barking up the wrong tree with that idea. Still, that's no odds. Fresh ideas are cheap."

" Oh," answered the inspector. " So that's a blank end ? Now there's another point that's rather worrying me, Mr. Brand. You gave sworn evidence about Trulock dealing in Dangerous Drugs. I take it you didn't do that without some grounds, but I'd like to know just what they amounted to."

" The symptoms I saw amongst that gang the other night," declared The Counsellor. " I consulted a good man, and he agreed with me that the stuff was probably a mixture with some hemp extract in it. I mean the dose that Querrin got, not the one I swallowed. And hemp extract means a skilled man of sorts, when it's a matter of giving just the right dose. And there was Trulock, that night, all present and correct, with medical knowledge and all. I felt justified in swearing that information. After all, short of actually seeing him make the extract and administer it, what other kind of evidence could one have ? My conscience is clear."

" And elastic ? " queried the inspector, with a grin. " Well, if there's a sample of a Dangerous Drug on these premises, I'll find it, if I have to take the place to pieces in the attempt. I've seen enough of Dr. Trulock to dislike his methods."

The Counsellor laughed, taking no offence at the inspector's insinuation.

" Good hunting ! " he said, heartily. Then he turned to Querrin. " Ever hear of live bait ? "

" In fishing ? Yes, I have."

"Care for a job of the sort ?" demanded The Counsellor. "It's just an idea of mine. Say No, if you don't like it."

" I'd need to hear a bit more about it, first," Querrin objected.

" I thought you'd leap at it, after all I've done for you," said The Counsellor in mock reproach. " You're giving me a poor opinion of American enterprise, Querrin. And that's not patriotic of you. But if you'll step a bit further down the avenue, out of earshot of the house, I'll put you wise."

Ten minutes later, they returned to the house to find Dr. Westhorpe awaiting them. Querrin, though he had kept himself under control, was evidently on tenterhooks, and it was he who spoke first.

" Is she badly hurt, Doctor ? Disfigured ? "

The doctor's smile reassured him more than words could have done.

" Not a bit of it. She's been heavily doped and she's still under the effects of the stuff. I've never seen anything like it before. If you hadn't explained beforehand—" he glanced at The Counsellor—"I couldn't have made head or tail of it. But she's physically perfectly unharmed. We took off the bandages with the utmost care, and then found we'd had our pains for nothing. Not a mark on her skin. Not a hair singed. Nothing. Once she gets over this dope, she'll be absolutely all right, I should say. A bit run down, probably, but that's all. At the moment, she's in a queer state, very rum. What she says sounds like sheer delirium."

"Fit to move in an ambulance?" demanded The Counsellor.

"Oh, I see nothing against it. Want me to fix up a nursing home?"

The Counsellor explained his plans, and Dr. Westhorpe agreed to them at once.

"I'll be interested to see the end of it," he admitted, with a lapse into professionalism. "Nothing of the sort's come my way before. Now what about an ambulance? I suppose we can ring up from here."

"You get an ambulance. And a couple of sympathetic nurses. Tell 'em to go to my house and wait," said The Counsellor. "I've made all arrangements there already."

"Pretty sure of your ground, weren't you?" said the doctor, chaffingly. "And now I come to think of it, you haven't seen my patient. How do you know you've got the right girl?"

Evidently The Counsellor had primed him with the whole story beforehand.

"The resources of civilisation are not exhausted, never fear," said The Counsellor. "Querrin, here, knows her better than anyone else. Suppose you take him in to have a peep at her."

When Querrin and the doctor turned away, The Counsellor leaned over to the inspector.

"Take my tip and get your prisoner off the premises before Querrin comes out."

"Something in that," admitted the inspector, taking a stride towards the sitting-room where Trulock was under guard. "You detain Mr. Querrin for five minutes, sir, till we get him away in a car."

20 UNDER FALSE COLOURS

WHEN it came to hospitality, The Counsellor never did things by halves. He set aside a suite in his house for Helen Treverton and her nurses; called a couple of specialists into consultation with Dr. Westhorpe; established Sandra Rainham on the premises to play her part in his guest's recovery; and invited Querrin to make the house his headquarters, so that he might be at hand if wanted. Then he firmly suppressed his curiosity until, after a few days, the doctors decided that Helen had recovered sufficiently to make a statement.

When she came into the room on Querrin's arm, the effect of three weeks under the influence of drugs was painfully evident. She looked pale and fragile, and the dimples in her cheeks had deepened into hollows. She walked with a hesitating step, as though she had not fully recovered the normal spring. Sandra rose and came forward.

"This is my cousin, Mark Brand," she explained, indicating The Counsellor. "No, you're not to thank him just now," she added, as Helen began to speak. "You're not to tire yourself in any way until you've told us about your adventures. Dr. Westhorpe's orders. This is Inspector Pagnell. But of course you know him already. He's going to take notes of what you say, but he won't worry you with too many questions just now. And this is Mr. Standish. I've told you about him also. And you know Dr. Westhorpe. He's here to see that you don't over-tire yourself. Now you know who they are. Take this chair, and go as slow as you please. There's heaps of time, and you mustn't let yourself get hurried or worried. You know we're all friends."

"Very good friends, I know," said Helen Treverton, with a rather weary smile. "What do you want me to tell you exactly?" she asked, glancing towards the inspector.

"Perhaps if I asked you a question or two at the start?" suggested Pagnell. "I'm sorry if it's painful, Miss Treverton, but we have to know some things. You and your uncle had a kind of a disagreement hadn't you? A recent disagreement?"

In The Counsellor's judgment, Helen Treverton was not the sort of girl to make a show of emotion in normal circumstances; but she had been sapped by the long course of drugs and her control was not yet perfect. They could see tears come to her eyes at the inspector's question.

"Poor uncle! I wish it hadn't happened like that," she began. "I'll tell you exactly how it came about. You know he'd set his heart carrying on the Ravenscourt Press on his own lines, although he could never make it pay. Things got worse and worse financially with him, and he came to me and borrowed some of my capital to make ends meet from time to time. I didn't mind that, for you see I was fond of him, and the Press was everything to him. But by-and-by, things changed without any of us meaning it"—she glanced down at a new ring on her engagement finger—"and then I needed my money, and when he came to me for more, I'm afraid we quarrelled, and rather badly. I wish it hadn't happened, now that he's gone. But, of course, I couldn't know what was coming. He was hurt and angry, and I was hurt, too, because he put the Press in front of me so obviously. It came to a head just a few weeks ago."

"Thanks," said the inspector. "I'm sorry, miss.

I had to get the point clear. Now would you tell us just how things happened on the day you disappeared—Thursday, September 8th, that was."

A look of slight perplexity settled on Helen Treverton's face.

"I'm trying to remember everything," she explained after a second or two, "but it's difficult in places. My memory doesn't seem to be working properly even yet, and there are gaps in it. You see, I've been living in a most extraordinary world—for some weeks, it appears—and it's so difficult to link up real things with the rest of it, that in some places I hardly know whether I remember things that really happened or whether I'm just fitting on bits of the nightmare, if one can call it a nightmare. Illusions, they were, anyhow. I'll do my best, of course, but you understand how puzzling it is, don't you?"

"Quite so," admitted the inspector. "Then suppose we go back to the morning of that day. Do you remember anything about your car? I'm trying to avoid leading questions as much as I can."

"My car?" Helen knitted her brows for a moment or two. "Yes, I remember taking my car into Grendon St. Giles, and going to the bank to draw a little pocket-money. Yes, that's quite clear. . . . And I remember meeting Mrs. Trulock in the bank and . . . Yes, she asked me if I would be sure to go over to Fairlawns that afternoon. I remember that distinctly enough. It's only later that things seem to get all muddled up. And I remember I took Mr. Whitgift into Grendon St. Giles with me, and brought him back again."

"You remember using your cheque-book at the bank, then," interrupted the inspector. "What did you do with it when you got home again?"

"I put it in a drawer in my writing-desk," Helen declared without hesitation. "I always keep it there."

"And you don't remember taking it out again?"

demanded the inspector, who had been well primed by The Counsellor for this examination. "You didn't take it to Fairlawns with you?"

"Oh, no," Helen answered definitely. "I'm sure of my memory up to that stage. I put it in the drawer and left it there. I haven't seen it since."

The inspector nodded as though he attached no great importance to the point.

"One thing's puzzled us," he explained, with a glance at The Counsellor. "You were going to a tennis-party that afternoon. Why didn't you simply drive over in your tennis things, instead of wearing that grey coat and skirt and having to change when you got to Fairlawns?"

Apparently Helen Treverton had no difficulty in recalling the facts in this matter.

"It was Mrs. Trulock who got me to do that," she explained. "She had begun to do some dress-making, just to amuse herself she told me; and she'd been making something like my grey coat and skirt, but she hadn't managed to get it just right, it seems. So when she met me in Grendon St. Giles that morning, she asked me to wear it coming over to Fairlawns so that she could see where the padding was put in at the shoulders. And I think she'd had trouble with the hang of the skirt, too, so she asked me to wear it that afternoon, so that she could see it, and of course I could change into my tennis things in a few minutes. Of course I was quite glad to help her, so I wore the coat and skirt as she asked, and took my tennis things with me in an attaché case."

"One moment," interrupted The Counsellor. "Do you remember any of the Fairlawns people taking photographs of you in that get-up, probably some-time earlier than that?"

Helen Treverton stroked her chin for a moment or two, as if in thought. Then her face brightened, and she turned to The Counsellor.

"Yes, I do, funnily enough," she declared. "It was some weeks ago, and Mrs. Trulock had just bought a cine-camera and was practising with it. She got me to walk about on the lawn and she took quite a lot of pictures of me, so as to accustom herself to working the camera. I remember that quite well, now you've reminded me of it."

"Ah!" said The Counsellor with some satisfaction. "I wondered how they managed to have that nannie ready fitted out with a get-up exactly like yours. This explains it."

The inspector made a jotting in his note-book and then continued his interrogatory.

"Do you remember what you did after lunch that day?"

"I remember taking my racquet and an attaché case with my tennis things to my car. . . . Let me think. . . . And I started for Fairlawns . . . Wait a moment, there's something else. . . . Oh, yes, I remember stopping in the avenue to talk for a moment or two with Mr. Whitgift!"

"Anything particular about that talk?" asked the inspector. "Think carefully, Miss."

"Oh, I do remember something, because this is where the thing seems to get weird in my memory. I seem to remember, most distinctly, that he said he'd filled up my tank for me. He was always doing little things like that for me." She hesitated for a moment. "You see, he proposed to me once, and he wanted, I suppose, to show that he was taking the refusal well. He was very kind in a lot of ways."

"What happened after that?" asked the inspector.

Helen knitted her brows for a moment, as though striving to be sure of her memory.

"This is where things begin to get hazy," she said, frankly. "I mean, they don't seem to fit together, somehow, and I can't be sure of . . . I can't be quite certain that I'm not . . . Well, what I mean is that perhaps I may have imagined some of these things and they got to seem real while I was drugged. I want to tell you the exact truth, but even to myself, they don't fit together properly."

"Just tell us them, anyhow," suggested the inspector. "Perhaps we'll find ways of checking them if they did happen."

"Well, I just want to be quite straight about it," Helen said, with a glance round the company. "It may be all imagination, and I don't want to pretend it's accurate. If you'll take it so, then I know you won't think I'm not telling the truth if it does turn out that these things never happened at all. What I *do* seem to remember is, that my car stopped suddenly somewhere on the road between our gate and Grendon Manor. I couldn't make it out; for Mr. Whitgift had filled the tank, and when I looked at the petrol-gauge it showed the tank *was* full. I remember I thought the feed had got blocked, and I got out and lifted the bonnet to try if the carburettor would flood. It wouldn't. Now, I remember that perfectly clearly, and yet it must be all nonsense, really, for the tank couldn't be dry after five minutes' running. I must have imagined it all . . . and yet, it *does* seem clear enough. That's why I warned you against pinning me down in details, which may not be real, though I seem to remember them well enough."

"Don't trouble about that side of the thing, Miss," the inspector interjected. "Just tell us the story as you seem to remember it. We'll look after the checking of it, once you've given us it. What happened after that?"

"A bus came along; I remember *that* well enough, I think. It was one of the Royal Defiance fleet—you know them, Mr. Pagnell, with the black and yellow stripes—and I remember it stopping beside my car. At least, when I say I remember it, you know what I mean. It's in my memory, but I can't be sure whether it really happened or whether it came in as part of the visions and delirium. I looked at the bus, and I saw Mrs. Trulock was the only passenger in it. Of course, I'd have had no hesitation in boarding a Royal Defiance in any case, but her being on the bus made it more tempting, since I was going to her house and might just as well have her company there as wait on the road until someone could be sent back to help me. So when the bus stopped and they offered to take me on, I got in, and Mrs. Trulock and I began to talk. She had some patterns in her bag, and we got interested in discussing them, so I never looked out of the window."

The inspector glanced at The Counsellor when Mrs. Trulock's part in the affair was mentioned. Neither of them had suspected this last convincing touch in the scheme.

"The first thing that surprised me was when the bus swung off the main road and turned into the avenue leading up to Grendon Manor. I suppose I looked startled, for the conductor made some sort of explanation about picking up a party; but he mumbled it out and I didn't catch exactly what he said. Mrs. Trulock said something, 'It's all right,' or something like that, to reassure me, and naturally I didn't get suspicious at all, because the Royal Defiance buses often are hired out to people who have a big party that they want to take somewhere or other. So I went on talking to Mrs. Trulock, expecting that the bus would be picking up some people at the Manor, and then going on past Fairlawns, so that she and I could get off there."

Helen Treverton broke off and leaned forward, resting her chin on her hands and her elbows on her knees. The puzzled look deepened on her face, but after a moment or two she resumed her story.

"The bus stopped, and the conductor said something I didn't catch. Mrs. Trulock was further from the door than I was, and she got up, saying something about our having to get out for a moment or two. I didn't grasp what she meant, but as she had risen to her feet, I did the same, and began walking down the gangway to the door. The conductor stood aside to let me pass . . . It's dreadfully puzzling. I seem to remember all that quite clearly, and yet it must be just a dream getting mixed up with my real memories. . . . I remember that man standing aside to let me pass down the steps of the bus . . . And then I remember nothing, nothing at all. There's a complete blank. . . ."

"Don't trouble about that, Miss," suggested Pagnell. "Just go on with the next thing you *do* remember."

"The next thing I remember? Well, that was finding myself in bed in a room I'd never seen before; a sort of bed-sitting room with a couch, easy chairs, invalid table, wash-hand basin with taps, and all the rest of it. And there was a woman in nurse's uniform sitting beside me. And my head was terribly sore. I made a movement to try and sit up in bed, but the nurse stopped me at once. "You must lie quite still," she said. "Perfectly still, you understand? You've been badly hurt in a motor-accident." And then I realised that my head was bandaged. "The doctor will be here very soon," the nurse told me. "You've been unconscious for a long time, for hours. You must keep absolutely quiet. Don't move your head an inch, whatever you do."

"I was feeling very sick and badly shaken, and my brain didn't seem to be working properly, so I was glad enough to lie quiet and try to think. I couldn't remember any motor-accident, and that puzzled me badly. But I was too sick to make any real effort, and my head hurt terribly; so I gave it up and just lay still.

"Some time after that, Dr. Trulock came in. He was very kind, but he insisted that I wasn't to worry myself whatever I did and that I was to lie perfectly still. I'd had concussion, a slight fracture of the skull. It would be all right in time, but I must obey orders and keep still at any price. Then he asked about my head, and I said it was very painful. That seemed to worry him, and after a few words with the nurse, he told me he'd give me a morphia hypodermic. He had a syringe with him, all ready, and he gave me the morphia. While he was doing it, I heard him say something to the nurse, and I picked up that they were afraid of my turning delirious. They spoke of it once or twice, so that I understood quite well, though they didn't say anything to me directly. Then Dr. Trulock warned me again about being restless. The morphia would give me ease and probably I'd get to sleep, which would be the best thing for me. If I was thirsty, the nurse would give me a drink from a lip-cup; and when I woke up, she'd give me some medicine. I began to ask questions, but he frowned at that and told me I was running a grave risk by letting myself get excited. I must keep quiet—at any cost."

Helen Treverton paused for a moment and let her glance run round her audience, as though she were trying to estimate whether they appreciated the difficulties in her tale. Then she continued:

"I asked where I was; but at that Dr. Trulock became very firm and said I mustn't talk at all and he gave the nurse strict orders about talking to me or answering my questions. Of course I wasn't suspicious at all. I was too sick to bother, for one thing; and for another, Dr. Trulock and his wife were friends of mine and it never crossed my mind that everything wasn't absolutely straight. I was quite content to be in his charge; and besides, there was the nurse, who seemed to know her work, so far as I could see. So I just shut my eyes and dozed off from the effect of that morphia. And that was the last time I seem to have had any connected touch with the real world, for long enough. I did, from time to time, half wake up to find the nurse attending to me, feeding me from a lip-cup, or giving me some draught or other with a bitter taste. But these were only a kind of spasm of reality in the middle of a delirium, if you can understand what I'm trying to describe. . . ."

She paused again and seemed to be making an effort to arrange her ideas. Then she made a pretty gesture of despair and let her hands drop into her lap.

"No, I simply can't describe it—that delirium, I mean. It wasn't exactly the kind of thing I thought delirium was like. It wasn't painful, or frightening, or unpleasant in any way, you see. It was just like being mad and not caring a rap whether one was mad or not. I seemed to have lost touch completely with the real world and to be living a life of my own, isolated entirely from all the normal worries and cares and anxieties. And yet the whole business was quite mad, from start to finish. I could see myself there in the bed, see myself from head to foot as if I were clean outside my body, and except for myself and the bed, there wasn't another thing in the world. I mean, there was complete emptiness all round, no room, no walls, nothing . . . and then on that emptiness there came all sorts of wonderful things, floods of colour, arches, arcades, the most intricate patterns in marvellous tints, with sounds welling up and dying away. And then even the bed vanished, my body vanished too, and I seemed to be all alone in some vast emptiness, cut off from my own world completely. And yet I wasn't frightened. I was just curious, intensely interested, I seemed to know that in a few seconds or a few years—seconds and years meant much the same thing in my state of mind then—I'd understand . . . everything. Everything! I'd come to the edge of the secret of the Universe and I'd know it and understand everything . . . And then I seemed to slip back, just as I reached it. . . . The colour films gathered again like mists and I was dragged back amongst these luminous arcades, endless vistas of them, and shimmering crystals, and living patterns that changed and wove themselves into one another, and weird living creatures all aglimmer with wonderful colours, moving here and there down the perspectives. It was all completely mad, outside one's normal ideas altogether, and yet as real to me as anything in the ordinary world of common-sense, while it lasted.

"Then I got a terrible shock. Sometimes I used to wake out of this delirium and see the walls of the room and the furniture just as they were at first; but once I woke up and found everything different: the windows in fresh positions, the chairs of a different pattern the quilt of a different colour; and when I spoke to the nurse about it, it was perfectly plain she thought I was delirious and wasn't able to recognise familiar things. I lay back in the bed and tried to think; and I shut my eyes and opened them, hoping that the old arrangement of the room would come back, but it didn't. And then I grew convinced that I'd gone quite mad, completely insane, through that injury to my head. And I began to scream with sheer terror. And then Dr. Trulock came in and gave me a morphia injection to put me to sleep. And when I woke up, I tried to tell myself that the old room must have been one of my dreams and that this new one was the "really real" world. But I couldn't quite manage to convince myself of that."

Sandra leaned over and put her hand over Helen's in a sympathetic gesture.

"It must have been dreadful," she said softly. "The people who did that to you must have been perfect fiends. But it's all right now. You know that it was only the effect of drugs. You mustn't let yourself think too much about it. It's all past and done with. You're quite safe now and you must let us take care of you till you shake it all off."

Helen Treverton smiled rather wanly.

"You can't imagine how real it was," she said.

"But you know what happened?" interjected The Counsellor. "They gave you morphia from time to time, and once, when you were insensible they shifted you from the Manor to Fairlawns. And when you woke up, the nurse pretended it was just delirium and that you'd been in the same room all the time. Just an extra turn of their screw, that. But now you know how it was done, you needn't worry over it."

"Oh, I know that," Helen retorted, with a certain fretfulness at his obtuseness. "But it was a shock, and I haven't got over it altogether, even yet. When someone hits your funnybone, Mr. Brand, do you say to yourself: 'It's nothing. It's all over. Forget about it?'"

"No," confessed The Counsellor frankly, "I admit that I jump about and say a few things. There's not much wrong with your brain if you can rake up an analogy like that on the spur of the moment."

"And what's the next thing you remember, miss?" demanded the inspector, who began to fear that these interruptions were going to break the thread of the girl's narrative.

"The end of it? I remember hearing Howard's voice—" she glanced across to Querrin—"and that gave me a start. I suppose I must have been just coming out of the effects of one of their doses. And then I remember being brought away in an ambulance, and looked after here. And then things seemed to grow normal again by degrees. But you can see now why I don't put too much faith in my memory, with all these things mixed up in it, along with the real things that happened to me. I can't be sure what did happen and what I just imagined."

"That's enough for your present purposes?" asked Dr. Westhorpe, turning round to the inspector. "You want Miss Treverton to sign those notes of yours? Well, when she's done that, I think she ought to get back to her own room again. I don't want to have her excited, and telling that tale has been enough for her at the moment."

Helen Treverton made a faint protest, but the doctor was firm. So she put her signature to the foot of the inspector's notes, and then submitted to Sandra taking her back to her room.

21 LIVE BAIT

STANDISH got up, helped himself to a cigarette, lighted it, and then turned to The Counsellor.

" Evidently they sandbagged that unfortunate girl as she was stepping off the bus. Then they told her that yarn about a motor accident. And then they doped her to make her think she was delirious. That's it, isn't it ? By the way, what did you mean, that time, when you mentioned Maelzel's Chess-player ? "

" Oh, that," said The Counsellor. " It was a fake automaton which played chess. Actually worked by a dwarf inside the box that was supposed to be full of the machinery. Maelzel used to open a door and show that one compartment was empty ; then he'd open another door, and prove that there was nobody in another compartment, and so on. Of course the dwarf shifted about from one compartment to the other as the doors were opened, so no one saw him."

" I see," said Standish, enlightened. " The natural place to look for Miss Treverton at first was at Fairlawns, but she wasn't there. Then when Grendon Manor got suspected, they shifted her over to Fairlawns, drugged with morphia and all bandaged up about the face because she was supposed to be someone who'd got hurt in that fire. And that let them throw Grendon Manor open to inspection from roof to basement. And when she waked up in fresh surroundings and was told she'd never been shifted, it helped to convince her completely that something had gone wrong with her brain. They fairly put that poor girl through it, damn them ! "

The Counsellor glanced at Querrin's face and decided that this subject was too uncomfortable.

"The 'second patient' that they took over to Fairlawns—the man—was one of their accomplices, of course," he pointed out. "If they'd taken a girl alone, it might have raised suspicions further, and they knew they were suspected already by that time. But by taking a couple of 'patients' across, they made it seem a bit more plausible. And, of course, the man-patient took his hook next day. It seemed all right on the surface. Trulock was a genuine medico. Quite reasonable that he should take these damaged articles under his roof to look after them."

"I suppose it was mescal they doped her with? Her description tallied more or less with yours."

"Obviously," confirmed The Counsellor. "Being a completely out-of-the-way drug, she couldn't possibly have recognised her symptoms as due to that, and she naturally swallowed their tale of brain trouble and delirium. Also, the story about a fractured skull was enough to keep her quiet and prevent her getting up and wandering about!"

"Have you got them all?" asked Standish, turning to the inspector. "There must have been quite a crowd: Trulock himself, that girl who personated Miss Treverton, Mrs. Trulock, the fake nurse, the fellow who personated Querrin, and two chaps who were in charge of the bus. I suppose they belonged to the gang who were running Grendon Manor's Hell Fire Club?"

"We've got the lot—now," the inspector stated. They're all under lock and key, on one charge or another." He glanced at The Counsellor. "It's really due to Mr. Brand that we've got them. He could tell you about it better than I could."

"Wait till Miss Rainham comes back," said The Counsellor. "She'll want to hear about it too. Ah, here she is! Sandra, they want me to lecture on the Treverton case. Take a chair if you want to listen."

Sandra took the seat she had occupied before, while The Counsellor stepped over to the hearth-rug and put his back to the mantel-piece.

"This is how it was," he began, without waiting to be pressed any further. "You remember how I came to be dragged into the business. Whitgift wrote a letter asking if we could use the wireless to help in tracing EZ 1113. I went down, and he gave me a lot of information; but Treverton didn't seem much interested in his niece, when I saw him. We know now, of course, that they'd got across each other over money matters, and I expect he was sore. That probably accounts for his attitude. 'She's her own mistress. She can look after her own affairs.' She'd been looking after her own affairs financially, just before, and he hadn't liked the results.

"The next stage was our looking into the route taken by EZ 1113. The more one thought about it, the clearer it was that somebody'd been laying a false trail. And that somebody wanted the false trail followed up. Not expecting that we'd actually unearth EZ 1113 in Lochar Moss, of course. The trail was to end at Stranraer. Now the wireless was sure to unearth that false trail quicker than anything else could do. So before long I inferred that the fellow who called us in was the fellow who wanted the false trail discovered. Not very difficult reasoning, after all. And that person was Whitgift."

"Whitgift?" said Sandra. "But. . . ."

"But he was keen on Miss Treverton, you mean?" interjected The Counsellor as he saw she glanced towards Querrin and hesitated. "So he was. Lucky for her, too, or perhaps she'd have gone the same way as her uncle. There it was, anyhow. I had my suspicions of Master Whitgift pretty early on. But one thing and another seemed to make it look as if I was barking up the wrong tree. He had a good alibi for the very time when she must have been kidnapped. Instead of going after him, I began to look elsewhere. Whoever did the kidnapping, it must have been somebody who knew Miss Treverton's programme for that afternoon. That limited the circle considerably, especially if you add in the fact that the kidnappers knew all about Querrin, here. So the Trulock family moved into the focus in my mind, though I had next to nothing definite against them. But they had invited her to Fairlawns that afternoon, and Mrs. Trulock had met her in Grendon St. Giles that morning and made sure she was coming to tennis. And, further, it was Whitgift who had contrived that Miss Treverton went into Grendon St. Giles that morning, and so gave Mrs. Trulock the opportunity of running across her."

"That seems to fit, certainly," Standish admitted. "I ought to have seen that myself. But I didn't," he confessed frankly.

"Then there was the personator of Querrin," The Counsellor went on. "The inspector here did his best to trace anyone of that description having stayed in the neighbourhood at the time. Nobody could tell him anything about the fake Querrin. Ergo, that young man must have been staying with accomplices till his time came to get on the stage. So, obviously, several people must have had a hand in the game: Whitgift, probably; the Trulocks almost for a certainty; and someone else who provided a refuge for the fake Querrin beforehand. In fact, a gang of some sort."

The Counsellor took out a cigarette and lighted it before continuing his narrative. Pitching the match into the fireplace behind him, he went on.

"The next episode was the murder of poor old Treverton, with its forerunner, the killing of Miss Treverton's dog. That served a double purpose, you see, Querrin. The actual killing was a dress rehearsal for Treverton's death, and by killing the dog they made sure that she wouldn't have it with her when she was kidnapped. It might have turned nasty and put them off their stroke if it had been there. Now Treverton was killed late in the evening in his study. You remember about the key being found on the outside of the door in the morning, which was suggestive. But his body was found in the garage. Somebody must have got into the house and removed him. Now Whitgift made a mistake when he admitted to me that on the night of Miss Treverton's disappearance he went into Longstoke House *with his latch-key* to ring up Fairlawns and ask about her. That proved he had access to the house whenever he wished. And therefore he, at anyrate, could have got in and removed Treverton's body to the garage without disturbing anyone. So my suspicions of his bona fides got another lift up.

" But for a while I was quite in the dark as to the motives behind all these manœuvres. Obviously someone wanted an uncle and a niece out of the way. Family feuds don't reach that pitch in England. So I looked for some other connection between the Trevertons. I found it in the affairs of the Ravenscourt Press, where they were the two biggest shareholders. But the company was an almost bankrupt show. Why should anyone go the length of murder in connection with it? I couldn't see through it. But I took a chance and quietly bought a share, to give myself a standing. Then I found somebody, acting through solicitors, was eager to buy up the thing, lock, stock, and barrel. Note the dates. The letter with the offer was received on September 12th. The next few days were enough to show Treverton's reaction to it: nothing doing. So on the 19th Treverton got finished off. And the abduction and the murder had been neatly timed to keep the Treverton interest off the map while the deal went through. Just out of curiosity—and also to protect Miss Treverton's interests—I stepped in with a rather better offer.

" That put the cat among the pigeons at once.

The interested party decided to push me off the map with the others. And—like Smith of brides-in-the-baths fame—he followed his previous procedure precisely in his second attempt. In my case, however, he misfired—and damned lucky for me it was. I had the sense to tell a few lies about being liable to seizures, so he was left wondering whether I realised that an attempt had been made on me. But still I was quite in the dark as to the object of all these doings. It did occur to me that they might be stealing valuable paintings under cover of photographing them ; but that notion was a wash-out. Nothing in it.

"Now you, Sandra, had picked up a bit of information which seemed to fit in, somewhere. That little typist told you that Albury had tried to persuade her to go with him to some place where they could have "a really good time, something out of the common." And that turned my mind to Grendon Manor and its Hell Fire Club. But I got no further on that line at the moment. The really important matter was to find out how Miss Treverton had been kidnapped. You all know how we got at the root of that. And that root led straight to Grendon Manor and these Children of Light. So Querrin and I got into one of the seances. I needn't explain how, at the moment, lest I embarrass the inspector, here."

He glanced towards Pagnell with something which was almost a wink. The inspector took the hint and asked no questions.

"We attended the meeting," The Counsellor went on. "I spotted Trulock and I recognised Albury, too. The whole affair was—h'm !—very free-and-easy, Liberty Hall in the fullest sense of the term. Querrin and I made a careful note of the symptoms produced by the drinks. Next day, I got in touch with a specialist in that line. My stuff was obviously mescal. Mescal's hard to come by. But you can get it in South America. And Trulock had been in

South America before he came here. Trulock, then, was the brain behind that part of the business. And he was up to the neck in the kidnapping, too, as we'd discovered. I put two and two together, then, and the result relieved me a good deal, I can tell you. Given these drugs, you could persuade any patient that she was delirious, and so prevent her from taking active steps to escape. So it seemed likely that Miss Treverton was alive and in their hands.

"Then I began to think over the Children of Light stunt. On the surface, it could be made a paying game simply through the fees for the séances. But there was the chance of bigger money behind. You know what happened to the crew who drank the second drug. And you can guess what chances of blackmail there were in doings of that sort. Even the mescal-drinkers could be put under the screw along with the others. Nobody wants to get their name mixed up with a stink of that sort, even if they aren't actually participants. Mud of that kind always sticks. So that seemed to suggest something. Treverton might have been mixed up in it. . . .

"But when I thought it over, that didn't fit at all. Treverton was almost a recluse. Nothing to connect him with the Children of Light and their doings, so far as one could see. And certainly it didn't cover Miss Treverton's kidnapping. So I came back to that bankrupt company and the struggle to control it. That was the only thing that did seem to bring things together. But for a while I simply couldn't get the key to the puzzle. When I spotted it, at last, I could have kicked myself for not seeing it straight away. So simple, and so very obvious. That was when I got in the epidiascope, Wolf," he added, turning to Standish.

"By that time, I was almost certain that Miss Treverton was detained in Grendon Manor. Then came that neat little touch of the fire on the premises, practically throwing the place open to the police so that they could search it from roof to cellar. *But,* two poor burned creatures were shipped away, smothered in bandages, before the police arrived on the scene. And where were they taken? To Fairlawns, in charge of the hospitable Dr. Trulock. All I had to do was to get Fairlawns raided by the inspector, after he'd primed himself about likely drugs. I hadn't even to wrestle with my conscience, for my pharmacologist expert had suggested the possibility of hashish being the second drug or at anyrate a component of it. So I could make a sworn declaration about hemp without feeling I was deliberately lying. It's not on my conscience, anyhow.

"You know what happened next. The inspector got in with a search-warrant and found Miss Treverton more or less as I'd expected. He swept all the Fairlawn's crew into his net, and I think he'll bring his case home to them in the matter of the kidnapping. Trulock kept his mouth shut. Wouldn't make any statement after he was arrested. I expect he'll talk before we're done. He'd better."

The Counsellor glanced at the inspector, who smiled rather grimly in return, as if endorsing the last remark.

"That brought us up against an awkward legal point. Somebody had killed Treverton. That somebody had also tried to finish me off. But you can only try a man for one offence at a time, so on the face of it the evidence in my case wasn't relevant against the suspect if he was charged with Treverton's death. But—especially after the decision in the Brides-in-the-baths case—you can adduce evidence of "system", and so drag in other examples of similar methods used by the prisoner. But then you want all the possible evidence of a "system", to make your case thoroughly convincing. We had the dog, and Treverton, and myself, all treated to carbon monoxide. One further parallel would convince any jury. So I persuaded Querrin, here, to act as live bait to catch that evidence. You tell 'em your share in the show, Querrin."

Querrin seemed rather unwilling at first, but he thawed in the course of his tale.

"The only part I played in the thing was a lay figure in your hands," he began. "All I had to do was to appear on the scene and speak the piece you supplied me with. There was no credit in doing that."

He turned to the rest of his audience and continued.

"Under direction, I wrote to Whitgift, as temporary boss of the Ravenscourt Press, asking for an appointment. I went down to Longstoke House to keep that appointment. They showed me up into the office Whitgift has taken it over, now Treverton's gone, I recited my piece, all about having talked things over with Miss Treverton and her having almost decided to accept Brand's offer when the matter came up for discussion. She was doing that on my advice, I said, but she wasn't quite fixed in her ideas. Still, it was only fair to let him know how things were going, etc., etc. And then I said I was a bit uneasy about the whole show. There seemed to be. . . something fishy about it somewhere. I didn't quite like the look of it, in fact. And before doing anything definite . . . Well, I'd make it my business to overhaul the whole affair from top to bottom. And so on.

"That seemed to shake him up a bit, though it was all Greek to me, personally. I just said what was put into my mouth. Anyhow, Whitgift pulled himself together and began asking about Miss Treverton. When were we going to get married, and so forth. So I told him 'almost immediately. No reason for waiting.' Then he went back to the other line, and wanted to know if I'd spoken to anyone else about these suspicions of mine. I said: 'Not even to Miss Treverton', which was quite true. So then he hummed and hawed. Seemed to be doing a bit of quick thinking, and finally said he'd like to consult Albury for a few minutes to see if he saw anything wrong. I said: 'Of course, I'll wait to hear what he says.' So Whitgift went off and left me alone in the office. Then I tried the door, as Brand told me to do, and it was locked. So I sat down and smoked a cigarette or two. And by-and-by Brand and the inspector came in and said it was O.K. and quite successful. That was this afternoon, and I'm still waiting to hear what it was all about. I've a glimmering, of course."

"This is how it is," explained The Counsellor. "The previous appointment was to give time for the criminal to make his preparations beforehand. The crucial bit in your playlet was when you let out that you'd told no one else about your suspicions. That meant that if you lived, things would be overhauled. But if you died, no one would know what you'd been thinking. Last night, the inspector chaperoned me whilst I cut the old acetylene piping leading out of the coachhouse. That made certain that you'd come to no harm by the old and well-tried method, which I was sure would be used. And I'd given you a pistol, just in case more open methods were tried. But the chance of that was small, I believed. Anyhow, you said you could look after yourself, so I took your word for it.

"When you walked up to Longstoke House front door, the inspector here was in the loft above the garage with his eye to a hole in the floor, just to see what happened. A couple of constables and myself were hiding within sight of the garage door. After a bit, Whitgift came out of the house, walked over to the garage, coupled up the piping, and started the engine of Treverton's old crock. Then when he'd seen this, the inspector whistled and the constables collared Whitgift and removed him with as little fuss as possible. So we had him absolutely red-handed."

"So it was Whitgift?" interrupted Sandra. "Why, I was sure it was Albury."

"It looked like the two in partnership at one time, especially after I spotted Albury at the Hell Fire Club that evening. But it turns out that the 'phone call which drew Albury away from the office and left me to be done in alone, came from the A.A. box near the gate of Longstoke House. Whitgift was an A.A. member and of course had an A.A. key to open that box. That adds another bit of confirmatory evidence against him."

"We've been hunting for evidence to confirm Albury's story about going to see about that rumoured fire at his house," interjected the inspector, "and we've managed to get someone who actually saw him in Grendon St. Giles at the time he said he was there. So he'd no hand in the attempt on Mr. Brand."

"No, we can put Albury down simply as one of the less desirable lot among the Children of Light, and let it go at that," continued The Counsellor. "He was a bad hat. But he'd no hand in either the abduction or the murder business. My impression is that he was enrolled amongst the Children of Light merely to have a sort of hold over him, on account of his little games there, if he cut up rough in the matter of the company manœuvres. But that's merely an idea of mine. Now perhaps the inspector can tell us if he found much at Fairlawns when he searched the house."

Pagnell stowed away his notebook before speaking. Evidently the facts were fresh enough in his memory to need no written data. He turned to The Counsellor with something very near a grin on his face.

"First of all, sir, to relieve your conscience, I'd better say that we found some 'dried or flowering tops of the pistillate plant known as *cannabis sativa*'," he began. "That's the legal description of Indian hemp, from which you can prepare hashish, bhang, and things of that sort," he explained for the benefit of the uninitiates in the audience. "So you were right enough in suspecting that they'd been mixing their drugs a bit and doping their members with hemp extract as well as the other stuff you told me about. And on the table beside the bed in Miss Treverton's room we found a glass with some mescal tincture in it. It's been identified provisionally by an expert."

"How could he do that in the time?" demanded Standish. "It's none so easy to identify a rare alkaloid in a hurry."

"Perhaps he swallowed a small dose and noted the effects, same as I did," suggested The Counsellor. "'Identified provisionally', was the inspector's phrase. Let's leave it at that."

"Another thing we found," went on the inspector," was the grey coat and skirt used by that nannie when she impersonated Miss Treverton. So that's that. When we produced them, the young lady collapsed and was quite eager to tell us all about it. So was Mrs. Trulock. And so was Trulock himself to-day, when he found what cards we held. I don't wonder at their eagerness to spill the beans."

He paused, evidently waiting for a question.

"Why?" demanded Standish. "I don't see what they gain by it."

"Why, sir?" echoed the inspector. "Why, because they're all in a holy terror lest they should be mixed up in the murder side of it. That's why. They didn't mind taking a hand in a kidnapping. Trulock thought he saw his way to turning that girl loose eventually in such a mental state that no one would believe a word she said and would put it all down to delirium. But into the middle of that nice little game came their accomplice's despatch of Treverton. That wasn't in their programme at all. That was a Whitgift move, pure and simple. They never heard about it till it was all over. And by that time they couldn't split without involving themselves in a nice set of other charges. Once they were nailed on the other counts, of course their only hope was to make a clean breast of it and give Whitgift away.

Which they did, pretty thoroughly. They were working along with Whitgift up to a point, but murder was no part of their programme."

Sandra made a gesture of incomprehension.

" But what was at the back of it all ? " she exclaimed. " I can't see it."

" Money, miss," said the inspector seriously. " Just money. But that's really Mr. Brand's part of the tale. I'll leave it to him."

" Tell us, Mark," demanded Sandra. " And don't make a long story of it, or I'll scream. I shall ! It doesn't sound like common sense. There was no money in that company. That was plain enough."

" Here's how it was," said The Counsellor, " staring us in the face from the start. A bankrupt picture-reproduction firm that never paid a dividend, and yet some parties unknown were sweating to buy it. Why ? Well, I thought of a theft of valuable pictures by substitution. All that idea did was to put me off the track completely when there was a far simpler solution."

He pulled out a note-case and skinned a one pound Bank of England note from a packet.

" Look at it : the colouring in the design, the engine-turning in the pattern, and the water-mark. Wasn't the Ravenscourt Press the very last touch in colour-reproduction ? Didn't they use photography in their work ? Wasn't Whitgift originally a paper-making expert ? And hadn't Whitgift a locked room into which he allowed no one else to go ? Why, it simply shouted ' Counterfeiting ' at one, if one had only ears to hear. And we'd actually come across two specimens of the stuff : one was in our museum, and the other I got later from that garage at St. Neot's, where it had actually been paid over by one of the gang. As soon as I thought of the idea, I got in an epidiascope, and put a genuine note and one of the forgeries side by side into it, magnified them up on the screen, and measured some of the engine-turning with dividers. The forgeries were almost exact facsimiles—but not quite. Under that magnification one could find slight differences, a constant error running through the measurements. That pointed straight to photography."

"But you can't make much out of a few forged banknotes," objected Sandra.

"I don't know what you call 'much'," said The Counsellor. "When the old Treasury notes were first issued at the start of the war, one young gentleman working in an old garage turned out £60,000 worth of them and nearly got away with it. Is £60,000 'much' by your standards?"

"But you've got to get them distributed," Sandra objected again.

"If you hand them out at half-price, plenty of people will do the distributing and be happy," said The Counsellor. "So that young gentleman found, in actual practice. So it's no good saying it can't be done. It's easy enough, if you go the right way about it."

"The whole lot were in it," interjected the inspector. "Whitgift turned out the stuff, and the Fairlawns crew help him with the distributing. When Trulock began running his Children of Light stunt, Whitgift spotted him as a wrong 'un, and took him in on the forgery side. That's how they got into double harness."

"But . . . murder!" protested Sandra. "Why did it get to that pitch?"

"Look at the conditions," said The Counsellor. "Whitgift had to work in a hole and corner way at Longstoke House, hampered for time, and by having to produce some kind of honest results to justify the hours he spent in that locked room. But suppose he had control of the whole Press. That would give him a respectable cover for his other trade: old-established firm, well-known for good work in its special line. Nothing could be better as camouflage.

That was why he was determined to get control of the company. And for all I know, there may have been a more urgent reason for clearing Treverton off the board.

" Meaning that the old man may have begun to suspect something ? "

" It's possible. We're never likely to know for certain," said The Counsellor. " But since Whitgift was content to get Helen Treverton kidnapped, I'm inclined to think that old Treverton got to know more than was good for Whitgift's health and so . . ."

" And of course when you turned up out of the blue with your offer to buy the company, he'd one death on his hands already, and couldn't be hanged twice. So he took the extra risk of polishing you off ? " said Standish.

" That's about it, no doubt," The Counsellor agreed, cheerfully. " But he'll find one hanging quite enough for his simple needs, I hope. Well, I've had one would-be suicide among my listeners. And now I've had a murderer. Really, it takes all sorts to make a world."

THE END

››› If you've enjoyed this book and would like to discover more great vintage crime and thriller titles, as well as the most exciting crime and thriller authors writing today, visit: ›››

The Murder Room

Where Criminal Minds Meet

themurderroom.com